THE VOLUNTEER

PEADAR Ó GUILÍN

The Volunteer
978-1499199529

Cover by Fiona Jayde -- http://fionajaydemedia.com/
Image copyright by diversepixel/Shutterstock

THE VOLUNTEER

PEADAR Ó GUILÍN

For the Dreaded Nork, its claws ever sharp.
Terror is my inspiration.

PART ONE:
WORLDS IN DARKNESS

I.
FOUR HUNTERS

Spearcatcher cried out once, and that was the last they saw of him. Their chests heaved as they ran. Muscles ached. The loudest sound was their own breathing and houses blurred past them in the darkness. Up ahead, the horizon glowed: fire of some sort, a haven surely, from the Diggers that pursued them. But the four survivors staggered to a halt when they saw what had caused the light. A thousand paces away, the streets of BloodWays raged with fire. Every house there was burning, so that even the stones seemed to spit sparks high into the air.

Whistlenose had no energy for shock. The eldest by far of the hunting party, he came in last and fell to his hands and knees on the damp and gritty street. He wanted to be sick. He wanted his head to stop spinning. He wished, just once, that his constantly blocked nose would allow him enough air.

They had been running throughout the night, driven farther and farther from the safe streets of home. Three men had died so far, disappearing one by one into the dark. But now the pursuit seemed to have stopped. Perhaps three corpses sufficed to satisfy the enemy. Or maybe ... maybe they simply wanted the humans to see what had happened to BloodWays; to show off what they had achieved.

The exhausted men stared. Many of the buildings had slumped into the earth. Of the inhabitants, they saw no sign. No guards waited to leap from the remaining towers to hunt them down; no drums thundered out in warning.

Whistlenose rested one cheek against the chill wall of a building. His left leg ached as never before, pulsing in time with his heart. Each burst of pain told him how few days of life remained to him now, regardless of whether he made it back tonight or not. Please Ancestors, he begged. He prayed to them out of habit only, because the world was ending, everybody knew it. The world was ending and there didn't seem to be a thing the Ancestors could do about it.

Highstepper waved his spear at the others. He had a long-limbed, awkward body and was far from the best hunter. But the Chief had put him in charge anyway. Gone were the days when men would decide such things amongst themselves. "All right, then," he said, "We'll have to go back."

"They'll be expecting us to turn around," said Whistlenose. "They'll lie in wait."

Highstepper nodded. "It's what I would do."

Nobody said anything else and BloodWays continued to burn. This was supposed to have been a simple hunt. An easy one, even. Many of the creatures that lived near human territory were battling extinction as the mysterious Diggers pushed in. Sooner or later, ManWays would suffer the same attacks, but for now, the hunting was easier than Whistlenose had ever seen it. "They run onto our spears," he had told his wife, while their infant son snuffled in sleep beside them.

"You don't sound happy about that," she had replied.

Too true. He should have been delighted. He was old now, coming up on fourteen thousand days, as his wife knew better than anybody. Hunting could be exhilarating: overcoming the terror; fighting for your life to bring home desperately needed food. And such adoration from the Tribe on a successful return! The embrace of wives. Nobody mocked him then.

But everything had changed for him when, so late, so unexpectedly, he had become a father. That was when Whistlenose,

7

a man with less than a thousand days of hunting left in him, learned the true meaning of fear. What if he died before his boy was named? Such children never grew to adulthood in a hungry, desperate Tribe.

So yes, Whistlenose ought to have been delighted with the easy kills that had been so common lately.

"Then why aren't you happy?" Ashsweeper asked him. She was a good worker with a sweet, sweet face. Some man would take her for a second wife surely, after he was gone. And the boy too.

"Husband?"

In the dark, the only sounds had been the pop of the fire and the faint hiss of his breathing that had given him his name.

"Most of them don't fight back," he said at last. "I think ... I almost think they're grateful for our spears ... "

Now, in the flickering light of BloodWays' burning buildings, Whistlenose looked around at the other three remaining hunters in the party. Highstepper, huntleader or not, still hadn't come to a decision. "We need to split up," said Whistlenose.

He could see they didn't like the idea. All three were younger than he was and probably, until that evening, they'd thought themselves farther from the soup. They had swagger and speed over him. And reputations already better than that of poor Whistlenose whose long life had gained him no more than three tattoos. And yet, he came from a generation that didn't let a Chief, no matter how clever, do their thinking for them.

"We can't fight these Diggers," Whistlenose said. "All night, they've driven us about like pups before the spear. If we are still alive now, it is only because they have not yet chosen to kill us." He waved back the way they'd come, through a tangle of dark streets, "They are going to catch us for sure. Some of us. But if one group holds them off, the other might make it home to tell of what happened here."

Highstepper chewed his lower lip like a nameless child. His sweat all but stank of panic. *My own too, probably.* Whistlenose winced as another wave of pain pulsed out from his knee.

"You," Highstepper said. "You."

"Me, what?" said Whistlenose, but with a sudden chill, he knew what the younger man was thinking.

"I saw you limping."

"I wasn't. I don't limp. I kept up with all of you." *My boy is too young! My boy!*

Leftear spoke up. "The huntleader's right." His eyes refused to settle on Whistlenose. "One of us might be enough to hold them off. The rest might make it back. BloodWays is gone. The Diggers have moved more quickly than the Chief expected. Word of this has to get out."

Whistlenose didn't care about any of that just then: not the Diggers; not the end of the world; or the men around him. The Roof seemed to be spinning above his head and beads of sweat itched their way down his face.

"Which of you will marry my wife?" he said.

They knew what he was asking.

"We're wasting time here," Highstepper mumbled.

Whistlenose wanted to scream into the huntleader's cowardly face. "Who will marry her?"

"Keep your voice down! The Chief decides such things now."

Ah yes, the Chief. Wallbreaker. Another coward, but clever to the point that many suspected the Ancestors spoke directly into his ears, keeping the Tribe safe. Clever, yes. And *practical*. Ashsweeper and the boy didn't stand a chance.

Eventually, Leftear looked up. "I will marry Ashsweeper. I will try. If *he* lets me."

Whistlenose nodded, feeling a sting at the corner of his eyes. It was the only offer he was going to get. "Go," he told the others. "As quickly as you can."

"You had many days left," said Leftear. A lie, but an honourable one.

Highstepper signalled the entrance of an alley and the three younger hunters disappeared into it, as though it had swallowed them whole.

9

Five times Whistlenose counted twenty heartbeats, giving them a chance to get away, but giving his own fears time to grow too.

The Diggers had come out of nowhere on the far side of TongueWays. They buried their living victims waist-deep in the ground where strange yellow or white grubs consumed them from below. The victims moaned in terrible pain but would actively resist attempts to rescue them, drooling all the while. Nor could these unfortunates be easily killed, except by fire. Which might explain why BloodWays was burning now.

He swallowed dryly. Would he have the strength to kill himself before he was caught? And shouldn't he try to stay alive anyway, in order to give the others as much time as possible? Leftear, at least. He needed Leftear to marry Ashsweeper.

But his own time was up. "Come, you flesh wasters!" he shouted. "Let me drink that slop you call blood! Sicken me on your marrow!"

Whistlenose felt a slight trembling in the road beneath his feet. He fought the urge to run for his life. His voice faltered as he forced the words out through his teeth. "I'll stuff your pups for my boy to play with! Your wives will be bedding for mine!"

A crack ran up the wall beside him. These creatures loved to attack from below. The Chief said that the hard surface of the ancient streets kept the ground from opening beneath a hunter, but that if enough holes were made farther underground it could cause the collapse of buildings. It seemed to be happening now. Ancient masonry popped, sprays of rust and flakes of stone stung Whistlenose, pushing him out of the shadows and into the centre of the street.

Now he heard the skittering sound of hard claws on stone. It came from all around him so that he turned again and again in a circle, his spear held out in front of him. In the shadows, far down in the direction of ManWays, something *flowed* across the street.

The hairs on his neck prickled and he spun around again, stabbing the spear at nothing. Then, the sounds seemed to be moving away from him. It made no sense, no sense at all, but in moments, he felt himself all alone once more.

He should shout again. He should draw their attention, but his mouth had dried up entirely and he hadn't the strength to hold tightly onto the shaft of his spear. He waited for what seemed like a thousand heartbeats, all alone with the burning buildings of BloodWays at his back.

The skittering sound came again, this time from the direction in which his fellow hunters had fled. He tiptoed towards it, although he only wanted run away. But that was the point of being a Volunteer, wasn't it? To give yourself so that your family might live, or, as the ancient saying had it, "That the Tribe Might Make it Home"?

He heard a shout—a human voice. No, voices! He reached the mouth of the alleyway to witness a scene worse than any nightmare. A dozen Diggers occupied an open space, their snouts round, their skins full of holes and seething with subtle movement. They weaved around Whistlenose's fallen companions. Leftear's right leg had bone poking through it from the inside. Twistedtalley might have been unconscious, while Highstepper crawled around in circles on hands and knees, shaking his head as though he had thorns lodged in it, but no hands with which to pick them out. "Mother!" he kept saying. "Mother!" It made no sense. He crawled to within a few spearlengths of Whistlenose's hiding place. One of the Diggers stopped him, its back so close that Whistlenose could have reached out and touched it. It became obvious now that the movement on its skin consisted of tiny grubs crawling over the creature's body. Now, one of these dropped from the Digger's hide to land on Highstepper's face. It was as wide as a man's thumb, but somehow it forced its way up the hunter's nose.

Highstepper's eyes widened. He screamed and gagged, rising up onto his knees, jaw working hard enough to dislocate itself. Then he simply went back to his crawling.

Whistlenose looked up to find Leftear's eyes fixed on his.

"Please," the man shouted. "You've got to kill us! You've got to help!"

And all at once, the faces of every Digger turned in the direction of Whistlenose's alleyway.

For the second time that night, he found himself running for his life. He might have a chance—humans on two legs seemed to run faster than the Diggers, above or below ground, but the creatures were masters of ambush and three times already they had appeared where the hunters had least expected. Speedywink had been taken from below when he leapt an ancient drain; Spearcatcher's legs had last been seen disappearing through a window. It was all so … *playful*, that was the word.

Whistlenose stumbled over a brick, felt something scrape down his bad leg and imagined talons. But it was only a piece of old metal jutting out of the masonry. He righted himself against a moss-covered wall and ran on. Leftear's cries had been silenced and the scrabbling claws seemed to be falling farther and farther behind him. But he wasn't fooled, not any more. *I'm just running where they want me to go.* It was as simple as that.

He found himself back on a street where he could see the remains of BloodWays burning and groaning in the night. Dawn could not be more than a Tenth away now, and the Diggers, for all their games, would want to bring him in before that. They were rarely seen by day and seemed sluggish then and stupid.

He thought about running back down the road in the direction of the human streets—ManWays, as they were known. But no, no. *They're expecting that. They've expected everything we've done.*

Between him and BloodWays, there lay a great open space—what the Ancestors had called a "no-man's land." Trees grew there while mosses of a thousand colours fought for the attention of poisonous insects. Even by night with only the tracklights of the great Roof for illumination, a hunter could be seen crossing this easily, unless he knew the area well and had planned out a route for himself from tree to bush to rock. Only a madman would go there otherwise, in full view of every predator.

Whistlenose turned his face towards the no-man's land and ran for all he was worth. One more street and he would be there.

Suddenly, the claws that had been so silent were rattling on every surface. He could hear them behind him, tens and tens of Diggers pouring into the road back in the direction they had expected him to go. But others, too, were skittering along in the streets parallel to his and one of these creatures, just one, slid out to block his way forward. He was still running at full tilt. Its triangular head turned towards him and its paws widened exposing a rippling chest, an unmissable target.

So be it. His spear shivered when it struck, biting deep, passing right through the creature's body only to snap off against the roadway beyond. He didn't know where the heart was, or if it possessed such an organ, but he expected it to die, at least to die. Instead, a shudder ran over it and its two widespread arms pulled him into an embrace.

They tumbled in the street together, round and round while the Diggers down the road clattered closer. Whistlenose felt his cheek pressed right up close against warm wiry fur, that stung, somehow, on contact. Something was crawling over his scalp, something finger-sized and warm. It tickled his ear. He remembered the grub that had shoved its way up Highstepper's nose and he screamed, shoving for all he was worth.

The arms fell away and he staggered free on hands and knees, but the rest of the enemies had arrived within spitting distance. He made it onto his feet and launched himself away towards BloodWays, weeping, his skin stinging.

Under his feet, the ground oozed. Rocks gave beneath his toes; moss pods opened to cause skids. They came after him, a great wave of them, greedy for his flesh. Their four legs would have the advantage here on the uneven surface, but Whistlenose, running upright, could better see what lay ahead: a Wetlane, what the ancient tales called a "Canal," with no bridge anywhere in sight. So, he kept running, knowing he had one slim chance of escape.

Whistlenose gritted his teeth against the pain in his leg and pulled in his last reserves of terror-fired energy.

Everyone knew there were creatures living in the Wetlanes.

PEADAR Ó GUILÍN

Sometimes Chief Wallbreaker's schemes tricked one of the monsters into the nets for the Tribe to feed on. But once in that water, unable to swim, the hunter knew that he would be the one providing dinner.

The reflections of the tracklights shimmered on the surface as he sprinted forwards. He didn't allow himself to think, to slow, to stop. Old Chief Speareye—from before Wallbreaker's time—had a son called Waterjumper, who had supposedly made it all the way across a Wetlane without falling in. Supposedly. But if he had, he'd been a young man, jumping in daylight, without a gammy leg.

Whistlenose remembered Waterjumper's boasting by the fire, shortly before the Armourbacks had killed him. "The trick is ... and, remember, this is my idea! Not Wallbreaker's, like he says. Mine! The trick is, you don't jump forward. You go *up*. High as you can and let your speed carry you to the other side all by itself."

"I don't believe he really did it," Whistlenose had said later to a comrade. "Who saw him, anyway?"

Whistlenose reached the edge and launched himself upwards. It seemed to take forever to cross the water. He had time to count reflections in it; to think about his miraculous son and his one remaining wife ...

He hit the Wetlane in a shock of cold that bubbled around him; that swallowed him down like a huge and slavering beast.

He panicked, clawing all around until his hands fixed on the lip of the wall. He pulled himself up, although the water sucked at him, sapping at his strength. He got his knees up onto the edge, hacking up water.

Behind him, the Wetlane churned. The far bank held a dozen Diggers, but others had made it into the water, their snouts peeping above the surface and writhing with grubs. They could swim? But they lived *underground*!

He had lingered too long on the bank already. One of the Diggers had caught up with him, but, hidden by the lip of the wall, he didn't see it until its clawed hand came up to fasten on his foot.

14

He would have died then, had not the inhabitants of the Wetlane arrived in force. Water frothed around the Digger. It released its hold on Whistlenose's leg, almost politely, and disappeared beneath the surface. A few bubbles remained, and then nothing. The other Diggers sank too, until only those on the far bank remained to stare across at him.

A promise, he felt. They were making him a promise.

He opened his mouth to shout defiance back at them, but closed it again in the face of that remorseless stare.

2.

A STRANGER

Whistlenose ran hard for BloodWays, although he had no intention of entering those dangerous, burning streets. He ducked behind the first rock big enough to hide him and then began crawling on his belly, parallel to the Wetlane he had crossed. Hopefully the Diggers wouldn't know which way he had turned in order to circle around towards home again. He was praying daylight would chase them off—and the Longtongues too, whose territory he was now approaching.

His crawling brought him at last to a small wood. He could stand here, but that didn't mean he could start running again. Longtongues loved to set traps: invisible threads they made inside their own bodies that a man would stick to and could not escape. He collected a branch and pushed it ahead of himself, wincing every time his feet crunched on dry leaves or snapped a twig.

He wouldn't have to go much farther. All he wanted was a place to hole up until daylight. He would cover himself in vegetation and muck and then—

He heard a voice—a human voice—a cry of anger. Whistlenose started forward and then froze. "Don't be a fool, boy," he told himself, although he was far from a boy now.

Nevertheless his feet, of their own accord, turned him in the direction from which the cry had come. More than once as he made his way through the trees, dizziness overcame him. Had he really killed a Digger and jumped into a Wetlane? Nobody would believe him back home. But *they* hadn't seen that thing crawling up Highstepper's nostril ...

The cry came once more, sounding more like frustration than outright terror. Whistlenose pushed the stick ahead of himself and pressed on.

The Roof was starting to brighten, thank the Ancestors! Whistlenose already fancied he could feel the heat of it under the trees. He came into a clearing, just as dawn broke, and stopped in surprise. One of the strangest creatures he had ever seen floated between two trees. It had a face that might have been a man's were it not for the hair that grew on its upper lip and the darkness of the skin. The rest of its body—other than the all-too-human hands—was made of a white flappy material.

Whistlenose stood there, frozen, until the creature's eyes swivelled and widened at the sight of him. He crouched, wondering how it would attack and knowing he was too exhausted to flee.

But nothing happened except that the tone of the floating creature's voice changed to what must have been curses.

"You're not really floating, are you?" said Whistlenose. Sure enough, as the daylight brightened, he could see the threads of a Longtongue net glinting around the tangled beast. For the first time, after that long night, the hunter smiled.

"Thank you, Ancestors!" Chances were, he'd make it back to ManWays alive now, and not only that, he'd bring the flesh of this creature home for his family. His belt-knife was made of that new material the Chief had discovered—Armourback shell. It would cut through anything, even the sticky threads of the Longtongue trap. He drew the weapon and stepped forward with a grin.

"It'll all be over quick, my hairy friend," he said to the creature, although he hesitated when he saw its eyes widen in all-too-human fear. It began struggling again as he approached. Spitting and shouting. It would attract the attention of other beasts if he didn't hurry. But just as he raised the blade the creature's struggles caused some of its flappy white hide to fall away and Whistlenose realised with a shock that it wasn't skin after all, but a form of clothing. The limbs beneath, for all their puniness and dark colouring, were every bit as human as that of anybody in the Tribe.

"I've seen skin like that before," Whistlenose murmured. And he had, too—that strange wife of the Chief's. The one his traitorous brother, Stopmouth, had stolen away. Whistlenose remembered the day she'd fallen from the sky and how she'd kicked some of the hunters in the face when they'd tried to subdue her.

"Shhhh," he said to the stranger. "Shhh." And the roofman seemed to understand that Whistlenose had decided on rescue rather than butchery.

After that, only the Ancestors knew how the pair of them made it back to ManWays alive, for the stranger crashed his way through the woods and caught his ridiculous clothing on every branch or stung himself on every patch of red moss. He didn't understand the most basic of hand signals. He had to be guided everywhere with tugs of his puny arms.

But Whistlenose had lost the strength to feel any fear at all. He too, would have made easy prey for any hungry creature that came along. He was limping by now and in between pulses of pain from his bad leg, he kept thinking how unfair it was that it was taking them so long to reach safety. The first streets they encountered had been part of ManWays when he'd been learning to hunt with his father and uncles. Once upon a time, human guards had manned these walls, each with a shell to blow warning in case of attack.

War had put an end to that. The Armourbacks had wiped out half the Tribe and the new Chief—as Whistlenose still thought of Wallbreaker—had pulled everybody back to a few small streets around Centre Square where they could defend themselves better.

The loss still hurt, especially amongst the proud older hunters.

The hairy-faced stranger stopped suddenly to stare up at the Roof. Oh, there'd been a lot of activity up there lately: metal Globes speeding through the air and spitting fire at each other, while sometimes, distant patches of the great Roof itself turned completely black. But there was little to be seen there now, and Whistlenose nudged the man back into weary motion until—thank the Ancestors!—the first of the rickety New Walls came into view and a sudden waft of cookfire set his tummy to grumbling. Even better, his wife was there, jumping to her feet. Ashsweeper! He felt a lump in his throat. Too young to be with a man who had so few days left in him.

The stranger saw her too. He all but licked his lips at the sight of her long limbs. Rude, very rude. Whistlenose glared at him, but the man, if man he was, kept on looking at Ashsweeper even as she wrapped her husband in a warm embrace. People came running from all directions. "What's that on its face? Should we kill it? Is it a man?"

Ashsweeper ignored all of it. "You took your time," she whispered. Whistlenose could barely stand. He wanted to lose himself in her, but the stranger's eyes were still there, like knives in the back of his skull.

In the Chief's house, Whistlenose's left leg continued its trembling while his belly cried out for food. Smoke from a single fire tickled his eyes and lingered over trophies on the walls: the skins of mankind's enemies and prey. Whistlenose kept such souvenirs in his own home, but here, Wallbreaker had laid them out in ways that showed off the inner workings of the creatures' limbs and muscles. He had even drawn charcoal lines on the skins to show where the sinews used to be.

"Our Chief is mad," he had told Ashsweeper once, as the boy tossed in sleep beside them.

"Well, he can be as mad as he likes, husband. He's all that's keeping the Tribe alive."

"No, Ashsweeper. It's strong hunters that keep us alive. And that... that *Chief* won't even lift a spear. As if that feud with his brother unmanned him."

"Say what you want, love. We eat better thanks to his strange ideas and lose fewer hunters now than we ever did before. I think our population has even increased since we ate the Armourbacks."

Whistlenose brought himself back to the present to find the Chief studying him, as though he were one of the strange creatures pinned to the wall. The magic ball known as "the Talker" lit up the Chief's body with an eerie glow. Its light picked out the skin of his belly, strangely soft, like a woman's breast.

"Thank you, Whistlenose," Wallbreaker said. "You did well."

What he really meant, Whistlenose knew, was that of the six hunters who'd gone out the day before, any of the others would have been a more welcome sight than this old man so close to the soup. "You'll get your share of the prisoner if he is to be Volunteered."

"Thanks, Chief. But ... " his tummy rumbled again. "But what about now? Could I ... for my family ... ?"

Wallbreaker's eyes narrowed and seemed to fly like slingstones towards Whistlenose's sore leg. "Are you still limping, hunter? You told me that injury was better."

Upstairs, a child was crying and one of the Chief's wives tried to soothe it. Whistlenose felt sweat beading on his forehead. "I got away, didn't I? When nobody else could? You don't have to worry about me, Chief. I'll Volunteer like a proper man when my time comes, but it's not today." *Please, Ancestors! Make him listen.* "I leaped over a whole Wetlane on that leg. But my family still need something to eat."

"You brought nothing back."

"I brought the stranger. That makes it either a successful hunt or a successful rescue, depending on how you count it."

All of a sudden, the Chief laughed out loud, making the hunter jump.

"Your mind hasn't blunted, anyway," said Wallbreaker. "Very well. You can take four days' rations for your family. There are only three of you, am I right?"

Whistlenose nodded.

"And a tattoo. You don't have too many, I see, but if you really jumped over a Wetlane, then, by the Ancestors, you've earned one. Now, sit down while I speak to the creature you brought home. He might trust you, since you were the one to rescue him. But," the Chief raised a finger. "This is like the Flesh Council. No rumours leave my house. Sit. Go on. Sit."

Whistlenose stifled a sigh and hoped his bones didn't creak too loudly as he lowered himself onto a cushion of stuffed Hopper skins. Shame they were extinct. Their hide softened so well when properly chewed.

Hunters pushed the stranger into the room. He shrugged off the helping hands behind him.

"Too proud for his own good," Whistlenose muttered and the man's head swivelled towards him. He had understood the words and it took Whistlenose a moment to remember the power of the magical Talker.

The stranger's mouth moved. A quiet, musical voice spoke words that should have made no sense, but again, the Talker's power made them real: "This world is at an end."

The Chief flinched. Ever since the dreadful struggle with the Flyers and the Armourbacks, people had been saying the same thing. "The world is ending." Barely more than a thousand humans remained alive, squashed into a handful of streets. Strange lights had been seen on the Roof, and a new, numberless enemy, the Diggers, swept all before them so that even the Longtongues teetered on the verge of extinction. Wallbreaker hated such talk. He sent his Flesh Council bullies from hearth to hearth to shut the pessimists up. But even the Chief was said to cry in his sleep.

"He's worried he can't save us," Ashsweeper used to say.

"Can't save himself, you mean … "

And now this dark-skinned stranger with hair growing on his face and perfect teeth, had arrived in their midst like a messenger of doom from the Ancestors.

Wallbreaker cleared his throat and licked his lips before speaking. "You mean the Diggers will kill us?" He waved a hand at Whistlenose. "Just today your rescuer told me the Bloodskins

21

are no more. Their streets were collapsed or burning."

"Yes," the man said. He sat forward then and grabbed Whistlenose by the wrist in his strange dark fingers. "So good of you to keep me from the Longtongues. It's a bad way to go, getting your insides sucked out while you're still alive." He released his hold, like discarding a toy. "But the Diggers are the worst I've seen. Not even entertaining to watch — they're far too ... too efficient." He looked from the Chief to the hunter and back again. "I know you think you're going to eat me now, but you won't. Or were you planning to sell me to the Clawfolk? You won't do that either."

"How do you know these things?" asked Wallbreaker.

"Didn't your runaway wife explain it to you, Chief?"

"My ... how ... ?" The Chief should have beaten the stranger bloody, but he only looked confused.

The man grinned. It had a strange and terrible effect, coming as it did from behind the hair on his face. "We see everything in the Roof. Everything. We know what you did to her. A few, like myself, found that funny. A stuck-up Commissioner's daughter! Ha! Most of them up there have you down as a villain. But don't you worry about your reputation, savage. They have plenty to keep them occupied up there right now. Plenty."

"Why are you here?"

"Oh, it's not for the cooking, I'll tell you that." The man grinned again, as if he thought that was funny. "This little trip to the surface was way down on my list of options. Let's just say I passed on information that should have been kept quiet. The punishment for that sort of thing has grown drastic all of a sudden and when I knew they were on to me, I said to myself, Aagam, my friend, if they're going to send you down to the surface anyway, why not pick your own spot? Go where the professionals are. The ones who already know how to survive. Rule over them!"

Whistlenose sputtered, "You ... you mean to rule over us? And how — "

"Oh, not by force! Don't you worry! I, Aagam, the conqueror," he winked, "will run this tribe through its current Chief. That's right, Wallbreaker. You will do all the work. Deliver me my food and hope I learn to keep it down. Give me a few of the prettier wives and a bodyguard and generally do as I say."

Whistlenose looked from one man to the other, amazed that the Chief allowed this stranger, Aagam the Conqueror, to speak to him this way. It made no sense, but Wallbreaker seemed to have overcome his earlier surprise. Now, he cocked his head, the expression on his handsome face one of polite interest.

"And in return for all this free food and protection?"

"Information."

Wallbreaker nodded and suddenly, Whistlenose couldn't take it any more. He leaned over and pulled the man by his black, black hair into a strangle-hold until Aagam's eyes seemed to pop in their sockets and his weak fists tore hopelessly at the old hunter's rock-hard muscles.

The Chief watched, waiting until it was almost too late. Aagam was kicking up the furs at his feet, his face under the hair even darker.

"Enough, Whistlenose." Wallbreaker waved him lazily away. "I think our guest has learned his lesson. Haven't you, *guest*?"

It took Aagam a hundred heartbeats of spitting and choking to recover. When he had finished, his voice emerged as little more than a croak, although the Talker continued to translate it perfectly.

"You will regret that, savage," he said to Whistlenose. "Next time your tribe is looking for Volunteers to be traded for flesh, I'll make sure your Chief here puts your name at the top of the list."

For the first time, Whistlenose began to fear the stranger. Aagam the Conqueror and the Chief looked each other in the eye like kindred spirits, and Whistlenose couldn't get his mind around it. A few dark utterances about "information" and suddenly this beast could make threats? Whistlenose remembered the Chief's stolen wife, Indrani. She had fallen from the Roof, and she too had escaped the pot by means of the strange fascination she had held for Wallbreaker, little more than a young hunter back then.

"What exactly are you offering?" asked the Chief.

"Survival," said the stranger.

"How?"

The man grinned, rubbing at his neck. "Let's talk about your brother."

The Chief stiffened. Everybody knew that Stopmouth had run away with the Chief's second wife a few hundred days earlier. That Wallbreaker had survived the disgrace that followed was testimony to how much the Tribe relied on his clever schemes and his meticulous planning.

"Stopmouth must be dead by now," said the Chief.

"Yes," replied Aagam. Wallbreaker looked away and Whistlenose couldn't tell whether it was from sorrow or relief. "But," Aagam continued, "this is the best part. He only died about ten days ago, when these creatures called Yellowmaws got him."

Wallbreaker leaned forward. "Only ten days ago? Impossible! Unless ... did you ... did you *see* him die?"

"As good as. I watched him fall right into the mouth of one of the monsters. He was surrounded, and the nearest help lay three hard days' travel away. He's dead for sure."

"But only ten days ago ... "

"I'm telling you this free of charge," said Aagam. "I'll even tell you how he survived so long. The answer is that he found more people. More humans. As many as you have here. They have a Talker of their own and a few streets like these, only, see, they're living now behind a set of *hills* ... " it took a few moments to explain what a *hill* was, but the important thing was this: the *hills* represented a rocky barrier that Diggers found hard to tunnel through.

"They have a far more defensible position than you have here. That's the first thing. The second, is that this new tribe are weaklings compared to you. Fresh down from the Roof with little experience of hunting. They need you, and make no mistake, Chief, you need them too. You're surrounded by men like this savage beside me — the one you will soon have killed for me." He pointed at Whistlenose. "Yes, you." He grinned horribly from behind the hair on his face. "Stopmouth's tribe do not think as clearly as you do. They will not yet have realised that their numbers have grown too small to survive into the long term, even if the Diggers had never existed. At most, each group has another generation or even two, shrinking all the while. You know this, Wallbreaker, and I know you know it. You have a daughter of your own already and two pretty wives who want to kill each other. You may see grandchildren, but there'll be no great grandchildren. And that's the *best* outcome. That's with no Diggers at all. But there are Diggers, aren't there, Chief? The Bloodskins, you say, have fallen. Even the Longtongues, for all their love of the dark, will be lucky to last a hundred days more. And after that? Well... you *know* what happens after that."

Whistlenose watched the men watching each other: one rubbing his neck, but smug and sure; the other more tense, calculating.

"But you will save us," said the Chief eventually. "You, Aagam the... the Conqueror. You will lead us to join with the Tribe my brother found."

"Exactly. I will warn you of what lies ahead every step of the way. And more than that. I studied the Diggers when I knew I would have to come here. I learned their weaknesses and committed them to memory, my *real* memory." Whistlenose had no idea what Aagam had meant by "real" memory, but nor did he care. He could only watch the Chief fall deeper under the spell of a man who wanted him dead.

"And this will help us beat the Diggers, Aagam?"

"Oh, nobody can beat the Diggers. Not with the primitive weapons available to you here. But I can help you identify weak spots to keep us all alive long enough to get where we're going."

"And you can guarantee all of this?"

The man laughed, his voice still hoarse from Whistlenose's attack. "Not at all. It is highly unlikely any of us will be alive a hundred days from now. The only thing I can offer you is your best chance. I, Aagam, I am all you've got. So, you'd best treat me like a *king*. Like a *god*! So, first things first. You will trade this murderer

25

here for flesh. Then, you will offer me my pick of the women."

"The *unmarried* women."

Aagam grinned. "Of course." He looked at Whistlenose as he spoke, however. The hunter remembered how the man had stared at his wife. "Or those women soon to be widowed."

Whistlenose opened his mouth to plead, to promise — he wasn't sure what — but Wallbreaker got there first.

"This man, you have ordered me to sacrifice, is the best hunter in the Tribe." A blatant lie. Even at his very peak, Whistlenose had never risen higher than a second spear. "I will not waste this great hunter on a whim."

The stranger's eyes narrowed. "Don't bargain with a master, Chief. I can count tattoos as well as anybody else." Whistlenose only had three, not including the new one he'd been promised.

Wallbreaker shrugged. "I can have you served to me as soup within the hour, stranger. I can trade you to the Clawfolk or even the Longtongues now that I have a Talker. Yes, it might be worth giving them a sign of goodwill."

"Oh, I don't think so. You'll want to know what happened to Indrani, won't you? That runaway wife of yours."

"*Kidnapped* wife."

"Whatever you like. You'll want to learn her whereabouts. She's still alive, you know. She made it all the way to that new tribe I was talking about. The one only I can lead you to."

Whistlenose held his breath. He could feel his life, his family's future, hanging by a thread.

"I could make you talk, stranger. I could cut bits off you until I had learned your secrets."

"Yes, and you would never know which things I told you were true and which invented."

"It's not as if I know that now, is it?" The Chief paused, his eyes like slits. "So, this then is my decision. You, stranger —"

"Aagam."

"You will tell me something useful now. Something I can see the truth of immediately. Prove your value first. Then, we will see about your demands for a wife and," he glanced at Whistlenose, "other things."

Aagam nodded and opened his mouth to speak, but Wallbreaker stopped him with a gesture. "You will tell only me. Whistlenose? You may return home. We will need a fuller account of everything you have learned this day. Go. I promised you rations. Collect them from Mossheart on the way out."

Whistlenose cleared his throat. "I ... I just wanted to say ... to ask ... "

"I will do what's best for the Tribe."

"Of ... of course."

3.
EXCUSED FROM WORK

Whistlenose had seen his wife by now and the Chief too, so everybody was free to ask him for news. First among these were some of the relatives of the men in his hunting party. "Highstepper died bravely," he lied, "spear in hand until the end. It came for him quickly." And so on, until, utterly exhausted he came down the steps into the cellar that was now his family's only home. They'd had a full house all to themselves before the Armourbacks had wiped out half the Tribe, but he loved the coziness he shared with his little family and never missed the extra rooms.

"I have flesh," he said to Ashsweeper. It was food from the communal stores now run by Wallbreaker's sad wife, Mossheart. Ashsweeper hugged him, her hair soft around his face. Another pair of smaller arms came from nowhere to wrap themselves about his knees.

The next thing he knew, he was lying on the floor, looking back up the cellar steps with Ashsweeper and the boy wide-eyed with fear above him. He had collapsed. Not from an injury, although his leg still tormented him.

"I'm all right," he told them, voice slurring. "Just need to sleep. How's my strong boy?" He never heard the answer, or gave his wife news of the stranger who wanted him dead. His eyes closed and that was all.

Whistlenose woke to the delicious smells of roasting meat. He wasn't sure what creature it had come from—Mossheart had failed to mention it. Instead, she had stared at his sore leg before picking out the food for him. But there was no need to think about that now. The aroma filled his senses and Ashsweeper laughed at the sight of him.

"Is it me or the food that has maddened you, husband?"

He grinned, remembering her on the day they'd jumped the fire together. How shy she had been back then! She was his third wife. Laughlouder had disappeared one day while out making rope. Nobody knew how. But Sleepyeyes had still been alive at the time and a little jealous when Ashsweeper had joined the family. She'd been proud too, though, to be senior wife, and hopeful the newcomer might finally bring them all a child.

Sleepyeyes had lived to see the boy born, but then the Flyers and their allies had come and the Senior Wife had died, knife in hand, while mother and child escaped out the back door. She wasn't really an Ancestor, but Whistlenose had heard Ashsweeper praying sometimes to the older woman and it filled him with love and pride every time.

"Where's our son?" asked Whistlenose, mouth full, hands wrapped around a hot skull bowl.

That's when he heard the slap of little feet on the stone cellar steps and he had to fend the child off until he could hand the food back to his wife. "Who's this?" he asked in mock surprise. "This hunter is far too big to be my child!"

"Men, papa," said the giggling boy. "There're men waiting for you!"

A voice called down to them from the outside. "You awake yet?" it was Whistlenose's friend Frownbrow.

"Not really," he called back, hoping Frownbrow would take the hint and leave him more time to play with his son. He wanted to speak to Ashsweeper too. She hadn't asked him a thing since he'd come home, but she would need to hear it all. Collapsing as he had done, had cost him a whole day and a night when he

PEADAR Ó GUILÍN

should have been planning on what to do about Aagam. At the very least, he could have spoken to Ashsweeper's brothers about finding her a new husband before it was too late.

"Sorry to disturb you, my friend," Frownbrow said. "Really. But the Chief wants to see you."

"Oh," he said, his heart freezing in his chest. *Already?*

"What's wrong?" his wife asked him.

He called back up the steps. "I haven't swallowed a bite since I got back. Can you give me a few heartbeats to finish up?"

He tensed, waiting for the reply. He heard Frownbrow saying to somebody else, "What's the harm? We'll tell the Chief he wasn't at home and we had to go looking…"

Ashsweeper stood patiently before him as the footsteps of the men above retreated. He looked into her eyes. No fear lay there yet, just puzzlement. An urge took him to lie to her, but time mattered in these things, so he said, "I don't think I'm coming back. I love you."

She nodded and scooped the boy up from the floor. "Give your father a kiss," she whispered. Another wife might have demanded to know what was happening. Ashsweeper never thought like that; she already had the important information and she would bind it up behind her serene face until she could be alone. He'd often caught her crying in the past and scolded her for not letting him help. But he was grateful now. Whistlenose hugged the boy. Then, as he was heading up the steps, Ashsweeper called him back. "Husband?"

He turned.

"Won't you flick a drop of blood at me?" It was something hunters did. A promise to come home. He shook his head. "I think… I think the Tribe needs my blood. All of it."

What could she say to that? All she could do now was prevent the giggling boy from chasing his father up the stairs, her face a mask.

Whistlenose staggered into the blue Rooflight of midday. Had he really slept so long when every moment should have been so precious to him? People smiled at him, around their communal fires.

30

"You really jumped a Wetlane?" asked young Fearsflyers. The boy—no, he was a full hunter now and one of the best—clapped Whistlenose on the shoulder hard enough to sting. He grinned around twisted teeth where half of his most recent meal rotted unhappily. "Why didn't the canal beasts get you? They weren't hungry?" He was tagging along and his presence gave everybody else permission to join in too. People always wanted to know the details of a hunt.

"I haven't spoken yet," Whistlenose said. "I haven't spoken to all the wives and children of the others."

"Oh, sorry! It's been more than a day!" said Fearsflyers. As quickly as it had gathered, the crowd was gone and Whistlenose was left to make the frightening walk to the Chief's house by himself. Still, though, it was true that he hadn't spoken to Spearcatcher's widow yet. He'd have to be allowed that first, wouldn't he?

His mind was racing. He couldn't stop it. He realized his fear of death wasn't just about Ashsweeper and the boy. He wanted to live for himself too. He wanted to be there when his son finally got a name. He wanted to teach him to make a spear; to butcher a carcass. To play the ambush game together; to sling at old skulls up on the wall.

But it was the Tracking game the boy enjoyed most of all: the carefully hidden clues to find the scrap of meat. They had such fun, the two of them!

Whistlenose found himself in Centre Square all too soon, the houses blackened by a hundred lifetimes of soot. He looked up at the Chief's home and found his eyes fixed on the empty sockets of a Bloodskin skull embedded into the wall. Gone now. All the Bloodskins were gone. Other extinct species watched him too: Hoppers; Armourbacks; Flim. As well as many others whose names the people had long since forgotten, but whose flesh had fed the Blessed Ancestors.

Would his own skull be decorating some beast's dwelling tomorrow? He wanted to turn back. Instead, he reached for the heavy hides concealing the entrance to the Chief's house. The curtains twitched back before he could touch them.

A woman stood there clutching the hand of a toddling girl. She was startlingly beautiful with her tossed blonde hair and her pale, pale skin. Her mouth, though, had a sad look about it, creasing towards the ground. People heard her shouting at her husband in the night and wondered if he would put her aside, or even trade her away. Outside of the home, however, she said little to anyone.

"Hello, Mossheart," he said.

"Goodbye, Whistlenose," she replied. "I think." She led her girl off down the street and even now, his head turned to follow after her lithe figure. But the sick feeling in his stomach brought the hunter back to himself. Go forward, he told himself. Volunteer willingly and Ashsweeper might be given another husband.

He stepped inside and turned right towards the main room. He had expected hunters to be waiting on guard, but the Chief had sent them away, maybe even to look for Whistlenose. He heard men's voices raised in argument. One wasn't speaking human, but Whistlenose understood every word.

"Half of us will die," the Chief was saying, "if we move from here."

"At least half," Aagam agreed.

In the dark of the hallway, Whistlenose imagined the man to be grinning. That's just how the voice sounded to him.

"We know the streets here, every building. We can defend ourselves."

"No doubt about it." Still grinning.

Neither man spoke for a dozen heartbeats more. Whistlenose squared his shoulders and was about to step inside when he heard the Chief's voice, little more than a whisper. "You think I want *her* back so badly, that I would risk ... everything?"

"Perhaps you want to kill her. Or to kick your brother's corpse. Or kiss it. What do I care? I, I Aagam want to live longer. That's what matters to me. Maybe I'll find a way back to the Roof when all the fighting up there is over. But not if we stay here, with the Bloodskins gone already and the Longtongues soon to follow. I need to be in that other place where the hard rock goes deep into the ground. I want it around me until the Diggers exhaust their food supply and die off."

"So, why didn't you land amongst Stopmouth's tribe instead of us? No—don't bother answering. You would have nothing to offer them, would you? Except your flesh."

Aagam laughed. "Exciting, isn't it? Look, I won't say I'm not wetting myself with terror at the thought of it. Aagam is no fool. Or maybe I am a fool. But look, the Roof gave me the odds before I left. I ran enough simulations. No chance of survival at all if we stay here, compared to one in eight if we leave. I'm taking the one in eight and your dirty savages will be running that risk with me."

"All except for one," said Wallbreaker.

Recognizing he'd been caught, Whistlenose stepped into the room. The Chief looked up from the hides he squatted on. "You were well-named, hunter. It took me a while before I realized what the sound was."

Whistlenose nodded, ashamed to have been spying, even now when it couldn't possibly matter. "You … you are going to give me to this … creature then."

"*Foreigner* is the word you're looking for," said Aagam. "Your language doesn't have it, but your Tribe might be needing it soon if they get where they're going."

"But not me."

"You should have been more respectful to me," said Aagam. "You laid hands upon me."

"I could make up for it."

Aagam grinned. "I have never eaten flesh, did you know that? Can you even imagine it?"

Whistlenose shook his head.

"But if I must, it would please me that yours was the first."

"I rescued you."

"Nobody rescued me. Aagam came here under his own

33

strength. That will be my story from now on, after yours has come to an end."

The Chief looked up at Whistlenose. This was his chance to Volunteer, he knew that. A willing victim always earned his family more respect than the one who had to be dragged. In spite of that, Whistlenose suddenly found himself on his knees in front of Aagam and Wallbreaker. "I will tell the Tribe you saved me. From ... from Longtongues or Diggers. I will tell them. Anything you want. But let me live."

Aagam grinned, saying nothing. A bead of sweat ran down Whistlenose's forehead and onto his cheeks, like a coward's tears. He turned his head to find the Chief looking at him too. He expected to see scorn on that handsome, youthful face, but instead ... could it be? *Understanding*? The look disappeared too quickly for him to be sure, however, and he swivelled back to face Aagam again.

After what seemed like a lifetime, the dark man nodded. "That wasn't so hard, was it? Begging is good. It shows who is the leader and who is the *servant*. Am I right, Whistlenose?"

"Yes, Aagam."

Aagam smiled again and turned towards the Chief. "I want him dead." And Whistlenose's heart turned cold. The stranger continued, "Sooner or later this old hunter will try to kill me. I know how these things work."

"That is how *you* work," Wallbreaker agreed.

"And who knows," continued Aagam, "what he heard while he was listening there?"

"We can trust this hunter."

"No, savage, great men can trust no one. Your brother showed you that much."

"He was so young," said Wallbreaker with a sigh. "I thought I would be glad to hear he had died. After his betrayal."

"You gave him everything. He owed you his very survival and still he wanted your woman."

"Yes." Wallbreaker smacked the ground with his fist. "Yes!"

Then, red-faced, he turned to the kneeling hunter. "You will Volunteer for the Tribe so that the rest of us might make it home."

Aagam laughed. "Do you even know what that means, Chief? That thing you all say, 'So that the rest of us might make it home'? Do you even know where 'home' is? *What* it is? It's *Earth*! It's—"

"Shut up! Or I will kill you myself."

"No, you won't," but Aagam settled down.

"I'm sorry, Whistlenose. The Tribe needs your flesh. But I, Wallbreaker, swear to you, I swear that if you can keep your mouth shut and do the right thing, your wife will remarry and your son will have a new father. I'll do everything I can to make sure the boy gets an early name. The pregnant women will confirm it if I ask them to."

Whistlenose found he was trembling. "When must I go?"

"We have a choosing tomorrow. We're sending some of our injured to the Clawfolk. We'll need a lot of flesh for … for our journey. You probably heard that much from the door. And it's a good deal for you anyway. You have to know that. You can't hide that bad leg forever."

Whistlenose nodded. He felt calmer now. He had the Chief's oath. "Can I spend the last night at home?"

"Yes," Wallbreaker replied, just as Aagam said the opposite.

"He'll talk!" the stranger said. "To his pretty wife."

"No he won't. Not if he wants to keep her from the pot."

"I do." Whistlenose swallowed. "I know this man promises to save our tribe. But he is a monster and he would see us all dead before Volunteering a finger."

Aagam shrugged. "I am. I would."

"Go on," said Wallbreaker. "Go home. Your wife is excused work today."

And there was nothing more to be said.

35

4.

SAVING THE Y⊕UNG

Clawfolk skittered everywhere along the roads, or hung from buildings by their fifth limb, the one that ended in a bony hook. They ran clumsily, careening off each other and scraping moss from the walls with impacts from their shell-covered bodies. The creatures chittered in voices only a Talker could understand. They climbed over each other and none of the nervous human volunteers had any doubt that they did so in an excitement of hunger and anticipation. The creatures were going to be getting a lot of flesh, after all: there were a good twenty men and women here, limping along as though half-asleep towards the end of their lives.

The Tribe needed to build up its stores and to leave the slow behind it. Of all the Volunteers, only Whistlenose knew why.

"They kill easy here," said Fearsflyers. He had been given the honour of leading the escorts. "Everybody says so."

Whistlenose nodded, but Cleanhair—whose husband he had seen captured by the Diggers only a few days earlier—snapped at the young guard. "And you've been slaughtered by the Clawfolk yourself, have you? You returned to tell the tale? How nice for you."

"Well … no, I … "

"Nobody knows how they kill here, puppy," she said. She turned away from him, had probably forgotten the unfortunate youngster already. Cleanhair would have a lot on her mind, even apart from her coming sacrifice. She had left two children behind in the care of a brother.

Whistlenose tried not to think about his own family. That joyous little boy who had wished daddy luck on "the hunt," not realising they would never play together again; and Ashsweeper, chin high and proud. No tears from her, but no words either from her trembling lips. What would become of them now when the Chief announced his great journey and its mysterious purpose?

The escorts allowed him to join them in guarding the other Volunteers. It distracted him for much of the day as they walked towards ClawWays. But now as they were coming to the entrance of a huge building with Clawfolk lined messily to either side, their yellow-splotched shells polished and decorated with lumps of moss, he had to hand over his spear to the younger men.

"It will serve you well," he said to Fearsflyers. He couldn't keep the shake out of his voice. "Give it plenty to drink."

The young man nodded enthusiastically. "I will make you all proud of me!"

"We're dead," said Cleanhair. "And the dead don't care."

"Of course not. I'm—I'm—"

Whistlenose interrupted him. "Good-bye, Fearsflyers." He gripped the youngster's forearm. Then, he pulled him close to whisper, "The Chief made me a promise. An oath."

"You told me, Whistlenose. I won't forget. I'll look in on Ashsweeper when I get home. You did the tribe proud, escaping like that."

"I ... I was rescued by ... " he was supposed to say "Aagam," but the lie stuck in his throat. And then they had reached the entrance of the huge building.

Whistlenose had travelled this far once before with a group of volunteers, one of whom had been his own brother. It seemed a very long time ago.

"We have to turn back now," said Fearsflyers.

"I know ... I ... I just want to say ... you performed this difficult duty with great honour. You bring pride to your Ancestors." A smile from the younger man, and then he and the other hunters were all gone, leaving the old and injured, the weak, the tired, behind.

By now, the heat of midday radiated down from the Roof of the world. Whistlenose felt it as a caress on his skin. All around the humans and the gathering Clawfolk, tiny glittering mossbeasts swarmed through the air or landed in impossibly co-ordinated formations on the crumbling walls. The Volunteer followed them with his eyes, marvelling at their freedom, at the flashing colours of their shells. Everything, everything shone so intensely, so suddenly beautiful.

Except... the Roof. He looked up at it one last time. No Globes hung there now—nobody had seen any for days—but it wasn't that that had drawn his attention. Something was wrong, as if the quality of the light up there had changed. It felt too dim for this time of day.

The Clawfolk didn't care. They pushed in to surround the Volunteers and Whistlenose felt a gentle pressure at his back. "All right, all right." His stomach started churning, but he moved forward into the darkness. Cleanhair was at his elbow and, as they moved around some shadowy corner, the last of the light disappeared and the smell of blood grew ever more pungent. He felt the woman grip his arm, although she said nothing. A few of the other Volunteers spoke nervously among themselves or muttered prayers to the Ancestors to accept their spirits. A few of them repeated the well-known story of the Clawfolk killing quickly. "They'll line us up and it'll be over and we'll be looking down on our children. You'll see..."

"How strange," he said to Cleanhair, although he couldn't see her now. They had been walking for a few hundred heartbeats. His own voice sounded strange to him. Instinctively he knew they had come into a vast, empty room. He couldn't stop himself talking. "A roll of Clawfolk meat—that was always my favourite food. And now—"

A man screamed—really screamed—hard enough to break something inside. The skittering of claws was suddenly everywhere and Cleanhair's grip, painful on his arm, tightened even more. But then, the skittering became louder. Something barrelled into Whistlenose, throwing him from his feet to roll on ground covered in stinging brick dust and cement.

"W-Whistlenose?" Cleanhair had been torn from his grip. "A-are you there." But then she yelped, as though her husband had playfully poked her in the side. It turned to a shriek, however. Something snapped in the darkness and she was whimpering and crying and begging. And all the while, he lay there, winded, stunned, shocked. It was supposed to be quick! His hand found a stone. He would not attack the Clawfolk with it—even if he could see one. They were Volunteers, after all. Volunteers for the future of the Tribe, for Ashsweeper; for a beautiful, nameless boy.

But his last act, he swore to the Ancestors, would be to finish off Cleanhair, whose sobs had yet to end. He scrambled onto all fours and reached for the source of her whimpers. He found her head with his left hand and raised the stone, but luckily, she had already gone to the Ancestors. "She had a thousand days left in her," he whispered, wondering when they would come for him, whether he would scream as much.

In a distant part of the building, a man cried defiance. He must have run, he must be trying to fight, attracting hungry beasts from all directions and away, it seemed, from Whistlenose. He strained his ears. *There's one behind me right now.* He imagined it standing perfectly still, its hanging claw poised above his head.

I can't run. Must stay. For the Tribe. Not that there was anywhere to run to, he knew.

His eyes were finally adapting to the dark: enough that he could discern the grey shapes of Clawfolk shooting over and back across the space and sometimes, too, the sight of their human prey, evading them, it seemed, all too easily.

He had seen the shelled beasts hunting many times in the streets of ManWays. As a child, he and his friends knew no greater entertainment than the watch them stalking Hairbeasts strong enough to smash through shell with a single blow of their bone clubs. But the Clawfolk were agile enough that they won more

39

often than they lost. Nor had they had never been particularly cruel with their kills. So, why had Cleanhair, and at least one other, been made to suffer so much?

It took Whistlenose a few moments to understand the difference between the Clawfolk he had seen in the past and those before him now. They're children, he realised. This was where they learned to hunt. Safely. On prey that was too weak or injured or confused to do them real damage. Cleanhair's slow death could be explained by nothing more than a lack of experience.

Through the palms of his hands, he felt the ground tremble. So strange was the feeling, but so slight that he couldn't be sure it had been real. *Like the way the light of the Roof dimmed before we came in here.*

Then he forgot all about it, because three shadows had coalesced out of the gloom around him: juvenile Clawfolk. They stood no more than waist high to him, their forelimbs waving hypnotically, embedded with the rocks or shards of old metal they used to kill. He should have stayed put and let them put an end to his worries and his bad leg forever. Instead, he was running suddenly towards the centre of the building, weaving and ducking as new figures popped into existence around him.

Up ahead, the room brightened. There seemed to be a door there and his feet took him in that direction, for all he knew that he would never betray the Tribe by actually escaping. Still, he ran, ignoring the growing, familiar ache.

Something hit him from above, landing hard enough to drive him to the floor, sending him sprawling, scrabbling on torn knees. He had forgotten they liked to hang high above street-level to drop on their victims! He rolled as claws smacked next to his face; felt the wind of another strike pass over his head. And he should have died then, but for some reason the attack stopped and he dove forward, aiming for the light he'd seen before. He should be right at it now, at the exit except ... except the door wasn't there any more. *Nothing* was there. His dark-adapted eyes were suddenly useless to him. He heard ... he heard a *rumbling* sound and felt it through the soles of his feet again. It made no sense: not the complete darkness; not the trembling of the ground. Whistlenose reached out to find himself standing before a curtain of hides. It moved easily under his hands. He opened it to the air beyond, he was sure of that, sure of it. But there was nothing outside either. No Roof, no streets, no houses. Nothing.

From somewhere high up in the air, there came a strange, screeching sound. The Roof flickered. Then the tracklights came on for a heartbeat, followed by the full, terrible glare of midday. The savage light pulsed once; twice.

And then, the entire building fell down behind him.

A voice said, "Twisted my ankle. Again!"

Whistlenose groaned, the whole world a blur. He had his back to a building, his various cuts and grazes stinging from contact with the moss growing there. He felt bruised all over and the words he was hearing felt like echoes, or the whisperings of a ghost.

"Who ... ?" He coughed, rubbed his eyes and found he was not alone. Dust hung heavy in the air, more than he had ever seen before. He couldn't tell where he was, although he had hunted these streets his whole adult life.

"Don't know why they still haven't killed us," said the voice. A man. "Probably need us to stay fresh. Don't want rotting meat in an emergency, right?"

Whistlenose knew where he was now and it didn't make sense. The giant building in which they were all supposed to die, lay in ruins. Walls leaned at impossible angles.

He had heard of this kind of thing before. Houses had fallen in his grandfather's time and the tunnels of the Diggers were said to have collapsed entire streets. But this was different; terrifying.

No more than a hundred paces away, a huge shard, like a spearhead made of bone, rose jaggedly from the wreckage of another collapsed building.

"It fell from the Roof," said the man beside Whistlenose. Charmer. A hunter like himself, beyond his prime and Volunteered

41

now because of a recent injury. He waved an arm. "You can see where it came off."

Sure enough, shielding his eyes from the glare, Whistlenose could see a black triangle in amongst the panels of the Roof. Other, nearby areas seemed dimmer to him than usual, but it was hard to say.

"Just as well we're getting out of this, Whistlenose. We can do some good for the Tribe as Ancestors."

Hundreds of Clawfolk swarmed around the wreckage of the slaughterhouse, pulling bodies free. They made a hissing sound—rare for them. He'd only ever heard it when they were losing a fight with the Hairbeasts. A sound of despair, maybe. Or defiance. Curiosity pulled Whistlenose to his feet. On the far side of Charmer lay another human, a girl whose name he couldn't remember. She looked healthy and he had no idea why she had been Volunteered. He left the other two and walked in amongst the crowd of his hosts, wondering if they would kill him for it, but uncaring. The mad panic that had made him run for his life earlier had left him. What did anything matter if the Roof itself could fall?

The Clawfolk ignored him, shoving him out of the way. Their long forelimbs were dressed in tubes of shell that humans sometimes fashioned into trumpets for their guards. But the tips, unlike the backlimb that carried the claw, were soft enough that tools could be embedded in them. The creatures made excellent use of them now to pull bodies from the wreckage. Dozens had died: appalling losses for any Tribe. No wonder they hissed, the sound all around him now as he picked his way amongst them.

To one side, a large group of Clawfolk piled wreckage up against one of the remaining walls, as though making a stair. They must have been working at it for several tenths of a day, for they had almost completed it. *How long was I unconscious?*

They finished as he watched. Without pausing for breath, three of them clambered up their new ramp and swung themselves onto the top of the wall with their hook limbs. But there, they halted, hissing and hissing, a whole row of the shelled beasts making a choir of despair.

Whistlenose followed, up the pile of shaky masonry, two stories high, until he stood balancing on the wall right in amongst them where any could have pushed him to his death.

He saw now what had upset them so much. A thin arch of stone separated this wall from another with a drop beneath so high, that not even the Clawfolk could have survived it.

Beyond the arch, on the far wall, a full dozen youngsters hung by their clawlimbs. They were smaller even than those that had chased Whistlenose within the building. Perhaps they had been left there by their elders to witness the hunt and learn from it. But they had been hanging for several Tenths of a day already and, as he watched, one of them lost its grip. It slid down the wall, tumbled and smashed itself amongst the debris below. More hissing. Several of the adults sidled up to the arch of stone leading across, but the human could see their bodies were too wide, too rounded to balance there.

"I'll do it."

Of course, they didn't understand and wouldn't get out of his way. He had to lower himself back onto the stair they had made and climb across until he could push up in front of them. Only when he stood at the arch, did they seem to get the idea and finally made room for him. The hissing stopped at once.

"What are you doing?" Charmer called up, but Whistlenose ignored him.

The light of the Roof was dimming now, but in a natural way, with the approach of dusk. He lay flat and pulled himself up the arch, wondering at the damage it had suffered and thinking it must surely collapse under him. "I'm already dead," he muttered. No need for his pulse to beat so insistently in his ears; no need for all that sweat. "Already dead. Food for the Clawfolk so the others can make it Home." For the first time in his life, he wondered where Home actually was. Aagam knew, the horrible stranger. *Earth*, he had called it, whatever that meant. Oh well. Whistlenose would learn the answer soon enough, when he became an Ancestor.

Another of the Clawfolk children tumbled, sickeningly into the rubble, and another. The hissing started up again and the Roof continued to darken. mossbeasts flew in around Whistlenose's body, tasting it, flying off again. He reached the top of the arch, slid forward on his belly, squealing in terror like an infant as he slipped sideways and hung with legs dangling over the abyss.

"Nothing to worry about, no need to hiss for me. I'm there now." Painfully, he pulled himself back up, until he sat on the far wall, the first of the "children" already within reach.

After that, it went quickly. The shelled bodies were much lighter than they looked and far from stupid. The first of those he rescued, moved out of his way and began pulling its fellows out of danger until all stood on the wall, their claws digging into its surface for balance. Then, it was half a night of waiting until the Clawfolk working at the front of the building had finally cleared a way through from below.

Whistlenose found his way back to the surviving two humans. "Thought they'd eaten you already," said Charmer. "Here, they gave us a few skulls of water. Look like you need some." Whistlenose did. More badly than ever he had in his life, although the Roofsweat had cooled him down as he waited on the wall. He collapsed beside the other hunter and the strange, silent girl.

"Wake up!" Whistlenose felt a dig in his side. The Roof was brightening again. He was stiff and cold, his leg aching. He dimly remembered feeling the pain in a dream. "Unless," said Charmer, "you prefer to die in your sleep?"

"That would have been a favour," said Whistlenose.

"Suppose so," said Charmer. "Sorry. Didn't think of that."

A dozen adult Clawfolk were gathering before the last Volunteers. They had sharpened bits of stone and metal embedded in their forelimbs. "They look hungry," said Charmer.

"I'm afraid," said the girl out of the blue. Her voice sounded hoarse. "I'm so afraid." And yet, she stood up. There really was nothing wrong with her. No limping, no shattered limbs. She strode right over to the nearest beast. And then, she was on the ground, gurgling and bleeding out.

Charmer was gasping now too, but from fear. "Wish ... wish ... " He couldn't walk, of course, with his injury, so the Clawfolk came for him. "I," he said. "Maybe—?" A creature shattered his skull with an embedded rock.

Whistlenose surged to his feet, breathing hard, heart hammering, desperate for life. He realised he wasn't as brave as the girl had been, that he couldn't look his fate in the eye. So, he lowered his head and forced himself to step forward. It was like walking with stones tied to his feet. Every part of him hurt. Even his eyes stung.

He jumped as he felt a brush of shell against his skin. He was hiccoughing with terror, ready to be sick. Another touch, a shove this time, and he stumbled forward. Another push, and yet another.

He raised his head, only to be nudged forward one more time. "You ... you're sending me away?" He was already standing on the far side of the group. He could see them butchering Charmer's body. He had witnessed such scenes all of his life, but only now did he feel sickened by it. *That should be me!* One of the Clawfolk kept pushing him farther and farther away, until eventually, he found the strength to turn around and walk off of his own accord.

5.
m⊕ss

Alone and helpless and old, Whistlenose had no idea where he should be going. *I'm supposed to be a Volunteer.* He couldn't stay out in the open, that was for sure. A friendless human was little better than a free meal. So he ducked into the first abandoned house he found.

He was thirsty again already, but he needed to think this through. He had a duty. He *had* to persuade the Clawfolk to take him back, even if it meant killing himself in front of them. Surely they wouldn't let his flesh go to waste?

He wrapped his arms over his head, hearing the wheezing of his nose working in time to the pulse of pain in his bad leg. The problem was that he still wanted to live. He had done everything he was supposed to do, had offered himself up. It wasn't his fault he had been rejected.

So, why not just go home and explain what had happened? He could be with his family again and feel their warm skin against his. Except ... nobody would believe his story. They would think he had run away. And even if the Chief used his Talker to ask the Clawfolk for the truth of the matter, his leg would get no better, his arm no faster, and Aagam would still be living in Centre Square, demanding his death.

All paths ended in the pot as far as he could see.

The least awful result he could hope for, was that his own

Tribe would get the benefit of his flesh. His own wife and child. He would try for that.

The walk home was a nightmare. Many creatures had been attracted by the disaster that had struck the Clawfolk. Guards were fewer, and everywhere, hunting parties haunted the alleys and staked out the sources of water Whistlenose so desperately needed. He spent a full day and half a night on a journey that should have lasted no more than a few tenths, passing through all of ClawWays and the no-man's land that lay between it and home. He avoided Pios, with their thin, sharp beaks, and padded around the tracks left behind by a pack of supposedly-extinct Climbers. Useful news, at least, for those back home.

Finally, the outer walls that had protected the old 'Ways of his youth swallowed him up. Humans no longer controlled these streets, but the older ones like Whistlenose knew them better than any enemy.

"I'll have one last night with Ashsweeper," he muttered. They'd grant him that much at least, before sending him off again.

He stopped uncertainly in the shadow of a building, cool with Roofsweat, utterly exhausted. Starving. What if he got home for that final night only to waste it by sleeping right through as he had done when he had returned with Aagam? The thought filled him with sadness. No, he would go into an old house. *His* old house. The one where he had grown up with an older brother and two sisters. He would rest on the same floor he had been born on and return home refreshed.

He found it without difficulty. The old place had seen better times. Parts of the walls had been scavenged to build the newer defences closer to Centre Square, leaving the ceiling to cave in and the first floor to collapse. Whistlenose crawled in through a gap that remained in the rubble, into what was left of the family room. He had not the energy to check it out for enemies or even to pound the stinging juices out of a bit of moss so that he might make a pillow for himself. He used his loincloth—the only thing he possessed in the world other than his flesh, and even that, he had stolen from his Tribe. *You can have me back, though. You can have me back tomorrow.*

Daylight woke him—a single beam swirling with dust, coming through a hole in the ceiling. Midday again already, by the looks of it. This time two days before, he had passed into the slaughterhouse of the Clawfolk to die. Chafe marks and scabs on his thighs showed where he had almost slid from the arch. It had really happened. A piece of the Roof had actually fallen to the ground with no provocation, to smash entire buildings.

Looking around the ruin in which he had spent the night, with its collapsed ceiling, he wondered for the first time if the greatest threat to his people might be something other than the Diggers. Aagam had said the world was ending, hadn't he? And who would know better than a Roofman?

Well, there's nothing I can do about that, now, is there? His one remaining responsibility was to turn himself in and win another last night with his family.

And yet, he stayed where he was. He found he was breathing hard. He kept hearing the screams of the slaughterhouse in the dark. His mind's eye returned again and again to the scene of Charmer's death and that of the nameless girl. He even found splashes of their blood on his skin. He had to force himself to lick it clean so as not to dishonour his fellow Volunteers.

And still he did not rise to turn himself in.

"Don't be a fool, boy. After all you've seen in your life!" He'd killed beasts himself, many times, for all he wasn't much of a hunter. He had hacked and chopped; stabbed and bludgeoned and crushed them. He had tripped them so others could finish the job. He had seen hunters die a dozen times and had been part of honour guards escorting old friends and members of his own family as Volunteers to the creatures who would end their lives. It had all been so normal. Yet now, his body refused to take its turn.

He froze. He heard human voices out in the street, all women.

Hunting parties would use hand signals and whispers to communicate. Voices—and the laughter that came next—could only mean large numbers. It meant safety. He pulled himself up onto his knees and crawled to the shadowy gap that was the only way in or out of his refuge. He saw the backs of two women. One had a sleeping child strapped to her chest—another sign that there must be a cordon of guards not too far away. Both of them wore the wraparound sheets of Hopper hide that women used when collecting moss or rubble.

"No, Chinwagger." said the taller of the two. She had black hair, tied in ligament twine to keep it out of her face. The shorter woman, the one with the child, had just struck at something with a rock. "No, I said! What are you doing?"

"What does it look like? I'm getting the juice out."

"He said not to do that, Chinwagger. The Chief!"

The shorter one threw the rock at the ground so that it bounced away. "That makes no sense! Who ever heard of *not* pounding moss? I don't want to bring all that poison home with me."

"Well, he was very careful to say he wanted it unpounded and to bring only the red stuff too."

"Ancestors, he's mad! The red stuff? Sure it's only good for smoking meat!"

The black haired woman looked around to see if anybody else stood nearby. Luckily, she didn't lower her eyes to where Whistlenose crouched, less than three spear-lengths away. But he had caught a glimpse of her face at least, and had identified her as Drumdancer, a friend of the Chief's first wife. "It's that new Roofman he's adopted. Aagam. What does that name mean, anyway?"

"If he even is a man!" said Chinwagger. "That skin ... like the false woman he took for a wife, remember? She fell from the Roof too. He's obsessed with them. She was no more a woman than he's a man, if you ask me."

"Oh, Aagam is a man, all right. Poor Ashsweeper had to marry him the very same day Whistlenose did his duty. Whoever heard of such a thing unless it was one of the man's own brothers?" She pointed up at the Roof. "I bet Whistlenose is up there now, fuming with anger."

"Well, he won't be the only one," said Drumdancer. "That new beast from the Roof wants more wives, and the Chief is going to let him have them."

Whistlenose didn't hear what came next. His ears were ringing, his vision blurred. He found himself lying in the dust of his old house, weeping. Some instinct made him smother the sounds of it in the flesh of his arms.

Ashweeper, made to marry without the proper mourning! He remembered the way the hairy Roofman had looked at his wife when they had returned together into ManWays. Of course. *That's the real reason. That's why he was so keen to have me killed.* His hands found his loincloth and throttled it between them. *Die, monster!* He fell back, sick and dizzy with hunger and despair.

He had no plan and no more strength. Less than a thousand paces from the place where he cowered, his family had passed into the hands of a Waster and there was nothing he could do about it.

"No more red moss here," said Chinwagger. "Stupid task anyway. Come on …"

Whistlenose barely noticed. His chest felt like it was in the grip of an ever-tightening noose. He gasped and a sob escaped that had been building and building since, who knew how long? Since the moment he had been Volunteered, perhaps.

"I heard something!" said Chinwagger, suddenly frightened. And then, the women's running footsteps slapped off down the street. No doubt they'd be back in a few heartbeats with a hunting party that would scrape him out of his shell.

But what then? There'd be no last night with Ashsweeper for him. There'd be no revenge. Aagam would have the pleasure of seeing him die, not once, but twice. Only this time there would be none of the honour of the willing Volunteer. Only the humiliation of a husband with no wife. And shame too for Ashsweeper, for he was sure now that Wallbreaker would say he had run away from the Clawfolk, regardless of truth.

Whistlenose staggered out into the light and the air. The hunters would be nearby now, signalling to each other, using moss to silence their footfalls. He had no idea even from which direction they would come. But presumably, the two women had been foraging within a cordon of protection, which would have extended out from the new walls. So, he turned in the direction of Centre Square slipping down narrow alleys, as fast as his exhaustion would allow.

All of these streets had been safe by day when he was growing up. But now, traps filled them and hidden pits. He had to keep stopping, to search his memory for a safe route, while sweat ran into his eyes and mossbeasts swarmed in colourful clouds from house to house.

Here a Flim skull hung above the doorway of a house he had played in as a child. Near it, some long-dead woman had practised drawing a tattoo in charcoal—the faint image of three six-legged beasts, each with a spear in them, could still be seen faintly under a generation of dust. He wanted to linger, to trace the outline of the picture with his hand. But a combination of inattention and a stray rock underfoot knocked him against the far wall of the alley to trigger a rain of pebbles.

"Down there!" someone cried, forgetting hunt discipline entirely. A youngster, then.

Whistlenose tried to stand up again as footsteps reached the mouth of the alley behind him. "Oh," somebody said, full of disappointment. A boy's voice. "I thought for sure it had come this way. Hey! Hey, you there!"

Whistlenose didn't turn around. "Clear off, lads," he said, his voice remarkably steady. "You'll catch it down towards the Wetlane if you hurry."

The tattoos on his back must be invisible under layers of filth by now, for the boy asked, "Who are you? I—"

But the others were already turning away, by the sounds of them, too excited to care about somebody who looked just about ready for the pot. As soon as they'd gone, he fell to his knees.

He had survived, but only because nobody was looking for a runaway Volunteer. He had been seen two days before, after all, walking right into the slaughterhouse. As long as nobody got a good look at his face or tattoos, Whistlenose could happily wander around these streets until he died of hunger and thirst. But the guards would identify him as soon as he tried to pass through the gates, and once caught, Wallbreaker wouldn't be foolish enough to let him approach his family. Not with Aagam there. Feasting and drinking in Whistlenose's house! Sleeping with a wife too kind for him. Poisoning their son with unworthy thoughts and hatred of his real father ...

But then, the Ancestors took pity and gave the ageing hunter the plan he needed.

Less than a tenth later, he had gathered up such a large pile of red moss that it filled his two arms and covered most of his face. There was barely a gap left for his eyes. Men did not do women's work unless they were too injured to hunt, but not so badly injured that the only cure was to Volunteer. So, he exaggerated his limp and stepped up to the new gates.

Of course, one of the guards, another youngster, asked him who he was. However, the moss muffled his reply, and the fact that everybody was still on the lookout for a "beast" that the women had spotted in the streets, allowed him to pass into the 'Ways unmolested.

As he walked, sharp fumes from the moss stung the inside of his nostrils and made his head spin. He managed to ignore it until he found himself in front of the steps leading down to his cellar home. Very few people were around. It looked as if the Chief had ordered the entire population outside the walls in the crazy search for a moss so full of poison, it couldn't even be pounded into blankets or ropes.

He dumped the bundle he had gathered in front of the door. The whole street seemed to be spinning and he found himself leaning against the doorway, drawing in huge gulps of clean air. And then, it was down the familiar steps and into the rooms he shared with Ashsweeper.

He found her there alone. She gasped, backing away, covering her mouth.

"It's me," he said.

"No."

"It is. Where's the boy?"

She didn't answer, still staring at him in horror.

"I'm not a ghost," he said. "I swear it! I'm not! And I didn't run away. You know me, love. I wouldn't do that!"

Slowly, she nodded, wiping the corners of her eyes. She *did* know him. A poor provider of few tattoos. But he was a tryer, too. Always doing his best. She must have known that. And when the day had come to offer himself up for the Tribe, she had seen, everybody had seen, how smartly he had stepped forward.

She came to him and made him sit, cradling him in her arms and crying. She never asked him for an explanation, but offered one instead, "The boy is off gathering. I was allowed to stay because … "

"I heard," he said. "They made you marry him. The monster."

She snarled all of a sudden and he jumped, for he had never, in more than two thousand days together heard such a noise from her throat. "I didn't let him touch me. That's why the boy is out gathering and him so young. Aagam went crying to the Chief with a bruise on each eye. At least that's what I think happened, because I can't understand a word of his mumbling. He is weak as a child, too. I punched him here," she patted Whistlenose's belly. "You wouldn't believe how soft it was! And he couldn't breathe then and I thought he would die and we would be Volunteered." She laughed and he felt himself laughing with her.

Then, they were hugging again. "You're trembling," she said. "You can barely stand, can you?"

"I'm fine, don't worry. It might be nice to sit, though. For a heartbeat or two."

"We have food, you know? For him, I think. He tried to eat some, but he must be sick, because he spat it out and crouched over for a long time in the corner. I … I could give you some of it." She knew what she was saying was wrong. But that didn't matter to Whistlenose. His stomach lurched. He wanted the flesh the stranger had rejected. Wanted it terribly and his head turned away from his beloved wife and towards the corner as though pulled to it by a rope. The food was right there, wrapped in pounded moss. The shape of it told him it was a joint of Bloodskin. His little boy's favourite. And now that those beasts had been destroyed by the Diggers, there would never be any more of it. Whistlenose's mouth watered for the smoky flavour he knew so well, for the crispy, fat-rich skin.

"I'm sorry," she said. "I ... I shouldn't have offered." For she knew, as he did, that he could be of no further use to the family or the Tribe. The flesh that might keep somebody else alive would only be wasted on him.

Except that wasn't true.

"I need the strength," he said at last. "The Ancestors saved me for a reason and that reason is to kill him."

"Who? You mean Aagam?"

He was already moving away from her. He fell upon the moss-wrapped parcel before ripping into the flesh beneath to the point of choking on it. Ashsweeper saved embarrassment by handing him a skull of water. He could feel her watching him. He stopped, amazed at his own thoughtlessness, and offered her the remaining scraps, but she shook her head.

"You can't, you know?" she said sadly. "You can't kill him."

"I thought you ... I *hoped* you hated him."

Ashsweeper's face glittered with tears and he felt a catch in his own throat. "You're clumsy, Whistlenose, and I was never supposed to marry you. I wanted Surestep to pay my bride-price, you remember him? But then, he broke his shoulder and it wouldn't fix right."

"I remember," he whispered. "Nobody had to ask him to Volunteer. He had a thousand days left. Ten thousand."

She nodded, wiping her face with the back of her hand. "And then you came along. The oaf, I called you," but she was smiling as she spoke, her voice fond.

"You did everything you could to discourage me."

"Of course I did! You already had one living wife! No way you could have supported the two of us with that shaky spear of yours. Or so I thought. But she was so lovely, wasn't she? Dear Sleepyeyes who saved us all."

"She was, she was. She watches over us still."

Ashsweeper sniffled. "But we can't waste what she's done, or what you've done, my sweet husband. If you kill Aagam, you might as well truss up our son and strand him out in no-man's land. The Chief... the Chief announced before the wedding that... that Aagam will save us all from the end of the world. I didn't believe it. But right then, the whole Roof went dark! Did you see that? The light... I was so frightened. I couldn't find the boy. Didn't know where he'd gone! And then... then a piece of the Roof fell down after the light came back. I didn't see it myself, but... "

"Oh, I saw it," he whispered. It had saved his life.

He didn't know what to do. He wanted to apologise for bringing Aagam into the 'Ways. For allowing the man to see his wife and fall for her... And yet, it was true what she had said. Removing the stranger would bring about the death of his family, and worse—infinitely worse—it might doom the whole Tribe. He shuddered, fighting against the hatred and the fear and the guilt.

Whistlenose looked around the room, wishing more than anything the boy were here, but relieved too that he wasn't, for the child was too young not to tell others what he had seen. Or did that even matter now?

"I know what they're planning," he said. "The Chief and his new friend. They want us... you, the Tribe, to go to a place his brother found. Stopmouth, his name was."

"His brother? But... "

"I know. He lived until only a few days ago, apparently. He was fast. I remember that much about him. I don't think his mind was right, but he always did his share. He was the one who won the Talker from the Armourbacks and the Flyers."

"He must have been a lot smarter than he looked, then," said Ashsweeper, "if he stayed alive so long away from the Tribe. But who could do such a thing? Who would *want* to?"

"Aagam was sure of his story. And the Chief believes him completely. There's ... there's supposed to be another tribe out there somewhere. And Stopmouth found it with the woman he stole."

She whistled. Then, all of a sudden, her eyes lit up. "But wait! If *they* survived, maybe you can too! Husband! You have so much more experience than either of them. You could make it to the ... the other tribe!" She faltered.

The whole idea tasted absurd to both of them. It couldn't work. Who would show him the way? He knew Stopmouth had headed towards Longtongue to begin with and had brought enough supplies to feed him and his woman for tens of days. Everybody had heard that much of the story, although the whole Tribe had learned soon enough not to speak of the incident in the presence the Chief.

He felt strength returning to him from the meal he had eaten. Her hand came to rest on his shoulder. "You can't stay, husband ... Whistlenose. You can't kill him either, if it's true the world is ending like he says."

He turned around and saw what those words had cost her. The Tribe came first and that's all there was to it. He felt the same.

"I should go," he agreed, at last. "Before ... before he comes back. I'm not sure I could stop myself if I saw him."

"There's still one of your spears here, you know?"

"I won't take it. You could swap it for flesh," he said. His second spear had seen a lot of use, but was in better condition than he was. It was one of the older ones from before the Tribe had learned to make tips from Armourback shell. It had a fine piece of flint at the end, however, that would buy a few good meals.

"We won't starve," she said, and he knew it was because of her new husband. A man who couldn't hunt, but whose position at the side of the Chief made him a far better provider than Whistlenose could ever be.

He nodded, unable to respond, and took the spear. Without a backward glance, he headed for the steps.

"Where will you go?" she asked. "Will you try to find Stopmouth?"

He didn't answer. He genuinely didn't know. But as he strode up towards the dangerous light, he realised suddenly that he would never Volunteer himself again. He was going to live, and that's all there was to that. He gripped the old spear and his face twisted itself into a smile.

6.
MOURNING A TRAITOR

Wallbreaker didn't think he would ever cry again, but after his first meeting with Aagam, he interrupted the evening meal with his wives and his child. He sent them to their room upstairs.

"I need to be alone."

Not even Mossheart had objected.

He found his face wet, and hot too, as though fevered. Stopmouth, of course. The only one he could trust. The worst of traitors and dead, it seemed, for a second time. But it hurt so much more now that the anger had faded.

"Take care of him," their father had said so long ago. Wallbreaker hadn't known what this was about. "Mind your brother. Your mother had to fight to get him named and there's plenty hungry enough to think he didn't deserve it."

Father had volunteered the next day and nobody had been expecting it.

Poor Stopmouth had been especially hurt. He'd trailed after Wallbreaker everywhere and couldn't string more than three words together without his tongue getting lost along the way. A sweet boy for all that, and sometimes when the older brother was courting Mossheart, she would joke, "Lucky for you, Wallbreaker! I almost forget myself sometimes and kiss him!" But her kindness to the boy, rare as it was in a Tribe that expected him to Volunteer early, had only caused Stopmouth to dream of her, to want her. It must have festered inside—Wallbreaker saw that now—it must have festered there until he thought Mossheart should have been his all along.

And then Indrani had fallen from the sky and changed everything. Wallbreaker had saved her life when all around wanted her Volunteered. Then, he had honoured her by taking her as a second wife, although she couldn't so much as make a blanket!

The life of the Tribe confused her. The whole surface of the world horrified her in a way only a really intelligent man like Wallbreaker could share. He alone had loved her: her marvellous dark skin; her bright teeth and the determined set of her jaw. No other woman in the Tribe could compare.

The thought that she was still alive, still out there. That she could be his again, filled him with joy.

She would have had time to adapt to the world by now. She would be thinking more clearly. And with his traitorous, wonderful brother gone, nobody would steal her from him ever again.

Two days later, Aagam stumbled back into the Chief's house sporting two black eyes and clutching at his chest.

Wallbreaker surged to his feet, heart pounding. "Who attacked you? By the Ancestors, I should have put a guard on you!"

"It was that slut you gave me for a wife!"

"You asked for her. And already you call her a slut?"

"Well, I want a different one now, and I want that one Volunteered. Along with her brat of a son."

"No," said Wallbreaker.

"No? You forget who I am." Aagam tapped his head with one finger. "I went to a lot of effort to learn what I've got up here."

"It doesn't matter," said Wallbreaker. "There's only so much the Tribe will swallow without chewing, you understand? We already have them harvesting moss now when they should be hunting—"

"—that was your idea, you ignorant savage! I wasn't saying to do that at all!"

Wallbreaker took a deep breath. "Are you trying to force me

to kill you? Is that why you came here?"

"You wouldn't dare! I'm the only one—"

"Sit down." And when the man ignored him and kept spitting and shouting, Wallbreaker kicked the legs from under him and knelt down hard on his belly. Even then, the stranger failed to shut up until he felt a knife against his throat. It was made of Armourback shell and quite capable of sawing right through the man's neck.

"I need you," said Wallbreaker. "The Tribe doesn't know that yet. They're not even sure they need *me*, although they do. They'd be gone already, every one of them, without me. But it doesn't stop the muttering over the fact that I don't hunt any more. The older ones especially don't understand it and every setback brings new cries for a return to the old days.

"And now, with your arrival, we have *two* men who do not hunt. One of these is practically a beast with fur on his face. He can't even talk, but already he gets a proven survivor Volunteered and takes over that man's family without so much as paying a bride price. People are wondering whose wife the Roofman will want next."

"But only I can—"

"Shut up, Aagam. You're barely human. You should be food for our spears. You're not Tribe." He tapped his chest. "We don't feel you *here*. If you marry again now, without showing your worth, it won't be just you that feeds the Clawfolk. It will be me too. And my wives and my daughter. Your knowledge might save us for tomorrow, but your greed will kill us for today. Do you understand?"

"I can't control that woman. She's a monster, I tell you."

"Her boy will go out gathering moss today."

"What? What are you talking about?"

Wallbreaker didn't like the man's attitude and he allowed his knees to sink further into that soft belly until he started struggling for breath. He expected there to be pleading, but Aagam wouldn't give him the satisfaction, preferring to sweat and gasp instead.

"Ashsweeper's boy is too young to be sent to gather moss," said Wallbreaker. "By putting him out, I'm sending her a message she will understand. You will find her less troublesome this evening.

"Now, to business. We need to plan the migration and you will tell me what I need to know."

7.
THE COWARD

On Aagam's wedding day, Wallbreaker had followed his usual custom of presiding over the feast from the first floor window of his house. He didn't like to go outside, but three days later, he forced himself to do so.

First, as always, he had his wives dress him in Speareye's famous cloak made of a dozen different hides. He liked the weight of it on his shoulders and the way the colours cleverly overlapped to form alternating layers of light and dark. He felt the breath of the Ancestors on his neck when he wore it. He became more than himself: he became every great Chief the Tribe had ever known.

Treeneck chatted away gaily, her palms gently weaving bones into her husband's hair. Mossheart, meanwhile, was tightening his tool-belt a little too much.

"I know you, woman," he said. "It's deliberate."

"Afraid you'll show your stomach? It's a judgement of the Ancestors that it has grown so much."

She was too clever to speak this way outside the home—she wouldn't give him a good excuse to put her aside.

I loved you once, he thought. She seemed so plain now when compared to Indrani. Her face was little more than a collection of angry lines, deepening by the day. And she made Treeneck's life a misery too.

"You're the mother of my child," he told Mossheart now.

"Bring her to me before I leave."

"She's asleep."

"I want to see her."

Mossheart softened. He always liked to flick a drop of blood at his girl before going outside. But he was even more nervous now than usual. Tomorrow he would finally tell his people what horror lay in store for them all. That was bad enough, but beforehand, he would have to put himself in real danger, something that hadn't happened since the great battle with the Flyers and their allies.

He stepped outside to where his men were waiting. Nobody had been allowed to hunt for several days. Faces showed signs of strain and frustration and no little curiosity. They were used to his surprises and his schemes, but he wagered they'd be more than a little shocked today. The younger hunters, the more loyal ones, were nowhere to be seen.

"You will escort me to the Hairbeasts," Wallbreaker told the men. He felt their resistance to his command. His predecessors, Speareye, and before him, Brainlicker, had always preferred to persuade their hunters. Direct orders were all very fine from a pack leader away from home. But in ManWays, the Tribe ruled, and the Chief was only there to voice its desires. Even the choosing of Volunteers was done by the Flesh Council, whose decisions the Chief carried out.

Slowly, slowly, Wallbreaker was dragging his people towards a new way of doing things. Just as a hunter must protect his eyes, so must the Tribe keep safe its Chief. He was their vision. His ideas were worth more than any ten of their lives.

Aagam was the only other person he'd ever met who truly understood this. The man had swaggered into the Chief's house with a magic word on his lips: *information.* Aagam had believed—no!—he had known it would bewitch the Chief, while that poor fool Whistlenose could only stare, never having seen the spear that killed him.

Wallbreaker felt happier every time one of the old hunters volunteered to be replaced by a younger man. But he knew too, that with the coming migration, he would need their experience more than ever.

He touched the tool-belt with the special pouch Treeneck had made him for carrying the Talker. That was one thing whose importance he didn't need to explain. Its power had made possible the alliance of enemies that had nearly wiped the humans out, while its capture had fed them many times since.

He held it up for the men. "Only I know how to work this," he reminded them. A white lie, of sorts, but one that made them nod and formed them into ranks around him. Then, the group was marching out beyond the rickety new defences towards what was left of the Wedding Tower.

Swirls of blood covered the walls in this area—typical Hairbeast art. The designs had meaning that the Talker translated as, "tunnel" and "life-into-blue" and other, even stranger concepts. The group paused. A few Hairbeast males regarded them from the roof of the Tower, watching for hostile hunting parties. Humans, who had been in alliance with them since time out of legend, didn't count.

"We have come to trade," Wallbreaker shouted up to them.

While they waited for a reply, one of his men, Laughlong, asked, "What if *their* Chief has gone out hunting?"

Wallbreaker ignored the veiled insult. The Hairbeasts preferred to hunt by night these days. They were few now. Twenty-three adults and an unknown number of mindless pups. They survived in the shadow of the humans' protection—something Wallbreaker himself had achieved. They'd proven themselves invaluable in the battle against the Flyers and more especially the Armourbacks.

Eventually, their Chief came outside. It was a female. With the Hairbeasts that kind of thing didn't seem to matter. It had painted its hands bright red with the blood of a relative who was probably recovering inside. Surrounding her came a delegation of her own: fifteen, a number exactly matching Wallbreaker's. These mangy beasts were the finest surviving specimens of their race. They stood half again as tall as a man, their bodies covered in fur that smelled sharp, like blood. It was always unpleasant and especially strong when the males fought each other.

"Flesh?" the female enquired.

"Yes," said Wallbreaker.

"We didn't even have a Council meeting about this," muttered Laughlong behind the Chief. *That's what you think.* Wallbreaker had had a meeting all right. But only with the younger men who weren't here now.

"You are our oldest allies," said Wallbreaker. "Our tribes have worked together since the time of Treatymaker."

"We have tasted your flesh forever," agreed the Hairbeast female. "Your marrow is sweetest of all."

"How many pups do you have in the Tower?" asked Wallbreaker.

"You have not asked this question before." The Talker gave the words a suspicious tone.

"We need a lot of flesh," said Wallbreaker.

"Why?" asked the creature and the Chief knew his men wanted the same answer.

"Now, that is a question that *you* have not asked before!" Wallbreaker grinned. "How many pups?"

"Sixteen."

"We'll trade for all of them."

"Three of our pups make sounds that might soon be words."

"As I said, we'll take them all."

"I cannot decide this," said the female, exactly as Wallbreaker had hoped she would. He kept the look of relief from his face, although the Talker did not translate such things as far as he knew. "My tribe must make sure all the pups are mindless. We will all decide together. In the dark."

Wallbreaker nodded. "I was aware this was your tradition. You will gather together and you will give us an answer tomorrow. Good. I will return then for the flesh."

Most of the humans went back to Centre Square muttering amongst themselves. But the Chief separated out three of the best: skinny little Quickbite, the lumbering Mossdrinker and the ever rebellious Laughlong. "Come with me." He led them away and then, doubled back, heading through the rear door of an old house that looked straight across a little square to the doorway where he had negotiated with the Hairbeast Chief.

"What are we doing here?" asked Laughlong. The others looked wary, but not worried.

Be quiet, Wallbreaker signalled. He felt nauseous. It had been a long time since he'd been away from his home with so little protection. He could hear his own pulse in his ears. It was ridiculous. He knew that. But the fear was not as bad as once it had been, when he had first escaped with his life from the Armourbacks.

He still bore the scars of their spears. He still had the nightmare sometimes, of swarming young with sharp little beaks, consuming him one little stab at a time. But he was getting better. He slept right through until morning more often. He allowed visitors into his house and even made trips away from ManWays to trade for flesh with the power of the Talker.

And now this. Away from home with the most modest of escorts. Across the road from the building where he'd consummated his marriage with Mossheart the very night that his courage had first been poisoned. He was doing well. Very well.

Darkness was falling. The light of the Roof dimmed and the tracklights came on. His disciplined hunters stirred not at all. They would keep their curiosity all penned up until they had the walls of home between themselves and the hungry night.

Wallbreaker stiffened as he felt a tap on his shoulder. Quickbite had spotted movement in the weak illumination of the tracklights. The Chief could only imagine the surprise of his escort as they realised the figures that now emerged from the darkness, creeping close to the ground, were human.

Good. Good. No alarm had sounded. That meant the Hairbeast guards were already dead. Generations of butchering Hairbeast pups had given humans an excellent grasp of how the creatures might be killed, while the trust between the two species would have allowed the young hunters to get right up close without arousing suspicion.

On top of the Tower, fires were burning and large silhouettes waved claw-tipped arms.

The young hunters were carrying something in their arms: moss. Bundles of red moss. Now there were a dozen of them crawling around, using their knowledge of the Wedding Tower to stuff holes with clumps of the plant. They built a large pile of it right in front of the only entrance to the Tower and set it alight with the help of the kindling and the embers they had brought with them.

Wallbreaker's escort stirred around him, agitated. Perhaps the betrayal horrified them, although when Chief Speareye had urged wiping out the Hairbeasts before, only Wallbreaker had spoken up for them.

Smoke began to pour from the moss. Just as a hole in the roof of a house could draw the smoke of a hearth, so now, the vapours of the moss passed up the stairs of the building and into the Tower. Even so, a few swooning human hunters, overcome by fumes, had to be dragged away by their comrades.

"I don't understand," whispered Quickbite.

"We need a lot of flesh," said Wallbreaker. "And quickly." He would explain to the tribe tomorrow about the journey they would all have to take. "This will get it for us without much risk." Just the way he liked it.

"Yes ... but won't the meat be poisoned?"

"Of course not. Women use it for smoking food all the time. As long as you don't eat the plant or consume the juices directly, all is well and the flesh keeps longer."

They waited and waited. How long before the Hairbeasts noticed there was smoke coming from fires other than their own? How good was their sense of smell? Strange not to know such a thing about humanity's oldest friends.

A boom of alarm sounded. "Down, down!" a Hairbeast

shouted, loud enough to be heard.

Wallbreaker turned to his escort. "They're going to come running out of there like blood from a throat. I need you to help the younger men keep their heads. Don't close with the Hairbeasts. Slings only. Got it? Make sure to tell them. Go on. Go on!"

The three men showed none of the reluctance they may have been feeling. No fear, either. The first of the creatures flew through the door and scattered the fire. It bowled two young humans out of the way and three more of the creatures, large males whose heads barely cleared the lintel, staggered out after. One of these had a club as long as a man's leg and studded with lumps of something that glinted in the tracklights. It swung at the humans who tried to swarm it, driving them back while more creatures pushed out into the square. Several fell to their knees, vomiting just as a human would have.

Wallbreaker's stomach knotted and squirmed. The fumes hadn't weakened the Hairbeasts as much as he had hoped. Already, seven huge adults had made it into the square, many armed with clubs or rocks that swung on the end of leather ropes.

Twenty young hunters clumped about the enemy, gathering themselves into groups, ready to charge stupidly. Wallbreaker poked his head out of the window. "Use your slings, you idiots! What I told you! Use your slings!"

But already, Quickbite was arriving to steady them, with Laughlong and Mossdrinker only a pace behind. Still, only seven Hairbeasts had made it out of the tower. Had the others all fallen asleep, then? Had the plan worked well enough for that, at least? But even seven was too many. Or eight, really, since another of the creatures had already run off into the streets. It wouldn't survive alone: nobody could.

A large male charged a clump of boys. It caught one of them—Wallbreaker couldn't tell who it was—it caught him in the centre of his body, caving in the ribcage, throwing the young hunter a man-length through the air to land skidding and bleeding amongst the smoldering moss.

Seven Hairbeasts. Only seven. More than enough to make the price too high ...

But already the enemy were down to six thanks to a shower of slingstones under Laughlong's shouted order. The other humans were beginning to get the idea, backing away, firing from a distance or charging the woozy Hairbeasts from behind. One young idiot, Gaptooth, kept laughing and ducking under the hapless swing of a club, bleeding the female Hairbeast with one shallow cut after another. Wallbreaker used to be like that himself. Fast and confident. Nothing could hurt him in those days.

Now, only three of the enemy remained standing. Laughlong was telling Gaptooth to get out of the way. "I'll kill it myself!" shouted the youngster. "It's already weakening. Look at it! Look!"

A smell tickled the Chief's nose. What was that?

It was all the warning Wallbreaker had. He had lost none of his reflexes and rolled immediately to the left, away from the window. Air washed his face a mere heartbeat before a massive club coming in from behind, shattered the windowsill. Splinters showered the whole right side of his body and he tumbled backwards into the shadows. It was in here with him! The Hairbeast that had run into the streets. It must have seen him shouting to his men and it had circled back.

"I will eat you while you live," it told him. "Your brothers are too far off to help."

"We can make a deal," said Wallbreaker. The sweat was pouring off him under the clumsy cloak while the rough wall seemed to burn against the scars left by the Armourback spears. He could see the creature's large, slow-blinking eyes, trying to fix him in place. "It's not too late to save your tribe," he said. "The rest are only sleeping in the tower. They—"

The change in its breathing sent him scuttling out of the path of the club. He scattered a fistful of dirt in the direction of its face and ducked under its grasping claws. If the moss smoke had made it dozy, the creature had already thrown off the effects of it. It yanked at his cloak, but he untied it, just in time, and staggered into the back room where—thank the Ancestors!—the rear doorway remained unblocked.

Wallbreaker made it out into the street. He could outrun it now. A human hunter should be able to do that easily. He would make his way towards the Wedding Tower, although the twisty layout of the streets in this part of old ManWays, would drive him away first for a turn or two and then—

—a line of fire ran down his side as the beast caught him with a lunge of its claws.

"I will ... eat ... you ... *living* ... "

He screeched like a child with the shock and the pain. He ran as fast as his legs would carry him. But things were not as they had once been. He hadn't properly hunted since becoming Chief. He spent much of his time now resting and thinking.

The largest share of the food from the hunts he planned always came to him and he ate his fill of it. Sometimes, it was to make the day pass more quickly. Sometimes he just wanted to show he could, in front of those lacking the proper respect. Symbols mattered more than ever when Chieftainship hung by the narrowest of threads. Meanwhile, his limbs had softened. His body had become listless, as though enemy Ancestors fed upon his spirit, slowing him down.

Wallbreaker's tormentor, a creature in its prime, pounded down the street after him, scattering moss and pebbles.

Go left! Wallbreaker thought. Go left around the next bend! A dozen paces after that would bring him to the hunters who must have finished mopping up the rest of the enemy by now. The Hairbeast was falling behind, its breathing unnaturally raspy. The corner, Wallbreaker was at the corner. Just—

That was when the creature decided to throw its club: an awkward flinging motion from arms not built for it. Maybe it had been trying to brain him, but the heavy, knobbled wood caught itself up in his legs instead. His face smacked hard down onto a patch of moss. His whole body skidded forwards while sap burned his face and stung his eyes. Only his left hand had made it past the corner.

The raspy breathing had reached him. He was weeping from the moss sap and everything appeared to float in his vision. "You turned your back on our ways," the Ancestors said. "Now we turn our backs on you."

He saw his enemy. Its fur hung bedraggled and wet in the Roofsweat of nighttime. It swayed a little, but managed to lower itself down onto its hunkers to grab his ankle.

"Living," it reminded him. It opened jaws lined with blunt teeth. Hairbeasts loved marrow best, he remembered. Looking into its mouth, he could see how they extracted it. It would crush his foot in a heartbeat. It would work its way up his leg.

He should scream for help, but he'd be dead before anybody got to him. The tears were still flowing from his face, but it wasn't the sap any more.

"I will give you anything," said Wallbreaker.

It raised his foot with deliberate slowness, and asked, its tone curious, "You would give your mate?"

"Yes!" shouted Wallbreaker, for his foot had almost reached the jaws.

"Your brother hunters?"

"Yes! Yes!"

It chose to mock him for a moment, licking his foot with a rasping tongue. All of a sudden, he voided his bowels, the stench filling the air between them and the creature wrinkled its nose.

"My hunters hurt your people. It wasn't me. It was nothing to do with me. You can have them. You can have any of them that hurt you. Any of my hunters! I'll give you anyone! As many as you want! I'll—"

Four slingstones flew into the Hairbeast, knocking it back. One of them must have got it in the eye or in that part of the head underneath the earhole that the skull didn't cover, because it didn't get up again and the rasping sound of its damaged breathing failed to restart.

Suddenly there were men all around Wallbreaker. He

managed to lift himself up onto his elbows. A mixture of older and younger hunters were looking down at him. One by one they wrinkled their noses at the smell. They had been lying in wait for the right moment to attack. They would have heard everything.

"Well," said Laughlong. "That's the last of them *murdered*."

"Go and butcher them," said Wallbreaker, but nobody moved. Finally, Laughlong nodded. "We can't let it go to waste," he said.

Only then did the other men move back towards the Wedding Tower.

8.
A GH⊕ST

Wallbreaker saw all of it from the top window of the Chief's House. A group of hunters, their faces covered in grease from the moss-flavoured Hairbeast flesh, had pulled Aagam by the arms and dragged the stranger right up to Wallbreaker's front door, while the man's new wife, Ashsweeper, kicked at the soles of his feet.

"Waster!" she cried. "To think they tried to steal my real husband from me for this!"

What did she mean by the words "tried to"? Wallbreaker wondered. Whistlenose had done his duty already and that was that, surely.

Now that they had dragged him into the presence of Wallbreaker's Talker, Aagam finally understood what Ashsweeper had been saying. He replied, voice shaking with fury, "I'm your husband now, woman! The Chief said so!"

"Not any more! He's not the … " Ashsweeper stopped herself. She looked up to find Wallbreaker's eyes fixed on hers. She lowered her head again and shut up. Everybody said she was a clever one and she had proved it now by stopping her tongue just in time.

Below, the men pushed open the front door and threw Aagam inside. "We don't need Volunteers. Won't need any for two whole tens! But after that … we'll be well rid of you."

A pair of the hunters remained on guard at the door to make sure that Aagam couldn't get out again. To make sure that *nobody* could.

After that, with Aagam downstairs, thumping the walls in anger, the feast in Centre Square took up where it had left off. No one had hunted in two days. They didn't think they needed to. The attack on the Hairbeasts had produced twenty adults and as many pups—more than their Chief had claimed. The creatures could lie as well as humans, it seemed. Such gluttony! Nobody had seen the likes of it since the defeat of the Armourback alliance.

A great fire was blazing, carrying the smoke of cooking all over the Square. Wallbreaker had yet to taste a single morsel. He hadn't even been offered a slice off that boy who had died, as tradition demanded. No, he and his family could only look on with thundering bellies.

People sang to ancient tunes with words that no longer made sense. A nameless boy and a girl of the same age performed the male and female parts of a courting song. He was offering her father the flesh of something called a "tract-ear," but it was not enough to win her hand.

Whatever a "tract-ear" was, or indeed the "ache-ears" he also claimed to possess, they must have been long extinct. And the girl's father didn't want them anyway.

Everywhere, people lay groaning, hands on their bellies, bursting with food. Wallbreaker couldn't stop himself, couldn't resist calling down, "You're wasting it! We need it!"

They must have heard their Chief, because the children's song stuttered to a stop. But nobody looked up. And then a woman brought out a wedding drum and everybody clapped in time to her clever hands.

Was that a good sign or a bad one? Wallbreaker wondered. The insults had stopped after they had imprisoned him in his own house. There'd been an angry meeting, despite the huge quantities of flesh that had been recovered. The people were confused, he realised. His cowardice had finally been proved beyond any doubt.

In the past, they must have decided, each in his own heart, not to see him for what he was. Wallbreaker brought them flesh, after all. He always found a way to feed them and wasn't that the point of a Chief? Of any man? He nourished the bodies of the Tribe along with the spirits of the Ancestors.

And yet, how could a coward lead? Tribe was everything. Women, children, hunters … all of them; their hearts and their marrow; the flesh of their backs should be, must be, sacrificed for the survival of all. When it came down to it, a coward, no matter how useful, was somebody who would do the opposite, who would betray the Tribe for himself.

It was a thought too horrible to contemplate. And so they feasted and sang and refused to look at him.

"They'll be back," said a voice behind him. "When they get hungry again." Mossheart. She had discovered his weakness before anybody else, on the very night of their marriage.

"Must you always eat my thoughts, Mossheart?"

"I don't like the taste of them. I would prefer some of that food."

"Where is our daughter?"

"With the woman, downstairs."

"Woman? Woman! Why won't you call her by her name? Treeneck? She's my wife, too."

He turned around, at last, to face her. He used to love her hair, the way it curled up around her face, a frame for glittering blue eyes. Now, it hung lank about her shoulders, as listless as the rest of her.

He wanted her to fight him more, as Indrani had done. He wanted her teeth to be straighter and brighter; her skin to be darker. He wanted her eyes to be black pools, swirling with passion and secret knowledge. Most of all, however, he wished he had not turned her into what she was now.

I'm sorry, he thought. *I'm sorry, Mossheart.*

He would never set her aside. Not just because she would tell everyone what she knew about him—the weeping in the dark, the sudden sweats—but because he could talk to her as though she were an Ancestor: in private; in full confidence that she would take his side, despite her growing dislike of him.

Aloud he said, "They will see sense eventually. But that's not the point. We must leave—"

75

"Must we? Why? So you can have again that black beast you tried to marry? She won't take you back. She ran away, remember?"

"She was *stolen*. By Stopmouth. You told me so yourself. You saw him."

"She will never willingly touch you."

"You're wrong about her. She was confused, that's all. Life in the Roof is different."

"Why? Don't they poison women up there in order to rape them? Is that what you did to the Hairbeasts? I hear their Chief was a female too."

His fist clenched of its own accord and experience made her flinch, but she didn't step back. Wallbreaker struggled to control his breathing. "It wasn't rape. I'm the Chief and her husband. And anyway, this has nothing to do with her. That flesh out there ... we need it. We need all of it. For our journey. We're never going to get another supply so easily, so quickly. And what of the other preparations we should be making? We could do with more red moss. We could toss it into the tunnels of the Diggers if we had to."

She stepped closer to him, half-flinching as she approached so that he knew she was about to say something that would anger him. She never let her fear stop her, though. From anything. She felt for the pouch that Treeneck had made for him, the one that held the Talker. "This ... " she said, "this is the only reason you still live."

He relaxed, having expected worse, something he hadn't already thought of himself. "Have you a suggestion, dear wife?"

"Him," she pointed downwards, so that he understood she meant Aagam on the floor below. "Didn't he tell you there were more humans? Another Tribe?"

He nodded. He hadn't told her this himself. She must have listened in on one of his conversations. He knew she often did that, but pretended not to be aware of it. He trusted her. "Well, you don't need those dancing fools, do you, husband? You don't need the Tribe at all. You have a Talker just as poor Stopmouth did. You have your own guide. One who won't try to seduce you away from your wife."

"Wives."

She pretended not to care. "So … Go yourself. Go with a small group. Escape. It must be safer and easier for a few to get away than a blundering mass of people." There was something about her words that made him feel dizzy and sick. He couldn't quite pin down what was wrong with them at first, but he found he was shaking his head and trembling all over. Was it fear? Was it the fear again? No. He saw Mossheart smile for the first time since Indrani had stolen his heart. His first wife was still lovely, he saw now. She took his damp palm in hers.

"The Tribe will die without you," she said. "Even you care about that, don't you?"

"Yes," he breathed. "Even … even me." He felt suddenly happy, almost giddy with it. He hugged her to him, then fiercely kissed her as he had not done is so long. "Even me," he said again, louder now, laughing, because, in spite of all the food he had brought to Centre Square since becoming Chief; in spite of the lives he had saved; part of him had believed himself a monster.

Just then, the drumming stopped in the Square and people were shouting. A few screamed. The Chief and his first wife turned back to the window. Below them, a hunter limped in amongst the packed members of the Tribe, while everywhere people panicked to get out of his way. He stopped, spotting Wallbreaker, and the two locked eyes.

Whistlenose.

"Don't speak his name," Mossheart said quietly. Of course not. For Whistlenose was a ghost. The creature's skin had been worn away in patches on its chest. It carried an old-style spear that trembled in its grip—as though spirits could feel exhaustion! When it spoke, its voice too, trembled.

"I'm not dead," it said. "Ask the Clawfolk. They sent me back. Ask them!" He wiped his grimy, pleading face.

Wallbreaker opened his mouth. "That was ten days ago, it was—"

"Don't speak to it!" cried Mossheart. "By the Ancestors!"

"I didn't know what to do," Whistlenose continued, his voice hoarse. "Who would believe me when the Chief himself wanted me dead?"

"We have no Chief now," said Laughlong from the far edge of the crowd.

Whistlenose shook that off as though he didn't care. "You have to listen to me. You all have to listen. The Longtongues ... They're ... they're leaving their nests. I've been ... I've been robbing their traps during the day." A dangerous business and one the creatures were usually wise to. "But today, I saw the Longtongues. Dozens of them. Maybe all that are left. They were streaming out the gates on this side of their territory."

"When?" asked Wallbreaker. Mossheart had pulled away from him as if she too might be caught by the ghost for acknowledging it.

"Just now. I ran all the way here when I saw it." He spun around, eliciting screams as people shoved away from him. "Don't you see? It's daytime. They're so afraid. The most powerful creatures we hunt. They're so afraid they're doing their running away *by day.*"

"He's not a ghost," said Wallbreaker. He surprised them all and himself by dropping right down from the window. He even managed to land all right, as though he had never been out of practice. He rolled in amongst the ashes of an old fire and strode across the Square to embrace Whistlenose. Everybody gasped, but he remained unharmed. "And you call *me* a coward?" he said to them, smiling hard enough to bring out the dimples they used to love him for long ago.

Oh, he knew himself for a craven, but somehow the arrival of Indrani and Aagam, and the conversations he'd had with them, had stolen away any fear he might have of such things as spirits. After all, the tracklights really were just lights—he knew that now. Nobody made their campfires up there. Certainly not the Ancestors, and that, that thought, right then, as he embraced Whistlenose, told him what he needed to do.

78

He faced the crowd, feeling a little of the old swagger return.

"You barred me into my house," he said. "And maybe you thought you had good reason to do so, because I am not like other Chiefs."

"You're no Chief at all," muttered Laughlong. That man would have to Volunteer. And soon.

Wallbreaker widened his grin. "And yet, Laughlong, my predecessor Speareye sent me a vision over ten days ago. He stood there with my father and other great hunters of our Tribe. Even the Traveller was there, although he did not speak. Speareye, had come, he said, he had come to beg me not to let the Tribe die.

"But how can I save them? I asked.

"The flight of the Longtongues will be a sign, he told me. You must leave too, for the safe place we have found for you. Use the Hairbeasts as your food supply. We will send a Roofman to guide you where you need to go."

"It's true," called Mossheart from the window. "I have heard him cry out in his sleep many times and always in the morning he has a new way to get us flesh. How could one man dream up so many clever schemes if not for the Ancestors whispering directly in his ears?"

Wallbreaker felt his cheeks burning. He wanted to laugh. For all her thoughts ran bitter as the red juice of a berry, Mossheart never failed to back him up in public. She now spoke with confidence of a place where Diggers would not dare to attack; where children could grow in safety, as in the old days.

But the reaction of the crowd was not quite the one Wallbreaker had expected. Laughlong, whom he had taken for an enemy, began to weep. Wives embraced each other. Hunters pulled their children close. Feast, it seemed, had turned to funeral.

He saw the drummer resting her head on her instrument, breathing fast, as though she had been running for her life. She was a hard woman called Tallythief, loved by her three named children and nobody else. Except when she was drumming. Then, she became beautiful and fierce and everybody adored her.

In neither state, was she a weakling, and yet here she was now weeping like so many others. And for what?

He felt Mossheart's gaze boring into his own. Her eyes were brighter than he had seen them in some time and suddenly he realised what had changed, what his crazy, self-serving lie had accomplished; why braver men than he shivered and sobbed.

"Finally," he shouted, "finally we have hope!" He had been hiding the preparations for the journey from them for fear they would have risen up and put a new Chief in his place, when all along, they would have loved him for it. An escape! An escape from the end of the world that everybody had felt was coming!

"You thought we were doomed," he cried. "As if the blessed Ancestors would let us become extinct. But we are not like the other beasts that feed us so well. This is our world—" he had heard as much from Aagam, "We were here first, brought here by the same Ancestors who will deliver us now to our new home. A place of safety!

"We have a hard journey ahead of us, and our numbers will decline every step of the way. But you must never lose hope, for other humans wait for us there. They are softer than you. Weaker than you are. Feeble as a nameless child! And that means that not one of us who gets there alive will be made to Volunteer, no matter how severe his injury.

"We will live, my people. We will live! We will live! The Tribe continues!"

And finally they cheered him. Those who had fallen to the ground leapt to their feet and the hugs became firmer. Tallythief screamed, but with joy and punished her drum as never before. "The Tribe Continues!" It was something said on the birth of a new child, but it seemed so appropriate now, so right that many shouted it. "We continue! The Tribe continues!"

He released Whistlenose and said, quietly, "You have saved yourself again. For an old man, the Ancestors like you a lot."

"I want my wife back."

"You know, I think Aagam might be more than a little glad of that."

"And that man needs to die."

"Not if you want your boy to get a name."

Whistlenose was on the point of collapse. Wallbreaker had felt it when the two had embraced. He felt exhausted himself now.

"Look, Whistlenose. With the flesh we got from the Clawfolk and the last of the Hairbeasts, we won't need any new Volunteers for several more tens of days. We might be safe by then. All of us."

"That man goes before any of mine," said Whistlenose. And with that, he pushed away from the Chief. Luckily, nobody seemed to notice his rudeness. The people continued to dance and to celebrate, while over in Longtongue the Diggers, presumably, were spreading their tunnels and collapsing the remaining buildings. He would have to put an end to this feast. And then, after a day's preparation ... two at the most ... He felt his gorge rise in sudden terror and had to cover his mouth.

The journey. Across a wilderness with a limitless variety of creatures waiting to gnaw on his bones.

9.

THE NEW REFUGEES

The forest here seemed full of magic to Whistlenose. Berries grew from the trunks of trees, bursting when ripe with tiny pops that made the younger hunters jump and look around them. But they weren't the only ones interested: glittering swarms of multi coloured insects, flashed through branches and leaves, each rushing to be the first to settle on a spattered trunk, leaving it clean behind them only to race towards the next little explosion.

Whistlenose had seen the same phenomenon twice before. Only the Ancestors knew why the berries chose one day to burst and not another. He didn't care, it was beautiful and he only wished his family could see it for themselves.

He motioned his pack forward. Three days travel from ManWays and in that time nobody in the Tribe had so much as seen another intelligent creature. Aagam had told the Chief they would be safe in the forest, but also that it wouldn't last forever. Sooner or later, trouble was going find them.

"Better if we find it first," said Wallbreaker when he briefed the scouts. "You're not there to hunt," he told them. "We have enough flesh for a while yet. Any non-Digger you find should be left alone unless you think you can bring it back alive."

"Alive?" That didn't make sense to Whistlenose.

"Information," the Chief had replied. That was an Aagam word and it made Whistlenose angry. But the Ancestors, it seemed, spoke through the Chief, so he swallowed the bitter morsels of resentment and nodded.

At least Fearsflyers had returned to him his Armourback shell spear. He had missed it while living as a "ghost."

The scouts had struggled through heavy growth for a full tenth, maybe half a day's travel ahead of the main body of the tribe. The cry of a baby would not carry so far, Whistlenose hoped. Nor the smell of blood from an accidental cut. But who could tell? Not even the Traveller had met all the creatures the world might hold.

The ageing hunter looked around at his men. First came skinny Chinjutter with the clumps of black hair that grew out of his nose and ears. Behind him, walked a boy who looked barely old enough for a name. But he did have one, and it was worse than even Whistlenose's—Browncrack. Whistlenose worried about him most of all. The boy had yet to properly wet his spear in the guts of a living enemy. He would be anxious: too enthusiastic and too scared all at once.

Three other men made up the numbers: Hoarseshout, Flatface and the trundling Mossdrinker. They had spread themselves out so far that with all the swarming insects, he couldn't be sure they'd see his signal in case of a problem. So he waved them back into the centre and crouched down until all were within whisper distance, but facing outwards with eyes peeled. Good men, he thought. Good men, after all. Better than he was and they likely knew it. But Wallbreaker had put him in charge.

"You're lucky," the Chief had said. And that was that.

"Anything?" Whistlenose asked now.

"A smell," said Chinjutter.

"You're sure it's not the berries? That's the sour scent we're getting."

"No, no. This isn't sour. Smells more hairy. Like wet fur. It's been growing stronger."

With that black growth in his nostrils, it's no wonder everything smells like wet fur! Whistlenose shoved the nasty thought away. Nerves, just nerves. "Anybody else smell it?" he asked. "I'm getting nothing."

"I didn't notice until you mentioned it, Chin," said Mossdrinker. "But now … " He pointed vaguely in the direction they'd been travelling.

Aagam had told them this route would be safe. He'd found a swathe of forest that ought to take them halfway to where they were going without encountering a single community of beasts. And where there were no beasts to feed on, there'd be no Diggers either. But anything might have changed in the meantime and everybody knew that.

"Very slowly then," he said, "and listen … you heard the Chief and you know he's right … The most important thing is not to give the Tribe away. There's no walls to protect our families back there. So, anybody who gets caught … No rescues. All right? We're just here to find out what's facing us. Then we run back and report."

"Unless we outnumber them, surely," said Mossdrinker, flexing one large fist.

"Maybe." Whistlenose looked around the group before settling on the youngest, the untried Browncrack. "You're the fastest of us," he said. He had no idea if that was true, but the boy looked like he was about to live up to his name and they had yet to so much as see a single enemy. He needed a kill to settle his nerves, but until then, he was just going to get in the way.

"At the first sign of trouble, even if we look like we're about to win, take a heartbeat to learn what the creatures look like. Then, I need you to run all the way back to the Chief. Can you do that? Straight back. He's to put guards out and if you do your job, they'll know what to look for."

"I won't let you down."

"Stay at the back, then."

The other five spread out and moved forward in a crouch. Ahead, the land dipped to form a clearing with a circle of mossy boulders around a still pool of water. The smell had grown strong enough that Whistlenose could get it now, too. Wet fur, indeed. A good way to describe it.

He felt a faint sensation in the soles of his feet. Diggers? Maybe. It seemed more gentle than that. It seemed distant. He signalled the two flank men, Hoarseshout and Mossdrinker, to run to the far side of the dip. They did so, slipping around the boulders and falling into a crouch.

He was raising his arm to move the rest of the team on, when Chinjutter touched his shoulder. The other man's eyes rolled in the direction of one of the boulders and Whistlenose had to stifle a gasp. The rock was *twitching*. Not a lot, barely at all, really. Slowly, he lowered his arm. But just then, the creature must have realised it had been spotted. The "boulder" suddenly rose up. The carpet of moss it had been wearing fell away to reveal a compact body of rubbery, glistening green flesh. It roared, deep in its chest, before springing forward with all the power and all the speed of a slingstone. It flew across ten paces to strike Chinjutter so hard that the man … *snapped*. There was no other way to describe it.

Other "boulders" came alive. They sprang on coiled green tails. Hoarseshout went down. Mossdrinker was shouting, cursing the Ancestors, while Flatface stabbed and stabbed at the monster that had killed Chinjutter, looking for a vital organ.

A flash of green. Whistlenose threw himself to one side as a beast shot past him. He rolled to his feet. It rose too, behind him now, while another, approaching on short little hops of its coiled tail, came up to face him. Like a human, it had two eyes. They hung unblinking over a wide, tube-like mouth where a tongue beat at the "cheeks" with a drum-like sound that might have been communication. It also had two arms. One of them slashed at him with a short, long-bladed spear. The other held a circle of wood that parried his two attempts to strike back.

There was no time for another attack. He rolled away, aware of the enemy behind him. Mossdrinker screamed. "Oh no! Oh no!" Flatface was grunting in time to the sound of a spear striking wood. The enemy were rattling their tongues, and deep in the forest, their rhythm was taken up by others. Many, many others. A swarm of them, it seemed. A dozen swarms, while the wet fur smell blanketed everything and seemed only to be getting stronger.

A long spear-point flashed past Whistlenose's face. He didn't have time to be afraid.

"Run, Browncrack!" he shouted. "Tell the Chief!"

He fell back against a tree trunk, a nice thick one. Whoever was behind him now wouldn't get much chance to attack. He pushed his spear in the direction of the nearest creature's round mouth. It raised the wood to block him and must have been shocked when the Armourback shell tip passed through far enough to cut. Whistlenose had already dropped the weapon, taking his knife to the now-exposed belly. If it even was a belly! It must have hurt, however, for the monster let out a terrible shriek, its tongue a blur against swollen cheeks.

And then, Whistlenose found himself lying on the ground, his face numb all down one side. The enemy that had been behind him, must have hopped far enough around the tree to smack him with the wood. More than just a defence then, his mind said calmly.

You should get up, boy. But his head was ringing and none of his limbs wanted to respond. Only the old injury gave sign of life, throbbing in time to his heart.

Beyond the far lip of the rise, he could see more of the creatures on their way. A swarm, he'd thought earlier, and he'd been right. More than a man could count, big and small.

He could see the other men from where he lay at the edge of the dip. Hoarseshout and Mossdrinker had done well, but would do no more. Each had taken an enemy with him.

I got one, too ... Not bad for a poor hunter.

A long-bladed spear rose towards the Roof. His enemy vibrated with triumph.

Make it quick.

Out of nowhere, Browncrack appeared, with an inherited Armourback shell spear of his own. It tore right through the green beast's face and out the far side.

"I hope you can run with that limp of yours," said the boy excitedly. "They're nearly on us."

"You were supposed to go back. I ordered ... "

Browncrack's voice had risen high enough to grate. "Well, I'll be going back now, won't I? Come on! Come on!"

The Ancestors still loved Whistlenose, it seemed, and the swarm of creatures, for all that they could spring forward at great speed in an ambush, came on now in harmless little hops. The humans left them far behind.

10.
THE SILENT TRIBE

Members of the Tribe knew how to stay quiet from a very young age. Mothers would gather wood with infants strapped to their breasts. They would walk from one clump of moss to another so that the juices stung their feet, but cushioned the sound of their steps too. They had signs of their own, just as the hunters did, and everybody watched and scolded everybody else's children—often with no more than a glance, lest some hungry beast hear them and swoop down from the sky or up from under their feet.

Even so, with over a thousand people of all ages clustered together for warmth and safety, the camp could be heard from a distance of two hundred paces. Thousands of twigs cracked under feet more used to streets than forest. Babies cried out for milk; adults whispered in argument while untrained boys made eyes at grinning girls who were far too haughty to show fear or excitement.

Whistlenose had mostly recovered his composure by the time they made it back. His ears still rang with a sound that nobody else could hear. His leg ached, of course, but he wasted no thought on that. He had run almost as fast as Browncrack.

"It's a migration," said the Chief when they reported what they'd seen. "Just like the Longtongues, these new beasts are fleeing the Diggers behind them."

Wallbreaker was sitting on the ruins of an ancient wall, legs dangling. He'd been piecing together shards of what might have been a skull, although Aagam called it *pottery* and insisted humans had made it. Every word the man spoke only made Whistlenose want to kill him all the more.

However, Wallbreaker was still talking. He had a magical ability to explain what he himself had not been there to see. "Our scouts ran into theirs, that's all. But what will the creatures do next? We need to double the guard. Bring Laughlong here. Get everybody ready to fight and to move."

"I killed one!" said Browncrack. "Do I get a tattoo?"

"No," said Wallbreaker. "You should have come back like Whistlenose ordered. How many times do I have to tell you, things are different now. That's not how we win."

"But Whistlenose would have been dead without me!"

"If they'd had slings and aimed one at you, the whole Tribe would be dead. They would have surrounded us in the night while praising their Ancestors for sending them an idiot like you to deliver us into their bellies."

"Perhaps you should make an example of him," said Aagam. "Does he have a wife?"

"Shut up," said the Chief. "You were the one who told us we would be safe in the forest. Half the journey, you said!"

"Then you should have left the day I told you! Things have changed. The Diggers are on the move. The more their population grows, the more food they need. The edges of their territory must be expanding *exponentially*. If we'd left at once, like I wanted—"

Whistlenose pulled Browncrack away and left them to argue. He didn't know why the Chief let Aagam talk to him like that, but it was beyond his power to change.

All he wanted now was to see Ashsweeper. But as soon as they were out of earshot of Wallbreaker's circle, he put one hand on each of Browncrack's young shoulders and looked him in the eye. "They're right, you know? You should have left me."

The boy nodded, a tight movement, almost a jerk of the chin.

Then Whistlenose pulled him into a tight, trembling embrace. "Bless you, boy. You are Tribe to me now."

"Thank you."

"Oh! And you have wet your spear. I can't call you 'boy' any more, can I?"

A dozen heartbeats later, he was back with his family. Ashsweeper sat him down without a word and sponged him off with water from a deliciously cold pool at the centre of the camp.

"He sends you out every day," she said, her voice a whisper. Everybody was speaking in the same tone so that it felt like they were surrounded by a constant, gentle hiss. "And you get all the most dangerous missions. You and Laughlong who displeased him."

"We're older than everybody else. You should know that."

Of course she knew. Hidden in her pack, she would have the tally stick on which she marked off his days. She recorded her own too. Only the boy, happily stalking mossbeasts around a rotted tree trunk, remained ageless and without a Tally of his own.

"How happy he must be," Whistlenose muttered. "We fight so hard to get him named, and yet, from that moment on, his every heartbeat will be numbered."

"Don't be sad," she said.

He shook his head. "It has passed again already, my bride." He hugged her. He would have to get up again now, he realised, to seek out the families of the men who had died.

Wallbreaker's orders for the Tribe to pack up arrived shortly after that. They moved backwards half a day's travel to a chest-high ring of crumbling old walls. Everybody tried to fit inside, so that whole families lay squashed in, one atop the other. They stayed there for two swelteringly horrible days, while women dug pits and every man who could lift a spear struggled through undergrowth, poking each rock for fear it should spring up at him.

The new beasts—people had begun calling them "Jumpers"—followed on. Their patrols sparred with humans. Hunters died in a contest of equals, and sometimes the bodies of heroes were carried back to feed the Tribe.

Small victories were won: ambushes that brought tangy green flesh to silent cheers and congratulations. But as the days passed, the Chief's agitation only grew worse. "How can I study them?" he raged, "if I can't get one alive? How can I make a plan?"

"Haven't the Ancestors told you what to do?" asked Laughlong, making sure there were plenty there to hear him. For all his Tally must be full by now, he was still a brawny man with enough tattoos that his words could not be ignored. "Or maybe you could go out on patrol yourself and bring the Talker with you?"

Wallbreaker sent the man on more and more missions, but Laughlong always found his way home to the Tribe without so much as a scratch.

Whistlenose, however, earned plenty of scratches. When he returned from patrol, he would bring his boy to the centre of the camp, stepping over families that joked with him or asked him how things were "out there." The boy had friends too and they called him "Blackie" for his tangled mop of hair that Ashsweeper tried in vain to keep tidy with decorative bones. The children waved to each other, but the boy refused to be parted from his father when Whistlenose was in camp.

"Why can't we play the tracking game any more, dada?"

"Because you're too good for me. But don't worry, when we get to our new home, we'll play every day."

"But I want to play now!"

A woman saved the boy from a scolding, "Ooh, there's a handsome little man."

"Thank you, Hightoes." Whistlenose smiled. The young woman, being with child, and therefore holy, got to sit in the centre of everything. The pregnant women received a constant stream of visitors asking for blessings and dream readings. Hightoes grinned again at the boy. "I hope my first child is as beautiful as you, little man."

The boy squirmed. "As fierce as him, Hightoes. That's what you meant, wasn't it?" Whistlenose said.

"Why yes, of course!" She grinned. Her husband, the young

Fearsflyers, was out right now, tracking down the Jumpers. She let none of her worry show. Instead, she said to the boy, "Why are you here? You need another story? Didn't I just tell you one yesterday?"

Whistlenose enjoyed the tales as much as anybody, and it was right here, at the centre of the camp, that they came to life. No more than two paces behind Hightoes, an enormous roll of furs held the oldest tally sticks from the House of Honour back in Centre Square. Many had been lost or damaged during the fight against the Armourbacks and Flyers, but Wallbreaker, to his credit, had ordered them packed up again. "We need them more than ever now," he'd said. How right he had been! Somewhere in the bulging furs, were sticks that had belonged to the Traveller, to John Spearmaker, to Treatymaker and other heroes of the Tribe. And many heroines too, thought Whistlenose, thinking sadly of poor Watersip. As a man, he dared not touch them, but he could feel their power from where he stood. It made his knees tremble.

The Tribe had worked for days to build extra sleds for the Tallies, despite Aagam's protests.

Now Whistlenose pointed to them. "You see the furs, son? You know what's in them?" A nod. "*This* is ManWays. Not the streets we left behind. This. This is us."

Beyond that large sack, lay another series of sleds that carried the tribe's food supply—mostly Hairbeast flesh and that of a dozen Clawfolk for whom he himself had been exchanged, back when he'd Volunteered.

"Half gone," he muttered. "And we've travelled less than five days from home."

"What was that, hunter?" asked Hightoes. She had been on the point of launching into a story for the boy.

He had no time to answer. A shout went up—shocking, when most people spoke in whispers. Men were running for the walls, hopping over and lunging past family groups, weapons held above their heads. "Mind him for me, please, Hightoes!"

He didn't bother going back to Ashsweeper for his spear, knowing there'd be weapons waiting at the wall.

Laughlong had returned from patrol. He had a wild look about him and there was no sign of the rest of his pack. There should have been others, five healthy men.

"The Chief has brought us into a trap!" he cried. "Let me through! We need to run for home! The Ancestors have abandoned us!"

And he must have been telling the truth, because something horrible happened then. Darkness fell—just like the time when Whistlenose had been in ClawWays. A darkness deep enough to hide men no more distant than the length of an arm. There was a sound, like the creaking of tortured metal, except that it came from everywhere at once and people started screaming, terrified the Roof was about to fall on them. And something did fall. Liquid, as warm as blood, in drops the size of a fist. Whistlenose felt them plopping down onto his skin.

"It stings!" somebody said nearby. Worse than moss juice, it was like a burn from the fire and everywhere screams and prayers rose...

And then, all at once, it was over. The Roof shone again, bright enough to blind, everybody blinking and afraid and rubbing at the red patches on their skin that the falling slime had etched there.

Laughlong recovered before anybody else and began pushing his way towards the Chief, his face white with anger and, under the fury, fear.

Whistlenose glanced quickly over the heads of the crowd to see Ashsweeper waving to him. She never seemed to be afraid! The boy too, could be seen at the centre of the camp where he had left him. Good, good. He followed after Laughlong to find out what was happening.

Wallbreaker had not been touched by so much as a drop of slime. He and his two wives and his daughter lived under a canopy he'd had built for himself. Now, he stood outside of it, poking his toe at a newly formed pool. "It moves! Do you see that, men? It's crawling... or slithering!"

Laughlong pushed him with such sudden violence that the Chief fell back into the arms of two hunters who were supposed to be guarding him and taking his messages.

"Enough!" Laughlong shouted. "Enough of this madness!"

Wallbreaker's response surprised everybody.

With his soft chest and belly, people forgot that he had once been the Tribe's most promising hunter. Whistlenose used to watch him sparring in Centre Square and remembered wishing he had even half of that speed.

Now, the Chief righted himself. Then, in a blur of movement, he kicked one of Laughlong's feet out from under him, before following up with a shoulder charge that threw the older man bottom-first into the pool of creeping slime.

"Maybe it will crawl up your crack and shut you up," he said.

He could be funny too, the Chief. That had also been forgotten. And a few people managed a laugh.

"Now, hunter. You have lost your pack and there'd better be a good explanation, for they were younger and better men than you."

"That they were," said Laughlong and he shocked everyone by starting to cry. He accepted a hand from Whistlenose, wiping the stinging slime away. "The green beasts," he said. "The Jumpers. Like you guessed, they can smell us even better than we can smell them, so, we covered ourselves in crushed berries and hid, hoping to take one alive for you to interrogate with the Talker."

But the patrols of the enemy had somehow missed the humans completely. To their horror, the men found themselves surrounded when the entire Jumper tribe had moved forward around them.

"That means they're coming," Laughlong said. "They don't have enough food to carry on this stalemate with us. They have no choice now but to fight."

"Foolish of them," said Wallbreaker. "We're dug in. We have walls. Small ones, but still. We can hold off twice our own number."

"But what about five times?" said Laughlong "I was able to do a count, I know what I saw."

"No, no," said the Chief, shaking his head vigorously. "It still wouldn't be worth their while. They'll have to go around us. They can't know how much they outnumber us. They can't know this isn't our permanent home with generations of defences. They couldn't be that stupid."

Whistlenose disagreed. "It's fight us or face the Diggers, Chief. That's the only choice they have now. And the forest is too narrow for them to pass us safely without going into the ... into the ... you know."

Everybody nodded. They knew. He was talking about the fields where the Diggers planted their food. In these places the bodies of living, captured creatures, were buried up to their waists, and there they remained, unresisting, as Digger grubs feasted on them from below. The moaning victims would even cry out to alert their tormentors if somebody tried to rescue them, or would try to grab at would-be saviours and trap them there. Humans had come to dread the fields. The Jumpers would not want to go there either.

And so, they would have to come here. No doubt about it now. They'd be passing this way and whether they defeated the humans or not didn't matter. They feared the Diggers more and that was that.

Whistlenose felt light-headed, as though his spirit were leaving his body. *My boy ... my boy will never be named ...* Everyone knew the Tribe could not long survive the losses of such a fight, even if it won.

He looked over at the Chief, hoping for some kind of solution. The man was crouching over the slime. Aagam had emerged from under the canopy to stand beside him.

"I don't like it," Wallbreaker was muttering. "Why me, Aagam? Why me?"

Whistlenose didn't understand what they were talking about. Was it another clever scheme from the Ancestors?

"Why you, what?" said Aagam.

"This slime stuff. It's crawling. Look. It has ignored Laughlong and everybody else. It just keeps moving towards me. It follows wherever I go. Look!"

That much was true. A few of the puddles had moved in his

direction, albeit slowly, as though hunting him. They clustered around his feet, although he scattered them again easily. "What is this stuff, Aagam?"

"How should I know?"

"Well, it came from the Roof!"

"I tell you I don't know and I don't care! We have a problem now. A real problem, you understand? These new beasts are coming to kill us."

"He's right," said Laughlong, wiping his eyes. He had recovered his composure; both anger and sorrow had been emptied out of him.

"But we have the Talker," said Mossheart. She too, had come out from under the canopy. Hunters glared at her. What was she doing listening in? "We can just negotiate. Why would they risk the losses?"

Instead of scolding her, as would have been proper, the Chief answered her question. "When they come out of the forest, they will be in new territory. They need a nice large store of flesh to keep them alive long enough to learn the streets, or to help them flee even farther from the Diggers. I'm not so sure they would negotiate, or that they would do so in good faith."

"Like us and the Hairbeasts," said Laughlong and Whistlenose could see by the way he said it that he felt ashamed by his part in the attack on humanity's ancient allies.

"Exactly," said Wallbreaker. "Besides, letting them know we have the Talker would just be another reason for them to fight us." But he seemed more interested in the slime than in saving his people. Fearful arguments broke out around him as he bent to study the strange puddles.

Laughlong looked like he wanted to take another swing at the Chief, but Whistlenose pulled him to one side. "How long?" he asked. "Before the Jumpers get here?"

Laughlong shrugged. "I was able to watch them for a full tenth. The little ones move slowly, and even the adults can't travel that fast in this terrain. Although I bet they're murder on a nice flat street. No, they'll be a full day and a night catching up with us here."

"And we definitely can't go around them?"

"The forest isn't wide enough. They'd smell us out for certain. They stink, but we must stink worse."

Wallbreaker had moved closer to Whistlenose, but only so he could watch the slime as it continued to track him. "It's slower now," the Chief was saying. "Look!" Many of the puddles had begun drying up in the heat of the Roof, leaving a faint metallic smell behind them.

Like the rest of the slime, Aagam too had followed the Chief closely.

"Remember," he said, "there are people where we're going, right? You can afford to lose more of these than you think. And this lot understand sacrifice. They will understand—"

Suddenly, Wallbreaker stood up. "The Ancestors have spoken," he cried. He didn't look as certain of his words as Whistlenose might have hoped, but still ... "Laughlong, Whistlenose, you two have done the most scouting."

"Yes," said Laughlong. "That's because you're trying to kill us."

The Chief shrugged, unembarrassed. An older hunter was supposed to make way for younger men and the whole Tribe understood that.

"You reported a mound half a day's travel behind us," he said.

Laughlong nodded. "I said it would be a good campsite, yes. But that was before we found this place. These walls make for a much more defensible position. We can hurt them here. We can fight them."

The Chief smiled. In the distance where the women and lower-status hunters watched, he must have looked confident with those dimples of his pressing deep. But Whistlenose stood close enough to see the tremor in Wallbreaker's limbs and the sickly look of terror in his eyes. "I do not intend to fight them at all," he said. "Everybody get ready to move."

And so the madness began and all without explanations, as if the Chief did not trust his own plan at all. Even so, they obeyed. Everybody obeyed.

Most of the Tribe packed up and began the short trek towards the mound. The rest had special tasks to carry out. Whistlenose, for example, stayed behind to help guard a gang of women that included Ashsweeper. *She shouldn't have been chosen for this. She's the mother of a nameless child.* Hightoes would have to keep an eye on the boy for them.

Ashsweeper showed no resentment and took charge of the other women with ease, although a few were thousands of days older and had borne many children.

"No talking," she told them. "We're here to work."

And what awful work it was, too! Around the site of the abandoned camp, they dug up latrine pits, gathering as much of the foul waste as they could, and piling it into blankets of pounded moss. They couldn't even sing as they worked for fear of attracting something hungry when they had less than a dozen hunters to keep them safe.

The forest was quieter now than it had been a few days earlier. The berries had stopped popping and the clouds of flashing mossbeasts had changed from perfectly co-ordinated swarms to individual insects meandering erratically from rock to branch to who-knew-where.

Whistlenose scanned the poor sight-lines of the forest looking for movement. The past few days had shown that Jumpers had infinite patience when on the hunt. They were as much at home crawling through the undergrowth in camouflaged moss cloaks as they were at balancing on coiled tails and springing to the attack. Could they climb? he wondered. Had the Chief thought of that? He signalled off to his left where Eatenfinger waited, just as nervously as he: *anything?*

A shake of the head.

In the other direction, no more than twenty paces away, his wife still worked, using a filthy skull to scoop excrement into a moss blanket. He risked moving over beside her, passing through a place where one of the slime puddles from the Roof had dried away to a fine white powder.

"What does he want this dung for?" she whispered.

"It must be their sense of smell," he said. "He'll use it to upset them in some way, or ... or ... "

"Or blind them?" she asked. "If their noses are as good as our eyes?"

"Maybe. They have eyes too, though. I don't know."

"The Ancestors won't abandon us, husband."

"No." But Whistlenose wasn't so sure. All his life he had heard tales of species going extinct. The story was always the same: numbers would drop below a certain level and then, crack! Gone within days. The Flim were destroyed when he was a boy. The Hairbeasts, by rights, should have been next if the humans hadn't sheltered them.

And now we are little more than a thousand. And fewer every day.

He had no doubt the Chief would get them through the next few days, but the real question was how many would die in the process.

Another filthy woman approached on silent feet. Whistlenose was surprised to recognise her as Mossheart. She too was the mother of a nameless child and shouldn't be here. Punished perhaps, for speaking out at what should have been a meeting of hunters.

"Why are you dawdling, Ashsweeper?" she asked, proud as ever. "There's a big pit left at the back."

"It's nearly dark," said Ashsweeper.

"All the more reason to hurry."

But at that moment, Browncrack and Shoulderbiter came sprinting out of the woods. They looked worried and tired, but they weren't calling out the alarm.

"Time to go," said Whistlenose.

He needn't have spoken. Everywhere, the workwomen were already wrapping up their sacks of filth and piling them on to the food sleds that had been freed up for that very purpose.

"How near are they?" Whistlenose asked the two young scouts.

Both were smeared with the poisonous juices of crushed berries and they stank like rusty metal. "Two thousand paces!"

said Browncrack.

"All right, that's all right. I thought we were going to have to put up a fight to allow the women to get away."

"To get away with the shit?" said Shoulderbiter. "We might have had to die for shit? Can't the women just abandon the sleds?"

"All right. Let's keep our voices down now. Listen, two thousand paces is plenty. Jumpers are slow when travelling, and when they get here, this whole place will stink of us and it will be night time. They'll have to stop and make sure we're not all around them ready to strike. We have plenty of time to make it to the new position."

And so it proved. Even in the dark, the gatherers and their escorts had no trouble following the trail left by the tribe earlier that day. The enemy were sure to find it just as easily, although they would have to worry more about ambush.

Whistlenose stumbled along, struggling to stay alert after a ten-day of incredible worry and fear. All he wanted was to curl up beside his family at the new position and forget about anything until the morning.

Up ahead, the dark shadow of the mound gradually became apparent. He had seen it only by day when scouting for a campsite, back before they had met the Jumpers. He wondered why no fires had been lit. There was no more hiding now, so why shouldn't the Tribe have one last hot meal to raise their spirits? Why no final dance to the sound of wedding drums?

He jumped as he felt something brush across his neck.

"You're dead," a voice whispered.

"Laughlong?"

"Is that you, Whistlenose? Oh."

"Is ... is something wrong?"

He sensed, rather than saw, the lowering of the spear. "I'm sorry, Whistlenose. I'm truly sorry."

"About what?" But he already knew. Deep in his guts, he already knew. The boy. It had to be the boy.

II.
WELL W⊕RTH IT

There were always children who did such things. "Don't run away!" were among the first words parents tried to teach. But every few hundred days or so, somebody's precious girl or boy walked around a corner and never came back. Things had improved after the attack of the Flyers and their Armourback and Hopper allies. ManWays had greatly shrunk and in the process its borders had become tighter, more secure.

But then, the Ancestors had sent the whole tribe running off into the forest.

Ashsweeper was on her knees, not even crying, her eyes as dry as a dusty brick, as if she didn't know anything had happened at all. The only sounds were from the great mound where crowds of people were digging pits with improvised shovels of wood and bone.

Hightoes had been brought out to them. *She* was weeping while her husband, Fearsflyers, stood nervously at her side. She explained it all again and again.

"He was too fast. In my state, I couldn't ... He said he wanted Ashsweeper ... he said ... he ... he ran back down the trail we had made. I hoped he would just run into you along the way, but he's ... he's not with you ... "

Her voice seemed to fade into the night. Here between the trees little chilling drops of Roofsweat spattered Whistlenose's face and rattled the canopy of leaves. He had that spinning feeling in his head, like his spirit was being sucked out of his skull. He was no longer an Ancestor: no longer anything at all. And poor Ashsweeper still made no sound. But the Roof made up for her—it always wept at night.

Nearby, men were getting ready to grab hold of him. They knew he would try to go looking and they couldn't allow him to waste his flesh that way.

Suddenly, everybody around him tensed. A warning was shouted and spears were lowered and then, just as quickly, relaxed. Laughlong started jumping up and down, as though he were trying to shout out something, but had lost his voice.

"Dada?"

The boy was there, clutching at his father's leg. Was Whistlenose dreaming? Everyone was babbling all at once until a sentry had to come back and shut them up. Whistlenose lifted the child into the air so that they were face to face. "What? How? What did you … ?"

"I hid," said the boy. "I saw you coming and hid. Then I tracked you back. Nobody saw me! I won, I won the game! I always catch you, dada!"

"Night tracker," said Hightoes.

"What?" Whistlenose felt dizzy.

"That's his name," she said.

Whistlenose still barely knew what was happening, but somebody slapped his back. Others were embracing Ashsweeper. And they were embracing the boy too with "welcome to the Tribe!" and "your Ancestors can see you now!" and other things. Surely it was too early? And the other pregnant women hadn't agreed to it yet, but nobody here had any doubts that the name would stick. Nighttracker. He had chased down his own parents and, in the process, he had evaded even the most experienced hunters. "Nighttracker."

Ashsweeper finally started crying. But not Whistlenose. Ever since the boy was born he'd felt a grip around his throat that had tightened and tightened so that it troubled even his sleep; so that at times he couldn't breathe. That was gone now, cut loose and all the cool air of night flooded into him at once. "Nighttracker," he said, his voice awed. A good name. So much better than his, with a good story behind it that people would tell around fires for hundreds of days to come. Nighttracker.

The following day, Wallbreaker revealed the full horror of his plan to the Tribe.

A Globe passed overhead, its metal body glinting in the light of the Roof, but not as brightly as it should have. It felt dark for the time of day. Or was it just fear that made him feel that way?

Whistlenose said nothing. Nobody did, stuck in such uncomfortable positions as they had been for two full tenths already. He wanted water. He was desperate to scratch his right leg. And worse than all of that, was the stench, the awful stench of human excrement, and the vomit too that the Chief had insisted on, despite all the food wasted in order to create it.

And yet, he still felt giddy. That was the word, "giddy," over the naming of his son. Nighttracker was a real hunter's name. And wasn't that how it often worked out? How people somehow lived up to what they were called? Speareye had been a great Chief; Crunchfist was every bit as powerful as he sounded, and Flimface ... poor Flimface! As cowardly in the end as those creatures he so uncannily resembled.

And then there was "Whistlenose," of course. A fool's name. Harmless and unremarkable, with no stories to leave after him for the fireside. But he *had* left a great hunter to continue the Tribe and *nothing* could be better than that.

A nearby woman, who must have been just as expendable as he was, coughed when the smell became too much. Somebody else hissed her quiet. What a fool! he thought. Can't she shut up?

And still, in the forest, nothing moved.

The mound, it turned out, had been terribly hard work to dig. People kept pulling away blocks of the stone known as *concrete*. The most disturbing discovery of all, however, had been the bones. Human, beyond any doubt. Crumbling away at the slightest touch. The Tribe had travelled five days away from ManWays. How could there be humans here? Did that mean the tribe had migrated once before, deep in the past? Or worse, that their territory had been slowly shrinking over the generations?

"None of those things," Aagam had said, but Whistlenose and the other hunters had been sent away before he explained the rest of it.

Something shifted in the forest and the hunter felt his heart speeding up. Another movement, and his eyes, which had been learning to spot them, made out the camouflaged shapes of two Jumpers crawling through the undergrowth.

"Ancestors help us," whispered the silly woman, but quietly enough that the creatures were unlikely to be able to hear it. Not that she could know that for sure!

The two enemies rose up on powerful tails. Whistlenose's fingers itched for a spear. They could see him now, he knew that. They could see he was unarmed and helpless.

Wallbreaker's schemes often cost lives before he "got them working just right." Whistlenose remembered in particular the Chief's use of nets to pull creatures out of the Wetlanes. Sometimes, it was the hunters who were pulled in instead.

Whistlenose tried not to think about that as the two Jumper scouts hopped closer to the easy meat. Were they hesitant in their movements? He hoped so. He would be, if he were them. What they were now seeing, were dozens of living humans—as well as a few of the larger men dressed in Hairbeast furs—buried up to their waists or chests, their limbs listless. A stench of bodily wastes hung heavy on the air.

The Jumpers paused. They lowered their weapons: the wood they used for blocking, which Aagam had called a *shield*; and their long-tipped spears.

Wherever they came from, these creatures had been fleeing Diggers. There was little else that could drive such a strong people with so many hunters from their homes. And now, they must be thinking, the Diggers had found them again. If Wallbreaker's scheme worked, the Jumpers would run away as far and as fast as they could, leaving the humans alone.

Unfortunately, these two scouts did not flee. Something must have been blowing the warning shell in their heads, telling them that all was not right here.

They hopped closer, coming all the way out of the forest, until Whistlenose, in the front ranks, could see them no more than a spears-length away from him. Sweat rolled down his forehead.

Of course the assembled humans could overpower these two enemies, even unarmed, even half-buried. But if they gave themselves away now, the green creatures would drum those tongues of theirs in an alarm that would quickly pass to a relay of their friends nearby.

One of the creatures hopped to a point just in reach of Whistlenose. *Ancestors help me.* He reacted, grabbing for the beast clumsily, just as a real victim of the Diggers might do. The Jumper swayed back and he brushed its moss cloak with his fingertips.

It rattled its tongue and Whistlenose moaned at it. Still, it didn't leave, although its companion stayed well back. The sweat ran into Whistlenose's eyes. He mustn't wipe it away! He couldn't react to the sting of it!

He wasn't the only one suffering. His neighbour was the woman who had been whispering earlier. What was her name? Stonedropper? He barely knew her, although they were close in age. How could that be? She'd been pretty when they were younger, he remembered that much. Hunters had offered ridiculous amounts of flesh to her father in order to woo her.

He heard her moaning now and she too grabbed at the Jumper—too enthusiastically, he thought. *No, no! They're not like that!* But then, how would a woman know? They had never been to the fields of the Diggers to see what a hunter saw. They'd never had the chance. She moaned again, louder now and Whistlenose imagined how afraid she must be, how she was trying to scare the creature away. He felt clammy with fear.

He knew it was wrong, but couldn't help turning his head slightly and in doing so, saw something horrible. The Jumper still wasn't sure one way or the other if these were genuine victims of the Diggers. It raised the arm with its spear slowly into the air where Stonedropper could not help but see it. The long, wicked tip of bone shone in the Rooflight and held there for ten full heartbeats.

Then, it flashed down and drove in through Stonedropper's belly and into the soil beyond. The pain! The pain must have been incredible! Great hunters, strong men with jaws of rock and chests black with tattoos had screamed their last moments away with such wounds. Whistlenose had seen it. He had seen them beg the Ancestors, their mothers, their Chiefs to save them; to take the pain away; to make it all end.

But the Diggers' victims did not react like that, would barely feel a thing.

Whisttlenose waited for the inevitable scream that would ruin the plan and condemn all off them to death. He would make sure to kill these scouts first, though. He tensed his body to leap out of the hole and could sense the other hunters around him preparing to do the same. They would start this last stand with one small victory at least!

Incredibly, Stonedropper held her silence, letting out no more than a quiet gasp when the cruel spear withdrew. The creature turned around calmly, and hopped away.

Nobody could move to Stonedropper's aid. Nobody. She bled to death in utter silence.

Later, just before the fall of darkness, when the signal arrived that all were free to move again, Whistlenose was first to get to her side. "Stonedropper," he whispered. Blood ran down her face from where she had bitten her lip through to keep from screaming. She had saved them all. She had saved the entire Tribe. It was the bravest thing he had ever witnessed.

"Good," Wallbreaker was saying from somewhere at the back. "I knew it. That was well worth it."

12.
TEN TH⊕USAND DAYS

In the days after Stonedropper's sacrifice, the migration went more smoothly again. The Jumpers had passed them by and although other species were seen trying to escape through the woods, they were nowhere near as numerous or as well organised as the green-skinned tribe had been. These new creatures fell easily, almost gratefully to human spears, and before long, enough confidence had returned to the Tribe that the Chief was allowing fires to cook the flesh and to smoke any extra for the long journey that still lay ahead.

In private, however, Whistlenose wondered at the madness of running towards the source of so much fear. He was sure that other members of the Tribe must be thinking the same thing, but nobody could complain: the Chief had been right so far and had saved many hundreds of lives with his clever schemes. The younger hunters admired him more than ever now. He'd heard Browncrack saying how the Ancestors—at the Chief's request—must have silenced Stonedropper to make the plan work. That was all too much for the older man.

"Listen," he hissed, grabbing the lad by the neck. "You saved my life. You're a good man and you'll serve the tribe well."

"Let ... let go my neck. Whistlenose! What—"

"But *you* didn't see ... you didn't see her lip. *She* did that. Stonedropper. Not the Ancestors, not the Chief. *She* did it. She had a thousand days left in her. Ten thousand! And you lessen them when you speak of her like that!"

"All right. I was just saying!" The young man wrenched himself free. He was going to be much stronger than Whistlenose soon, but he didn't realise it yet. He had red marks on his neck from the older hunter's fingers. This wasn't how a man should lead others and Whistlenose felt ashamed. And yet, not even Ashsweeper had really understood when he'd told her. "I was cursing Stonedropper before it happened," he said. "I thought she was a fool! But there's no way I could have done what she did. I couldn't."

"Of course you could, husband. You're always putting yourself down. I saw how you volunteered to feed the Clawfolk."

And so the days passed.

The Tribe was no more than a short journey from the end of the forest when the Roof turned black again. It was Whistlenose's third time to see such a thing and he should have been ready for it, except it went on for so much longer than before.

Utter silence reigned in the darkness. Nothing moved. Even the mossbeasts had frozen—he should have felt them whizzing past his ear!

Whistlenose was holding his breath, waiting for normality to return, and then ... then he saw a glow in the distance. A faint blue light that flickered as a fire would. Some creature, perhaps? But, before he could think of trying to track it, the Rooflight came back on.

People had a name for these periods of total darkness: the Blindness, they called it. This time, no slime fell on the tribe, but another half a day's travel revealed hundreds of crumbling trees caked in the white residue it left behind when it dried out.

"It would have killed us just as easily," Whistlenose told Ashsweeper. "There was so much of it here!"

"But it didn't," his wife replied. "The Ancestors wouldn't let that happen." She was starting to talk like all the others now, as if she believed in Wallbreaker's mystical pronouncements.

Whistlenose wasn't sure how he felt about that himself. There didn't seem to be any other explanation for all the things that had happened. And yet, why would the Ancestors have sent somebody as awful as Aagam to guide the Tribe? And why would they speak through a coward?

Speareye had been a great Chief: the man every man should be, but the Ancestors had allowed *him* to die in full view of the Tribe.

He dug into one of the trees with a bone knife. Dry bark flaked away to reveal more solid wood beneath. "This is where I saw that blue glow," he said. "During the Blindness."

"Have you told the cChief?"

"He didn't seem very interested."

Ashsweeper nodded, turning her head to keep an eye on Nighttracker digging for mossbeasts with a sharpened stick. Whistlenose raised his eyes to the great Roof, something he'd been reluctant to do for the past few days.

In the distance, four great squares the size of ManWays had turned black. One of these now flickered back into dull life. The other three hung over the world like a hole. Like the mouth of a Digger's tunnel.

13.
A REMEMBERED KISS

Wallbreaker's daughter looked more and more like Mossheart had when they were growing up. She had her father's blond hair, however, and just the slightest promise of dimples on those red cheeks of hers when he made her laugh. Which he did as often as possible. But there was no getting away from those full lips, or those eyebrows that each seemed like separate living things in their own right.

As the child giggled on his lap, Wallbreaker remembered the first kiss he had shared with her mother. Those strange eyebrows had risen in surprise—her father had barely turned his back, after all!—before settling gently again. She had whispered, "He'll want a big bride-price."

"Will you talk him down?"

"No." She grinned, keeping her lips close enough to his that an insect couldn't have passed between them. "You will work hard to win me and you'll work hard to keep me too."

He had leaned forward, but she pulled away. "And that'll be the last kiss before you leap the fire with me!"

It wasn't, of course. Tens of sweet adventures had followed: embraces they had hidden from her parents, from the Flesh Council and poor Stopmouth. But Mossheart had been true to her word in one thing at least: Wallbreaker had handed over a bride-price of five full creatures—the highest in living memory.

He had won love and a reputation, all in one go, and nothing back then, nothing, could touch him. Oh, how quick he'd been! And clever too. How strong!

"Enough of this time-wasting," said a voice behind him. The child stiffened in his arms. Like him, she had grown to hate Aagam.

"Go to your mother," he said. "Or Treeneck. Your mother's digging today."

They were camped in a place where the slime had killed a hundred trees. But farther on, the health of the forest had suffered even greater indignities, where Digger tunnels riddled the ground, and where fields fat with victims spewed waste in every direction. Scouts were out there now, looking for a way through while the Tribe consumed the last of its supplies.

"You told me we could pass here," Wallbreaker said.

Aagam shrugged. "The way has closed. Possibly only in the last few days. Remember the information the scouts brought back to us?"

"Back to *me*. I am the Chief."

Aagam grinned. He had lost quite a bit of weight in the early days, but now he ate flesh with gusto and claimed to enjoy it even more than the civilised food of his home in the Roof. "I told you how the Diggers work. The creatures planted out there are being eaten from below by the Diggers' young, yes? So far, the victims have sunk very little into the soil, and most of them are Jumpers or other creatures we have encountered fleeing through these trees. So, they are newly arrived here. And that means the great Eastern and Western Digger families have only just now met in the middle. Their territory will be thin for a little while yet. If we can bull through the centre, the hills lie only six days to the north of us."

He had explained what hills were already, although Wallbreaker had a hard time imagining mounds so large that it could take a day for a fit young hunter to cross over them.

"I don't like it," Wallbreaker said. "Planted creatures will grab at us as we run past. And what about all our food? What about the pregnant women? What about the Tallies?"

Aagam sneered. "All this *superstitious* junk. Pregnant women and sticks! You are worse than the *Religious* in the Roof. Just leave them behind. That is the answer you are looking for."

"Leave … the pregnant women?"

"For the love of the gods, you're savages! That's what you do, that's what you're supposed to do! Sacrifice the weak so the strong can eat better, right? That's what it's all about!"

"It's about the *Tribe*," said Wallbreaker. "About getting Home." No human, no real human could accept the loss of his people. They bustled all around him as they had done his whole life. Both his mother and his father had stepped forward proudly with thousands of days still to live. The very thought of abandoning the tally sticks, of a Tribe with no pregnant women amongst it to name the children, was abhorrent. Both past and future abandoned! No, no. And then, the pitiful survivors to throw themselves on their knees and beg mercy from a tribe of strangers that included Indrani, his unfaithful wife? Why would those strangers not simply volunteer him and his people? It's what he had planned for them, after all!

Aagam scowled and wagged a finger in his face. "You still care about home, Chief? Even after I explained to you where it was? What that phrase really meant?"

"It's what it means to us now that matters."

"Oh, as if you, the great Wallbreaker, really care about any of that! I've seen you from above, *Chief*. You can't hide from the Roof. Everyone up there knows you're a coward. I've been counting on it. Yes, counting on it! Above all else. Above even your dirty little tribe of cannibals, above your … your *home*, you want to live. It's as simple as that, and I, Aagam, am here to grant your wish.

"So, listen to me, Chief. Listen. We make a run through the middle of the planted creatures. The slow will do as they've always done—"

"We *never* volunteer pregnant women."

"Well, that's about to change, isn't it? The Ancestors are going to send you a new *vision*," he grinned fiercely. "The Ancestors will tell these women to volunteer so the rest of us can make it *home*, but, get this: *home* is going to be the other side of the hills. You'll tell them that's where it always was, and now, you'll be bringing them right to it, yes?"

"One moment, Aagam," Wallbreaker said. He fished around for a good Armourback shell spear. Then, he stabbed his shocked adviser with it in the arm—no farther than the depth of a thumb. The weapon was free again and blood welling out of Aagam's flesh before he could so much as yelp. "I want you to see that I am serious."

"I—"

Another quick stab with the spear. "From this day forth, you will speak only when I ask direct questions. Yes, you have convinced me there is no point in torturing you, but *I* have decided I quite like it."

The man's mouth opened once more, but before he could utter a word, the spear was nestling gently under his chin. "I don't want any plans from you. You will tell me what you know about the Diggers. What they're afraid of. What will hurt them. What they want. Wives? I will give you wives and your life because I like to know things. But *I* will do the planning here.

"Now, the Diggers, Aagam. What are their weaknesses?"

Aagam surprised him by spitting at him and grinning. "You are an idiot—" he grunted as the spear drew more blood. Sweat was pouring down his face. "You'll need to stab a little deeper, Chief. But where's the need? I'll tell you what you want to know. I'm sweet natured, after all." He smiled again, his blood dripping onto the moss and his filthy clothing, the sweat rolling down his face. "The Diggers," he said, "fear fire and light."

"Fire and light? We have seen them even at midday. Not often, but still..."

"Take the spear away."

"Answer me, or you die."

"I doubt it."

Wallbreaker put the weapon away and even handed the stranger a cloth of pounded moss to staunch his wounds.

"They don't fear for themselves," said Aagam. "That's why you'll see some of them wandering in the full glare of the Roof. It's the grubs that will die after too much exposure to heat and light. The grubs. Those little darlings feed on their parents until the adult can find another host for them instead."

"By the Ancestors! They eat their own parents?" It explained so much. Everybody knew by now how difficult it was to kill the poor creatures planted in the fields. The grubs had a way of keeping them alive right up until the end and, according to tales Wallbreaker had heard, adult Diggers too had been seen "coming back to life," crawling away from the hunters that had "killed" them. The grubs must have been responsible for all of that.

"Yes," Aagam nodded. "The greedy little darlings have their parents in constant torment, yet the adults who are … blessed by motherhood, avoid light and heat at all costs. Even unmated Diggers have an instinct to keep away from flames."

"So, we can simply surround ourselves with torches and cross the fields?"

"Do you really think it's that easy, Chief? These are intelligent creatures we are dealing with. I imagine they are well aware of their own fears. Remember, they have already consumed fire-wielding tribes far larger than yours. Every time they do it, they learn new lessons and grow more numerous."

"What about my brother? How did *he* get past them? You said he went a longer way around." Of all his tribe, Wallbreaker alone knew Stopmouth had been no fool. Shy, yes. Nervous and jealous too. Incapable of putting two words together without biting the tongue out of his own head. But no idiot.

Aagam grinned, taking great pleasure in the next bit. "Your runaway wife told him to tie some old trees together. Then, they floated down the Wetlane until they had passed almost to the far side of Digger territory. She *helped* him. She helped him every step of the way."

Wallbreaker grabbed the spear again. His face grew hot. "You know she was kidnapped. Stopmouth must have forced her to tell him what to do."

The grin grew only wider. To avoid killing the man, Wallbreaker moved his gaze off to where his daughter played among the trees. She had found a little boy and was attempting to boss him around. "How like your mother," he said fondly. Humans had come across creatures, such as the Hairbeasts, that did not love their offspring, but the Diggers were not among them, it seemed. There must be a way of using that to get to the hills with the main strength of the Tribe intact.

The light of the Roof flickered and everybody held their breaths, but this time the Blindness lasted less than a heartbeat and Wallbreaker chose to take that as a good sign. It was getting better up there, whatever the sickness was. Everything was going be all right.

14.
THE BURN

It was no work for a man to be doing, but none of the hunters objected. And even some of the children were involved, cutting brushwood and pulling down trees. They were carving a path through the forest, straight from the Tribe's camp and out into Digger territory.

"It's got to be as wide and as smooth as possible," the Chief said.

He even came out to supervise and people worked harder under his gaze. For once, he had explained his plan to them in detail and nobody wanted to be counted among the slackers for fear of being chosen for the more suicidal roles that the scheme demanded.

"We two will be picked anyway," Laughlong told Whistlenose. "He thinks we're trouble."

"He thinks *you're* trouble, Laughlong. Hey, you are trouble! Me? I'm just lame."

"Funny that," said the other hunter, wiping sweat from his brow. People said he hadn't laughed even once since getting his name. Some men accepted themselves, while others fought against it their whole lives. "You're a better hunter since you hurt that leg of yours, Whistlenose. How many scrapes have you got out of in the last hundred days? And I heard you were the first to wet his spear in the guts of a Jumper."

"We brought no flesh home that day."

"Still … The Chief would be mad to throw you away. You're a better provider now than you ever were as a youngster."

Whistlenose tried to hide his pleasure, but wasn't sure he'd managed it too well. The other man patted him on the arm. "We'll be picked, though, no matter what. You'll see."

It didn't stop either of them from bringing down trees under the orders of an older woman, Hairtosser. "This path will save your lives," she kept telling them. As if they didn't know it better than her! She was famous for stating the obvious, though, and now she kept repeating, "If they catch you, you're dead!"

"Thanks for the hunting advice, Hairtosser," Laughlong muttered. "Ancestors bless your bottomless wisdom."

It took the entire tribe three days before the path was complete. Four hunters could run along it abreast, and children, including a very proud Nighttracker, now climbed trees to hang swathes of moss cloth from the branches to either side. Gangs of women, meanwhile, had been clearing away rocks and smoothing down the larger bumps in the path.

Here and there, a tree too proud to bring down forced twists and turns along the route, and that worried the hunters. Wallbreaker made them walk the length of it several times, while Hairtosser, representing the women, kept saying, "You'll only get one chance, boys! Just one!"

Finally, all the brush was carried away and Whistlenose felt his bones turn to water. *The time has come, boy.* But he was wrong.

Despite the fact that food supplies were shrinking fast, two more days passed while everybody rested up. Whistlenose couldn't help thinking that Wallbreaker, Ancestor visions or not, was trying to gather up his own courage too. Death would threaten everybody in what was to come. Everybody.

And then, with the Roof reaching its brightest point, Wallbreaker gathered the hunters together to assign them their roles. Whistlenose heard his name called out, along with Laughlong, Boneless and a few of the more experienced hunters, as well as some of the women. However, he did not expect what came next. "You lot are to be part of the second ambush."

"Not the runners?" Laughlong asked, relief obvious in his voice.

"Oh, your job will be hard enough, old man, don't you worry." He indicated another group that consisted of mostly younger men, although Wallbreaker had toughened it with older meat too—hunters such as Spitback and Kneebiter. "We need stronger legs for the hard part, right lads? The bravest of the brave!" No insult was intended to other groups. It was simply the way a Chief spoke to those whose flesh was most at risk. They cheered him, and it seemed to Whistlenose that the less experience a man had, the louder his approval.

"The runners will depart a tenth of a day before dark. You know what to do? Browncrack?"

The youngster nodded eagerly. "Go into the planted fields. Steal as much flesh as we can."

"But don't get carried away. Don't let them grab you, because they will be trying that. Packs of three to tackle each body. A limb each with the third man to stab through to the brain—but only in species that have an obvious head. Leave the Pios alone, or anything too unfamiliar. Pull the corpse from the hole. What then, hunter?"

Browncrack showed no fear at all. "The Diggers will come when it gets dark."

"If not before … " the Chief agreed. "But probably it won't be until the tracklights come up. From what I've heard."

"Did the … did the *Ancestors* tell you that?"

"Of course. What happens then, hunter?"

"Then, we kill the Diggers! We—"

Wallbreaker slapped Browncrack hard across the face. "Weren't you listening? To the plan? *You* will kill no Diggers. You are to run. All of you." He turned to Spitback and Kneebiter. "I'll be relying on you two to make sure nobody tries anything stupid."

"You could always go yourself," said Laughlong. "I'm sure the boys will make room for you."

"I'm sure they would," said the Chief. "Or for anybody else I chose to send." But he showed no signs of anger and he repeated, "Nothing stupid! You bring the flesh back here to the first ambush point."

"What if..." Whistlenose couldn't help himself, "what if there are too many Diggers following? Those fields go on a great distance. And there are tunnels everywhere. All the buildings are tipping into the soil, as if the ground was sucking them down."

"You let me worry about that," said Wallbreaker. "Now, wait." He beckoned Hightoes out from under the trees where she had been watching. She was a fine-looking woman, Whistlenose thought, but she was here now because she was closer to giving birth than anyone else in the camp.

"You men," she said and then coughed, nervous under their stares, although she spoke now as the Heart of the Tribe. "You men are my hands. You are the strong arms and the swift legs that will carry me Home. I am the fire that waits for your gift of flesh. I am the voices of your children; the embrace of your wives."

Each of the runners produced a knife and cut his fingertip. They flicked beads of blood at her until she was speckled with it. Rarely did so many hunters leave on a single venture, but she didn't make the mistake of wiping her face clean; rather, she honoured the men by licking her lips and smiling shyly at them.

"Your blood has returned to me," she said, "and so shall you."

Cheering was no longer appropriate. The men wrapped the cuts in moss so as not to make tracking them any easier. It was habit more than anything else, for this was one occasion in which they wanted to be followed.

Then, the hunters, in total silence, turned up the path the Tribe had created together and broke into a quick jog. Whistlenose wondered how many of them would make it back, despite the blood they had just shed. He felt afraid for them, but very proud too, for not one showed any hesitation in his step.

"We have the hardest job now," said Laughlong. "Waiting. Worrying."

Whistlenose knew what he meant, but didn't feel it was right to say so. He had been chased by Diggers before and dreaded to think what it would be like in a forest, at night, where every step on the rough, root-covered ground might bring a hunter down to be overrun.

Sometimes, when he closed his eyes, he still saw the grub pushing itself up Highstepper's nose. Now he feared that many of those young men would not be coming back from their deliberate attempt to provoke the world's most powerful species.

The ambushers were allowed a final visit to their families, no more time than it would take to hug their children and flick a drop of blood at their wives. The women and other hunters had plenty of work of their own to do. By now most of the food was gone. Maybe no more than three days' worth remained and this was divided out amongst everybody, along with tally sticks for the women to carry. The sleds were to be abandoned entirely, left at the old camp, which was also to be the site of the planned ambush.

"Don't worry, husband," said Ashsweeper. "The Ancestors have inspired this plan. It can't go wrong." She was preparing a cloth to tie around Nighttracker's little shoulders. The boy's share of the tribe's goods would be symbolic: a few strips of meat that he would bear proudly for the length of the journey. Ashsweeper would have preferred that he be carried instead, but the fact that he was named now made that impossible. Whistlenose constantly prayed to the Ancestors that the boy would be able to keep up with his mother.

"Don't let her out of your sight, you hear me?" he told Nighttracker. "She won't be safe without you."

"No, dada."

"And no hiding for the rest of the day."

"I don't do that anymore. I'm big now. I have a spear."

And so he did. A sharpened stick. "Good boy. Give me a kiss." It was getting dark. The runners would already be in amongst the planted bodies that would be moaning to warn the Diggers of attack. Whistlenose shuddered. He took up his position with the other men in trenches dug especially for them, with cover provided by moss camouflaged blankets copied from those of the Jumpers. Would that be enough to hide them from the Diggers? Wallbreaker seemed to think so.

"The Diggers' hearing is good enough to see with," he said. "They make a sound we can't detect, they create echoes with it that ... "

"Echoes?" Everyone was staring at him except Aagam who sneered openly at the men.

"Oh ... never mind," said the Chief, "it doesn't matter. Just duck down and as long as you've never taken flesh from their fields and keep quiet, they won't be able to tell you apart from a pile of rocks."

Afterwards, Laughlong said to Whistlenose, "Maybe they *will* be able to see us. "Maybe Wallbreaker is counting on it and we're the real bait for his trap. He could rid himself of all us older men in one go."

Whistlenose didn't believe that, but who knew with the Chief? Who knew what the Ancestors were whispering in his ear. Or was it only Aagam who did that?

The last of the Rooflight dimmed and the grids of tracklights came on to cast wild and frightening shadows through tangled branches. Whistlenose tried to ignore them, to stay present. He felt suffocated by the moss he had wadded up his left nostril to block the sound from it. The rough camouflage blanket spawned a thousand itches all over his back.

Men were used to ambushes. They trained for them before they were even named. They learned stillness and silence and patience. It was the one part of hunting where the old surpassed the young. But Whistlenose twitched and sweated, his mind on his family as well as the young men who surely should have returned by now from their taunting of the Diggers.

He started at the sound of a *crack* nearby. *Calm, be calm.* It was just another branch succumbing to the residue of the slime that had dried it out. And then, too late to save that dying tree, he felt the first chilly drops of Roofsweat trickling into his hiding place. He suppressed the urge to shiver, to move at all ...

Was that ... ? Yes! The cries of men; the pounding of running feet. He wasn't imagining it! The young hunters were returning, a long line of them sprinting through the darkness, their skin streaked with the blood of the planted bodies they had killed. Each man would have consumed a sliver of flesh along the way too, to ensure the Diggers would come after him.

Whistlenose counted more than twenty survivors. Not too bad! Although some had abandoned spears they would be needing shortly. He hoped Wallbreaker had foreseen that possibility too and would have provided for more weapons at the far end of the old camp.

The hunter tried to still his own excited breathing. He gripped the shaft of his spear. The second to last man passed him by and he appreciated the Chief's cleverness all the more now, for none tripped on the smooth path or lost their way in the darkness. All that chopping of wood made more and more sense as the night progressed.

Poor Treekisser was bringing up the rear, carrying a leg wound. *Ancestors help him!* He wouldn't last too long. A slick black swarm was already nipping at his heels, its members too numerous to count. They flowed past, silent and vengeful, their skin writhing with grubs that shone silver in the tracklights. They kept coming and coming. More than any human had ever seen and surely more than the ambush at the far end could cope with.

Don't think about it, boy! It's not your problem.

The experienced hunters didn't lift a finger as Treekisser went under with a pitiful cry. They bit their lips waiting for the last of the Diggers to pass. Then, as silently as they could manage, hunters sprang from their burrows. They uncovered smouldering embers from pouches of tanned hide. They set light to piles of undergrowth that the tribe had been building up for days. Then they blocked the path down which their friends had fled with branches and tree trunks set aside for that very purpose. These too were set alight.

Roofsweat began to fall a little more heavily, but it did nothing to protect trees that had been parched dry by the slime. Whistlenose had never seen a fire take so quickly or burn so fiercely.

Everywhere, the old camp site blazed as men, and even a few of the younger women, scattered their store of embers. There hadn't been enough hunters to carry out all the many parts of the Chief's plan and, just as the migration had forced men to dig and bring down trees, it now brought women into close proximity with living enemies. None of the women had complained.

"Ready?" shouted Laughlong. "Get ready!"

The fire fed greedily on the slimed trees, but was beginning to spread to parts of the forest beyond the camp too: to trees that drank from the Roof every night and that should have been far too wet to succumb. The hunters now faced a real danger of being caught in their own trap.

"Here they come!"

Two dozen Diggers charged back towards them along the path. They would have had nowhere else to go. The younger band of hunters had led them into a huge ambush at the far end of the old camp. Now their one path to escape lay through a much smaller group of older men and untrained women.

"Slings!"

Stones smashed enemy bodies. Diggers tumbled, tripping those behind and giving the humans time for another shot. But many of the creatures remained unhurt and the first of these threw their bodies straight onto the flaming branches so that others could scamper over their writhing flesh. Grubs fell away, hissing and popping in the heat.

"We can't let them past!" Laughlong was shouting. "Not even one!"

But it was all going horribly wrong now. A bridge of bodies had been created, three wide. Yet more of the enemy had come running out of the forest behind, their fur singed, their grubs tumbling off them. Fifteen or so made it out of the trap to throw themselves at the defenders.

Whistlenose thrust his spear as a Digger charged him so that the Armourback point disappeared far into its chest and was pulled from his hands. Another creature, coming on behind, hit him hard and the two were rolling in the moss as flames roared all around and above them. Claws raked his side and then tried for his throat. He wanted his knife, but couldn't reach for it; his two arms were busy fending off the forelimbs of the beast. It was stronger than he. The creature wrenched itself free, but it had no intention of killing a human this night, it just wanted to escape. It clambered over his body only to meet somebody else's spear.

"Up, get up, Whistlenose!" shouted Laughlong. "I've killed it for you. We've killed them all! Up! Everybody! Run now. We have to run or be boiled in our skins!"

Whistlenose obeyed, remembering somehow to retrieve his spear. Smoke had spread everywhere. The men and women coughed, stumbling over corpses of friend and foe alike. The fire had spread far beyond where they had intended it, but somebody shouting, "I found it! It's here," brought them all onto a second, smaller path.

They were in a race now against the flames. It licked at their heels as they ran, pulling each other along, choking, eyes streaming. "We're cooking, Ancestors save us!" Whistlenose couldn't see who'd said that. By day, the route had seemed so short and he began to fear they had turned the wrong way in the confusion. But then, the stench of Digger fields overpowered the smoke and they knew they had made it beyond the reach of the fire.

They fell, every man and woman, gasping into the muck.

The cold Roofsweat soothed the scratches on Whistlenose's skin. He panted and panted and every breath scorched his lungs going in and coming out.

"Are you all right?" That was Laughlong, his voice a rasp. Whistlenose didn't answer right away. He was looking up at the tracklights far above, blurred and glittering behind a veil of mist.

When he was growing up, people said the tracklights were

the fires of the Ancestors in a grid of streets such as you saw in some places. But people had stopped saying that since that cursed woman Indrani had fallen from the Roof. Whatever she was, she was no Ancestor.

"Whistlenose? We have to catch up to the Tribe. We can't stop here."

"Their fires are going out, Laughlong," he said.

"What?"

Just as had happened in the daytime, large areas of the Roof were dark by night too. The Diggers didn't like light, didn't need it. Were they were taking over up there also? Is that what this all meant?

He allowed Laughlong to help him to his feet.

Bodies had replaced tree trunks in the murky darkness, hanging listlessly and stretching off into the night. Nobody dared stand too close to them, despite the heat of the forest so near at their backs and still growing hotter.

"You made it! Thank the Ancestors." It was a new voice, undamaged by smoke. "Did you kill them all?"

"Of course," wheezed Laughlong. "Is that you, Fearsflyers?"

"It's me. I'm to bring you to the new camp."

"Camp?" said Laughlong. "I thought we were supposed to keep pushing through the night. All the way to those magical *holls*."

"*Hills*," corrected the young man, unhappily. "You're right. But they've stopped. I don't know why. I was just told to come back for you. Come on, everybody, come on."

A ragged crowd of maybe fifteen stumbled nervously into the field of the Diggers. With luck its owners were all dead now, following the ambush.

While the fighting had been going on, while poor Treekisser was dying under a swarm of enemies, the main body of the Tribe must have been sneaking out of the forest. First would have come men with Armourback spears to stab planted aliens in their brains. This would stop them calling out in alarm or grabbing at people. Then would have come the heavily laden women, the children, a scheming Aagam, a cowardly Chief…

The hunters sidled past a swathe of eerie but now harmless bodies. Whistlenose couldn't help goggling at the wonders around him. He saw tentacled monsters, all beaks and eyeballs. There were creatures of scale and fur, of feathers and shells and spines: creatures with wings; with claws or hands or pincers.

In spite of the terror he had been through, in spite of the choking stench all around them, the field was starting to feel like a magical place to him. "I would love to taste every one of them," he said to Laughlong, wiping the drool from the side of his mouth.

"I know, my stomach has been going crazy. It can't decide whether to rumble or to throw up!"

But nobody so much as unsheathed a knife, of course. The Diggers paid special attention to those who stole from them.

"But then ... " said Laughlong, "then I can't help thinking ... "

"Thinking what?"

"All of these beasts ... The Diggers beat them all eventually. What chance have we?"

Whistlenose shook his head, although he had been avoiding the very same thought himself. "There's every kind of beast here, my friend. Every kind but human."

Up ahead, Whistlenose could see torches and knew they were already catching up on the rest of the Tribe. He was limping yet again by the time they reached a rearguard of men who nodded in greeting but didn't speak otherwise, even through signs. A returned hunter was supposed to see his family before anybody else and Whistlenose wanted that more than anything now.

"Everybody looks so worried," Laughlong muttered. That was true. As Whistlenose moved forward, he found people to be more and more bunched up, their torches waving uncertainly.

And then, warm arms wrapped around him and Ashsweeper's breath was tickling his ear. "Welcome, husband."

"Where's the boy?"

"Nighttracker is with his cousins. I'm going straight back there after one kiss." She took more than one, her lips soft against his. "I need to clean all those cuts for you, husband, but you'd better go on, first."

"Go on where? What do you mean?"

"*He* will want to see you. The Chief."

Whistlenose asked no further questions, pushing right through the crowd until the reasons for the Tribe's stopping here became obvious. A great line of bewildered, worried people were spread out along the shore of a Wetlane. On the far side, the planted bodies continued, although many of these had sunk so far into the ground as to be little taller than a man's knee.

He limped over to where the Chief raged at Aagam.

"This is not supposed to be here, Roofman! You said we were clear through to the hills!"

"How do you expect me to remember every little detail without the Roof? I had to store all the information, absolutely everything in my head. Have you any idea how difficult that is?"

Whistlenose thought that was a strange argument. Where else was a hunter supposed to keep his wisdom if not in his own thoughts?

"And, anyway," Aagam continued. "This should be easy. We just need a few tree trunks to bridge the thing and we can all be on our way. Send a few of these men back to the forest for some." But he was not as confident as his words made him sound. The stranger's eyes kept darting in one direction and another. Morning could not be too far away surely and there appeared to be no end in sight to the fields. And how long before new enemies came looking for them? For all anybody knew they had already moved into the territory of another Digger Tribe—what Aagam himself had called a "family."

"We have *burnt* all the trees," said Wallbreaker. "Remember? We need something else. You have to give me something else!"

At that moment, his eyes settled on Whistlenose. Not speaking to anybody in particular, he asked, "Has this man seen his wife yet?"

"I have," the hunter answered, surprised that Wallbreaker could sometimes still be polite.

"Tell me the truth, then, hunter. Is it true you leapt over one of these Wetlanes? Like Waterjumper did?"

"Almost, Chief. I landed just at the lip on the far side. I was lucky to be able to pull myself out."

"Could you do it again?"

Whistlenose looked around, struggling hard not to show his terror. After what he hoped was long enough to make it seem as though he had considered the matter seriously, he shook his head. "No. There was a road back there where I did it. The ground here is too rough to get a proper run up. Not even the younger men would make it. And even if you got somebody across, what then? How would we move the rest of the Tribe?"

The Chief nodded and Whistlenose struggled to keep his composure. His sore leg started throbbing enough to make him wince. But everybody had turned back to the Chief again by then.

Wallbreaker pointed up and down the Wetlane.

"There's no point going back now," he said to Aagam, "Which way? Which way for the hills?"

"Why ask the Roofman?" Laughlong had come up too from the back, his voice so rough from smoke as to be barely human. "Haven't the *Ancestors* already told you what to do?" He smiled. "In a *dream*? Here's what I think: the Ancestors wouldn't have wanted us to lose so many hunters for the privilege of starving in the middle of this Digger larder."

His words spread out through the crowd and Whistlenose realised then how stressed and afraid the Chief must have been to hold this meeting in public. His eyes, like the bottomless pits of a skull, had known little sleep recently.

"Look," said the Chief, at last, "didn't I promise you hills? Didn't I say they were giant rocky mounds? Well, there they are!" The Roof had already began to brighten with daylight, apart from a few diseased patches here and there. Sure enough, in the distance, beyond the stinking field of almost sunken bodies, a low green line bumped along the horizon. It might have been anything, but many people shouted praise for the Ancestors at the sight of it.

"I told you, didn't I? Only the Traveller saw sights like these before us."

And your brother. With your wife. But Whistlenose kept that to himself.

"We're not so far away now," Wallbreaker continued. "A hunter could run there in two days."

"Ten for the rest of the tribe," said Laughlong. "If the Diggers don't catch us first. If we can even get across the Wetlane."

"I am your Chief," said Wallbreaker. "I am telling you the Tribe will survive this. You have my word the Diggers will not catch us. You have the word of the Ancestors themselves!"

"Then you won't mind," Laughlong said sweetly, "if you and your family travel at the back from now on?"

A silence fell, broken only by the dripping of water and the whir of mossbeasts waking at last to greet the day. It seemed to last forever.

"Of course not," the Chief replied finally. Any other response, in the tense, terrified atmosphere, might have finished his leadership, because if he didn't believe the Ancestors protected him, why should anybody else? He smiled, although inside he must have been screaming.

We're nothing but slowly moving food, Whistlenose thought. *Ancestors protect my family. Ancestors bring us all Home.*

15.
THE BRAVEST OF THE BRAVE

For some people, flesh was flesh. They would eat smoked Armourback with the same enthusiasm as the liver of a Hairbeast pup. But most people delighted in endless debates over flavours and textures. The thrill of breaking through bone to the sweetest of marrows; the properties of various organs that differed subtly from creature to creature.

As a man who knew himself for a coward, Wallbreaker had spent more than one night in consideration of the many types of terror with which he filled his belly, unable to resist chewing and chewing at them until little of his real self remained.

He had rarely experienced fear as a child. His father had fed him and Stopmouth with tales of bravery; of close encounters with sneaky Bloodskins; of daring escapes and heroic kills made to feed the starving back home. It was all a game that Wallbreaker longed to play for himself and when the chance finally came, he displayed a wondrous talent for it, such as the older men had never seen before. "The bravest of the brave!" dear old Flimnose had called him. And, when Mossheart had asked him once, "Do you never feel afraid?", he could answer, with perfect sincerity, "Not so much as a tremble!"

Looking back, he saw now that all this "courage" was born of the mistaken belief that he could not be hurt at all. The shock, then, when his invulnerability had turned out to be a lie, had destroyed him. He understood that. He wished with all his heart, he could fight against it, fool himself once more with the lovely lies he had grown up with. But, as mother used to say, "You can't uncook a liver."

Fears were all he had now and he spent his life balancing one off against the others. Should he worry more about Laughlong's efforts to unseat him or an imminent attack of Diggers? How important was his personal safety against that of the tribe? After all, not even he could survive without a people! And what about his family? His little girl? So like her mother, but unpoisoned by the world and still content to find him and sleep in his arms.

He always felt strongest when she was close, but cursed her too, because her arrival into the world had brought a whole new type of fear for him to deal with and one that Laughlong had made worse with that challenge of his. Now Wallbreaker's treasure would have to walk with her father at the back of the migration—the worst possible place to be when the Diggers came looking for revenge.

Whose life would Wallbreaker save first when that happened? His or hers? He feared he knew the answer and hated himself all the more for it.

"Aagam, come here."

The man looked so much fitter and younger than when he'd first arrived in the Tribe, although his skin had broken out in an unsightly rash of pimples that everybody joked about.

"We can't cross, so which way do we need to go? For the hills?"

"I don't know. This isn't what I planned for." Aagam sweated and twitched in the heat while mossbeasts crawled over the hair he called his *beard*. "Maybe ... maybe ... "

"Maybe's not enough," Wallbreaker said.

"You think I don't know that, savage? This is my death sentence too." He paused, scratching his scalp, eyes tightly shut. "By the gods ... "

Wallbreaker, recognizing calculation when he saw it, let the man take his time.

"It's no good," Aagam said at last and shrugged. "You should have left ManWays when I said and we wouldn't be in this position now."

People were watching, so Wallbreaker had no choice. He took Aagam by the neck and dragged him right up to the edge of the Wetlane, forcing him to lean over the water so that drops of sweat from his brow spattered its surface. In the murk beneath the hot blue reflection of the Roof, something swam, its movements excited by the approach of food. But the threat Wallbreaker meant to make died on his lips when the Roofman said something curious: "You *barbarian*! You mean to waste clever Aagam like this? I can't swim!"

"Of course you can't swim!" Wallbreaker sputtered. "A man is not a twig that he can float away!" And then, as though possessed by a crazy Ancestor, Aagam started laughing. "Wait, wait! I know the answer! I know which way to go!"

"You're just lying now."

"Am I?" a grin had spread over his spiteful hairy face. "The twig—you said it yourself—the twig! It floats along the Wetlane, but not at random! No! It's got to be heading for the *river*."

Aagam explained what a *river* was. He claimed to remember seeing it on a map flowing right past the place where their new home would be.

"How long will it take us to get there?"

"I don't know. I didn't learn that route. Longer. A lot longer. But we can't cross here, now that you've destroyed all the trees."

"And Diggers?"

"Of course, there'll be Diggers along the way. They're already everywhere. Except beyond the hills."

Wallbreaker pulled him back. "We will follow the twig then."

A whole day stretched in front of them, but a great amount of organizing needed to take place before the Tribe could follow a new plan. Scouts moved forward, but slowly, so slowly. They had to stab hundreds and hundreds of creatures in the brain or risk capture and Wallbreaker knew their arms would tire quickly. So, he sent four or five times more hunters than would have been normal, and when he set the Tribe to moving again, he caused more grumbling among his veterans by ordering that some of the younger women be armed too.

"You're killing the Tribe in two ways now, *Chief*," said Laughlong. "Our Ancestors won't recognise us, won't want us like this."

"As long as we don't join them too soon," said Wallbreaker, "I'll be happy." He was relieved to see younger men nodding behind Laughlong's back. Survival was the only real law and everybody understood that, no matter what they pretended to believe.

Slowly, the Tribe made its way down the narrow track of dead planted bodies, and eventually, after a full tenth of nervously watching the Roof at the back of the column, Wallbreaker got to follow them, along with Mossheart, Treeneck and his sweet little girl. His stomach roiled with fear, threatening to make him waste his breakfast.

"It's flickering again," said Mossheart. She was looking up at the Roof, shading her eyes. "The rhythm, it's like the heartbeat of a pup as it bleeds out."

"Enough of that, wife. I don't want anybody hearing that kind of talk from us."

"They have eyes of their own," she replied.

Aagam, on the other hand, seemed to have become less worried by the phenomenon. "I figured it out," he said. "It's just the rebels interfering with the way the Roof works. But they can't win, you know? Not with everything that's against them up there. And the funniest thing? The Roof is self-repairing. It's filled with tiny *machines* that can fix anything. No, this can't last. All we need to do is to get beyond the hills and when the Rebellion is over and everybody has calmed down, Aagam will find a way back. You see if I don't."

That first day, the Ancestors seemed to be with them. The scouts discovered another stretch of forest, and even Wallbreaker, right at the very back of the migration, growing ever more anxious with the falling light, made it under the cover of the rotted, tilting trees. The only shame was that none of the wood seemed strong enough to support a man's weight, or they could have used it to build a bridge to the far side of the Wetlane.

Everybody seemed excited and happy. Even the night passed peacefully, except that a young scout shook Wallbreaker awake shortly before dawn and beckoned him out to the edge of the wood where it grew right up against the Wetlane.

"Look," whispered the young man who bore the unhappy name of "Browncrack." "Over there!"

Wallbreaker stared and stared, not sure what he was looking for, but then he saw it: a blue, flickering glow, moving between the knee-high bodies the Diggers had planted on the far side of the Wetlane. It came closer to the hiding hunters, seeming almost to float.

"The bodies aren't even trying to grab it!" breathed the younger man and Wallbreaker saw this was true. The Diggers' victims lolled as they always did, drooling in private agony, while the blue creature floated on past them. It glistened and flickered, yet, the strangest thing about it was that it bore the unmistakable shape of a human woman, her head seeming to quest this way and that. When drops of Roofsweat touched her, they turned into a sudden mist that hung around her, sharing in the glow.

"Why is she growing smaller?" asked Browncrack.

Sure enough, even as they watched, the woman became completely transparent, before fading away altogether. "An Ancestor," breathed Browncrack. "Lots of people have seen them by now," he said. "Scouts anyway. They've got to be protecting us."

Wallbreaker was not so sure. It wasn't just that he alone knew he'd been lying about the communications he'd pretended to receive from the after life. There was something else too: something about the quality of the glow from the creature that felt familiar to him, although he couldn't quite identify the taste of it.

And then, the tracklights turned black, plunging the world into pure darkness. He felt the young hunter's grip on his arm, but for once, he wasn't afraid. Part of him was counting down the heartbeats to measure the blindness. Another part of him was thinking about the glowing creature he had finally seen with his own eyes. Did it assume the form of the prey it hunted? he wondered. Why had the planted bodies not tried to grab it? He would love to catch one and speak to it with the Talker!

And that reminded him of something.

He took the magic ball out of its pouch. "Activate," he said, and it glowed gently with a warmer light than that of the spirit creature.

"We'll find our way back to the others with this," he told Browncrack. And so they did.

On a normal night, the tracklights would have faded away as Rooflight slowly replaced them. This time, however, it was suddenly mid-day and people, frightened by the darkness of a moment before, cursed angrily at the unexpected glare.

"Get everybody ready to move," Wallbreaker said, pretending to be unruffled. "We all need a good breakfast, but give more to the scouts. Laughlong! Get up here! How far does the forest extend this time?"

"Two days' travel. I don't like it, though. See the trees? They have that Digger rot about them. And look at how they're tilting! Half of them have sunk into the ground like the bodies do."

"At least they won't try to grab us. Listen, Laughlong, we need to keep following the direction of the Wetlane."

"Well, we'll only get a day and a half in the cover of the trees if we do that. And what about food? The women say we'll be lucky to get three more days out of what we have."

"That's no worry of yours, hunter."

Laughlong wrinkled his lip. He looked like he wanted to spit, but even he wouldn't go so far, even now when extinction seemed certain. "A day and a half, Chief. A day and a half. And what will you do then, I wonder?"

16.
THE TUNNEL

When total darkness had fallen in the woods and the tracklights seemed to die, Whistlenose had been dreaming of the Clawfolk's slaughterhouse. He woke up sweating and blind.

"Where are you?" he whispered.

"I'm here," his son replied.

"We both are," said his wife, her hand finding his without so much as a fumble. "You should have left us to sleep through the Blindness, husband. It's not as if there's anything worth looking at."

Ancestors, but she always made him smile! He replied, "And it's not as if you couldn't find me in the dark!" He was referring to the sound his nose made, hoping to amuse her and trusting that she wouldn't push the joke too far.

Nor did she. They rested together in silence, as Nighttracker drifted back to sleep.

Whistlenose tried to take comfort in their warm presence, but he couldn't help wondering what would happen if the dark-loving Diggers ever decided to attack during a blindness. How could a hunter possibly save his family?

Light returned far too quickly and painfully. He cursed, shading his eyes, blinking away the glare. "It's too early for midday!" His stomach told him that much if nothing else. But the sudden brightness might have caught the Diggers by surprise too and fried a few of their grubs.

All around them, the camp stirred into life. He smiled across at Hightoes, waddling around with an armful of moss. She grinned but didn't come over, still embarrassed, he supposed, about the night she had lost track of their boy.

"She looks tired," said Ashsweeper quietly. "All this walking is bad for pregnant women."

A few hunters came looking for him. The previous day, everybody who had been involved in the forest ambush had been allowed to stay with their families, but Whistlenose had a feeling his time off was about to end. He smiled at Laughlong, who said, "I'm to go scouting forward."

"You want me to come too?"

Laughlong shook his head. "No, and too bad for you! You have to take charge of the rear. Worse. You'll have *him* for company."

"All right."

"And I'm telling you, Whistlenose, you should stop up your ears with moss. He'll only fill them with lies and promises."

"And what about food, Laughlong?"

"Oh, there's plenty of that in the fields. Just lying there." But nobody would want to risk another big fight with the Diggers so soon, so it might have to come back to Volunteers.

Thank the Ancestors Nighttracker had a name! Some of the other children weren't so lucky and might be picked. Especially during a migration when they were slowing the Tribe down.

He collected together his weapons, before eating a twist of dried flesh—he had no idea what kind—and helped his wife and son get ready. "I'll be at the back today, but I want you both walking in the centre. Look after Hightoes. We'll probably be fine for the next two days, but you know ... "

She did. Ashsweeper would keep her guard up.

And then the Tribe trundled into motion, everybody trying to speak quietly, helping their friends, shushing children or hoisting them up to carry on their shoulders, food and Tallies packed away. Whistlenose allowed them all to pass him by until finally the Chief and his family and that awful man, Aagam, left him alone with the rearguard. It was a tired bunch of men he commanded: seven hunters other than himself, all of whom had been involved in the forest ambush. A few of them limped almost as badly as he did, but he smiled at them. Brave lads every one, and the Tribe lived on thanks to them.

He didn't speak to them, of course. Hand signals sent them left and right, except for Browncrack—the fastest and best recovered—who would keep watch over the path behind them. The young man smiled thanks for the responsibility before slipping in amongst the rotted trees without so much as breaking a branch. When had he learned to do that? He was growing up fast, that boy!

Time to go.

He sniffed at the air in case it hid some clue, but the Tribe had spent so long surrounded by the Digger stench already that he might as well have buried his nose in his own armpit for all the good it did him.

The day passed easily enough. Dried out moss cracked underfoot. Light glittered from the Wetlane when the trees allowed it. The only strange thing was how the Rooflight failed to dim properly and he couldn't keep proper track of time.

The whole Tribe came to a halt several times when obstacles were encountered ahead: like the small stream that must have been terribly difficult for Hightoes to cross; or an ancient wall that seemed to be made of nothing but uncorrupted metal that shoved itself right out of the trees.

"Deserters," he heard Aagam say with a sneer. It meant nothing to Whistlenose, but Wallbreaker seemed intrigued and lingered to examine it some more until Whistlenose threatened to leave him behind with it.

"Have you really no curiosity, Whistlenose?"

"Will it help us escape the Diggers?"

"Who knows? Who knows how such things could help us if we learned their secrets."

"Won't Aagam tell you?"

138

"I don't think he understands this wall any more than I do. He is as incurious as any of you hunters." The Chief rubbed his hands over faded symbols. They swam under Whistlenose's gaze, crawling together to form meaning:

"In honour of those who died in the great crossing."

The strange sight brought a gasp from his lips and Wallbreaker chuckled. "That's the Talker, making you understand the words."

"But ... but there's no creature here to speak any words!"

Wallbreaker shrugged and even winked at this man he had sent, more than once, into death. "Come on, then, hunter. Let's go. You're supposed to keep me safe."

That was when it happened—screams from up ahead.

The two men ran forward without hesitation. Whistlenose could feel the new threat in the soles of his feet: an angry, rumbling shaking of the earth. The rotted trees were feeling it too, and to the left and right, a number of them sagged suddenly, while others, just out of sight, must have fallen altogether with a tremendous crunching and snapping that urged the men to greater efforts.

The Diggers had found them again and were no longer content to wait for darkness. Instead, Whistlenose realised, they had been busily burrowing under the humans to ambush them in a place where the forest shade might protect their grubs.

All of this sped through Whistlenose's mind as he ran through the undergrowth, stumbling occasionally as his leg let him down, or when a root tripped him up.

The Chief had no such problems, it seemed. Although his spear had not tasted blood in the longest time, Wallbreaker, the supposed coward, fled towards danger. It made no sense.

The screaming had grown louder. Directly in Whistlenose's path, a great old tree, began to topple over, groaned its agony as it fell. It would come down between Whistlenose and the Chief; between him and the tribe. He would be too late to help if it blocked his way.

With a great cry of pain, he launched off his injured leg and dived forward into a roll, even as one heavy branch raked across his back. He came up on the far side of the trunk, spearless, helpless. In front of him, there was only chaos. Women and men seemed to be fighting the ground. They screamed or wept. They stabbed spears into the soil while dust filled the air and whole clumps of people fell suddenly into nothing.

Immediately ahead of Whistlenose, Wallbreaker was shouting orders: "Don't stop! Leave them, it's too late for them. Run! Everybody run!" He had gathered his own family about him and was pushing them forward away from the action, until others started to obey, and in moments, everybody was fleeing for their lives.

Whistlenose felt he had no choice but to join them. He too ran, ignoring the pain, leaping over holes in the ground where people cried piteously. He wept, knowing he must stop to help; knowing he couldn't. The rule was to keep running, after all. The Tribe, the Tribe needed to survive more than any individual. But he heard children down there too and knew that by nightfall, they would be buried in a field somewhere.

Whistlenose had seen a planted human once. While the expressions of beasts were unreadable to him, the agony on the man's face had been obvious, and horrifying. And now those children would suffer like that for fifty or a hundred days. How could it be borne? Was the life of the Tribe worth so much?

But of course it was. Tribe was everything. And so, still crying, he kept running.

Although the trees had stopped falling around them, nobody slowed, their movements still full of panic. Even packs of food lay abandoned in the path. But Whistlenose had almost caught up with the main body now and he breathed a little easier. He felt wretched, knowing he would never forget the cries of the lost.

Wallbreaker's family, at the very back, began falling further behind. Mossheart hobbled along on an injury she had picked up, while Treeneck carried the girl and the Chief kept watch for enemies, his face shining with sweat.

Whistlenose came to a stop, not wanting to catch up with them. He was supposed to be the rearguard, after all. And he wasn't sure he was ready to talk to a Chief who had ordered him to abandon children to the Diggers. *You wanted to run, though, boy.* But how he hated it! How it hurt!

Wallbreaker and Mossheart started arguing in heated whispers, while Treeneck walked on ahead with the girl. And then, as if, Whistlenose had merely imagined them, the woman and child were gone. Straight down into the earth without a sound.

The old hunter didn't even think about it. He sprang forward, all pains forgotten. He passed by the Chief and Mossheart. He had no spear, but it didn't matter. His mind knew nothing. He dropped into darkness, landing amongst a writhing pack of Diggers with his knife already in his fist. He was yelling and stabbing all around him. The brain. Go for the brain and maybe, like the creatures in the fields, they wouldn't come back to fight him.

He left his knife in an enemy's skull. He bit at their faces, he clawed at their eyes. One of the monsters served him as a shield, as others, a stream of them, their pressure relentless, forced him up against the chill damp walls of the tunnel.

All was darkness. But then, suddenly, a ball of the purest, blinding light, dropped down from above—the Talker, of course. Heartbeats later, another man was in the tunnel beside him, both of them fighting and screaming together, possessed by an insane Ancestor. A Digger threw itself over the Talker and it was as though dusk had come, allowing the enemy to surge forward once more. Whistlenose's companion went down, swamped. Now, Diggers tore at the creature Whistlenose was using as a shield until it came to pieces in his hands. But they weren't trying to kill the old hunter. No, they fought to pin his limbs down, to steady his head to receive a grub ...

He shouted, "Ancestors, kill me! Kill me!" He could feel tiny beasts crawling down his scalp. One of them pushed up into his left nostril and he lost control of his bladder. The slimy creature's boneless body met an obstruction and began to eat through it. The pain! Oh, the pain!

But out of the corner of his eye, he saw the other man rise

again. Wallbreaker! It was Wallbreaker, the coward, the Chief! He was on his feet, stabbing about himself with a spear when he should have been calling for his "mother." And the strange thing, the really strange thing, was that the Diggers were just ... taking it. He killed them and *none* of them fought back. It was as though they couldn't even see him.

He uncovered the light of the Talker, and all at once, the enemy fled.

Whistlenose, crying his disgust, flung grubs away from himself and pulled out the one that had got stuck in his nostril. A stream of blood followed it to the ground.

"Daddy?"

Gore dripped down Wallbreaker's cheeks, glistening in the light of the Talker. He seemed not to notice. He was shaking and weeping and hugging his daughter to him. Treeneck's body lay trampled beside them. At least she would never be planted.

"Treeneck had a thousand days left in her." Whistlenose said. Or wanted to, anyway. He couldn't quite make anything come out of his mouth. His throat was raw. He kept seeing images of Wallbreaker killing Diggers without any of them fighting back. He couldn't understand it.

"Give her to me," cried Mossheart from above. "Give me my girl!"

They cut a little flesh from Treeneck to remember her by. That was all there was time for. They left their kills behind them too. Then, they climbed out and resumed the march.

Whistlenose should have gone back to the rearguard, but couldn't quite manage it any more than the Chief knew how to give orders. So, it was Mossheart who took charge, shouting at Browncrack and the others to spread out.

And then, night fell, normal in every way, except it came too early, and instead of Roofsweat, human bodies rained from the sky.

17.

THE FALL

Nobody knew what was happening.

A hundred heartbeats after the tracklights had come on, great thumps and clatters in the forest sent dozens of hunters running for their spears. "It's an attack!" somebody cried. How wrong he was. But nothing could have prepared the exhausted men for what they saw: a dark-skinned woman lay dead in the first clearing they came to, her body twisted, her face mercifully out of view beneath her fine black hair.

Whistlenose and Fearsflyers were at the back of the group that discovered her. "In the trees," whispered the young hunter, pointing up. Right above their heads, the branches had caught another man in a weave of foliage and floppy limbs. Nearby were others, all Roofpeople: men with beards like Aagam's, their faces stark with fear, their arms spread wide as a Flyer's wing; a mother who had wrapped herself around a boy in the vain hope of cushioning his fall; a creature so shrivelled and wrinkly, it was some time before they could even recognise it as human. On and on through the trees, in bushes, burst against rocks, were ever more corpses, covering an area as large as ManWays …

Here and there, men began to weep. They hugged each other or threw themselves down on their knees. "Thank you, Ancestors!" they cried. "Oh, thank you! Thank you!" In the Tribe's hour of greatest weakness, when food had run low and

Diggers pressed from all sides, their forebears had sent them a feast of brave volunteers from the Roof itself!

The night that followed was the most joyful of the migration.

"Dada! Dada! I'm eating liver! Like a real hunter!"

"Your father's tired," said Ashsweeper. So he was, but Whistlenose grinned, clutching a hot bowl of brains and watching those with greater energy who were dancing or arguing over the fantastical array of garments with which the Roofpeople had been clothed.

"There's enough for everyone," said Ashsweeper. "Even the Diggers. A pity they wouldn't take their share and leave us alone for a while."

Whistlenose smiled, or thought he did. He felt his eyes glaze over as he scooped little bits of food into his mouth. He tried to savour the taste, but his mind kept wandering. There were those who asserted loudly they could tell the difference between a male and a female brain. "A man leaves richer flavours behind," they would say, only for the nearest woman to scoff back with "More simple, you mean!"

Sadly, Whistlenose wasn't quick-witted enough to join in these games and, truth be told, it all tasted the same to him in the end.

The last time he'd had this much human meat had been after the passing of Laughlouder, his first wife. The body of his second wife, brave Sleepyeyes, had never been recovered, so he hadn't been able to honour her in this way. *Are you there, my sweet?* he wondered. *Have you been protecting us all this while?* He felt arms around his shoulder, and for a moment, he really thought—but no. This hug came from the woman whose life Sleepyeyes had saved. Ashsweeper.

"There's something different about you, husband," she whispered. "I know, I know. I said I wouldn't bother you, but you're not the same since you came back from the rearguard."

He tried to guess what she meant, but he was so, so tired. He had fought Diggers in their own tunnels. He had seen more people fall from the sky than he even knew were alive. Of course he was different … But that wasn't what his wife meant at all.

"Your nose," she said, at last. "It doesn't whistle any more."

"It doesn't?" if he hadn't been so exhausted, he would have realised it himself, but yes, yes, it was true! A Digger grub had tried to eat its way through a blockage in his left nostril, the one that had caused him such humiliation all his life.

Whistlenose had no recollection of dropping the bowl, but he found himself hugging Ashsweeper and laughing like a fool. That was how the Chief found them a few heartbeats later.

"Whistlenose?"

He looked up to find Wallbreaker waiting for him at the edge of the fire.

"Won't you join us, Chief?" asked Ashsweeper. "We have more than enough."

"No, thank you. I wish to consult with your husband."

"We were sorry about Treeneck," Ashsweeper continued. "She had a thousand days left in her."

"Ten thousand," agreed the Chief, but he was too agitated for real courtesy. "Come with me, hunter."

He sighed and put down his bowl. The two men trudged away from the firelight, although the breaking of branches all around them told Whistlenose that they were never completely alone or unprotected. They pushed through bushes and over drooping trees until soon, the nearest hearth was little more than a flicker between the branches.

Whistlenose struggled to stay focused. Part of that was tiredness and part of it was all the attention he paid to his own breathing. Amazing, he kept thinking. The sound is gone!

The Chief too seemed lost in his own mind. He said nothing for what felt like hundreds of heartbeats. He was just a shadow to the older hunter and when at last he spoke, it was barely louder than the voice of an Ancestor heard in the heart. "I ordered you dead."

Whistlenose froze. "What? I—"

"No, no. I don't mean now." The Chief actually gripped Whistlenose's shoulder, as though they were the dearest of

145

brothers. "No. I mean before. Aagam wanted you gone, and anyway, everybody knew about that limp of yours. It was nearly time." He snorted. "It's funny, that, because since then, you've been a better hunter than you ever were as a young man."

He paused, breathing heavily now, his grip still tight and sweaty. "You saved my daughter today."

"No, Chief. I only delayed her capture. You were the one to save her ... And ... I'm sorry to say this. I always believed you were a coward, but you jumped right into that hole too."

"I *am* a coward, hunter. More than ever now. That's *why* I jumped into the hole."

"I ... I don't understand."

"I don't care. What matters is that if you'd had the decency to die when I ordered it," his voice shook, "my daughter would be gone."

"Wallbreaker ... Chief. I am a father too. You're welcome. And ... and if I may say so, the way you used the Talker down there in the tunnels was amazing. The light drove them right back! You gave us time to fight and ... " Whistlenose's words died in his throat. He was just remembering something else that had happened in the tunnel, something truly miraculous. Why had the Diggers, having covered the Talker and brought down the Chief, let him escape again so quickly? And afterwards, why had they seemed to ignore him even as he slaughtered them?

The old hunter strained through the dark, trying to see this man that the Ancestors loved so much. They must have been involved in such a miraculous escape! There could be no other explanation. And in that moment, the last of Whistlenose's doubts about the Chief flew off like a cloud of insects.

"I'll be honest," Wallbreaker said. "I never thought of using the Talker as a weapon before. Even though it's obvious now ... I just ... it was dark. Darkness is especially ... I mean, I just wasn't sure I could go down there, even for my own daughter. That's the truth of it. So ... hunter, ask a favour of me. Ask anything and—" But he never finished the sentence. The grip on Whistlenose's shoulder tightened suddenly. "There it is again! Look, the creature!"

Sure enough, another light shone through the branches all around them, but with a bluish hue that showed it was no campfire.

"It's on this side of the Wetlane," Wallbreaker breathed. And then, although there was a very real possibility of Diggers in the area, the Chief was off running through the trees. Whistlenose followed, only to find that a lot of slime had fallen here in the last tenth or so. He skidded through puddles of the stuff, burning his feet. He found the Chief at the edge of a clearing and slid to a halt beside him, breathless; shocked at what he was seeing.

The usual, gentle sounds of a forest night assured their ears that all was as it should be. There were cracks and creaks; rustles and the fluttering of tiny wings; and then, the *crunch, crunch, crunch* of pounding feet as the Chief's guards finally caught up. "By the Ancestors!" said the first of them. Whistlenose didn't look to see who it was. It didn't matter. His eyes couldn't leave the bright figure in front of them. It was a woman, as they had seen before. Except ... except they could look right through her to the other side. She glowed with a slightly blue colour, her body shivering like a bowl of fat.

"It's slime," said Wallbreaker. "She's made of the slime that fell from the Roof. Remember the way it moved sometimes? Remember the way it seemed to follow *me*?" Whistlenose did. And now the strange substance had made a woman out of itself with features that reminded him more of Aagam or Indrani than any member of the tribe.

"Who ... who are you?" asked Wallbreaker. "*What* are you?" He had the Talker of course, and the creature may have understood him, for she drew closer, her steps leaving tiny, moving puddles behind her.

"It's an Ancestor," said one of the honour guard.

"Then why is she so sad?" said another, and Whistlenose realised it was true: she looked like a mother whose child had just been Volunteered.

"I am," she said in a voice like a bubbling stew. "I regret. I am ... *regret*." She said other things that made no sense at all, and the Chief in frustration held out the Talker, as if bringing it closer to her might make its magic stronger. Instead, the effect it had was quite astonishing: the woman simply exploded, soaking all of them in drops of slime.

"That's it?" Wallbreaker shouted. "That's it? You came all this way for that?"

But that wasn't it. The next day, the Talker, their only weapon against the Diggers, their one way of communicating with Aagam who was guiding them, started leaking slime. It would never work again.

PART TWO: UNDER THE SUN

18.
MAKING ENEMIES

The Warship ruin glittered in the light of the *sun*. Stopmouth shaded his eyes with one hand while bouncing his daughter with the other. She was chewing the leather strap that held her firm against him, her drool running down his shoulder.

"You like that, little one?" Flamehair she was called, despite her dark colouring and the fact that it was unnatural to name a child before she could walk more than a few steps. Other children played near the wreckage and not all of them were human. A Fourlegger pounced in amongst them and that too, was wrong, or, as Indrani would have said, "new."

"Well, love?" His wife had arrived. He felt an arm snake around him from the far side and he smiled, couldn't help it. None of the strangeness mattered. He had everything a man could want.

"It's the hole," he said, nodding upwards. "The one you burned in the Roof."

"With the Warship's *lasers*. Yes, love."

"It's bigger," he said. "It's growing."

"That's just your imagination, Stopmouth. It was huge to begin with. As large as a *city*. But ... " she sighed. "I keep thinking of all the people we must have killed when we did that. We—"

They'd had this conversation before. "Those people were dead already," he insisted. "You know that. Or dying. Look at the rest of the Roof! Look!" He pointed away from the sun-filled gap and out towards the hills beyond. Here and there, a few tracklights still worked or blinked on and off. But the rest of the world lay smothered under a thick blanket of darkness. The Roof was gone for good, along with all those who had remained in it.

But down on the surface, although Diggers waited just beyond the hills, down here there was a chance to survive. The *sun* dropped warmth and light through the massive gap Indrani had created. And the crashed Warship had brought with it little kernels of magic called "seeds" that could be tricked into making food. It would take time, apparently, despite the fact that the seeds had been altered in ways beyond his understanding to grow faster. There were *rations* too. Disgusting stuff, and not enough to feed everybody, but they would help a lot until the harvests came along.

It better work, he thought. There are too many of us now who don't know one end of a spear from another.

Toiling in the glare of the sun, hundreds of Newcomers, woken from the freezing boxes in which they had thought to sleep for generations, were clearing rocks away and pulling up plants. Another group, faces screwed up in disgust, raided latrine pits for excrement, while still others, cursed and wrestled with a thing called a *pump* that produced water out of nothing.

Indrani sniggered. "Oh, they're paying the price now! Look at them!"

He wished she wasn't so open with her distaste for these people, but he was finding it hard to care right now. The warmth and the strange new light had a lovely relaxing effect on him. Here, with Indrani by his side and a milky, squirming child in his arms, Stopmouth couldn't have felt happier. Let every day be like this, he prayed. This place and these people. Let it be home for us all.

A tap on the shoulder banished his peace.

Why did it have to be Vishwakarma? A great sadness had descended on the man since the awful attack that had happened when Stopmouth was in the Roof. But his over-excited nature was never too far away. "Uh... Chief? Um. Yeah, what you were expecting. The Fourleggers. Amazing!"

"They're here?"

"Just three of them."

"Of course. Thank the Ancestors. All right, Vishwakarma. Get everybody up from the … the fields and arm them all."

"But, Chief! Those people. *Farmers.* They haven't a clue how to fight!"

"Don't worry about it. Just get them together. Give them spears or sticks. Anything."

Stopmouth could no longer tell the time without the ever-changing brightness of the Roof to guide him, but perhaps a tenth of a day later, a crowd of up to a thousand humans confronted a ragged band of Fourleggers.

Stopmouth had seen the lead creature before, recognizing it by its smaller size and the slightly darker shading of its rusty colouring. It bore new injuries: welts and parallel lines of missing scales that could only have come from a close encounter with Diggers. It limped forward to meet him.

"Hunger needs flesh," it said through the magic of the Talker.

"Hunger needs flesh," Stopmouth agreed. *But not forever. We'll be eating plants soon, Ancestors help us!*

"My sisters are few," the Fourlegger said. "Diggers have brought darkness to all the world and have buried us deep in their nests. Only ninety trios remain, many injured. Many failing."

It was the longest utterance Stopmouth had ever heard from a Fourlegger, but even so, he felt it had not yet finished speaking.

"The land needs our bones," it continued. "It will have them in thirty, or ninety days. No more before our last trio fills Diggger bellies."

Here it comes, thought Stopmouth.

Humans and Fourleggers had made a sort of alliance some time before. They had promised not to hunt each other and to exchange food. He had been expecting a plea for aid. It's what he would have done if his own people had been in such a desperate position.

However, the leader of the Fourleggers surprised him. "Hunger needs flesh," it said again. "Your numbers are greatly increased. My sisters and I prefer your bellies for a bed. We will sleep more quietly there."

Stopmouth looked uneasily at the ex-priest Kubar who stood beside him. "Did it say what I think it said?"

Kubar was grinning. "This is marvellous! There must be nearly three hundred of them left and they're offering to Volunteer? Why, we might not have to hunt before our first crop! We wouldn't even have to eat that monster Dharam! I suspect he'd only poison us anyway."

Stopmouth sighed, saddened by the loss of such firm allies, but knowing he had no choice but to accept their brave offer. He opened his mouth, wondering how to phrase it, when he felt something brush past his leg.

It was the infant Fourlegger his tribe had adopted. It bounded across the space between the two leaders and swarmed up the body of the adult of its own species until it came to a rest behind the triangular head, its forelimbs wrapped firmly around the throat. The adult stooped a little under the weight, but neither creature spoke.

"Is that … " said Stopmouth aloud, "is that your child?"

"All children need me," it said. "This one's heart needs comfort."

"Of course … "

They stood on a street, soft moss beneath their feet and the light of the sun streaming in through a ragged tear in the Roof. Already it had moved most of the way across the hole. Darkness would fall shortly after it reached the end of the gap.

"Tell them we accept," whispered Kubar.

At that moment, the Fourlegger leader lifted its snout high, an action mirrored by the younger one on its back.

"The Diggers need darkness. They are already near."

"See?" said Kubar. "Get the Fourleggers inside the new perimeter, at least."

"How far away are they?" asked Stopmouth. "The Diggers, I mean."

"Half an old day's travel," said the Fourlegger.

"Your hearing is that good?"

"Yours is not, human? The earth suffers the bite of their claws even now."

Stopmouth felt the decision settle on him with such certainty that he knew an Ancestor must have been speaking to his heart.

"We will not eat you," he said.

"What?" said Kubar.

"Does your hunger have no need?" asked the Fourlegger.

"What we really need, more than your flesh," he said, "are your talents." "We could do with those ears of yours, and your powerful claws. You will join us inside our walls and tomorrow, when the ... the sun comes back into the sky, we will raid the Diggers' fields and find flesh enough for all of us."

"This is madness!" said Kubar. "We can't go back to hunting! Those new people from the Roof have no skills, they—"

"Agreed," interrupted the Fourlegger. "We will come inside your walls. Humans are now my sisters."

Stopmouth found himself laughing and a great many of the men and women around him cheered when he moved forward to touch snouts with the beast. "Sisters!" he said, still smiling and wondering, as Kubar had, if he was truly mad.

Not everybody was delighted with the idea of an alliance. The Newcomers had greater reasons to fear it than most.

Before Indrani had hijacked their ship, they had planned to spend decades asleep in little boxes with only enough food for those who would be waking every few thousand days to tend their machinery. But now, these aliens would need feeding too, and that meant hunting and the risk of a horrible violent death.

Stopmouth was on his way back towards the U with its new set of defences that everybody had been building, when he smelled Rockface's foul breath. He would have known the man was there anyway by the sudden appearance of hip-high children, armed with better weapons than most of the adults here could make.

"You've taught them well," he told the older man.

The children grinned and passed hunting signs amongst

themselves as though they had been born to them. Indeed, some of the gestures they used were wholly new to the Chief and only the presence of the Talker allowed him to fully understand what was going on.

"Where did they learn to do that?" he asked.

"They're good, hey?" said Rockface, clapping the younger man all too hard on the back. "They were having trouble getting through to me without that Talker you always keep to yourself, and the little Fourlegger can't make half the sounds she needs either."

"Of course..." Stopmouth couldn't take his eyes off the children, as they mocked each other with supple hands or made jokes that the hunting language of home could never have coped with. "That's wonderful," he breathed and Rockface's chest swelled with pride.

"I'd nearly take them hunting now," said the big man. "They'd do a better job than any of the Newcomers, but they still lack the strength in their arms..."

Those words seemed to be some kind of signal that caused three of the children to launch themselves at the old hunter, and with the stiffness in his back, they almost knocked him over. "Not yet, young ones, hey? Wait 'til you're shoulder-height before you try bringing *me* down! Listen, Chief," he sent the children running ahead with a *go* signal and an extra wave of the fingers that somehow meant "home." "Listen, these new people you've given me to train, these Ship People... They're worse than the others. They won't learn anything. Won't even try. All they do is weep. The only time they'll fight is against our lot. Ancestors but they hate each other!"

"I know." Stopmouth sighed. He had really hoped the secular Ship People and the Religious tribe he and Rockface had saved from destruction hundreds of days before, would have united, if only because they were humans together against a sea of Diggers and other beasts that wanted them for the pot. "Indrani says the new ones are unlikely to come around until they get as much of a shock as our lot got back in the beginning."

Another great backslap from Rockface. "We showed them, though didn't we, hey? What fights we had back then! We were stacking up flesh like the Ancestors intended. A sharp spear and a strong arm. No tricks!"

The two men were walking past a new set of walls. They wouldn't provide much protection against the Diggers the next time they crossed the hills, but they might deter the few other beasts that were still around. Besides, everybody slept a bit better for being inside them.

Beyond the gate, Yama was shouting at sweating Ship People, who were building up the defences. "That's all you're good for," he cried at them. "You'll never be a real killer like me! Yama of the Bloody Hand!" The builders glared at him, but saved a little of their hatred for Stopmouth who had brought them here against their will. Two men and a woman halted work long enough to spit as the Chief walked by.

"Don't worry about them," said Rockface. "We'll Volunteer anyone who tries to murder you in your sleep."

"Thanks," Stopmouth muttered, wondering how he could trust any of these people to fight for the tribe, or even themselves. He could understand why they disliked him, but he found it incredible that they had started listening to Dharam again. Surely they knew who had destroyed their world?

Or, maybe not. The vast majority of them had been frozen in little boxes when Stopmouth had taken over the Warship. They had not heard Dharam condemn himself from his own mouth. And even if they had, they might prefer to continue on in the belief that it was the Religious or some other enemy that had poisoned the Roof. And now, when they had expected to awaken in paradise, they had instead been "kidnapped" by a cannibal and condemned, as they saw it, to a life of flesh-eating and murder.

"They would have died anyway," he muttered, remembering how the slime had contaminated all their machines. Never mind. Already a plan was forming of how he was going to win flesh for his tribe and their Fourlegger allies. It wouldn't work without the cooperation of the Ship People, so they would be coming along whether they liked it or not.

"Rockface, I want to talk to the Tribe tonight."

"Even Dharam's lot? I mean, how is he still alive? They keep feeding him, but I don't know where they get the food."

Stopmouth knew that a proper Chief would have Volunteered the man. Indrani wanted him dead too, but she thought it more important that Stopmouth take no part in it.

"It's a new world now, love," she'd said. "Or will be when the fields are producing. We can't be seen to Volunteer anybody, although even the Diggers are a better death than the likes of him deserve! And remember, if we kill him, he becomes a hero for them, a *martyr*."

Now, Rockface was saying, "I'll bring them. The ones who will come."

"No," said the Chief. "You will bring them all."

A stinging backslap followed and a final gust of foul breath. "That's the spirit, hey? That's what I like to see! I'll have every one of them there even if I have to eat their arms for them."

"Feast well," Stopmouth muttered.

No Roofsweat fell tonight, for the hole created by the crashing Warship lay open above their heads, and tiny bright dots twinkled eerily in place of the reassuring grid of the tracklights.

Other than guards and scouts, all of Stopmouth's people had gathered together in one place, just in front of the ruins of HeadQuarters. They perched on tumbled masonry, or leaned back against walls. They huddled in rival groups such as the one led by the madman, Dharam, who had killed the Roof and who now whispered and gesticulated amongst his followers.

"They have a secret stash of food somewhere," Indrani said to her husband. "They're keeping Dharam alive with it. We should take it from him."

"You're the one who won't let me Volunteer him!"

"Yes, but there's nothing stopping you hurting him, though!

You should break a leg to match his broken arm."

Stopmouth shifted uncomfortably at the thought. Volunteering a man made sense, but to cripple him? He shook his head. Even so, yes, he already knew about the stash of food, and was counting on finding it.

Stopmouth looked around the faces in the firelight. The Religious exiles of what he used to refer to as his "New Tribe" all sat together at the front, clustering around Kubar for the most part, or the grinning Yama in some cases. They were few now—no more than a hundred fit for the hunt. Yet, their spears had drunk deep; had bitten into squirming flesh. They had been through trials that the two thousand newly woken Ship People could not imagine.

But there was no getting away from the fact that it was the soft newcomers who were the future of the Tribe. Knowing their precious machines must soon die, they had brought huge amounts of knowledge with them in flapping boxes known as *books*. They were the ones who would make food come up out of the ground; food that wouldn't even fight back, that would just lie there, waiting for the butchers ... But all of that would only happen if Stopmouth could keep them alive.

The Ship People hated him, though, most of them. He could feel it like a spear poised at his neck.

He took a moment now to look over them, to gather the courage he still lacked sometimes when so many eyes rested on him.

"Why have you kept us waiting here so long?" asked a woman too deep in the crowd to be identified.

Kubar shouted back at her, "And what else would you have been doing tonight, you Godless *whore*?"

"Enough!" cried Stopmouth. There'd already been several fights over the last few tens of days that had come close to killing people. "Sit, Kubar, please." He had expected better of the old priest.

"Listen now!" continued the Chief, and when they still failed to settle down, he tried a fierce glare. As always, it surprised him to see how well it worked. But it saddened him that his people feared him so much. As if he would ever hurt them!

He had grown since the days when he had first taken Indrani away from his brother's house. He had the strong limbs of a man, and while he would never be as muscular as Rockface, whenever he spoke to his old companion now, he found himself looking down into the hunter's creased brown eyes. The Ship People saw his growing strength as a threat. Well, so be it. He would use that if he had to.

"We have new allies," he cried, "the Fourleggers. They have kept treaty with us since before my time in the Roof, and we can trust them to keep it now. They are fierce in the hunt and have excellent hearing, but their claws have not tasted blood lately. We need to feed them before they can be of help to us."

Mutters rose from the crowd and it was only then Stopmouth realized how odd his statement had been. What would his original Tribe have thought if they could hear him now? Trying to persuade men and women he loved to risk their lives to save beasts from extinction? Wallbreaker had urged something similar for the Hairbeasts, but on that occasion, nobody had had to lift a spear for the creatures or Volunteer on their behalf. The idea made him dizzy.

"Why should we give those monsters our rice?" shouted a Ship Person. "We don't even have enough to last us until our first harvest. And what if they can't eat rice anyway?"

"Nobody wants your filthy rice!" Yama replied. "We want flesh! We want to kill it ourselves!" and his crowd of youngsters cheered.

"Enough, Yama! Everybody, quiet! Quiet!" The glare again, pinning the crowd to the spot as surely as a spear. "I don't know if they can eat your rice, but there's not enough of it in any case."

"How would *you* know that?" shouted the woman who had spoken before.

Stopmouth ignored the question. "The fact is, we need flesh. There's no other way out of it. So, tomorrow at dawn, we will cross the hills and steal as much of it as we can from the fields of the Diggers."

159

"We?" an outraged newcomer.

"*Everybody*. We are all needed. The Fourleggers will kill the Digger victims for us. Then, with own brave hunters to guard us, every single person who can walk will carry joints of meat up over the hills and back down here."

"—Disgusting!"

"—I'm not touching ... touching ... *meat!*"

"—I feel sick."

"You have no choice," Stopmouth told them. The Seculars weren't listening, they stood to shout at him or to argue with each other or the Religious at the front. Nobody noticed the arrival of Rockface and little Tarini, who had saved him in the Roof. She winked at him, smiling with crooked teeth.

Stopmouth smiled back. The presence of his two friends was enough to tell him that the secret stash of rice and other foods had been found. A small, loyal group would already be moving it elsewhere. Now, all he had to do was wait for the yelling to die down. Then, they would *have* to listen.

But a voice whispered in his heart, they will hate you more than ever if you make them do this thing. And he knew it spoke the truth.

19.
⊕URS T⊕ KILL

The old and the lame stayed behind to make a show of guarding the children at HeadQuarters. Humans in ManWays had long ago learned that most of the beasts they fought had difficulty distinguishing a fighter from any other person. Then again, nobody back home lived long enough to have more than a strand or two of grey in their hair. That would change now if the new crops worked. People wouldn't need to Volunteer at all, but would instead hang around, uselessly, getting weaker and weaker forever. It made no sense to the Chief that a hunter would want to live like that.

Rockface felt the same and Stopmouth knew that if it weren't for the loving attentions of Sodasi and the pleadings of his Chief, the older man would long since have found a glorious end for himself.

Well before dawn, the whole tribe moved out—nearly two thousand people. Stopmouth already regretted it as he watched his few experienced hunters roaming the edges of the great crowd, making targets of themselves with the torches they carried to guide the ungrateful newcomers.

Stopmouth had no idea how to bring about peace between the two groups, and he knew in his marrow that many would die as a result of this failure.

The human river passed along streets of rubble and moved through Slimer territory. The almost extinct creatures would not bother such a mass of well-guarded people. Or at least Stopmough hoped not! His plan was to get everybody to the hills by the time the sun passed over the hole in the Roof. The Diggers disliked its glare even more than Rooflight, so, with luck, his people and the Fourleggers could carry away a few hundred of the creatures' victims while they were still dreaming in their tunnels.

"Hunger needs flesh?"

He jumped and nearly stabbed the Fourlegger leader. "Yes," he said, heart thundering, as he cursed Vishwakarma and Yama. Not one of the scouts had spotted the Fourleggers, emerging silently from the last ruined houses along the road.

"Ancestors watch you," he told his allies. "Are your sisters ready?"

"Their weakness needs flesh," the creature told him.

"You will feast tonight," he responded. "We all will."

The creature didn't nod, but somehow—perhaps it was an effect of the Talker—he knew it was content.

And then, it was a long climb up the hills with Ship People cursing and even weeping all around him. Most people had been hungry in the Roof as their food supplies had slowly dwindled. But those who had come with him to the surface had been amongst the privileged. Many had already lived five times longer than any of Stopmouth's Ancestors—or at least those he knew of! They were beautiful in appearance and their minds could hold ideas that would terrify any hunter.

These few had feasted their lives away, even as the rest of their Tribe starved, and finally, as their home died around them, they had bent all their resources and their considerable genius in trying to save themselves—and nobody else. Deserters, in other words. Deserters. Like his own far-off Ancestors who had fled the Earth. The Ship People hated him, but he struggled every day not to return the feeling, because he needed them if Flamehair were ever to grow up. If Indrani were to be safe.

"A great sight, hey?" Rockface was beside him now. The sun was coming over to the gap in the Roof and to Rockface, who had never left the surface, the new tribe must have seemed numberless. Sodasi had come along too. The young slinger had taken it on herself to be Rockface's protector, although the big man didn't seem aware of the fact. She had saved his life at least once that Stopmouth knew of. The woman had no problems with the slope. None of the surviving Religious did, not even Kubar, one of the oldest-looking people in the community. He chivvied his Secular enemies along, keeping his spite to himself for once, as yellow beams of light picked out the scales of Fourleggers formed into a spearhead at the front.

Stopmouth called a halt at the top of the hill. The Ship People looked exhausted, their dark skin sheened with sweat, their eyes open a little too wide at the thought that they were about to go into danger now, albeit very little compared to that of their Fourlegger allies who were already streaming on ahead.

"This is it," Stopmouth shouted. He pointed down the hill towards the plain on the far side, lined with rows of what looked like black dots. "Indrani says the sun will only light up a little of the plain and only for two tenths of a day or so. After that, nothing will keep the Diggers away from us. So, we run down there. Everybody will take one joint of meat, or two if they think they can handle it, and then, head straight for home. Understood? It's easy, and nobody needs to get hurt. If we're on our own side of these hills before nightfall, we should all be fine."

"And what if we refuse?" said a woman in the torn remains of a blue Warden's uniform. She looked muscular enough to rip Stopmouth's head off, but the rivers of sweat dripping from her was proof enough that she had never been one of the Elite.

"You can refuse if you like," said Stopmouth. "Just don't try coming back inside the walls without flesh. You won't be welcome."

There. He had said it. He might not be allowed to Volunteer anybody, but every member of a Tribe needed to work for its survival. He had expected more anger from the woman, but the ex-Warden surprised him.

"I am Ekta," she said. "I am going to live." She nodded and he

163

nodded back. Not friends, but allies, if only for a little while.

"Traitor," said an older man, who saw them talking, but he winced when Ekta glared at him.

"All right," cried Stopmouth. "Enough! Let's go! Come on, now! You don't want to be here when darkness falls!"

And they didn't, nobody did. The Ship People found a new lease of life, and, aided by a downward slope, the whole tribe surged after their nonhuman allies. In no time at all, the stench of the Digger fields rose to meet them and they could see individual Fourleggers dodging the flailing limbs of Digger victims to skewer the brains.

Experienced butchers followed on, mostly women and children from amongst the Religious exiles who had long since lost the squeamishness that had killed so many of their friends. They didn't bother with the more difficult cuts—a waste that made Stopmouth squirm to think of it. But the Talker, translating the cries of "mother!" from the planted creatures of a hundred species, quashed any misgivings he might have had. The tribe would need to get out of here quickly.

Limbs were piled up: parts of local creatures like Slimers, along with the milkier flesh of Skeletons, while mounds of squirming grubs shrivelled in the sun.

Ship People wept and vomited. They cried out in horror at what they had to do. Many had to be prodded with spears by the sneering Religious, but in the end, every one of them headed back up the rocky slope with an armful of bleeding flesh.

Stopmouth took in the endless fields of bodies, scanning for the Diggers, but finding no sign of them yet. The light had spread over a greater area, but very soon, the sun would complete its short journey. He could feel the Ancestors in the air around him, warning him to make haste. The Diggers would spill out of the night at once, and they *always* followed after those who stole from them.

A commotion came from down amongst the fields. People seemed to be fighting with ... with Fourleggers? He was running before becoming fully aware of it, his young legs powering him

164

over moss-covered rocks. "Stop it!" he called, "Stop it!"

He was shocked to find Vishwakarma and Kubar amongst those in the thick of the struggle. Vishwakarma bled from claw marks that ran the length of his ribs. A little deeper and he would have been finished. But his face was more angry than afraid. Stopmouth had never seen him like this before.

"What's wrong? Stop fighting!"

He pulled Vishwakarma away from a Fourlegger that topped him by a head. One on one, a Fourlegger should beat a man, especially a relatively inexperienced one like Vishwakarma, and this creature was particularly large.

"Calm, now," Stopmouth told them. And to the Fourlegger. "Thank you for not hurting my people."

"Do they not hunger?" it asked.

"What's going on here?" Stopmouth demanded.

Vishwakarma couldn't speak, such was his outrage. Even now, he didn't realise that he should be dead. But Kubar found his voice easily enough. He pointed at the nearest body—one that was calling for its Digger mother like so many others. A human. A man Stopmouth recognized, who had been stolen when the Diggers came over the walls of HeadQuarters. "This *alien* was going to kill Sanjay."

Sanjay continued to cry for help between drooling and moaning. His eyes rolled in their sockets, first one way and then another. He was sunk up as far as his own thighs.

"His feet are gone," Stopmouth whispered. "You can see that, can't you? If...if we got him out and managed to carry him over the hills, he would be in terrible pain. He'd never be able to hunt..."

"He's my friend," cried Vishwakarma. "I knew him back...back..."

"I'm sorry..."

The Fourlegger picked that moment to speak again. "Has your hunger no need?"

Vishwakarma roared and it was all Stopmouth could do

to hold him back. But in less than a heartbeat, all strength left Vishwakarma and he was weeping instead. "This one is ours to kill," Stopmouth told the Fourlegger. "Please tell your sisters that we must go back now. Darkness is falling."

"We ... we're going to kill Sanjay?" asked Vishwakarma. "We're really going to kill him? *Sanjay*?"

"*You* are," Stopmouth told him gently. "His friend should free him from this pain." Poor Vishwakarma nodded.

The last of the Fourleggers were pulling back. Ship People were scrambling up the slopes, weighed down by delicious fresh meat. All they had to do now was get home.

"This was too easy," Stopmouth told Kubar.

"The Diggers are scared of us," said the priest. "After the way you burned them when you landed the Warship. You must have killed thousands of them."

"What are thousands to them? They cover the whole world."

"True enough," responded the priest with a shiver. "Come on then, Chief. Let's get going."

They gave Vishwakarma the privacy he needed and turned up the hill after the others. A few hundred Fourleggers came running on behind, adults and children all together. They caught up with the burdened Ship People all too quickly. "Hurry now!" Stopmouth told them. None of the Roof people carried very much, but they were far weaker than he had feared. Darkness would overtake them long before they reached the top.

"Shall I tell them to abandon the flesh?" asked Kubar. "I doubt any of these have run anywhere since they were children, and in some cases that was a *long* time ago!"

Already the moaning from below had stopped and the stench was easing off. The Diggers would come now, Stopmouth felt sure of it. A great wave of them surging up the hill. His mind raced with plans that he should have come up with the day before. He could hold a line here with the experienced hunters and the Fourleggers. But would that be enough? And how many Diggers would come? If they broke the line, the Tribe would be lost within days. Even if they beat back the enemy now, the cost of such a fight would jeopardize everything...

He felt a soft touch on his elbow. Kubar. "Don't forget, Stopmouth, you have a Talker."

Of course! "Thank you, Kubar." The priest had shown how its bright light could drive the Diggers away.

"But use it sparingly," warned the old man. "It needs light to refill itself."

Stopmouth scanned the base of the hills, and thought he detected the first signs of sinuous movement. "Hurry up!" he shouted to those around him. There was no point in trying and hide their presence from the enemy. The Diggers knew perfectly well where the thieves were already. Stopmouth could feel them watching him...

And yet, no attack came. Nobody screamed as they were dragged away. Every single human and Fourlegger made it safely back to the useless walls. Exhausted people were getting sick again, flinging the precious meat away from them. Others were cursing his name for the crimes he had forced on them, or collapsing as though they had done something incredibly difficult.

Stopmouth didn't care. It was over now. He found Indrani and the sleeping Flamehair. He hugged his wife tightly. "Not a thing went wrong," he said. "Not a single thing!"

The next day, he learned otherwise.

20.

CH⊕⊕SING A SIDE

Stopmouth woke well after the sun came up—almost everybody did that. "The days are too short now," they said to one another, but they still marvelled at the chaos of sprinkled stars that came by night, and greeted the first yellow beams of light with joy and relief as though fearful that one day the sun might fail them. But here it came again now, and spiral clouds of glittering mossbeasts rose up to meet it. He had never seen them do that back when the Roof shone for them.

The passing of darkness brought children out to play at hunting, and sent groaning adults to trudge down to the fields. They hadn't planted anything yet, or so Stopmouth had been told. Most of what they had been doing was clearing rocks away and releasing beasts too tiny to see into the soil so that human food might be welcome there. He understood none of it. Instead, he spent his time worrying about the fact that the guards—mostly Religious—had no love for those they were supposed to be protecting.

They were doing their jobs, however. He saw Sodasi directing men to nearby hides and fortified positions. These had been her own idea. "We're not hunters any more," she had told Stopmouth, while Rockface sputtered with outrage. "We just need to stay alive until the farm starts feeding us."

Whatever about Rockface, the rest of the men had seen her hunt a dozen times now—enough to have forgotten she was a woman. They obeyed her without question. Mind you, when he thought about it, just as many women in the Roof seemed to command as men.

"Sodasi!" he called down to her from the one remaining roof of HeadQuarters. "Where's Vishwakarma? Wasn't he supposed to be leading a patrol with you today?"

"Yes!" she said. "I've got to run now!"

"What was that about?" asked Indrani, putting an arm around him, while her other cradled Flamehair.

"I don't know. Maybe she didn't hear me properly. Or maybe the Talker is having problems." He squinted at the little sphere, looking for tell tale droplets of slime on its skin. He had been very careful on his return to keep it away from the technology of the Warship. So far, the device had survived, but he dreaded the day when it died or became lost.

"We are much too dependent on this," he said. "We need a ... a language for all of us. Just the one. And a way of communicating with the Fourleggers too. We should start working it out before it's too late."

"Hmm ... " said Indrani.

"You disagree?"

"I don't disagree at all, love. We'll need to teach everybody to write as well, before the skill is lost. But forget that for now. What I think, is that Sodasi is avoiding you."

"Avoiding me?"

"She didn't answer your question and it has nothing to do with the Talker."

"Oh ... But I just asked her where Vishwakarma was."

"Exactly, love. And where is he?"

The Chief looked around. From here he had a great view over the new fields and the collapsed buildings that had seemed so strong before the great Digger attack. Now, the rubble stretched most of the way towards the hills that protected the tribe, with the odd house, here and there, miraculously untouched. A single large structure—what Indrani called a *warehouse*—had survived too, and this was where the Fourleggers had made their new home.

Immediately below him, shelters made from salvaged materials from the Roof or the Warship, huddled inside new walls of rubble. This was where most of the people lived now, not trusting the stability of the houses. A hunter like Vishwakarma could hide in a thousand different places here. But why would he want to? Was he concealing an injury?

But no, there had never been any forced Volunteering in this tribe. People would have different reasons for hiding here, but for the life of him, Stopmouth could not think what they might be.

"I should find him..." He kissed Indrani good-bye. "But listen, love. I have a new job for you."

She bristled. Indrani did not take orders from anybody. Not even her husband. A lot of Roof women were strange like that. "I mean, I was hoping you would take care of the language thing. The *reading*. Before the Talker dies."

She relaxed and smiled. "I'll talk to Rockface about it."

"Rockface? Oh, of course, you think we can use the sign language of the children?"

"Exactly," she said. "I'll take it up with the big lunkhead." And she meant that term affectionately. He hoped. "Now, love, you go find Vishwakarma."

He meant to do just that, but when he had passed down the stairs and travelled no more than twenty paces farther on, he heard shouting from behind one of the makeshift shelters.

Four women were rolling in the dirt, while a fifth hovered nearby with a rock as though she meant to strike one or more of the fighters. She dropped it and ran as soon as she saw the Chief.

He pulled three of the women away to find a smaller one at the bottom of the pile, scratched and bloodied.

"Tarini?" Most of the passengers from the Warship had one thing in common: beauty. Women and men alike had arrived on the surface with clear skin, straight teeth and perfectly even features. Roof magic had made them this way—particularly those born before the so-called Crisis. The same magic had not been available to the younger ones.

However, although Tarini was thinner and shorter than the other women, it seemed that she had taken four of them on by herself and marred their perfection somewhat with a few bruises and one broken tooth.

"What's going on here?" he asked.

Nobody said anything, not even Tarini herself. Stopmouth had a horrible intuition that they had intended to kill her—his only friend from the Roof. He'd been foolish to leave her with them, to use her as a spy against them. He saw that now.

Growing up in a Tribe where people who fought amongst themselves were Volunteered, where justice was meted out by the Chief, and where the highest law was the survival of humanity, none of this would ever have happened. So, he had made no real effort to hide his friendship with her and now, with the food stash of the Newcomers betrayed, they wanted her dead.

"Go to the fields and do your work," he told them.

"Do it yourself, savage," said one of the women, tall and wide-eyed like a Goddess from one of the Roof's religions. "I hefted carrion for you yesterday. Over the hills. No more. I've had enough." The others nodded, but timidly. "I'm an *engineer*, not one of your *brood mares* or your *peasants*. We could have gone to Earth if it weren't for you. *Cannibal.*"

They left, of their own accord, perhaps heading for the fields as he had ordered, perhaps not.

He helped Tarini up from the ground. The girl had saved his life in the Roof, aiding his escape from a prison of his own fear. She looked even thinner now than she had up there.

"Haven't you been eating?" he asked her.

She shrugged. "I'm used to it. That lot didn't like sharing much, but we have their food now, right?"

"Right." He smiled, but she failed to respond and that worried him. In the Roof, with the whole world collapsing around her, Tarini's funny little grin had never faltered. Now, as the sun passed right overhead, she screwed up her eyes against it.

He couldn't help asking, "Do you think it's growing?"

"The sun? Of course not."

"No, I mean—"

She grabbed his arm. "Listen, Stopmouth, listen. There are two thousand of them and only maybe, what? A hundred and fifty of the rest of us?"

"What are you talking about?"

"The Ship People, of course. They hate it that they're here. They hate you. Us."

He shrugged. "Where else can they go? They have to live here now and only I can show them how. Or Rockface."

Tarini shook her head. "They don't believe that, you see? Not like the Religious who came before them. They don't believe it. Because they don't want it to be true, any of this. They've started paying attention to Dharam again. Have you noticed?" She stopped talking for a moment, cocking her head to one side. She checked the nearest shelter, making sure it was empty. Then, she whispered, "Some of them are planning a takeover. They want a new Chief, one of their own. They're still scared of you, but sooner or later they'll get you by yourself just like they got me." He followed her gaze as it swept around the walls. Everybody was gone: working in the fields or on patrol or watching for attack.

If he were rushed now, if those women had enough friends … none of his allies would get to him in time. He shivered once, but then he got control of himself again.

"These people are weak as pups," he said.

"Two or three of them were Wardens."

"Maybe they were. But I can't believe it, anyway. Humans will not fight humans with so many enemies around us."

Tarini kept looking at him, her face a mass of bruises—from human fists. And he knew better anyway. He had been to the Roof, after all. People had been fighting each other up there for a long time, even as their world died around them.

"You're right," he admitted. "They're capable of anything." It was a whole new way of thinking for him and he wasn't sure he wanted to get used to it. "Have you actually heard them plotting?"

She shrugged. "A lot of them don't speak my language or anything similar to it. But I know. Trust me. I should be on their side, after all. Except they're all filthy deserters."

"Like me?"

"Not like you, Chief." She grinned, finally coming around after her fright. They really would have killed her!

"You still don't like the Religious much, though, do you, Tarini?"

"Nope. But I guess I'll be living with them now, right?"

It was his turn to smile. "Rockface says you'd make a good hunter. You're fast enough."

"I am. Does that mean I don't have to go the fields today?"

"No, you can start your training by keeping me safe instead. Just look fierce. The bruises are helping a lot! Come on. I need to find somebody." But already his mood was beginning to darken. He thought of the woman with the rock. And of the glares he received every day from the Seculars.

"I'm looking for a hunter called Vishwakarma," he said. "Do you know him?"

"He's the one who talks too much."

"That's him. And a bit clumsy, but he's turning into a good hunter. Even back home, his spear would have drunk often, I think. If he could only learn to sit still!"

"What about Yama? He's a sort of leader too, isn't he? I've heard him say so."

"Hmm…" Stopmouth wasn't sure he wanted to talk about Yama. There was something about that boy…

Nearby, a man groaned, a sound of despair. "Did you hear that?" he asked.

It came again, uttering, this time, a single word: "Mother…" it said. "Oh, mother…" Stopmouth froze, his heart beating fast. He grabbed Tarini's arm as she tried to pass him.

"No," he said. "Let me go first."

He had no spear with him, so he held out a knife in front of him and stepped carefully towards the entrance of a shelter that looked as though a sneeze would tumble it.

"Ohhh ... motherrrr ... ."

Diggers. It had to be Diggers. But how? How?

A figure emerged and Stopmouth almost gutted it with his knife. He caught himself just in time. "Vishwakarma? Are ... are you all right?"

"I'm all right." Very few words indeed for a man who normally unleashed an excited stream of babble.

"Motherrr ... " the sound came from inside.

"You didn't ... you didn't kill Sanjay, did you?"

Vishwakarma hung his head and tears leaked from the corners of his eyes. "I had to do it. You rescued Indrani, didn't you? I heard that story. I heard Rockface tell it more than once how you took her back from them."

"They'd had her less than a day," said Stopmouth. "Her feet were still intact."

"You said she had a belly full of grubs, didn't you? And that she threw them up later on? I thought ... I thought Sanjay would do the same. But they won't come up." He squeezed more tears from his eyes. "He won't stop calling, he won't stop ... He's ... he's more than a friend to me. Do you understand?"

"You are brothers?"

"Motherrrr ... "

Vishwakarma groaned too, as though he felt the pain caused by the grubs himself; as though their cry for help were his own. "I know he has to be killed. I know it, I know it. But I can't. It should be me, his ... his friend. But I can't. That face of his. I can't do it."

"It's all right," said Stopmouth. "I would be proud to end his suffering for you."

Sanjay's cries grew louder, so loud in fact, that it was almost enough to smother the clumsy footsteps of a great crowd approaching. Stopmouth looked up to see at least twenty Ship People emerging from between the gaps in the dwellings. The cruel women from before were there, but so too was Ekta, the

Warden with powerful muscles under her dark skin. Nobody said anything. Vishwakarma continued to weep and even Sanjay quietened. Stopmouth could feel Tarini grow tense at his side.

Finally, the crowd split apart to allow two large men to come forward, carrying Dharam between them. At his back stood Dr. Narindi, nervous, but curious. Dharam gave that famous grin, the one that lifted only one side of his mouth, while his left arm hung before him on a sling.

"I thought you would be more of a challenge, savage," he said. "Less than a month, it took to bring you down. Did you really think you could turn us into labourers? Really? We who gave everything, who risked everything, to reach the stars?"

Stopmouth should have been afraid—fear kept a hunter alive, after all. But instead, the sight of Dharam brought only anger. "What choice do you have anyway?" he said. "Your Warship can never leave this world again. You will have to fight the Diggers. You will have to eat too, and all of that means you'll either be hunting or working no matter what you may think."

His words made the people around him uncomfortable and more than one face turned to Dharam to see how the Commissioner would respond.

"It's not what I *think* that matters, savage, it's what I know. There is another escape route from this terrible world you cannibals have made for yourselves—"

"*We* did not make this world and everybody here knows that!"

"You make it every day, savage. Through your barbarous actions. Your killings, your feastings on the flesh of others. We tried to give you a chance. To let us get on with growing our food, but no! You forced us to kill, yesterday, just to feed the beasts you invited to live right in our midst. Alien killers and human killers together. For many of us, it was the last straw."

Stopmouth felt his face go red, but he managed to control himself, to not fly at this monster before him. "If you hate killing so much, Dharam, then I expect you will be letting us go?"

A pause. Dharam's followers were uncertain again. "We will

have a … a trial," said the Commissioner. "There will be no murder."

"Apart from the murder of the Roof that you committed?"

"Your Religious allies did that, Stopmouth, not me." And he spoke that monstrous lie with such assurance that even the Chief found himself believing it. Almost. But the words had strengthened Dharam's supporters, no doubt about that.

And then, Stopmouth saw something that chilled him to his bones. A few of the men to either side of Dharam produced shiny black objects from pouches at their sides. *Guns*! He had seen their like in the Roof. The men carried the weapons awkwardly, but eagerness showed on their faces and they swapped excited grins.

"Where did you get those?" he asked. "We could have used them a hundred times before today!"

"Oh, there was plenty of cargo in the ship, known only to me, savage. We don't need you any more; we don't need you at all now. *I* will protect the people."

Stopmouth tensed his muscles. It was time to leave. Tarini could skip through far denser crowds than this one and Vishwakarma would be stronger than any of them would be expecting.

But Vishwakarma chose that moment to fall to the ground, weeping.

"Don't worry, Vishwakarma," Dharam said, misunderstanding. "Your crimes will be forgiven and when we leave this terrible place, they will never be spoken of again. You were civilized once. But this other, this Deserter who corrupted you, who has tried to do the same to the rest of us … "

Stopmouth reached his hand slowly towards the Talker and Dharam's grin widened. "Remember, the Talker is the only weapon the savage has now. When he commands it to brighten, don't forget to close your eyes. You see, cannibal? I am wise to all of your tricks. I advise you now to surrender. We cannot afford mercy otherwise."

The Chief touched Tarini's back and whispered. "Surrender if you want, but I don't think you can trust them."

"I know I can't."

Still whispering he told her what he meant to do. Then, suddenly, he raised the Talker and shouted, "Brighter!" But he never finished the command. Instead, he and Tarini charged forward just as everybody else was closing their eyes as tightly as possible. Many had dropped makeshift weapons to cover their faces. A gun went off with a tremendous *bang*. Everybody flinched, or screamed as though they had been hit.

The Chief powered through the Ship People, knocking two of them aside. Nearby, Tarini too passed through the line of enemies using that uncanny ability of Crisis Babies to dodge through crowds as though they were made of air.

The Warden, Ekta, had been too clever for Stopmouth. She appeared right in front of him, her face determined. "Now, stop right there, Chief—"

That was all she had time to say before a sling stone sped past Stopmouth's ear and struck her in the side of the head. Vishwakarma! It had to be! Other cries of pain from behind Stopmouth told him the young hunter had fully recovered from his weeping fit.

More hands were reaching for the fugitives.

"This way!" shouted Tarini, running off down the narrowest of gaps between the lean-tos. He pounded after her, ignoring the sting of weakly thrown stones and curses. All of this area was new to him. Real buildings had collapsed into the earth, leaving rubble behind them, or entire walls in some cases that fooled the eye into thinking a full house lay beyond. Much of this lay hidden by the maze of shanties. They had been built of plastic scraps and sheets of torn metal that flickered in the sun as though alive.

The cursing continued behind him. Ahead, Tarini had come to a stop at the back of a lean-to. A dead end, it seemed. "Get out of the way!" he shouted, still running. He picked up the pace, ignoring the risk of tripping and the jagged metal edges that threatened to rip him open if he strayed too close. He smacked hard into a wall of plastic, knocking it over, so that the roof of the shelter, heavy enough to trap them if it fell, swayed dangerously.

He plunged in through the darkness, choking on the fumes of poorly pounded moss, before passing through a curtain of the same material to come outside again.

"This way!" Tarini cried, pushing past.

More Ship People must have come from the fields. He could hear them calling one to the other, combing the narrow alleys for the fugitives.

"Where are we going?" he asked her. "I need to get to Indrani before they do!" The Ship People regarded Indrani as a traitor of the vilest sort, and even his own followers, the Religious, still disliked her. That was mutual, of course.

"I found them!" shouted an excited man. He and two women came rushing from the right bearing sticks. Stopmouth wasted no time in charging them, knocking them all in a terrified heap.

"You're pretty," Tarini told the man as she passed, before calling, "This way, Chief! I know where we are now. We can get in to HeadQuarters through here." And it wouldn't be a moment too soon. A large group with Ekta at their head and another man beside her in the torn garments of a Warden were running towards them. Shots rang out, punching holes in a nearby wall.

"Stop wasting bullets!" Ekta shouted. "We've got them trapped!"

"Come on," said Tarini.

Stopmouth needed no further urging. The shanty dwellings had been built right up to the walls of Head-Quarters. One whole side of the 'U' had fallen over, and stones from the barrier had been taken away to make new defences farther out. It was simplicity itself to slip in through the curtained entrance and run up towards the roof where he had left Indrani and Flamehair. This was where he had hidden the food of the Ship People, filling entire rooms, and leaving only a narrow entrance at the top of the stairs. He and Tarini might be able to block themselves in for a while. Then he could use the flashing of the Talker to signal for help from the Religious patrols. With better fighters and control of the food supply, he would soon put Dharam back in his place and then, by the Ancestors! Then there would be a Volunteering! That man ... that man would feed the Tribe before he destroyed it.

Stopmouth and Tarini had risen two flights of stairs before the first of their pursuers could be heard entering the building below. Just as well, since Tarini could barely put one foot in front of the other now. For all her courage, she would need more than rice in her belly before she ever became a proper hunter.

The sun, almost directly above, blinded him when he came out onto the roof.

"You led them quite a chase, Stopmouth!" Who was this? Most people called him "Chief" now, except Indrani and maybe Kubar. It took Stopmouth a moment to recognize Yama, back from patrol with his "pack." They were all there: a group of fifteen young men who used to cause trouble when all had lived in the Roof together. Now, they had found a better way to use their high spirits by serving the Tribe.

"Guard the stairs," Stopmouth told them. "Don't let anyone up here!"

A few moved to obey him at once, but only a few. Then, even these ones paused, looking, not to Stopmouth, but to Yama. The boy grinned.

"You taught us all about sacrifice, didn't you, *Chief*? Threatened to Volunteer me when I took this wound on my leg for the Tribe. Remember that?" The leg still bore a bubbling scar from the burning spit of a Skeleton Hunter.

Stopmouth felt suddenly dizzy at the sight of so many spear points turned towards him. "I don't know what Dharam told you," he said quietly, speaking as quickly as he could. "There is no escape from the world, you know that, right? You know you can't believe anything he says. He even blamed your people for what happened up in the Roof. Surely you remember that?"

The young men stirred uncertainly.

"I don't care if we can't leave," said Yama. "I like it here. I like it when my spear drinks, and it *always* drinks. Right, boys?" That got them grinning again, although Stopmouth knew some of

179

them still wept in their sleep and wet themselves before a fight. They wanted to go home even if Yama did not. "But we need a new Chief around here. And real women. Proper beautiful ones who'll do anything. Right boys?"

"You can't ... Yama! You can't!"

Tarini's eyes opened wide. "Stopmouth!"

He had barely time to look around. Ekta's fist was waiting for him. She knocked him hard onto his bottom, his head spinning. "Sorry, Chief," she said, with real regret. That didn't stop her hitting him again, harder this time, cursing under her breath at the knuckles she must have bruised. "Tie him up!" she said. "Tie them both up!"

"I don't take orders from you," Yama said. The voice seemed to come from far away. Where was Indrani?

"Tie them up, *please*," said Ekta. "Or I'll rip your head off."

Stopmouth tried to resist when he felt them loosen the Talker pouch from his belt. But somebody hit him again. Not Ekta this time. He felt woozy, he felt like being sick. He heard a chorus of Ancestors cursing him for his foolishness. "Too trusting!" they cried. "You have killed your Tribe!"

21.
THE TALK OF CHILDREN

"That wasn't so bad, hey? A little knock on the head?"

Stopmouth wrinkled his nose. He knew that smell, that voice.

"They wanted to volunteer us, boy—I mean, Chief. But our lads, Kubar and them, even some of Yama's lot, wouldn't stand for it." Rockface paused. "Is he even awake yet? Am I talking to a corpse? Thin-skulled like his father."

Another smell he knew and the hic-cough of a baby.

"Leave him, Rockface. Not to touch." Indrani's voice. She was speaking strangely, with difficulty. Almost as if...

Stopmouth opened his eyes and tried to sit up—too quickly. A high dark room was spinning around him with miserable looking, blurred faces. He felt his gorge rise. "Ekta hit him hard with those muscles of hers, hey? What kind of a woman is that? She'd crush her own babies if she hugged them, so she would, and smash a man's tally stick!"

"You are idiot, Rockface. Sit, love. You must to ... to *down*."

"Lie down," Stopmouth croaked. "I must l-lie down. They took the T-talker?" Of course they did. Half of the Ship People didn't even speak the same language, although they had made plans for dealing with that problem, he remembered. Still. The Talker would save them a lot of trouble.

His vision began to clear. Light leaked through a crack in the wall of a building he didn't recognize, seeming to redden everything it touched.

Apart from Indrani, Flamehair and Rockface, there were two others with him in the large room—Tarini, her clothing ripped, her face speckled with dried blood; and Vishwakarma, also lying down, staring at the ceiling.

Something flashed by Stopmouth's hand. He brought it close to his face: a Fourlegger scale. They were everywhere. It explained the rusty-looking colouring of the floor and told Stopmouth exactly where he was: in exile; sheltered by allies he would never be able to speak to without the Talker. All over the room, were balls of moss and twigs. It looked like some kind of art, like the charcoal pictures of home, or the bloody swirls of the Hairbeasts.

"I'm hungry," he said. Indrani and Rockface nodded. The big man looked suspiciously cheerful for a hunter who had been exiled from his Tribe. But it wasn't the first time for either of them, and maybe that explained it. Nevertheless, a shudder passed through Stopmouth's body.

He felt Indrani's warm touch on his shoulder. "We still live," she said. "We still will win. We kill Dharam and we take Talker and we ... " she shrugged, lacking the words, but her expression revealed everything: anger, ferocity, strength. She would not be anybody's Volunteer and she had survived far worse situations than this. The death of a world, for one thing; Wallbreaker for another.

He managed a smile for her and the others. What a tribe they made! Six starving humans: one infant; an old man with a twisted back; a younger man with a broken heart to whom nobody could talk; a Crisis Baby—also confined to vague gestures; a nursing mother; and an Ancestor-cursed Chief.

"I love you all," he said. Vishwakarma didn't look up and Tarini didn't understand, but he grinned at her anyway. They might survive another twenty or thirty days, even a hundred if the Diggers failed to come again. That would have to be enough. Despite what Indrani had said, he would make no attempt to win back the Talker or to persuade the Religious to fight for him. He would not endanger the main body of the Tribe by becoming the cause of a split. On the contrary: he would do everything in his power to see that it survived.

Dharam must have won the Religious over to his cause. Stopmouth didn't understand how, but he suspected it was something to do with Dharam's insistence that there was another way to escape the surface of the world, to get back to civilization.

It was something all the Roofpeople yearned for, and that evil man, that magnificent liar, must have turned their longings on a spit, until they glistened and dripped with delicious fat. The bellies of the Religious, empty but for fear, had been maddened with it. It was the only explanation Stopmouth could think of.

He forced himself to sit up, ignoring the desire to be sick, and the sudden pounding of his head. He needed something to help him stand. "Where is my spear?"

"Oh, they took your weapons. But they couldn't get mine! And I've been making more all along. Like the old days, hey?"

"We will to attack them!" Indrani insisted, but both hunters shook their heads together and she spat at them and turned away, as though unable to look at them further.

"But what about f-f-food …"

Rockface grinned. "Let's just rest a little, Chief."

"That's … that's not like you, Rockface."

The big man made an exaggerated yawning motion as if he didn't have a care in the world, trying and failing to suppress a grin. "It's nearly night, hey? When a man should be squeezing his wives and lighting fires. Let's just wait for that ridiculous 'sun' of yours to pass the edge of the hole Indrani made."

Stopmouth nodded, uneasily. He always hated it when Rockface had a plan. The lack of weapons only made him more afraid. "W-what are you up to?"

"What does it look like?" The big man lay down on a bed of moss. "Going to sleep, hey? To listen to the Ancestors a while instead of your moaning."

Stopmouth slept too, without meaning to. His eyes closed just for a moment, and then a few heartbeats later, or so it seemed, they opened again in total darkness. He heard whispers and he heard giggles. Kindling flared into life and then a torch. Children were everywhere, perhaps as many as a dozen, their hands flying in hunting gestures too complicated for Stopmouth to follow. Their leader was a fierce little girl called Fulki who bossed them from task to task.

Even the little Fourlegger was there, its claws distinctly making the sign that meant "hurry," but evolving it into "split" and then "go" in a way that made no sense at all.

Somebody grabbed one of the Fourlegger rolls of moss and twigs from the corner and used it to create an instant fire. And soon, flesh, delicious flesh, began sizzling over it.

"What's g-going on?" he said. He felt better already, barely able to speak for the drool forming in his mouth.

Rockface grinned. "We can talk to the little Fourlegger and she can talk to the adults, hey? And they have thirty days worth of food that we gave to them only yesterday! Eat up! Only the Ancestors know what creatures they came from, but what a feast!"

Stopmouth saw Sodasi, looking beautiful with firelight wrapping around the curve of one cheek. She too spoke with her hands, much more awkwardly than the children, but Rockface seemed to be following along because he laughed from his belly and rubbed her face. Her smile grew wider and the big man grinned shyly back.

Indrani whispered, "First time he *see* her. What a fool! Does he think she wants another father?"

"He'll g-get to it," Stopmouth whispered back. A man had to decide he wanted to live before he could even think of getting married.

Afterwards, everybody ate the unidentifiable flesh, except for poor Tarini who wept and gagged. All the Roof people had that problem to begin with. Nobody had the words to help her, but a few of the smaller children gave her hugs before gobbling up whatever she couldn't manage. They fought, laughing, over Vishwakarma's substantial leftovers until every scrap of food had been consumed.

Stopmouth played with his Flamehair for a while. Sometimes he thought he could see bits of his brother in her, especially in the way her cheeks seemed to dimple when he made her smile. But she was *his* daughter now and that's all there was to it. He would find a way to get her back into the tribe, even if he himself could never be part of it. She would need somebody to marry in the years to come and to bring flesh when she had children of her own. "But you'll fight like your mother, won't you, little one? You'll kick hunters in the face if they say so much as a bad word to you!"

The other children were yawning by now, relaxing against the walls and chatting, sometimes with words of human or their own language, sometimes with gestures.

"Are they s-sleeping here?" he asked Rockface.

"Well, we can't be putting them outside."

"But, I mean … " he waved the hand that wasn't holding the baby. "Shouldn't they be getting back to their parents?"

"These are the ones with no parents, remember? We're all they've got now."

"They n-need a Tribe."

"I know, hey?" and Rockface actually looked angry. "But they won't obey me when I tell them to join Dharam's lot. And why should they? Who will teach them to hunt? Who will make sure they eat?"

Stopmouth nodded. "I d-don't know what the right thing for them is either. Or for the Tribe." Dharam's reign as Chief might come to a sudden end when everybody learned he couldn't bring them back to civilization. *Or could he?* There would have to be something behind his lies, surely, to win over clever men like Kubar.

Indrani had been with Tarini, trying to get the girl to eat some more and to keep it down. Now she came back to sit beside him.

"What do you think, love?" he asked her. "The Roof is dead, everybody can see that. Why would anybody believe Dharam could help them escape from here now?"

She shrugged. "The Roof has many things of your Ancestors

185

up there. Many things like Warship."

He nodded, making sense of what she was saying. His people, once known as the Deserters, had fled from Earth a long time ago. In the process, they had abandoned Indrani's Ancestors to what everybody had thought was certain death. Eventually, the Deserters had been overtaken and captured, condemned for their selfishness to a life of primitive cannibalism, while their spacecraft, became trophies and monuments in the parks and gardens of the victors.

Later, the strange slime that fed on the sophisticated machines of the Roof, had left the more primitive technology of the Deserters completely untouched.

"You think Dharam knows where to find a Deserter ship?" he asked.

She struggled to explain her thoughts, "Dharam is waster. Is ... not a hunter to tell ... right things."

"You mean he's a l-liar?"

"Yes! A liar. You, my man. You will eat his heart."

"I will," he said, grinning. But he couldn't help turning over in his mind the idea that another ship might really be found. Dharam's followers would get the escape they clamoured for ... Or would they?

Stopmouth had seen one of these Deserter craft for himself, and one thing he knew for sure, was that it was a lot smaller than the Warship. There was no way everybody would fit.

But in the end, none of that mattered. Dharam would never be able to fly up into the Roof to retrieve the new ship. And even if he did, nobody could survive the horrors up there. Stopmouth had seen that for himself. In the end, the Tribe would be staying put to face the Diggers, and that was that.

He sighed. "I'm sorry, Rockface. You know there aren't enough of us here to keep the children properly safe. They can stay tonight, but they have no future here with us." *Because we have no future.*

Then the moss curtain over the door opened and Stopmouth

jumped. They hadn't even set a guard! What was he thinking?

But it was only an adult Fourlegger sticking its head inside so that a few rusty scales fell away to the floor. The young Fourlegger rushed forward to rub snouts with it before turning to Rockface and signalling the "all clear" with its claws. The Chief grinned and relaxed. There had been guards after all. Inhuman ones. And suddenly Stopmouth found himself dizzy all over again, but not from the knock on the head. Indrani was grinning at him, her eyes shining. "We not few as you think, husband!"

"No," he said, smiling back, his eyes prickling for some reason. The Fourleggers were Tribe to him! He saw that now. There might be a future, after all. A bizarre one, maybe, in which the shattered remnants of different tribes learned to work together as one body, with one heart.

22.

THE DARK

The Ancestors had performed such miracles to keep the Tribe alive in the wilderness that few people remained who doubted their power or love, or Wallbreaker's connection to them. Even the loss of the Talker had failed to dampen spirits.

A few days after the sighting of the Slime Woman, the Roof fell dark for the last time. The despicable Aagam cried out in a mix of anger and horror, shaking his fist and screaming gibberish until Fearsflyers silenced him with a smack to the back of the head. Nobody was afraid anymore. Not of the Blindness. Not of the Diggers. Every horror that had come their way was beaten back, and just when hunger struck, bodies had rained from the Roof.

When the sea appeared in front of them, just as Wallbreaker had promised, the Tribe's faith only strengthened. They could see little of the water beyond the range of their torches, but men laughed and stabbed it with their spears. Children lapped at it, spitting it out, throwing cold handfuls at each other. It tasted saltier than blood.

Only the endless darkness oppressed them, but even in this they were offered hope.

One day, trudging along the endless road of sand that ran the length of the sea, the ground shook hard enough to throw everybody from their feet. Ashsweeper cried out and Nighttracker forgot he was supposed to be grown up and called, "Dada! Dada!"

until Whistlenose wrapped him in his arms.

In the distance, a portion of the Roof was glowing.

"The light is coming back!" somebody cried.

It turned red first, and then intensely white, as flaming fragments of it tumbled and burned. A column of fire followed on from this and whole hills seemed to be ablaze. Whistlenose felt vibrations through the sand, in every part of his body that touched the ground. *How many times can the world end?* he wondered.

But calm returned and soon a new set of *hills* interposed themselves between the Tribe and the distant fires they had witnessed. Then, after what felt like a number of days, the Diggers, who had not been seen since the forests, began to mass again just beyond the range of their torches.

"They were fighting elsewhere," Laughlong growled. "But they must have missed us all along."

Nobody panicked, and word came down from the Chief so that when the enemy finally struck, the Tribe knew exactly what to do.

"Into the sea!" Wallbreaker shouted, and people waded fearlessly into the freezing water with torches held high and children floating on bundles of tally sticks. The enemy, shorter than men, proved very awkward in this new element. They had to swim where men could still stand, and Whistlenose stabbed one after another until a carpet of the hapless creatures surrounded him.

"We'll feast tonight!" said Laughlong from somewhere nearby. "If they let us back onto the beach ... " But even he had ceased to criticize the Chief lately.

So easy was the fighting in the water, that many suggested the Tribe could live here forever. And another miracle happened there too, something extraordinary. Hightoes gave birth right in the water! Nobody had seen such a thing before and they all marvelled at how easy the birth had been, even as the Tribe had been battling for its life against the Diggers. It was a fine baby boy that brought tears to the eyes of his father, Fearsflyers. "The Tribe continues!" he cried. "Even here! Even here!"

But the sea, it seemed, had life of its own. After a ten, or maybe fifteen days, people began disappearing, pulled under before they could so much as cry out.

The Tribe moved on.

They reached a place where the air hissed like burning fat and a fast-moving Wetlane—or *river*, as Aagam seemed to call it—poured into the sea. Here it was that they saw daylight again for the first time in nobody knew how long.

It was some distance away from them—in the very place where they had seen the Roof burning when the earth had shaken enough to knock them over. It was burning again now, but much more gently and with a kind yellow glow. Whistlenose knew his jaw was hanging open. He hugged his family tightly to him and everywhere men were doing the same. Nearby, Aagam gibbered excitedly, speckling his speech with proper human words like "good" and "tasty."

Daylight! Daylight! It seemed to lie in exactly the direction Wallbreaker had promised to take them, the one from which the *river* came. "It's not that far," Laughlong was saying to his own surviving wife, Sweetfoot. "Four or five days for a hunter. More with you to distract me!" Sweetfoot giggled like an unmarried girl.

But to get there, they had to leave the safety of the sea. So, they clung to the tops of the hills along the river, while just beyond the circle of torchlight, the Diggers seemed to be moving with them.

The enemy never attacked, however. Even when the distant daylight disappeared night after night.

People speculated why—everything from the protection of the Ancestors, to something the Chief had come up with, to the enormous losses the Diggers had suffered in the sea. But as the tribe stumbled towards the daylight over slippery rocks, with the rushing water of the river to one side and the whispering darkness to the other, Whistlenose felt his own fear growing stronger and stronger.

He kept remembering the day he had seen Bloodskin burning, when he and five companions had been chased among the houses of no man's land. His small group had not been attacked immediately then either. "Playful" was what he had thought at the time, as if the Diggers revelled in a cruel sense of fun.

"They even move away when we go scouting," Browncrack told him. "They stay just out of the circle of our torchlight, but you can hear their claws and it's louder than the hissing of the *river*."

"They must be afraid of us," said Whistlenose, hiding his real thoughts.

"Of you, maybe, with your bad knees and worse breath," said Browncrack.

"Well, it can't be as bad as the breath from that lower mouth of yours that gave you your name!"

"Ha, old man. I've wiped it clean on hides that were fresher than you ... "

They clapped each other on the back as if they were home in ManWays after an easy hunt.

Three days travel later, sort of—the new, far-off, daylight didn't seem to last as long as it should—brought them to the remains of a great stone structure that hung halfway over the river with a slope leading up to it and a small stand of dying trees to provide them with firewood. Of course the Tribe camped there, up high, with the rush of the river beneath them. Of course they did.

Wallbreaker stood at the edge of the stone structure, with the river hissing along directly below. He beckoned Whistlenose to approach. "Give me your torch," he said. The Chief flung the burning wood out as far as he could. It smashed into something on the far side, exploding into a shower of sparks. "Ha!" he cried. "I knew it! Did you see that? It collapsed into the water, but this used to be a bridge."

"A what? Like a tree trunk?"

"Exactly! Like the tree trunks we used to use to cross the Wetlanes back home. Or the metal ones you find sometimes."

"But this is stone!"

"Sure, sure. What a shame it collapsed. I wonder how they got it to stay up?"

In the distance, in the direction of their future home, the

sky turned pink and bright yet again and the people cheered as was their new habit. But suddenly the sentries were crying out in alarm. They had built fires down at the bottom of the slope. Whistlenose and most of the other men ran down to join them there in case of attack.

But there was no fighting. At the very farthest edge of the firelight, the Diggers had finally shown themselves. They waited in their hundreds. Thousands maybe. A great mass of them, just standing there. "Use your slings!" Wallbreaker shouted when he arrived. But nobody dared. The two sides simply stared at each other.

"What are they waiting for?" whispered the Chief. There were enough of the creatures that they could have overrun ten times the numbers of humans that remained. Nobody spoke for a while, but eventually, Laughlong, from over on the right, provided the answer.

"The fire," he said. "They knew we'd camp here with all this wood. Three days worth to keep ourselves safe from them. But we've only trapped ourselves to get it. There's no defences here and we've left the sea far behind. There's no way out at all unless … Chief? A new plan? From the Ancestors?"

Wallbreaker didn't answer. He turned and stumbled back up the hill.

Three days, Whistlenose thought. After that there could be no more fire. And the Diggers, in masses never before seen, were waiting.

But they were not as patient as they seemed.

23.
EVIDENCE ⊕F LIFE

Scouting, that was the first thing. Stopmouth's new hybrid tribe would only need to survive until Dharam's lies became apparent to his followers. Until then, the young hunter wanted to know where the Diggers had got to. Surely they should have tried to launch an attack by now? Their cowardice made no sense to him. They needed to feed like everybody else!

So, for the good of the Tribe, for the future of his wife and daughter and all the other children and friends he still had, Stopmouth needed to find out what was going on beyond the hills.

After slipping from the warmth of his moss bed with Indrani, he crouched next to the lump that Vishwakarma had become.

"Get up," he said.

The hunter spoke no words of human other than weapon words such as "spear" and "sling," but his eyes opened, glittering in the darkness.

"You can't stay dead f-forever. I need you." Vishwakarma understood none of this, of course. Nevertheless, he sighed and allowed himself to be helped up. He accepted one of Rockface's new spears, as well as a sling and a Slimer hide skin of water. He must have suspected then he would be heading into danger and seemed glad of it.

"Don't be reckless. The Ancestors w-will be angry if we w-w-waste our flesh this day." All gibberish to Vishwakarma. That didn't stop him nodding and grimly gripping the spear. "W-welcome back, hunter."

Stopmouth cut his finger and flicked a drop of blood at the wall. Then, covering the tiny wound with a bandage of moss, he led the other man outside. As he had hoped, the short night seemed to be coming to an end. Already a gentle breath of golden light was brightening one ragged edge of the hole in the Roof.

The men passed by a motionless trio of Fourleggers that stood guard on the building, before breaking into an easy jog and heading for the hills. The light of the rising sun followed them all the way, warming their backs and waking swarms of mossbeasts into glittering, rising spirals. Way back in time, when there had been no Roof, and no hunters either, these insects and the sun must have greeted each other like this every morning.

The run up the side of the hill went so much faster with no Ship People to slow them down. They were young men at the peak of their strength, and in Stopmouth's case, even old wounds and scars had been scoured away after exposure to Medicine during his time in the Roof. The slopes and the coloured mosses, the sliding scree, were like meat to him after a long fast.

And then they were at the top, looking down as the light sped across the fields below with their lines of bodies stretching back and back farther, into the darkness where the sun would never reach.

"S-something's not right."

The human raid had cut swathes in the line and Stopmouth wasn't surprised to see that the gaps had been refilled with fresh bodies. The familiar stench too, tickled his nostrils, even from this distance. And yet …

"Let's g-get closer."

They jogged down the slope. They were no more than halfway, when Vishwakarma, whose eyes must have been better than Stopmouth's, hissed and fell back on his bottom, smothering a cry of alarm before signalling frantically for "retreat." It took the ex-Chief a few heartbeats to realise what was wrong.

Diggers! Dozens of them. Rarely seen by daylight and certainly

194

not in such numbers! His heart caught in his throat, but he calmed himself and signalled Vishwakarma to "halt" and to be "silent." A human could outrun Diggers most of the time, as far as he knew. So, as long as this wasn't an ambush, they should be all right.

The creatures showed no interest in the distant hunters. None at all.

"I think I know w-what's happened." He signalled "forward" and was glad to see Vishwakarma nod back at him, much calmer now. He too, must have realised what was going on.

They proceeded more cautiously down the slope until they were within slinging distance of their listless enemies. Like the other creatures around them, these Diggers had been planted, their lower legs buried in soil, their claw-tipped upper arms limp at their sides. Either the enemy had run out of creatures to hunt in the rest of the world, or they were fighting amongst themselves now. Both cases implied a level of desperation. Stopmouth knew better than to see this as a good sign.

The creatures eaten by the Diggers' young tended to sink as they were consumed from below, until only the head remained to be fought over by the remaining grubs. The last grub, the victor, large enough by that point, would consume the entire skull and bury itself deep in the ground, only to emerge later as a full-grown adult. Stopmouth had seen this himself when the Roof had sent him visions of it.

Now, he imagined something different. His mind's eye saw how the fields in the heartlands of the Diggers must be empty, depopulated of anything the creatures might live on. This had forced them to expand and expand until no other species remained alive anywhere in the world, so that they must turn on each other.

"Oh Ancestors," he said. "W-we're all they have l-left." He'd always known the enemy would not long delay their attack over the hills, but any hopes that the Diggers' fear of being burned again by the ship's engines would keep them permanently away, failed him now. The Diggers simply had no choice but to keep going.

195

And yet, they *had* waited. But why?

The men moved down to the bottom of the slope where the soil became too rocky for planting. He stepped as close as he dared to the first of the creatures, while Vishwakarma kept well back. These Diggers in front of him did not look well. Many lacked claws or bore terrible wounds. "Knives and spears did this," he said. "Not claws or teeth."

He walked carefully along the lines and then stopped dead. A piece of wood still jutted from the chest of one of the beasts, although the wound had long since ceased to bleed. It was the handle of a dagger, much like the one a human would have made back in ManWays, just the right size for a man's hand. Could it be … ? No, no. Of course not. But he was holding his breath all the same.

Vishwakarma gasped as Stopmouth darted within range of the Digger's claws. He ripped the wood free, falling back again on his bottom in time to avoid the clumsy strikes that could have disemboweled him. The other hunter grabbed him under the arms to pull him further out of range, but Stopmouth shook him off and crawled back to where the weapon lay. He felt his jaws working, but no sound came out. He couldn't believe what he was seeing, couldn't believe it. He held it up to where his companion might see. But Vishwakarma didn't get it.

"Armourback," said Stopmouth. "It's Armourback shell." He and Rockface had both owned similar weapons, but nobody else outside of ManWays ever did or could. Stopmouth's people had fought the Armourbacks to extinction and this wonderfully strong material had been their reward. Stopmouth himself had discovered how to shape it with fire after his brother had first betrayed him. It seemed so long ago now.

He was breathing hard and his eyes were blurring. His people had to be close by, surely, and yet, none of them were planted here along with those they had been fighting.

Stopmouth found himself on his feet again and running with no idea of how that had happened, but Vishwakarma was calling out his name, falling farther and farther behind. With an effort he stopped himself to wait for the other man to catch up. There was no point in exhausting himself without reason.

The two hunters slipped into a more natural hunting jog. Vishwakarma asked a few questions and Stopmouth guessed the man wanted to know where they were going, but Stopmouth didn't know himself. He was following the line of planted Diggers. It was all he had to go on. Eventually, however, as they came to a place where the hills met the rushing river, they began to leave the sunlight from the hole behind them. The line of wounded Diggers stretched off into the darkness beyond, but the bodies along the river bank lay too thickly together to pass safely.

What do I do now, Ancestors? No buildings stood nearby that he might have climbed for a better view. But the hill would do just as well, maybe better, for it would help prevent the Diggers from getting underneath them. But what would he see from up there anyway? Nothing could possibly survive out in the darkness other than his enemies.

He sagged, exhausted from the day; frustrated and afraid. The whole idea of scouting seemed absurd. Other than a tiny patch of light under the hole Indrani had made, the entire world belonged to the enemy. If some human band from his lost home had tried to follow in his footsteps, then they must have wounded a few dozen Diggers and been swallowed up. And even if they still lived, the sheer mass of bodies between him and them, meant he would never meet them.

He should have been glad of that. They thought him a traitor, after all, and maybe he was.

Vishwakarma made a frantic gesture. "Down! Alert!" The men dropped behind a boulder. The ground shook. Soil sprayed from a small clearing amongst the planted victims nearby and suddenly Diggers appeared. They had bodies with them—more wounded Diggers to be planted here and there while the hunters held their breaths. The men didn't have to wait very long. In less than a tenth, the enemy had gone again, leaving the tunnel

197

exposed behind them and a trio of fresh plantees.

"They've been burned," Stopmouth whispered. "You see that? Somebody knows they d-don't like fire." Vishwakarma neither understood nor cared. He grabbed Stopmouth by the shoulder and pointed up the hill. The Chief nodded, and the two climbed up above the river as quietly as they could, keeping two spear-lengths between them so that one might escape any ambush the other fell into.

About halfway up, a sharp blaring cry echoed across the fields and over the rushing river beneath them. A Clawfolk horn. There could be no doubt about it. The alarm sound that had quickened his pulse so many times back home. The sound that brought hunters stumbling out of their beds, weapons in hand.

When he turned now, a red glow lit the horizon. A fire: several fires, more likely, hot and bright.

The river cut through a ravine back there, he remembered, just as it did here. A ruined structure stood right up over the river; easily defended on all sides with plenty of rock for flinging at an enemy, and wood too, for the fires he could see now.

His people! Oh, Ancestors, how he missed them! The greatest hunters the world had ever seen! They were no more than a day's run away. An impossible gap to bridge in the Digger-controlled dark, even if he had every Ship Person on his side to help him. Even if they knew how to fight. He felt his chest tightening and his vision blurring.

Suddenly, he was on the ground with Vishwakarma's arms clamped around him and the man babbling and pleading in his ear. Had he tried to run back down the hill? Had he really come so close to wasting his precious flesh?

"You think I'm s-stupid, Vishwakarma? B-but imagine what they could do for us, those people trapped down there! They can hunt like your spirits or *gods*, or whatever you call them. It's only the dark that makes them weak and the Diggers strong. We have to get them back to HeadQuarters to f-fight along with us. We *have* to." And what he didn't say—not that the man could speak human in any case—was that his brother might be there. Hated so much, but loved too by a younger version of himself that still lived in his heart; a version that hadn't yet learned to give up.

They headed back along the ridge of the hill, Stopmouth's mind filling with memories of home. He had been bullied and mocked as a child in ManWays. But none of that seemed important now; not against the weight of his mother and other beloved Ancestors; not against the Tribe, the *real* Tribe that was his marrow and guts and heart. Nothing mattered more. He had learned as much from his first breath.

The light grew stronger as they came under the hole in the Roof again, but it had a deep, orange quality about it that Stopmouth was learning to associate with the coming of night. He could see HeadQuarters from here and the ruins that surrounded it. He could hear the river too, hissing like a living thing, too wide to cross, although the far bank bore matching ruins. He had never spotted any life over there. But he was glad to have the river as a defence against the Diggers should they ever appear from that direction.

Vishwakarma grabbed his arm and signalled "alarm!"

Two hundred paces away in the failing light, a woman-shaped, glistening beast rose up out of the ground. It glowed with a faint blue colour that seemed familiar to Stopmouth. And it was camouflaged too—he could see the colours of the rocks and moss behind it.

He still had the Armourback shell knife in his hand. Some other man had made it, but the Ancestors guided Stopmouth's throw and the weapon flew true. It struck the creature right in the chest. But rather than sticking, it passed fully through to fall out the back in a spray of transparent liquid.

The hunters stared. A mouth appeared in that female face. "Shtop-mou ... " it seemed to say. Almost as though ... almost ...

Vishwakarma grabbed him by the shoulder and pulled hard. They could not kill this creature of pure liquid! So they ran again, fearing an ambush that never came.

Whatever that was, it can wait.

They reached the first, rubble-strewn streets, not stopping until they had returned to the building of the Fourleggers, panting and exhausted after the day, calves aching from the hills.

"Rockface!" Stopmouth called. "Rockface, I need you! Indrani!"

His wife appeared first, shushing him, until she saw the look on his face. Then, she had her arms around him. She smelled of milk and baby and he remembered again, for the thousandth time, that little Flamehair had been fathered by his brother and not him. Rockface turned up a moment later with Sodasi at his side, both of them smiling.

"Ha!" said the big man, uncaring that Flamehair must be sleeping nearby. "You're not going to believe it, but I've caught myself a new wife. At least I think that's what's happened. We'll need to borrow that Talker to be sure, hey?" And he laughed while Sodasi shyly took his huge hand in hers.

"Aren't you happy for me, boy? I should be meat, of course, I know it, hey? But you're to blame as much as I am. I Volunteered, you may remember. I Volunteered! But it'll be a while before—"

"R-rockface! Indrani! Rockface … you h-h-have to listen to me."

"A man on his dowry day, doesn't have to—"

"The T-tribe. Our Tribe. F-f-from ManWays. They're still alive. Less than a d-d-day away."

"No!" Indrani and Rockface both said the same word simultaneously in very different tones of voice.

"T-they're trapped on that big rock down by the r-river. W-w-we need them here. Those Ship People are useless. They won't even learn to hunt, most of them."

He felt Indrani leave him. He saw her run out of the room from the corner of his eye, but he couldn't think of that right now. The Tribe, the Tribe! And Rockface felt the same way, his big face writhing with emotions too powerful for words. Meanwhile, Vishwakarma and Sodasi were talking rapidly in their own tongue.

Finally, Rockface, with tears on his cheeks, let out a roar and grabbed a spear from the wall. "No! R-rockface! No! It's impossible. We need help on this one."

"The Ship People? Are you crazy, hey? The Ship People?"

"No, no. There are a f-few dozen of our hunters still around. The Religious. And we'll need a p-plan."

Rockface threw the spear down again. "Why would they help us? They're with Dharam now. They don't want to eat flesh any more. He's meeting them all tonight to tell more lies. They lap it up from him like soup."

"We can't d-do it without them, Rockface." Stopmouth felt sick. But he felt alive too. He hadn't even eaten the strips of dried flesh he had carried with him all day, but he forced some down now and made his friends do the same. Then he went to look for his wife, but she was asleep beside the child and wouldn't wake even when he shook her.

"You're angry with m-me," he whispered. "He's probably not even alive anymore. This isn't about him. You must know that, love. Or me or you. It's Tribe. It's more than flesh." No response came until he bent down to kiss Flamehair on the cheek.

But then, she murmured, "You said before *we* are Tribe. Flamehair and me, your womans."

"Of course, you are! Of course, you are, love!"

But she said nothing more after that.

24.
THE DANGERS OF RELIGION

When they were growing up, uncle Flimnose used to tell the children stories of heroes from the Tribe's past. At the end, he'd always point up at the grid of tracklights that dotted the Roof at night. "And that's where they're living now," he'd say. "The fires of our Ancestors, watching over us until the day we all go Home."

But fires weren't like that, were they? All laid out as neatly as the streets where hunters lived and died. Wallbreaker was always the one to annoy their uncle by pointing that out, but Stopmouth had wondered the same thing. Later, as an adult, he had travelled into the Roof and had learned that the tracklights were simply objects of dumb-metal and other materials whose names he had since forgotten.

However, now that Indrani had torn a hole in the Roof, something new had come into the world: random speckles and clumps of light, sprawling across the night sky like true fires, except that they were as numberless as the Ancestors themselves. While the daytime sun could not be looked at, these *stars* always drew Stopmouth's eyes and filled him with new hope that the tales of his childhood had been more than mere lies.

He dragged his gaze away from the hole to look down at the ruins of the Warship. Dharam was to hold his meeting here, and already the Tribe was gathering. Bedraggled Ship People, no longer so confident of immortality, along with the remaining

Religious, all together in a defensive clump. The latter, having spent time on the surface, knew the value of strong walls and were probably wondering why this meeting had been called at night, so far from HeadQuarters.

Stopmouth wanted to know the same thing, but he had more urgent questions to answer. Where was Dharam himself? Where was the Talker?

And then, he got all of his answers at once. A light shone from the top of the ship, as bright, or brighter than the sun, and Dharam appeared up there from a door where he seemed to be floating.

"You see, my friends?" he cried. "You were wrong to bet against me. We have already uncovered some of the old technology of the Deserters. I know—only I!—where in the Roof to find one of their ships. It will whisk us away soon and we will leave this place to the Diggers and ... and our other enemies." He rambled on in this vein for some time, using terms and ideas that made little sense.

"They don't b-b-believe him," he said to Rockface.

"So, why are they listening, hey? They even clapped for him when he spoke about the other ship."

"They *w-want* to believe him. Because they hate us, but if he's wrong they have to become like us."

"Bah," said Rockface. "I will have Sodasi hit him with that sling of hers. She's a very lucky shot for a woman."

"She's a g-g-*good* shot," said Stopmouth. And she'd only improved since the death of her sister. "But if we k-kill him, they will only hate us forever ... But y-yes. We'll be using Sodasi's skills very soon ... "

They moved closer. There seemed to be no guards of any kind. Were these people suicidal? Only the Religious seemed to be worried about security, and they kept throwing nervous glances towards the hills. Stopmouth's small group of hunters—himself, Rockface, Sodasi and Vishwakarma—was able to get within a dozen strides of the wreckage without being seen. At that point, Sodasi, always quick to understand what Stopmouth wanted her

203

to do, stood up and let loose with a slingshot.

She was supposed to hit Dharam on the wrist of the hand holding the Talker. Instead, the stone cracked into the metal between his legs. She may have looked abashed, but Stopmouth didn't notice because in his shock at the attack, Dharam had dropped the Talker anyway and Stopmouth barrelled through the crowd fast enough that he was able to leap upon it just as it hit the mud and moss below.

Stopmouth was on his feet again instantly.

He didn't get very far, however. The Warden Ekta appeared out of nowhere and pointed a gun right at his face. "I can't let you have that, Chief," she said quietly. But in spite of her artificial strength, she had none of the great speed of a true Elite. She grunted as she felt the tip of Rockface's spear caress her neck.

"I like this," Rockface said, grinning. "Maybe Vishwakarma can marry this one and all three of us will have women who can fight, hey, Stopmouth?"

"Shoot them!" Dharam shouted from above. "Why is nobody shooting?"

"Lower your weapon, Ekta," said Stopmouth to the Warden. "I just want to speak to them. No flesh should be wasted over a few words."

There came another crack, and a man to Stopmouth's left fell over clutching his temple. The gun he had drawn fell from his hands into the muck and he lay there moaning.

"We have slingers out there watching you from the dark," said Stopmouth. "And Fourleggers."

"Fourleggers?" asked Rockface.

"Enough, Rockface!"

Ekta lowered her pistol at last and Stopmouth strode forward.

"Go away," a young man shouted at him. "Nobody wants you cannibals here!"

"I will go away," said the hunter. "Let me have my say and I'll leave." He fixed his stare on the man who had shouted at him. "And nobody else need get hurt."

They were still afraid enough to quieten down after that.

"So, you think you are safe. You trust this man above me. A man you must know is lying when he says he can save your lives."

"His story makes sense," said Ekta. "There *are* Deserter craft in the Roof. You have seen them yourself, I imagine. And while there's not enough fuel left to allow the Warship to take off, there's enough for the small craft we are building. Enough for a few pilots to get up there and bring one of those ships back here!"

Murmurs of agreement followed, and more than a few faces glittered with tears of hope. Stopmouth realised then the futility of his mission as he looked at these people. Even the Religious wanted to believe, even Kubar.

He imagined Sodasi crouching out there in the darkness with her sling, wondering now if she had made the right choice. For although in its last days the Roof had been a place of horror, it had been nothing but a long wedding feast when many of those around him had been born. There'd been food and comfort for everybody, with nobody to fight but themselves. Stopmouth could not hope to compete with such a dream. Strife was all he could offer them. A short life of terror, ending in a monster's belly.

Ekta must have seen it on his face. She held out her hand for the Talker.

Then, somebody laughed out in the darkness. A woman's voice. *Indrani's* voice. She strode into the gathering, her beauty extraordinary to his eyes. "Those ancient spacecraft will not work," she asserted. "Why else did that lying fool above us go to all the trouble of building the Warship if he could have *deserted* without one?"

"You were just as quick to run away," Dharam shouted from above.

"I was," said Indrani. "I *begged* for a place on that craft in order to save the life of my child." Her eyes glittered as her gaze swept the gathering. "So, ask yourselves this: why am I not begging for a place now?"

"Because you *want* to stay," said Dharam. "Among the

PEADAR Ó GUILÍN

cannibals. You have a taste for those foul practices that civilized people long ago abandoned. No wonder you came back here instead of letting us wait for Earth to rescue us."

Many nodded vigorously at his words, but Indrani had not finished speaking. "Fuel burns," she said. "That's the whole point of it, is it not? Do you really think our ancestors would have been stupid enough to hang spacecraft full of fuel above our public parks? And would there have even been any fuel left to the Deserters anyway after their long journeys through space?"

One of the older women in the crowd stood up. "Actually ... I'm an engineer."

"Sit down," Indrani told her, "Without the Roof to hold your memories, you're nothing."

"I'm not nothing," the woman replied. She kept her feet, her grey hair and the lines on her face lending her a strange unruffled dignity. "We have books here, remember? It's clumsy, I know. But still, I have learned some things for myself. Our Warship was only ever meant to orbit this planet while we slept and waited for ... well, never mind that. The point is, the Deserter ships are likely to have used a thing called nuclear technology ... "

Indrani interrupted her. "Whatever that is, it will still need some form of fuel."

"But we can get it!" said the engineer. "I have seen only hints in the books so far, but I'm pretty sure we can dig the fuel it needs right out of the ground!"

Indrani burst out laughing, her voice startling the older woman. "You are fools, every one of you if you think you can get craft that are hundreds of years old to live again. Look around you! I have no Roof, but I remember the Deserters had centuries of their cruel civilization behind them when they built those things. They had ... what do you call it? They had *industry*. They had our ancestors working for them like armies of slaves. If you are very lucky, it will take you years to get one of them down from the Roof and to get it working.

"But you don't have years, do you? Do you? Your lives ... your

206

lives are now measured in *days*."

"She's lying!" shouted Dharam. "Where's your courage? Take her down. Ekta!"

"I will hear her out," said the Warden. "She, at least, is no coward."

The two women exchanged a nod.

"The Diggers must cover 80% of the surface of the world by now," Indrani continued. "And the darkness of the Roof will only have helped them against whatever creatures remain to resist them. Here, only the rocky hills and the memory of how they were burnt out last time keep our enemies focused on easier prey. But already they are running short of food. That will force them to try us again very, very soon. And what will they find when they do?"

She looked around her, lingering on the Ship People who had never fought a day in their lives, before passing on to the miserable, unloved Religious with barely a hundred left among them who could raise a spear.

"We have better weapons than the savages," said Ekta. She waved her gun to show everybody what she meant.

"You can fight them," agreed Indrani. "But I have yet to hear any target practice. Not a single day of it. And do you know what that tells me? It tells me you don't have enough bullets for your guns. And that you don't know how to make any more of them. Tell me I'm wrong. Tell me, Ekta, and I'll leave you all in peace."

But the Warden looked away, unable to contradict her.

A few cries of fear and shock greeted these words. Stopmouth felt so proud to be married to her, although, it seemed strange she had turned up here to argue in favour of rescuing the Tribe. She would have had to leave Flamehair with Tarini to come out here tonight. And this after all that scowling she had done when they spoke of a rescue back in the Fourleggers' warehouse. Stopmouth had assumed then it was because she feared his brother might still be alive. Now, he didn't know what to think.

Indrani smiled grimly. "Only savages have any hope of keeping you alive long enough to grow more food. Only savages can win you the time to retrieve one of those useless Deserter craft so that Dharam and a dozen of his cronies can leave the rest of you behind again."

"Oh, rubbish," cried Dharam, "how could any of you believe that?"

He may have been surprised by the laughter that broke out amongst the crowd. They knew, of course they knew he wouldn't hesitate to leave them behind. They themselves, after all, had deserted the Roof in its hour of greatest need, and many of them felt terribly guilty about it now.

Stopmouth took this moment to step forward, holding the Talker high like a trophy. "My people are nearby," he shouted. "My people that I grew up with. They are trapped down the river from us on the great rock that rises above it there. I think that's why the Diggers haven't been pushing us here so much. My tribe have been taking all their fury and they have bought us time. But if we can bring them back here, they could keep us all alive. All of us. For tens of days, maybe, or even longer!

So, who will come with me?" His voice rose to a shout, without—thanks to the Talker—the slightest hint of a stutter. "Who will come for the Tribe?"

Nobody moved.

"Oh, they're useless!" cried Rockface. "But with all the Diggers down there, none of them would last a dozen breaths and—"

"Will nobody come with us?" Stopmouth asked again, his heart breaking.

"I will." It was Kubar, looking older than ever. He stood up, his back straight and his head high. "Twice, I owe you my life, Stopmouth. I have only repaid you with betrayal." Behind him his Religious friends stirred uncomfortably, although he had carefully avoided including them. "Stopmouth, you have always been truthful with me and loyal. When you ran off to the Roof, I begged to go with you, because I was ... because I still am, a coward.

"I will go with you, though it terrifies me. I will go with you and die today rather than live five more days in the service of the liar Dharam. The monster. The Deserter." He turned to the Religious behind him. "You know what Indrani said about the Diggers is true." And then, his gruff voice rose in what might have been song:

"Do not become a coward, because it does not befit you. Shake off this trivial weakness of your heart and get up for the battle!"

As he sang his voice grew stronger and the words seemed to have a special meaning to his people, for all at once they cried out in rage and leaped to their feet.

Stopmouth felt Ekta's breath right at his ear. "This is why Religion is so dangerous. A few magic words and they'll do just about anything."

"They might be saving your life," he said.

"Oh, I know. That's why I'm coming too."

"What about Dharam?"

"If he's right, then nobody here needs a Warden to protect them. Besides, somebody should keep an eye on you savages, right?"

209

25.
THE END OF THE TRIBE

They had burnt all the wood. The fires had gone out.

Whistlenose cried and grunted and spat and cursed. He and the Digger rolled down the side of the hill, locked together. It was stronger than him and barely reacted when he bit the wiry hide of its face—no surprise for a creature used to being consumed alive by its own young.

The pair had fetched up on an overhang above the *river* as other knots of human and beast fought around them with only embers to see by. He could feel his muscles weakening under its insistent claws, although he still lived because it seemed reluctant to damage him. No, its real weapon was a single grub that it tried to place on his cheek so that the thing could crawl into an eye or a nose or an ear.

One of the grubs had already made the mistake of pushing in between Whistlenose's teeth. *You feed me, not I you…*

The pressure increased, forcing a grunt out of the hunter. The Digger's breath came in rapid sighs, the sounds swallowed by the *river* below. He cried out, trying to get a foot underneath to launch both himself and his attacker into the water. The current ran rough here. He and his enemy would die quickly together if he could only pull back far enough.

But the Digger knew what he was trying to do and kept the old human pinned down, his right arm trembling, but bending too, the first hairy tendrils of the finger-sized grub tickling his cheek. With a cry, he allowed his arm to collapse all at once, using the strength of his enemy to squash the grub against his face. But more followed it, crawling down from the top of his scalp.

And then, the weight was gone altogether and the Digger tumbled silently into the churning foam below. "Get up!" shouted Fearsflyers. "Up, old man! Up the slope!"

He obeyed, not sure what was happening. There was fire all around them. Fire everywhere and the Diggers fleeing before it. "How ... ?" he asked. "The wood is all used up! I saw it!"

Fearsflyers was too tired, too *sad* to answer. They had fought all night, and Whistlenose knew that it was night because in the distance they had seen the magical, longed-for daylight disappear, only to return again now, too far away to help them; too beautiful for words.

In that time, they had piled enemy bodies up three high, while their own losses had all been taken alive—dragged away before they could be rescued, or screaming as grubs found a path into their heads.

And yet, this supposed final assault had been beaten off and, at the top of the hill, fires burned everywhere once more. Fires. "Where did the wood come from?" he asked Fearsflyers again. Other hunters were staggering back to safety now, too.

The young man would not answer him. He was weeping. Everybody was weeping. The Diggers' reluctance to kill meant that maybe eight hundred people still survived, less than a third of them hunters. None looked happy to be alive.

There was something strange about the wood that had saved them, that burned so merrily. Whistlenose's eyes couldn't quite make out what was wrong with it, but then, with a spasm of pain that snapped through his whole body, he understood. Tallies. Tally sticks.

"No!" he cried. "No!" and he too was weeping. He found Ashsweeper and Nighttracker as soon as he could. He hugged them hard enough to hurt.

"I'm glad you did not end up in the fields, husband," Ashsweeper said. "We'll have one last feast," she added. "Then ... then the boy will sleep."

All around them, other parents had the same idea. Digger and human flesh were both abundant. Children would sleep when they were full and wouldn't feel a thing. Whistlenose was glad of that, but inside him was nothing but emptiness. The burning Tallies had done that to him.

He realised now, that nothing had been real: not the voices of the Ancestors speaking to the Chief; nor the Ancestors themselves. There was no future and no past. Even his flesh would go to waste in the end, for the Diggers seemed to have no use for corpses. And that didn't matter either. It had never mattered.

Off to his right, the Chief sat with what remained of his own family, while Aagam crouched by the side, understanding little or nothing.

"You're a liar," Mossheart kept saying to the Chief. "We were better off where we were. These people should throw you to the Diggers right now." Their daughter sobbed, not understanding why they fought.

At the edge of the light, the Diggers had gathered once more in a silent mass. These little fires shouldn't have been able to hold them back, but they must have been caught off guard when the cowardly Chief had given the order to burn the Tribe's history. The creatures could wait another tenth or two, and after that the humans would be no more.

Two days travel away, the Roof glowed a strange orange colour as the morning there came into its full strength. "You are so cruel," Whistlenose muttered to his non-existent Ancestors. "To bring us this close ... "

"Are we going to win?"

Nighttracker had come to sit by him. His little body trembled, but he held a spear firmly in his hands.

"Of course we are, hunter! One more sleep, my fine boy, and we'll push the last of them away. But it won't work, you understand

212

me? It won't work if you don't sleep."

"I don't understand, dada..."

"It's what the Ancestors want. Good children sleep when they're told. Especially the ones with names! The ones who will be heroes some day." Whistlenose's voice held steady; his eyes stayed mostly dry throughout. He could lie now as well as anyone because nothing was real and all would be quiet soon enough and forever.

Away from the Chief, another group of hunters had stood up, gathering their spears and knives. Fearsflyers stood amongst them, making stabbing gestures down towards the Diggers. "We need to go," he was saying, "while there is still firelight to see by." That lot did not care, it seemed, if they were planted in agony for tens of days before death found them. They wanted to go down fighting rather than take their own lives.

Whistlenose had had enough of that, however, and of pain too. He hugged his child and gently, gently moved his free hand up towards the boy's neck. How to do it quickest so there would be the least pain?

He felt a hand on his shoulder. Wallbreaker crouched down beside him. "I know how to do it," he said.

"What? What are you talking about?" Why had the man interrupted? The man who had caused all of this.

"Remember when we fell into the tunnel with my daughter and Treeneck? And the Diggers covered up the Talker with their bodies?"

"I remember. What does it matter now?" Whistlenose just wanted to get on with killing his son before the Diggers came back. At the same time, he grasped at any excuse to delay this awful task.

"And remember how they didn't attack me after a while? I was killing and killing them and it was like they couldn't even see me? Well... I know now. I know how I did it. We could defeat the Diggers!"

"Now? We could defeat them now?" Hope surged in Whistlenose's heart.

"Well ... no ... I don't suppose we could do it *now*."

"Then why are you telling me this?" Whistlenose could hear the sob in his own voice and could feel his shoulders tense up to push the Chief away or to stab him or to pluck out the man's hated eyes.

But just then, a searing blue light exploded on the far side of the hill. It was brighter than anything Whistlenose had ever seen. Brighter than the Roof itself! A great boiling mass of Diggers was suddenly revealed. More of the creatures than could ever have been imagined, pushing back against each other, climbing one atop the other, desperate, desperate, to escape.

They surged around the base of the slope, trampling their comrades, even diving into the river to be swept away, away from that awful blue light.

"It's a Talker!" shouted Aagam in perfect human, "a Talker!"

Not all of the Diggers got away fast enough. People were attacking them from behind. *Humans!* Humans! And that was impossible, because Whistlenose didn't recognise a single one of them!

"The Ancestors!" somebody cried, although the attackers looked like Aagam, like Indrani.

They slaughtered the enemy in great numbers with the strangest hunting style Whistlenose had ever seen. They swarmed about in little packs. Not all of them carried spears. They had women amongst their numbers, often as slingers or diving in close with knives. Each pack worked together, protecting each other as some of the Diggers, trapped against a wall of their own species, fought back.

"Let's go and meet them!" shouted Fearsflyers.

Whistlenose surged to his feet. "Go back to your mother, Nighttracker. I need you to protect her with your spear!"

He and the other men ran pell-mell down the slope to crash against the panicked enemy. He had lost his fear of capture, of being buried. He brushed grubs from his face and stabbed all around him.

The enemy wished only to flee, but more than one hunter felt their claws in his belly or across his throat. Several screamed and disappeared as tunnels opened at their feet or the ancient streets collapsed beneath them.

Soon, however, only a thin line of stubborn Diggers separated the Tribe from its rescuers. At the head of the newcomers fought a pale-skinned hero. His speed with spear and knife; his fierce, flashing eyes and sleek muscles, all showed him to be an Ancestor reborn. There could be no other explanation. Why he had been born to these foreigners and not the Tribe from ManWays, made no sense to Whistlenose, but in that moment, he did not care. Directly behind the great hunter, a woman, as powerfully built as any man and wearing strange clothing, held the Talker high above her head. A few heartbeats later and the hero faced him over the body of the last Digger.

"You are Whistlenose?"

"You ... you recognise me?"

"Of course! Don't you recognize me?"

"I ... " Was this John Spearmaker? The Traveller?

"Never mind," the stranger said. "We have to hurry. We have to get you all out of here." The hero strode past, while the powerful woman with the Talker tried to follow, but then gave up.

"I'm not walking on that," she said.

"On what?" asked Whistlenose. Her face was perhaps the most beautiful he had ever seen, but to his eyes, it sat strangely on such a large frame.

"On *them*!" She indicated the Digger corpses that had piled up as far as her knees. She shuddered, although she had been killing the creatures herself until moments earlier. "I'll wait here until you all come down again. But tell him to hurry up. We'll need to get back while it's still light beyond the hills."

"All right," he said. "I'll ... I'll tell them."

All along the lines, people were looking at each other, the light-skinned members of the Tribe and their darker saviours.

"Can I see?" Fearsflyers said to another young man. "Can I see your spear? Why did you make it that way?"

Whistlenose left them to it and followed the hero back up the

215

hill, racking his memory for where he had seen the man before. He would never have forgotten such a skilled hunter, surely. The Tribe would have songs about such a man and fathers would have fought each other trying to marry their daughters off to him. The blue light of the Talker stayed at the bottom of the hill and the old man saw the newcomer pause at one of the fires, his brave face in a frown.

"T-t-tallies? Are those t-t-talley sticks?"

"By the Ancestors! You're Stopmouth!"

The young man grinned. "Who else would I be? We have R-rockface too, you know?"

"Rockface? That madman is still alive?"

The grin widened. "He's tried hard enough to get himself k-k-killed, but still has a way to go."

"Of course, he does. He would!"

Stopmouth's voice turned to a whisper. "And my b-b-b ... And m-m-m ... "

"Your brother?"

A nod. Whistlenose should have remembered that the young hunter had been condemned as a traitor. His own tally stick had been snapped in two in Centre Square. Surely that would all have to be forgiven now.

"The Chief is just up a bit farther."

People had been wandering down the hill to look in wonder at the newcomer, mostly children and women who had not taken part in the last fight. Not one of them recognised him any more than Whistlenose had. As if the Ancestors had slipped a mask over his face.

"You're supposed to be dead." There was no fooling Mossheart. She had come to the front of the group.

The young hunter nodded, still reluctant to speak, but he met her gaze in a way he would never have done before he had left. He'd been so shy, Whistlenose remembered. And then his handsome mouth set itself into a hard line. Somebody else had pushed his way forward.

"Where is my wife?" asked Wallbreaker.

The two brothers looked so alike now and their faces seemed to ripple under the weight of powerful emotions. Hatred, love, violence and fear. The crowd stepped back to form a circle, as though they might be caught between falling buildings.

"She was mine, Stopmouth. And you stole her from me. And a Talker, the one you have below! You stole that too when we might have saved ourselves with it. Instead, you use what is ours, what belongs to the Tribe, to act the hero. We lost ... we lost *everything* because of that.

"Well, you can give it back to us," he continued. "We don't need your rescue. Give it back and we will drive the Diggers away all by ourselves."

It was true, Whistlenose realised! Surely no strangers had been needed to save the Tribe if only the extra Talker had not been stolen before! "Grab him," said Wallbreaker. "While his puny hunters are all down at the bottom of the slope. We can ransom him for it. It belongs to all of us."

Somebody bowled Whistlenose aside and swept Stopmouth's feet from underneath him. A few other hunters piled on top. The young man roared and threw them off again as though they were dried twigs, but others piled in, pinning him to the ground, his face against the dirt.

Stopmouth struggled to speak. Finally, he managed: "W-w-we came for y-you. C-c-came f-f-for T-t-tribe."

"Then you won't mind returning the Tribe's property."

"W-w-wouldn't w-w-work. Talker f-f-feeds on d-daylight. No d-d-days here. It's already h-h-hungry."

People glanced nervously down the hill. Sure enough, the blue light of the Talker did not seem as strong as it had before. Whistlenose could feel everybody growing more tense around him.

"You don't know what you're talking about, brother," Wallbreaker said. "You barely knew how to swallow soup until I showed you! Now. What about the other thing? My wife? Where is my wife?"

"*Stopmouth's* wife is here. Let me to pass."

217

And so, Indrani had arrived. Stopmouth seemed as surprised as anybody else to see her. "G-go b-b-back!" he cried. "G-go back!" He bucked harder than before, upsetting the hunters on top of him.

Indrani looked as beautiful as ever, maybe more so, as she had left her girlhood behind her and wore comfortably the hides of exotic creatures. Everybody made space, as they would have for Speareye, or one of the great Chiefs of the past.

She faced her ex-husband, nothing in her fist but a black stone, watching him as he drank in the sight of her.

"You came back to me."

"I am here to kill you," she said. Her face betrayed absolutely no emotion.

"N-no!" said Stopmouth, but Wallbreaker laughed.

"Oh, yes! I remember those high kicks of yours and how some of the older men lost a few teeth over them. What about you, Whistlenose? Were you one?"

"I never lost a tooth to her, no." It had hurt, though, he remembered that, when they had first attempted to catch her.

"Well, wife. You tried your tricks on me, remember? But I was faster. I'm famous for it. You can't beat me. You can't touch me. And—"

She raised the black stone. A loud *bang* sounded and everybody jumped, looking around for fear of a new attack. Wallbreaker was on the ground, there was blood everywhere, spilling from his shoulder. Mossheart was screaming.

A hunter ran towards Indrani, but she pointed the black stone at him, until he backed away from her. Then, she was right beside the Chief, pressing the strange object up against his skull, while Mossheart screamed and everybody fell back and away from her.

"What do you say now?" she asked. "What do you say? You will to hurt no person again."

"Wait!" he cried. "You don't understand. The Tribe needs me! I know how to defeat the Diggers! I have a way to defeat them!"

"You say anything to live. You lie."

Whistlenose surprised himself by speaking up for the Chief when none of the younger men would. They all wore expressions of shock. "Wallbreaker does have a way out. He told me so himself just before the last attack. There was no point in a lie. We thought we were all going to die."

Indrani's face showed some confusion and the black stone might have moved a little away from the Chief's head and then, Stopmouth came forward, having pulled free of his captors. "He's r-r-right l-l-love. If anybody could think of a w-w-way to defeat the D-Diggers..."

"*You* could think a way, Stopmouth!" she said. "*You* could. He is nothing, no better than ... *Pah!*"

"But I *haven't* thought of anything, l-love. We can use the T-Talker to drive them back for a while, b-but they're not stupid. They will l-learn to overcome it. Think of the Tribe. Think of F-F-Flamehair."

His last words were a mistake. All the confusion left her face at once. The black stone returned to the Chief's skull and a loud *click* sounded. Whatever she was trying to do, hadn't worked this time, but Wallbreaker jerked suddenly and Whistlenose might have thought he had died if he hadn't screamed out, "Ancestors save me!"

Then, Stopmouth was beside Indrani, pulling her away from the Chief and into an embrace. She shouted at him, kneed him in the groin so that he ended up at her feet.

"The Tribe," she spat. "The Tribe! Stopmouth, you said I am your Tribe now! When all these tried to kill us. You said it!" She threw the black stone into the dirt next to his face so that he winced. And then, she was gone back down the slope, with nobody thinking to stop her.

Stopmouth staggered to his feet, struggling to breathe.

"I want her back," said Wallbreaker. "She's mine."

Stopmouth smiled through his pain. "You have w-wet yourself in t-t-terror of her, brother."

It was true. Enough firelight remained to see the glistening stain in the Chief's leg and Whistlenose, who thought he could feel no more of anything, felt shame on the Chief's behalf.

Stopmouth, despite his youth and a lack of scarring, looked more a Chief than his brother now. The two stood together and for what must have been the first time in their lives, the younger brother looked down on the older. He turned to the crowd.

"Follow me to the *river*," he said. "There is a way to s-safety, but you must t-trust me."

"We will do what you say," Wallbreaker agreed. He recovered himself long enough to address those around him. "The Ancestors have kept us safe," was all he said. He was bleeding from his shoulder and it seemed he might faint at any moment. But he managed to lead his family to join the crowd following after Stopmouth.

The next tenth brought its own share of terrors to everybody. Stopmouth's strange followers moved the Tribe towards the banks of the rushing water of the *river*. Their hunting signs were familiar, but somehow more elaborate than those used back in ManWays. The Talker still provided some light, but it was much dimmer than it had been and everybody fretted that the Diggers would return when inevitably it died.

But what followed scared Whistlenose even more.

He was left on the bank, staring into the blackness for a return of the enemy, while his family were set whimpering onto sheets of some strange material that floated on the river. Nighttracker called out to him as the flimsy craft fell away with the current, and men and women on board beat frantically at the water with pieces of wood.

He winced as a hand clamped over his shoulder.

"They'll g-g-get across, Whistlenose. We m-managed it on the w-way here. And this is a calm spot."

"Aren't there Diggers on the other side?"

"Oh yes. But too r-r-rocky for f-fields. I h-hope they w-won't know we were there until we have returned home safely."

The numbers of hunters around Whistlenose dwindled, until, eventually, he and Stopmouth along with a dozen other men abandoned the empty bank of the river for a *raft* of their own. It felt like a living thing beneath him, yawing and bucking to throw them all into the deadly water. They spun around more than once.

On the last occasion, he saw, in the pitiful firelight they had left behind, a single Digger staring after them.

26.
BRINGING THEM HOME

Stopmouth felt exhausted. He desperately wanted to talk to Indrani. Something had happened between them back there by the ruined bridge when he'd tried to stop her from killing Wallbreaker.

He hadn't even known she'd come along as part of the raid, or that she had borrowed a gun from Ekta. But it was obvious to him now, why she had changed her mind about rescuing his old Tribe and why she had argued for their return. She just wanted to remove the thorn from her heart that Wallbreaker had put there. She needed it, almost more—he feared—than she needed to live. And Stopmouth, her own husband, who was supposed to love her, had got in her way.

He wanted to see her, to explain himself better ... to explain why Wallbreaker had to live.

But there was no time for that. First, the Tribe had to be ferried across the river. Then, on the far side, they sneaked through ruins on a route that would keep them as far from the nearest Digger fields as possible. Finally, they would cross the river one last time, back to the relative safety of HeadQuarters.

The journey took two whole days with the Talker barely strong enough for a gentle glow. That didn't seem to bother Stopmouth's old Tribe, however. They seemed to have lost their fear of the dark. Every one of them appeared strange to him now:

purified; with a feverish light in their eyes to match that of some of the Religious fanatics he had met in the Roof.

Even stranger was the way they argued over who should be allowed to carry his wounded brother around, as though their Chief were a pregnant woman or the skull of an Ancestor! What had he done to deserve it, after all? During the fighting, Wallbreaker's spear had stayed dry as old bones. The supposed Chief had hidden at the top of the slope where the bridge hung out over the river. He hadn't even come up with a plan! Instead, he had been rescued in a way that nobody could have predicted, and at the end of it all, a woman who had once humiliated him had done so again. Only a miracle had spared his life.

But Stopmouth received his own share of love, too. The Tribe welcomed him back, touching his arms, marvelling at the new muscle. "That brother of yours must have known you'd come for us. How clever of him to send you away all that time ago, waiting for this day."

"What? I don't ... "

"Oh, I suppose it is the Ancestors we should really be thanking. They speak to him. He's never wrong."

Stopmouth shook his head, his confusion greater than ever.

The two tribes could not converse except in the presence of the Talker. Even hand signals created problems, because the signs of the New Tribe had evolved beyond anything the Old Tribe had ever needed. The subtle differences between the two systems only deepened the confusion.

When finally everybody had been brought safely to the vicinity of HeadQuarters, Indrani ran back alone towards the Fourlegger Warehouse. Stopmouth wanted to follow her at once, but some of his brother's men appeared around him. These were little more than boys, being about a thousand days younger than he was. But they carried themselves as bravely as any hunter with a house full of trophies.

"He wants to speak to you," said one of them, whose whole left side looked as though it had been scorched not too long ago.

Stopmouth swallowed, containing a sudden surge of anger.

"Good. I want to talk to him."

Wallbreaker lay alone by the bank of the river where the rushing water would hide their words from anybody else. Always clever, even now.

This time, you're in my territory.

But the words would not come to him. His brother looked exhausted and thin. The muscles of his shoulders and arms seemed too soft for a grown hunter and his whole body lay bent over to the right, as though trying to escape the seeping hole Indrani had made in his left shoulder.

"So, here we are again, brother," Wallbreaker said.

"Tell me the plan," said Stopmouth, not trusting himself with anything less practical. His every word had to fight its way free of clenched jaws and grinding teeth. "You said you knew how to defeat the Diggers. Can you?" He wanted to hit this man. To embrace him. To drown him in the river so that he would never see his face again. Poor Indrani!

Wallbreaker grinned. "Amazing how the Talker has fixed that tongue of yours, isn't it, Stopmouth? Well, that's too bad. I have to take it back now."

"You'll get nothing more from me, brother." One thing the Talker couldn't hide was the catch in his voice.

"On the contrary, I am the one who gave you everything and I'll have all of it again soon. That spear you use so well? I taught you those skills after Father had given up his flesh for the rest of us. I was the one who protected you from the bullies. It was I who spoke up for you back when many were thinking of not naming you. I protected you when your legs were broken. And even after mother Volunteered to save you, it was me and my hunting tricks that kept you from the pot. A thousand times you would be dead, Stopmouth. And the Tribe would be dead a thousand times too if it wasn't for me, with the Ancestors looking down on nothing and nobody for ever and ever." These words were true. Every one of them.

"But my kindness to you," Wallbreaker continued, his voice

thick, "all counted for nothing the first time an unfaithful woman looked over her shoulder at you."

Stopmouth stepped closer. His whole body thrummed with emotions he couldn't quite identify. He swallowed painfully and tightened his lips into a line. Wallbreaker ignored the potential threat and kept talking. "And here you stand now, young and healthy, and so full of your own importance as to think you are a Chief! Do you really think you could lead our people?"

"I don't 'think,' Wallbreaker. I *am* Chief. Here at least." Now was not the time to discuss the situation with Dharam. "*I* have my own people and you have yours ... "

Wallbreaker laughed, despite the pain in his shoulder. "Are there two tribes of Bloodskins? Two tribes of Armourbacks? Of course not! Nowhere in the world do you see two Chiefs. Such a thing cannot be and you know it as well as I do. My people are the stronger. That much is already obvious. We will dominate your dark-skinned weaklings, who probably aren't even human anyway. The Tribe would never follow you."

"Why not? I rescued them, the Tribe. My *weaklings* rescued them."

"No, Stopmouth, you didn't. That was all my doing."

"That doesn't make any s—"

"The Ancestors work through me, brother. To save humanity. That's the way it's always been. I summoned you and you came. That's how my magic works. I am the Chief, the only Chief, for that very reason."

Stopmouth growled at this madness. "Would the Ancestors save you if I threw you into the river? Can you swim?"

Wallbreaker lowered his head, breathing hard, and when he looked up, the sight of tears in his eyes astonished the younger man. "You wouldn't hurt me, Stopmouth. After all that has happened, we still love each other."

"You tried to have me killed! You had my Tally broken!"

"Yes. Of course I did. I have always done what was necessary. Whereas you, poor Stopmouth, you were never strong enough

225

for that kind of thing. You always needed me."

"All I need from you, brother, is the plan."

"Oh, you need it, do you?"

"It's not for me. It's for the Tribe."

"Not for you, you say? So, I suppose you won't get to benefit from it, will you, Stopmouth? Living with *my* wife and thinking to steal *my* people from me too?"

Stopmouth swallowed back his fury as best he could. "We can argue about these things some other time, Wallbreaker. None of it will matter if the Diggers plant us all. The Tribe *must* live. The Tribe is all there is after we are forgotten."

"It's not true that we are forgotten, brother, not true at all. There are always heroes. The Traveller. Treatymaker. John Spearmaker. I was born to be one of those."

"You're no Traveller!"

"Why not?" There was anger in Wallbreaker's voice now too. "I've achieved far more than he ever did. I brought an entire people to the far side of the world." He paused, panting with the pain from his wound. "You see, Stopmouth … that thing about the Tribe being more important than any one of us? The thing that's been spooned into us so often it comes out in our sweat? Well, I've learned something. Every few generations special individuals appear, individuals that can't just be replaced."

"Like you?"

"Why not? There would be no Tribe without me. I am *necessary*, and I found that out the day I was captured by the Armourbacks. I wanted to live so badly. And not for the Tribe, but for me. For me! Does that make me a monster?"

"Yes," said Stopmouth.

"I knew you'd say that. It's what any hunter would have to say or be Volunteered on the spot. But I am more than a hunter. More than marrow and flesh and a spear. That's what I learned that day. I knew I had so much to give and ever since, I've proved it again and again. And I will do so one more time with this new plan of mine: the plan that will save us all in the end."

"So, why not just tell me?"

"Oh, I will tell you, Stopmouth. I'll do that. But I need something from you in exchange."

"You're not getting Indrani," said Stopmouth. "Even if she was mine to give. You'll never touch a hair on her head."

"I don't want her." Wallbreaker spoke the words as casually as a wounded man could. "I hear there are lots of women here now. Dark-skinned women that make Indrani look *rancid*. Ha! I see you clench your fist, brother! You are angry at me, but still you will not push me into the river because you know you need me. Good. Good. Let's put you to the test then. The Tribe is what's important to you, yes?"

"Of course."

"Good. My foolish, sweet brother. Listen, Stopmouth. You must never be Chief. I love you. I couldn't hurt you. But your betrayal has been too much. I can't stand the sight of you or the looks people give you despite what you did to me. So, here are the rules. I won't touch Indrani, or Volunteer her or your child. You have my word on that. I swear it on the memory of our mother." He locked eyes with his brother. "Your family will live."

"But ... " Stopmouth took a deep breath. "But I will not."

"You *must* not, Stopmouth. I can whistle now and those men will come here and kill you because the Ancestors, through me, have told them to do so. Then, they will hunt down your Indrani and anybody else here you call a friend. Or, or, you can choose to help me in my plan. Help save the Tribe forever. And then ... then you must disappear."

"But ... but I could stay out of your sight, Wallbreaker, I could—"

"I will mourn you, Stopmouth, you know I will. All will be forgiven when you're gone. But first, you will help me. Help me take control and make my plan work. Then ... then you will find some way to leave and all your ... your friends will be safe. I promise it."

Kill him, a voice said in Stopmouth's head. Kill him. His

fingers gripped hard at the haft of the knife on his belt. *Why should I be the Volunteer? He's the monster! The coward!*

"Tell me the plan," he said at last, as numbness replaced his earlier anger. "Tell me the plan and if it's good enough, I... I will agree to disappear. As you asked."

27.

HUMANS

Whistlenose would never get used to the *sun*—all the world's light concentrated into a single point that was powerful enough to blind anyone who tried to swap stares with it. Other things made little sense either: like the two thousand men and women who would not hunt and who hated hunters. What contemptible cowards! They had their own horrible food and claimed that more of it would grow magically up out of the ground. These were the Ship People: terrified of real humans; waving the black stones, the *guns*, at any hunter who came too close.

Then, there were Stopmouth's allies, who lived in the company of beasts, speaking to them with their hands. But while Stopmouth commanded this group, a single meeting with Wallbreaker by the *river* had convinced him to accept orders from the Chief again. "It's w-what the Ancestors w-want," he would mumble to anybody who asked him, although he would never meet their eyes.

The Talker too, he had handed over ...

In spite of this surrender, the three Tribes of humans kept to themselves until one morning four days after the rescue, when terrible cracking sounds like the noise of shattering bones were heard from the fields of the Ship People. A great plume of dust rose up into the air and Whistlenose found himself running over there along with Stopmouth, struggling to keep up with the younger man.

They arrived in time to see dozens of dead Diggers lying twisted in the dirt. They had attacked by day, probably in an effort to catch so many people out in the open at their strange work. However, without the Talker present, it was difficult to figure out the details.

Perfectly healthy people were screaming and running around the lips of pits. Whistlenose guessed that while the first group of Diggers had attacked in the open, a second wave must have come up from below.

Now, a sweating, wild-eyed man jumped into one of the holes, clutching a gun. A grey-haired woman tried to follow, while others fought to restrain her. Perhaps these people were not as cowardly as Whistlenose had assumed!

Whistlenose caught up to Stopmouth. "Those guns..." he was panting, but at least his nostrils no longer embarrassed him by squeaking with every breath. "He waved at the enemy corpses. "The Diggers paid dearly for this raid. I'd say they lost at least as many as they captured."

"Yes. B-but they made the Ship People use up all those b-b-bullets. The ... the stones that they sling out."

"So? Stones are everywhere!"

"Not these ones. B-bullets have to be m-made and either the Ship People d-don't know how, or it's t-too difficult away from the R-roof."

The grey haired woman who had tried to jump into the pit, pulled herself free and ran over to Stopmouth babbling and babbling at him, her face streaked with tears. She made one of the strange hunting signs that seemed to be spreading everywhere. "I will," he told her, although he couldn't have known what she was saying. "I'll g-get them back for you if I can."

But others dragged her away again and the broken-armed leader of this group, a man called Dharam, arrived in the company of a large group of people with guns. He shouted and shouted until every gun in the area turned to point in the direction of the two hunters.

"T-time to leave," Stopmouth muttered. "Where is my brother? I need to see him."

Wallbreaker was working on some new weapons of his own when they arrived. He had wrapped a sling around the shaft of a spear, and now Browncrack tried to throw it while keeping hold of one end of the cord. It caught on his hand and hit the ground no more than a short jump away. A group of watching hunters laughed.

"We'll get it right," Wallbreaker said, grinning as much as anyone. "First one to throw the length of the camp will get his pick of the Ship Brides after the Diggers are gone."

The words made Stopmouth angry for some reason. "You will give women out now like prizes? Without even asking their fathers?"

A hard stare from the Chief, however, silenced him at once. Stopmouth even lowered his head in respect. "Brother..." he said, "I'm sorry. I'm sorry. Chief. I'm upset because the Diggers have struck the Ship People at their farm. They may have carried away a hundred of them, maybe two hundred. I can't tell without the Talker. We need to raid the Diggers to get those people back. If they stay planted in the ground too long, we won't be able to wake them up at all."

The Chief grinned. "A hundred or two hundred, you say, Stopmouth? But they hate us. Remind me again why we should risk our hunters to save them?"

"We need them. When you finally defeat the Diggers there'll be nothing left to eat but all that... *lentils* and *beans*. Only they know how to grow food and we'll die without them."

"Oh, we need *some* of them, of course, Stopmouth. But what we *don't* need are a people more numerous than we are. Especially a people armed with those gun things. Let them waste their weapons on the Diggers. Let them lose a few hundred and they'll be over here in no time begging us for protection. Right Aagam? That's what they'll do?"

"Of course, Chief," said the foreigner.

"There's one favour we will do for them, however," said Wallbreaker. "We'll tidy away those Digger corpses and have a nice feast for ourselves." Everybody cheered except Stopmouth.

"They're strange," said the younger brother now. "And you're right that they hate us. But this is our chance to end all of that, don't you see? This is our chance to become one people, when they see us give our flesh to spare theirs."

"They are not Tribe," said the Chief.

"But they're human, right? Men and women are suffering," he waved an arm, "out there somewhere. If we can get to them quickly ... "

Wallbreaker shook his head. "Of course I value their knowledge and their flesh. But we'll be getting all of that anyway when they come crying to us for help. For now, I say the Tribe, the *real* Tribe, has suffered enough. I will not waste a single hunter on them."

Stopmouth protested a few more times. He even shamed himself by going down on his knees. The Chief seemed to like that and laughed at him along with the young men of the Flesh Council.

Whistlenose didn't join in. He did not like to see anybody humiliated, and when the young man stormed off, he followed along after.

Once again, he found the Chief's brother too fast for him and he had to stop once, leaning against a building when his sore leg felt like a sharp stone had been hammered through it. The pain passed quickly, but when next he saw his quarry, Stopmouth was a tiny figure, running alone out past the ruins of the Warship. *Why do you bother, boy?* But Whistlenose's curiosity about the young man was stronger than the pain and he pushed on.

Their route took them away from the river and across the now empty fields where tiny green stalks ran in rows towards the hills. Bizarrely, Stopmouth's footprints avoided the little plants, sticking awkwardly to the lowered spaces between. This might be what gave the older man a chance to catch up in the end. By that time, he had reached the exits to the tunnels the Diggers must have used on returning from their attack, and the ground had grown rocky once more.

Stopmouth was waiting at the top of the first hill—a baby

compared to the fully grown slopes that lay beyond it. The light of the sun struggled to reach this far, as the hole in the Roof above them had come to a jagged end.

Whistlenose was gasping for breath. He leaned on his spear and watched the horrible sight below. There was a dip between the smaller hill they stood on and the greater one behind it, with rich deep soil down at the bottom.

And right there, without fear of counterattack, a Digger swarm was planting a hundred humans in rows every bit as neat as those back at the farm. Those who had yet to be buried writhed in agony, their moans loud enough to be heard by the two men.

"They're d-doing it on p-purpose," said Stopmouth.

"Of course they are! Burying people is what Diggers do!"

"N-no. I m-m-mean they're planting humans deliberately close to where we live. They expect a rescue. They w-want it. And look!" He pointed at his feet and for a moment, Whistlenose had no idea what was supposed to be wrong with them. But then he understood. A line of shadow lay there, right along the top of the hill. The dip would never experience a light stronger than that of the murky dusk down there now. The Diggers would be able to fight there unimpeded.

A trap then. Either the humans must abandon their people to feed the enemy, or they must attempt the expected rescue. Either way the Diggers won.

"You're right, Stopmouth. They're not even trying to chase us away." Whistlenose shook his head sadly. "Come on, son. I'm sorry, but those Roof people are lost to us now." Wallbreaker would be happy with that. He wanted the Ship People helpless. He wanted them on their knees begging him to save them.

But Stopmouth refused to move. "Do they look h-human to you, Whistlenose?"

"I suppose ... I don't know. The only Roofman I know well, I want to kill. Aagam, he's called. He's a real monster, that one. He doesn't think like a human should."

"There are good ones and b-bad ones," agreed Stopmouth.

233

"I've hated some of them too. Most of them sometimes. And they do think differently, but that's a good thing, isn't it? A hand isn't a f-foot, but I need them both to hunt."

"I … I don't know," said Whistlenose. "We really shouldn't stay here where the Diggers can see us."

"And listen to their p-pain! That sounds human, doesn't it?"

Of course it did.

Stopmouth allowed himself to be turned around, but despite Whistlenose's attempts to hurry him away from danger at their backs, the young hunter lingered near the top of the slope. He was deep in thought and that expression made him look so much like his brother.

In the distance, the river glittered. The plain glittered too where metal fragments of the Roof had fallen the day Indrani had broken through. Beyond that, lay the Warship and the abandoned farm that ended where the first ruined streets began.

"Stopmouth, we can't stay here if we want to see our wives again."

"I'm n-not sure mine w-wouldn't be happier that way."

"We all have troubles at home, sometimes, we—"

"Oh!"

"What? Stopmouth? What is it?"

"She *is* c-c-clever. My wife." And with that, Stopmouth surprised Whistlenose by breaking into a smile as handsome as any his brother might have managed. And then, he started running—leaping down the slope like a Hopper, saving himself from accident only with the shaft of his spear. The older man cursed and tried to follow, but he had lost Stopmouth by the time they got back to the streets.

28.
THE DIP

Stopmouth wasn't sure if his brother had deliberately sent Whistlenose to keep an eye on him, but he made sure to lose the man now. He wanted to speak to Indrani alone.

That would be hard. As the earth slapped against the soles of his feet and ruined buildings sped past him, he wondered at how he had managed to lose his wife's love all over again. She glared at him all the time these days when she even bothered to acknowledge his presence. She refused to sleep near him or talk to him. Except in front of Flamehair, who remained as cheerful as ever. The little thing had no idea who Wallbreaker was, but whenever Stopmouth walked into a room where she rolled around, she would smile and point in his direction, raising her arms until he had no choice but to lift her up. She liked to see everything from an adult's viewpoint and she ordered him around by pointing from one distraction to the next.

He lifted her now, while her mother pretended to be unaware that anybody had entered the room at all. They were in the Fourleggers' warehouse. The children were off skinning Digger corpses or causing trouble. Rockface, Sodasi and the Religious were nowhere to be seen.

Stopmouth jiggled Flamehair and let her try to catch the shining dust motes in her pudgy fingers. But his eyes were focused on his wife's back.

"Indrani. I need your h-help." She failed to respond. She was pounding an unusual black type of moss found near the river. The stuff had no use that he could think of. "Indrani? The Diggers took more than a hundred of the Ship People today. Wallbreaker doesn't want them back, but I know how we could save them. Will you help?"

She paused and he could see she was unsure. "Indrani ... love ... I know you can speak to some of them, the Ship People, I mean. Wallbreaker won't give me the Talker for this, but if you could explain my plan ... "

"To Dharam?"

"Well, no. He w-won't like it either. Find somebody else. Please."

She sighed. "So, neither of them want the rescue to happen? All right, then. Good." Still she would not look at him. She hadn't even spoken his name. But she would help and that was enough for now.

Dharam had been furious when he heard about the plan, but the anger and fear among his people had been too much for him to control. And so, early the next day, Stopmouth and the Warden, Ekta, led a full three hundred of the Ship People, as well as the remaining one hundred Religious hunters, over the top of the small hill to where they could look down into the dip.

Stopmouth heard the groans even before they had crested the rise. Then, the smell hit him, the usual stench that told him the Diggers had moved in below: that stomach roiling mix of excrement and vomit, concentrated here between the hills.

He was reminded too of how dangerous the situation was.

"This is great," said Rockface, only increasing Stopmouth's misgivings.

"Is it? The Diggers w-want us to d-do this." They would love for a good proportion of the remaining humans to waste themselves foolishly.

To either side of the hunters, other people jostled for a view,

Religious and Secular alike. Even Yama, who worked for Dharam now, was here to keep an eye on them, although Stopmouth knew the boy wouldn't be able to resist taking part.

Nearby, Ekta was talking rapidly to somebody in her own language. She had arranged for people who could understand each other to coordinate everything. Right now, she was probably ordering them to extinguish their torches, for the sun was already on its way.

Everybody looked afraid. It didn't stop them peering down at the rows of planted people, seeking out the faces of friends, exclaiming in dismay when they saw one. They had been warned to silence, but Stopmouth supposed it didn't matter. The Diggers knew they were here anyway.

"Will they come at us from below, do you think?" asked Rockface.

"I d-doubt it. I've never seen them destroy one of their own fields."

But in that case, how was a trap to be sprung? The only thing Stopmouth could think of, was that the enemy were hiding just beyond the brow of the far hill, on the other side of the dip. As soon as their precious grubs used the mouths of their victims to cry for help, the mothers—if that's what they were—would come streaming over the top of the hills. It wouldn't leave the humans enough time to get away, not if they were burdened with those they sought to rescue.

"All r-right," he muttered. He tried to give the order to move, but found his muscles unwilling to obey him.

What if his plan failed and he died while Indrani was still angry at him? She had spoken to the Ship People on his behalf, but her manner had remained distant.

She would forgive him anything, he knew, after he was dead. But that wasn't how their life together should end. No, more than anything he wanted to patch things up with her first. To make her understand that there could be no future for her and Flamehair without the Tribe. To tell her that her safety was the reason he had made peace ... and worse ... with his terrible brother.

237

With a wrench, he pulled himself back to the present. "Move!" he told himself. "Move!"

He passed the signal along the line. He saw a great many faces he recognised here, scattered in amongst the strangers: Vishwakarma, his eyes so sad; Ekta, rippling those great muscles; Tarini—surely too small for this part of the plan. Why wouldn't she stay on the crest of the hill with Kubar, who would be organising the work gangs?

Rockface saw the signal and passed it along the lines. "Oh, I can't wait!" he said. "This is going to be glorious!"

Everywhere, breathing grew faster, faces more anxious. The Diggers would be waiting for them, had to be! And yet, when Stopmouth flung his arms forward, every woman and man, Religious or Secular, launched themselves over the ridge and onto the scree on the far side. There were at least 200 of them running down the hill, at least that many. Far too many to waste should things go wrong, but it was too late to think about that now.

Stopmouth slid down the slope, jumping, stumbling, running. Clouds of dust sprayed from under his feet. A woman tumbled past him with a screech and tiny stones rained all around. In a dozen heartbeats, he had reached the bottom, where human bodies drooled and suffered just beyond the light of the sun.

As he came within touching distance of them, the victims began grabbing at him and a great moan rose up from those at the front, spreading and spreading towards the rear. "Mother!" they cried, each in his or her own voice. "Mother!" Although he didn't know the languages spoken, the various words were eerily similar to the one he had used as a child.

Stopmouth stayed clear of their arms. He had a spear with him and he poked at the ground with it for tunnels, while others watched the ridge of the far hill anxiously. Hunters fanned around to the edges of the crowd, ready for the attack that must soon come. But it was the unskilled men and women who would be doing the real work now.

In teams of four, they fended off the arms of the victims and dug them out of the soil, one at a time.

"It's f-f-far too s-s-slow ... "

"But where are the Diggers, hey? Where are they? You think they're coming around at us from behind?"

"N-n-not b-by d-d-d—"

"Not by day? They'll come from the front instead? You'd better hope so! But shouldn't we have sent somebody up to the top of the far hill to watch for them?"

Stopmouth had thought of that, of course, but figured the Diggers would be just out of sight and he'd lose whoever he sent up there. But now he wished with all his heart that he could have had some kind of warning. Oh, how he wished it!

And then, the Diggers struck.

By that time, only five or six of the Ship People had been dug free of the earth. They lay insensible in the semi-darkness on the slope nearest to HeadQuarters while their rescuers worked on freeing others.

But while Stopmouth was watching the ridge in fear that Diggers might appear at the top of it, something far worse occurred. The whole of the far slope began to move as what must have been a thousand Diggers or more threw off a covering of stones and moss.

Humans used camouflage, of course, as had other creatures they encountered over the generations. But the Diggers had never done so before now, preferring to strike from below ground through tunnels. I have underestimated them, Stopmouth realised, mouth hanging open in shock.

The enemy boiled down the slopes. Their claws scrabbled for purchase, raining stones and scree, much as the humans had done arriving from the other direction. "Watch out!" Stopmouth shouted pointlessly. Everybody had seen the threat. Some stood motionless; others ran for home. Not one of the Ship People stuck to the plan that had been agreed for the inevitable Digger ambush.

"Don't run!" Stopmouth cried, signing furiously with his hands for *attack*. "Forward! Forward! We have to fight!"

Luckily for him, several dozen of the ex-Religious had followed him into the dip, and these at least, held their nerve. It was they who had clung on together when the world had turned dark and Diggers had swarmed up the walls of HeadQuarters. No cowards remained among them, for half considered themselves already dead, while the rest now believed in their own invulnerability.

They charged around the edges of the field to meet the Diggers, to keep them from advancing too far into the dip, while the Ship People ran, or milled about or started dragging the few who had been saved back up towards safety.

The two species came together on the flanks of the field.

The Diggers had come looking for more victims. Grubs covered their bodies so that their skins seemed to ripple with silver, even as their claws tore up the earth in their eagerness to find new homes for their young.

The enemy did not slow at the sight of human spears. They crashed into the Religious, dragging men and women to the ground, fighting for access to the fresh meat.

One of the creatures impaled itself on the tip of Stopmouth's spear and the weight of its comrades shoved its body all the way down the shaft. He had to let go of it at once, pulling a dagger free from his belt. Beside him, Rockface roared and a Digger flew backwards through the air. Humans were writhing and screaming, trying to protect their ears and noses and mouths.

Claws swept towards Stopmouth's face, but they were only meant as a distraction—the Diggers didn't want anybody dead. He kept the creature from pinning him down. He ducked, he stabbed with his knife, feeling it catch, pulling it free, slashing it around himself in a circle.

A Digger threw itself at his legs, but when he jumped aside, he collided with some other hunter and both men hit the ground together and stayed there too as claws pressed them into the mud. Stopmouth kicked with his feet until they too were pinned. He raked at a Digger belly and tried to bite too, when one of them came close enough. But then, he saw the grub they were going to put into his ear or his nose and all he could do was throw his head from side to side, screaming in rage.

It landed on his cheek, warm and ticklish, until he threw it off, but another was there already and more were making their way up from his chest. "I won't!" he shouted, "I w-w-won't!" One of them had reached his left nostril and claws were now tangled in his hair, pinning him still.

Are you happy, brother? This is what we agreed! That I would disappear. Indrani, Indrani, I'm so sorry!

But then, the sun came out and blinded him.

It swept into the dip. The Diggers on top of him let go, staggering backwards. The grubs on his face writhed and stretched and fell away. Stopmouth felt his hand come free and he wiped them off himself in a panic. He could see very little with the spots in front of his eyes.

"Get up," he croaked. "All of you get up! We don't have long."

He hoped everybody would remember what to do now, because they certainly wouldn't understand a word he was saying. On top of the low hill, the Ship People were reflecting the sun's rays into the dip with polished pieces of wreckage from the Warship. But they wouldn't have more than a few hundred heartbeats of light before the angle of the sun, already very poor, made the task impossible.

At least half of his hunters writhed on the ground with grubs already inside them, causing horrendous agony. These had to be helped away by terrified Ship People whose courage lay trembling in their hearts as lightly as a leaf.

He pulled out his spear from the Digger that had taken it. The creature was properly dead, for its grubs could not restore it to life in the reflected glare of the sun. A great many of its comrades had died from their wounds too and they scattered up the slopes.

"Leave it!" he shouted to Rockface who was carving a snack for himself. "We've no time!"

"Just taking what I'm owed, hey? The Ancestors hate waste."

At the top of the far slope Diggers continued to flee the light

241

as it followed them up. It was actually much easier to direct it up there, or so he'd been told, than down into the dip. That was why his hunters had been forced to engage the enemy as close to the far side of the dip as possible even if it meant fighting uphill.

"C-come on," he told Rockface. "We've all g-got to help with the rescue now b-b-before the Diggers come back. And they will."

"True," said Rockface. "They nearly had me there, you know? It was like the old days. I feel great!" He slapped Stopmouth far too hard across the back and then joined in with those who were digging people out of the dirt while others carried unconscious bodies all the way up the small hill.

29.
THE HERꙨ

Whistlenose watched the return of Stopmouth's raiding party from the roof of HeadQuarters. Mossheart stood quietly nearby, but the Chief, under the full glare of the sun and with a temper to match it, paced up and down. He kept muttering, "I told him not to save them! I forbade it!"

But everybody was cheering the triumphant raiders. Even the young men from Wallbreaker's Flesh Council. They had run down to the streets and were now clapping their hands and hanging onto Rockface's every word.

Whistlenose leaned over the wall as far as he could, watching the line of rescuers with their moaning victims, parading through the streets. Now and again, one of those who had been saved, would double over and void their stomachs to great cries of relief from all who watched. It meant the grubs had left them for good. Another one saved—really saved, from the Diggers.

When he straightened up again, the Chief and his wife were arguing about something. Mossheart didn't seem to care if Whistlenose overheard them or not.

"He *agreed* to that?" she said. "No wonder they love him more than you."

Wallbreaker's eyes slid over towards Whistlenose who pretended to be fixing the binding on his spear. "Enough of that, woman. Shut up."

But Mossheart was not cowed. "That's the difference between the two of you. I used to think it was that you had better dimples and that Stopmouth was just a boy. It's all anybody saw back then and look at you now! Look at him!"

"Ha! Well not for much longer. I know my brother. He will stick to the deal we made. Now, enough of that gristle, I said."

A huge group of weeping Ship People arrived—men and women who hadn't gone on the raid. They were begging forgiveness and Whistlenose had no need for a Talker to understand that. They hugged their friends and family. They laughed and sang, while the returning heroes grinned and preened, or collapsed with sudden shakes as they realised the enormity of what they had experienced.

One female voice was shouting loud enough to be picked up by the Talker: "It was brilliant. The mirror trick! We got all of them out. We didn't lose a single person and we scared those Diggers senseless! That Stopmouth's a god, I tell you. A beautiful terrible god!"

That was too much for the Chief. He called Whistlenose away. "All right, old man. Remember the orders I gave you. You're to take the Talker. I'll kill you myself if you lose it. Go down there and find out where they're putting the captives. The ones who haven't puked yet. Remember what I said to do. It's important."

Whistlenose did remember, although he wasn't happy with it. Not one bit.

"I'll join you shortly, hunter."

As Whistlenose walked away, the Chief and his wife started back at each other with their bitter, bitter words.

Whistlenose gathered some of the Flesh Council together, and with their help, he made sure that any Digger victims who had yet to recover, were made to do their throwing up in a dark room beneath HeadQuarters.

"You can have them back later," he told worried relatives. "When they've recovered. I promise it. You have my word." And he kept it too. But more importantly, about thirty men and women ejected their parasites in a place where the strongest light was that of a torch.

Wallbreaker had come downstairs by that time and he dismissed the younger hunters.

"How long can we keep the grubs alive, Chief?" asked Whistlenose.

"A tenth at the most," said Wallbreaker. "Or so Aagam assures me. If we can believe a word that comes out of his mouth."

Whistlenose spat at the mention of the stranger's name, but otherwise said nothing. Instead, he looked at the helpless little worms, questing and questing about. A Tenth of a day was nowhere near enough time to prepare for what the Chief had in mind. Nowhere near enough. A few of the grubs were getting tangled with each other and he surprised himself with a burst of laughter. "Are those ... are they making love?"

Wallbreaker cursed. "You idiot! You idiot, no! They're eating each other!" And suddenly the two men were down on their hands and knees gingerly pulling the precious grubs away from each other and stranding each one on a separate rock or clump of moss where they curled into thumb-sized balls.

From outside came another cheer, this one large enough that the whole complex seemed to shake with it. Wallbreaker gritted his teeth. There was no getting away from it. The Ship People loved Stopmouth now. Just as the Real Tribe did, for had he not rescued them too? Oh, of course, Whistlenose and everybody else knew that the real saviours had been the Ancestors themselves. But who could forget the sight of the young hero's first appearance amongst the burning tallies? Like a Chief out of the stories!

"It is ridiculous," said Wallbreaker. "I'm the one who's going to ensure their future! I bet he hasn't told them that!"

"I know, Chief," Whistlenose said quietly. "And everybody else will know too when the Diggers are gone for good. So ... what are we going to do about keeping the grubs alive?"

"I've made arrangements, Whistlenose, don't worry. They should already be here ... Ah!"

PEADAR Ó GUILÍN

Footsteps came down one of the corridors leading from deep inside Head-Quarters itself. It was a young hunter of Stopmouth's new Tribe, the one called Yama. He had a knife to the throat of a much taller man who had been gagged and who'd had one of his arms bound in a sling.

"Good," said Wallbreaker. "Just in time."

"I told you which woman I want," said Yama.

"You'll have her, hunter, don't you worry."

"What's going on?" asked Whistlenose.

"My brother and I have both agreed that there should only be one Chief from now on. That makes sense, doesn't it, Yama?"

"Yes, Chief," said the hard boy who only reached as far as Wallbreaker's shoulder. "We want a proper leader here. One who knows how to reward his followers. This one," he kicked at his prisoner, "wouldn't give me what I deserved. Worse than Stopmouth if you ask me."

"Don't worry, hunter. You'll find that I won't be making the same mistakes."

The captive rolled over and managed to spit out the poorly tied gag. "Savages!" he hissed. Then, he raised his voice to a shout. "Help! The savages have me! The savages have me!" until Wallbreaker kicked him hard enough that it must have cracked a rib.

"They're all celebrating my brother's victory outside, so nobody heard you." He paused, contemplating the Roofman. "Dharam? Is that your name?" The man was growling, as though unafraid. That was about to change. "I hear you've lived a very, very long time, Dharam. Maybe what happens next won't kill you either, you never know. But I can't have any rivals for the story of the future, you understand me? Oh, Ancestors, I know you do. Maybe *only* you do."

"I understand you too, Chief!" said Yama. "I'll be your man all the way."

"Then help me dig a hole in here, hunter. Knee high should be enough."

"What ... what are we going to do?" asked Whistlenose. But a sickening clenching of his stomach had already told him the answer.

246

"We need to keep these grubs alive a little longer," said Wallbreaker. "Come on, let's show the Ship People they aren't the only ones who know how to ... to *farm*."

And with that, the Chief, and an excited, laughing boy, began placing grubs over Dharam's face. The Roofman screamed and screamed. Until he stopped.

Whistlenose tried not to look, but he couldn't help remembering how the Diggers had played with poor Highstepper that day long ago when BloodWays had burned to the ground. He felt sick.

Afterwards, there were plenty of grubs left over, maybe too many. "We should dig another hole," said Yama eagerly. "What if those grubs eat him right up? We can find somebody else, or maybe one of your brother's Fourleggers. I'd love to see how the grubs would take to them!"

"This isn't right," said Whistlenose. "We ... we can't do this to another human. Please. Let's dig him back up!"

Unfortunately, the Chief agreed with Yama that the remaining grubs should not be wasted, and the two began to scoop out dirt for another hole, as though it were an everyday thing to torture somebody.

"I know a few people we could put in here, Chief. As a lesson to the others. What about Kubar? He's popular with the Religious. Used to be one of their priests, the old hypocrite! Oh! Even better! Much better! You'll like this one! Indrani! She spat in your face and made made a fool of you. It would teach the others a lesson, right? If you're the wife of a hunter, you can't be running off with their brothers! If it were me, I'd put her in here and come down and visit her every day. How'd you like that? How do you like it?"

"We shouldn't put anybody else in here," Whistlenose insisted. "Even one is too many."

"Maybe we should put you in, then, old man," said Yama. "Right, Chief? You going to let him talk to you like that? Right?"

Wallbreaker pushed the boy backwards. "What ... ?" was all Yama had time to say before he felt arms wrap around him from behind and a voice—Dharam's—right in his ear groaning, "Mother ... Mother ... ".

"Get him off me! Get— Oh, gods, no! No, what are you doing?"

Wallbreaker dropped a grub onto the boy's scalp and watched as it slowly crawled down, questing at the eyes, and finally the nose.

"No room here for troublemakers," the Chief said. "Or big mouths. Or people who change their loyalties too easily ... " He looked at the horrified Whistlenose and shrugged. "I don't like this either. I don't enjoy it as he would have." He indicated Yama. "But I do think that after this, in our new world, there will be more ... respect for me. Now. Fetch me my brother."

Whistlenose was horrified. "You don't mean to ... "

"I'm just going to send him scouting. Fetch him, or by the Ancestors, Whistlenose, you can start digging a pit for yourself in here."

"Are you going to show your brother ... this?"

Wallbreaker seemed to consider it. But finally, he shook his head. "Maybe not. Have him meet me on the roof."

Whistlenose turned to leave, but Wallbreaker called him back. "And there's one more thing you can do for me, hunter. I want you to test my idea for beating the Diggers." He held something in his hand, something that twisted to get away from him.

"Can't ... can't somebody else do it?" Whistlenose hated the sound of fear in his own voice. They had come so far to be safe! And now that he and Ashsweeper and Nighttracker had finally reached the hills, Wallbreaker asked *this* of him? *This*?

The Chief sighed and his face softened. "Do you really think I want you hurt, Whistlenose? You, of all people? Who saved my girl?"

"I ... it's just ... "

"Other than you, only my brother knows the plan, hunter. There is nobody else I can trust with this, and nobody else I know who is as lucky as you. Now, fetch Stopmouth for me. I will give you the grub later."

"Later," Whistlenose agreed, almost sagging with relief. "Later."

248

PART THREE: SUNSET

30.
SUNSET

Stopmouth saw his brother for what he knew would be the last time, up on the cracked and shattered roof of HeadQuarters where the blood of past battles stained the concrete.

The man was mostly a stranger now, or so it seemed, until he looked up, his eyes an echo of their father's from so long ago. It felt like a haunting.

"You've done well here, brother," said Wallbreaker. "I had always meant to cut you out of my story, but I won't do that now."

"W-what are you t-t-talking about?"

"I'm saying... I'm saying that your betrayal of me will be forgiven. Completely. You, your woman, your child, all forgiven, the moment you keep your promise to me."

"You st-still... I was hoping you would change your m-mind and let me live."

Wallbreaker rubbed his eyes and looked away over the smashed streets to where the sun was beginning to fade. "I hoped that too," he whispered. "I did. I asked the Ancestors to give me the strength, but they refused me. No. Your disobedience has made your existence here impossible." he sighed. "A body has only one head, Stopmouth. One spine and one heart. That heart must be me, and so you... you need you to go scouting."

"Scouting?"

"Yes. I need you to go scouting and to never come back. You

do that and your woman can live as she pleases. I'll even make sure your child gets a name. Wait! Let me prove it." He raised his voice. "Whistlenose? Get up here. Bring the others."

As many as a dozen hunters came crowding up through the skylight. "Listen, men," Wallbreaker said to them. "Listen now as I make this pledge before the Ancestors. I am setting aside my traitorous wife, Indrani. This man, my beloved brother, is her only husband. I am rewarding him with forgiveness for the bravery he has shown. If Stopmouth dies, I will not give her to another or take her back for myself. I will not Volunteer her or her child. Tell anyone you want. Tell them I said this."

The men broke out in grins at these words, slapping Stopmouth on the back, and each other too. Stopmouth had not realised until that moment that they liked him. For the first time in his life, he felt respected by other hunters of his Old Tribe, loved even; admired. Whistlenose hugged him and then, the younger men were lining up one after another to do the same.

All that time, Wallbreaker smiled, the muscles on his jaws clenched hard enough it seemed his teeth would shatter.

"I thought I should say that now," he said. "In front of my Flesh Council in case anything should happen to my brother. I have kept a promise to him, and he is going to keep one to me, isn't he, Stopmouth."

"Y-yes, brother … Chief."

"He's going to do some dangerous scouting, as he knows this area better than anyone. Then, in a day or two, we will all confront the Diggers for the last time and we will win!"

Stopmouth saw her with the baby, with Flamehair. They sat out in the open, the child playing with rocks, full of angry protest when forbidden from eating them. Indrani soothed the baby in her own language, whatever that was, and it saddened him that he had never learned any of it and probably never would. He realised now, it would have brought him closer to his wife and not just for his benefit, but for hers too. She never seemed to have any friends.

251

Too proud, maybe. Too strong to need them. Worse, every group here, from the Old Tribe, to the Religious, to the Ship People, had reasons to hate and fear her.

In spite of all this, his heart swelled at the sight of the two of them. The sunlight sat gently on their shoulders and slipped over strands of black, black hair. He wanted to rub his face in it and fall asleep.

"Come out!" Indrani called. "Your ambush not very good today."

"I was j-just…" He found himself suddenly reluctant to approach. For days she had refused to even look at him, but now, he realised, if he wasn't careful, she might pull the secret of his promise to Wallbreaker out of him. She wouldn't allow him to keep his word, even though it might be the only thing that could hold this world together. He would be the last volunteer ever needed, but she might not see it that way.

He sat beside the two of them and was gratified when Flamehair offered him a stone so that he too might have something to play with.

"Thanks, little one," he murmured.

"He will to Volunteer you," Indrani said. "And then us."

Stopmouth didn't need to ask who she meant. "He promised me he w-would not." And she snorted at that, angrily shrugging off the arm he had meant to comfort her with.

"You are much very idiot, then, husband. Of him, I make fool twice and the Tribe see it. Once, I leave with his stupid brother and two, I sling him with *gun*. He can not to let me free. His promise is nothing and you must know this. Once before he say you can to marry me if you get Talker for him. Remember that? Do you?"

"I r-remember."

There was no point in trying to convince her that Wallbreaker was different now. Not always in a good way, but he too had a daughter, and nobody who had grown up in ManWays would ever do anything to compromise humanity's future.

Wallbreaker was going to be Chief or Commissioner or whatever the new Tribe would call the post if they survived the Diggers and became farmers. There was no changing that other than through murder, and Stopmouth was not capable of it. The only chance his little family had of survival now, was if his brother kept his promise. And he would have to keep it, surely, when he had spoken the words in front of his Flesh Council!

"I will to kill him," said Indrani. "If you do not."

"No!" he tried to jump to his feet, but she restrained him with a hand on his arm.

"Do not worry, husband. I wait for him to save the stupid Tribe," she said. "That much, I do for you. But for Flamehair too. You are right this once. Let him to save us. And then, let him to die so we stay safe after."

Indrani refused to bed down with Stopmouth that night and he wasn't sure he wanted to anyway. His thoughts were swirling and confused. She had spoken as if victory over the Diggers were certain, which of course, it could not be. Wallbreaker's terrible plan, which she had not heard, was full of uncertainties. The Diggers could not be underestimated: their use of camouflage in the fight at the dip had proved that much.

He watched the two of them sleep, his little family, for the last time, for as long as he could stand it. Then, his body surprised him with a yawn. He should be staying awake, shouldn't he? Savouring these last heartbeats?

He rose shivering when morning came and made his way past the walls. Ship People paused in their work to pat him on the back or to hug him outright.

"Thank you," he said. "T-thanks."

He walked right out the gate without so much as a spear or a knife. His only job today was to die and he saw no reason to deprive the Tribe of decent weapons.

As he left the buildings behind him, he felt more sad than he did afraid. Sad to be leaving Indrani, to never see little Flamehair again. "My girl," he whispered, as though she might hear him and be comforted. Only the Ancestors were listening, he supposed;

253

or maybe the gods of the Religious; or the nothing of the Ship People. He would be learning all too soon who was correct.

He made no effort to watch for ambushes or tracks. If any Slimers still lived, they'd have made an easy dinner of him and a much quicker end than he would have faced in the fields of the Diggers.

"I don't have to die," he said to himself. "I just have to disappear. Weren't those the exact words? I can run and run to the other side of the world. I can find the mountain that touches the Roof..." But he didn't believe any of that. He had brought no food, nor even a strip of cloth to form into a sling, and there could be no life anyway without the Tribe.

And so he walked until he found himself at the base of the very same hill he had descended with Rockface when first they had come to this place. They had fought a gang of Skeletons, who'd been lying in wait to ambush a single, terrified man. It seemed a lifetime ago.

He spun around at the sound of a skittering pebble.

Three Fourleggers were there waiting for him. They seemed too small at first, so that he thought it must be a trick of the strange sunlight. But then one of them started signing at him, far more fluently than he could ever have managed himself. Nor could he follow it too well, but nevertheless, and in spite of everything, he found himself laughing. "You're the Fourlegger child!"

"Flg," it agreed and signed the affirmative.

"You've found some friends?" and he accompanied his words with the sign that meant *good*—a thumb pointing upwards.

He had nothing else to say. His stock of signs was far too limited. He shrugged. Then, he waved goodbye and made as if to continue, but the little creature got in his way, waving its forelimbs furiously. The only signs Stopmouth could make out were *stop!* and *danger!*

"I know," he said, pushing the beast gently aside. *Thank you.* This last sign was one that had been adopted from the Roof People: two hands pressed together in front of the face.

Then, he made his way up the hill.

The Fourleggers had placed a line of boulders right at the top, right where the world came to an end. It was a warning, maybe, to go no farther. Or an offering to the Ancestors or gods of their own.

Some sunlight made it over the crest. He could see it caressing other hills in the distance, but immediately below Stopmouth lay a vale of blackness so complete that when he descended into it a hundred paces or so, he couldn't see his own feet beneath him. The Diggers could sense him, he felt sure, the sacrifice coming towards them.

He strained his ears. Had a pebble fallen nearby? Did claws approach? All he could hear for sure was the sound of his own frightened breathing; the occasional chattering of his teeth. He had walked slowly from the settlement, and descended towards his death even more reluctantly. He imagined the sun must be getting stronger off behind him and regretted that he would never see it again.

It's cold, he thought. Like in the Roof, in the parts that the virus had destroyed. He shivered, remembering all the bodies that must still lie up there.

His plan now was to find the Diggers before he could change his mind. Then, he would fight them as hard as he could, forcing them to kill him before he could be planted. Even so, he did not pick up the pace, nor did he stop jumping at every imagined sound or turning to look back up towards safety at the top of the hill.

Something cold and wet landed on his face. He jumped and shouted without meaning to, even as it slithered off him onto the ground, leaving a stinging track behind it. Then came another and another: heavy lumps of slime falling from the Roof to burn at his skin. In this complete blackness, the globules seemed to glow slightly, so that soon, the faintest of faint embers stirred everywhere on the hillside and all over the plain below him. The victims in the Digger fields must have felt they were under attack, for he heard them raise a great moan that thickly filled the darkness, so that even his bones hummed in awful sympathy.

"Oh, Ancestors," he whispered. "I don't want to die. I don't."

255

He had to swallow back his terror before he was able to move again, and even after that, he felt it waiting at the back of his throat, ready to spew forth.

The pools of slime, meanwhile, seemed to be moving. That didn't bother him: he felt sure it was the same stuff he had seen in the Roof. It used to move up there too and he had even wondered if it might be intelligent.

But then, his heart stopped altogether. The imagined scratchings had become real. Some creature—several creatures—had begun moving out there in the darkness, attracted, no doubt, by his earlier cry. It was almost as though he could feel them surrounding him: the slide of claws over moss; the scattering of sleeping insects. Why hadn't he brought his weapons? How could he force them to kill him without a credible threat?

Down on his hunkers, he picked up a fair sized rock…

He never got to use it. A great bruising blow struck him in the ribs, knocking the wind out of him. All of a sudden he was tumbling down over stones, leaving skin and blood on every one, only to land face down in a puddle of stinging slime. Claws clattered towards him from every direction.

Stopmouth got his toes planted beneath him and sprang straight downhill into the utter darkness, no thought to it, only instinct. He crashed into the warm, wiry body of a Digger, ripping its flesh with bare fingers as they went down together. One less! He'd make one less for the Tribe to face!

It fought back, ignoring the pain it must have felt, struggling to pin his right arm with all its weight, while his left continued to tear at the holes in its skin.

Another weight landed over his legs and now he screamed, enraged, horrified that in the end, it had come to this, that his brother had wasted his flesh so uselessly.

But that had been the point, hadn't it? To remove Stopmouth from the story of the Tribe and of the world, with nobody to even know he had Volunteered.

And still more of the enemy converged on him. Grubs

crawled in his hair, catching there. He fought to grab them until finally, claws transfixed his wrist to pin him to the earth and there was no part of him that could move at all.

He had a vision then—just like when he had lived in the Roof and the giant machine-goddess had spoken to him and had shown him anything he cared to know.

He flew over shattered metal caverns filled with burnt, or frozen or asphyxiated corpses. Places where men and women had been crushed to a pulp, their flesh uneaten, and great parks where the grass had been consumed by the starving until the air had turned to poison and finished them off. Their numbers were beyond counting. The achievements of the dead—and there had been many—lay corrupted about them, as lifeless now as they were themselves.

I'm sorry, Shtop-mou. I'm sorry.

Who was sorry? The Roof Goddess? But the Roof is dead!

Stopmouth blinked. He knew somehow that a great deal of time had passed: perhaps several tenths of a day. And he saw before him a woman of light. No! Of *slime*, of glowing slime with the slightest tint of blue. Like the one he had thrown a dagger at that day with Vishwakarma. It stood before him, in its barely human form, quivering all over in an effort to stay in one piece. The Diggers, like all shadows, had been driven back, but not very far. They waited patiently less than five paces from their intended victim.

I'm sorry. I will fix it. Then, the slime creature collapsed back into a puddle and the light disappeared once more.

The Diggers paused, perhaps wondering if another slime woman might appear. He could hear their breath all around him, shallower and faster and hissier than a human's. When the sound stopped completely, he knew they were about to spring. But this time, he made no effort to grab a rock to defend himself with. He couldn't get his mind off the slime creature and kept wondering if it had really spoken to him or if he had imagined it. And what could it have wanted with *him* anyway? Addressing him by name!

Such strange last thoughts for one who should have been

257

thinking of his family and dedicating himself to his Ancestors.

"Shtopmouth!"

A voice called out from up on the hill. *Indrani.* No! he thought. No! She would get herself killed with him. He surged to his feet. "Get back!" he cried. "Get back!"

He expected the Diggers to take him then, but they did not move. He couldn't possibly escape, surrounded as he was, and he realised then, that they *wanted* him to call out to this would-be rescuer, that nothing would please them more than for other humans to rush foolishly into their realm. "Please," he shouted. "Go away! Go away!"

He heard a rumbling, but had no idea what it was. Something massive flew past his face and warm liquid sprayed over him. More objects crashed and bounced down the hill all around. Finally, he realised what was happening and threw himself flat. Boulders! Somebody was pushing boulders down the hill!

"Shtopmouth! Shtopmouth!"

"Go away!" he screamed.

Another crunch as rocks rolled past him. But that wasn't the end of it.

Next came fire: rolling bales of dried sticks and moss that turned end over end, with dozens of Fourleggers charging along behind them. They were going to save him! He couldn't believe it, but nor could he allow it. He *had* to die, that was the deal. He *had* to. Yet, he couldn't make himself run further downslope into the darkness.

In spite of the rolling fires, the shadows of Diggers in great numbers surged up the hill just as the first of the Fourleggers reached him. Both sides fought silently and better than humans would have, with senses superior for killing without light.

"Shtopmouth!" a torch appeared right in front of him. "Come on! Come on!"

"I can't, Indrani. Please, leave me. I *agreed*."

"To him. To *him*!"

"He knows a w-way to save us all, but I have to—"

She shrieked as a shadow appeared suddenly between the two of them, but she overcame her surprise quickly and smashed the flame down hard over its skull, scattering sparks everywhere.

"Fourleggers die for you. Come! Come!"

"But—"

"He tells not true all the time, your brother! Now, you do the same."

"We need him, the T-tribe needs him!"

"*I* need *you*. So, we tell not truth too. We sleep you with Fourleggers until he kills Diggers. Then, he not to needed again and I kill him!"

The Fourleggers were beginning to pull back, as their balls of wood and moss began to burn out. And Stopmouth found himself running too, rushing up the slope with his wife. He didn't want to die, had never wanted it. He would hide out with the Fourleggers as she asked, while Indrani would say he had disappeared. And it would be true, wouldn't it? It's exactly what he had agreed. To disappear. And no more than that.

Yet, as he ran after his wife, he knew the Ancestors would see through such double thoughts and they hated liars. Hated them.

Indrani tripped, her torch falling away.

"Forget it," he said, catching up to her and lifting her by the elbow. "Forget it!"

But the Diggers had not given up on them yet. His legs were taken out from under him and Indrani yelled in rage. Stopmouth had fallen flat on his face and couldn't move at all. He heard his wife snarling over him and then screaming enough to chill his blood, but then, the Digger rolled off him.

"Come," she said, entirely out of breath. "Come! Oh Gods!"

They had nearly made it to the top of the slope. The sun still managed to shine for them up there, although when they finally saw it, it was only a few hundred heartbeats away from sliding past the far side of the hole. They would have to hurry if they were to make it to the Fourleggers' warehouse. And what if somebody saw them creeping in? How would Indrani persuade his brother

259

of his disappearance then?

Sodasi was waiting anxiously for them beyond the brow of the hill, along with the fourlegger child. This then, was how the news of his attempted suicide had been spread.

"Indrani?" She had come to a stop. He turned to look at her in the fading golden light. Sweat covered her face from all of her efforts so that now she seemed to sparkle.

"You must to live now," she said, the words spilling softly from between perfect lips. "Flamehair ... for her." And blood came too, then, from her belly, where claws had ripped her open.

"Oh, no," he whispered. "Ancestors ... " they *hated* oathbreakers and always punished them. She collapsed, and he didn't even manage to catch her in time, although she had stood but the length of an arm away. He fell down beside her, pulling her beautiful head up onto his lap, his mouth working uselessly.

"I never know ... " she said, "why you love me, Shtop-mou."

"What!" her words made no sense.

"I did ... very much bad things ... I am monster ... but you ... "

"No! No!" Indrani was hard, yes, hard as metal and stone. But loving too. Just like the Tribe, the way it needed to be to survive. She had once told him that he was her heart. But if that was true, then she was his backbone. He couldn't be brave without his Indrani; he couldn't be anything.

He didn't know how to say that to her here and now. His idiot clumsy tongue and his panicking heart, each tripped up the other so that the only sound they could make was an awful, wordless moan.

And then, as suddenly as that, she was gone. He trembled, his throat a swollen, aching lump. He rocked her body, their skin sweat-stuck together, as the sun that she had brought to the world disappeared at last.

31.
FINDING M⊕THER

The time had come for the last battle that would decide the fate of the world. Scouts had spotted huge groups of Diggers. They gathered in the darkness beyond the hills where the light barely reached, even though the hole in the Roof seemed to have grown slightly in the time since the Tribe had arrived here.

"They're coming," people said. "For sure, this time."

And so a meeting had been called for the Tribe—the *real* Tribe: men and women descended from John Spearmaker. He had taught them to hunt; to feed and to clothe themselves. Sacrifice and bravery had been handed down through so many generations of these people, you could taste it in their marrow.

Heavy moss bandages covered the Chief's shoulder, but Indrani's magic weapon had failed to kill him, and he was finally back on his feet. He grinned, brimming with confidence as in his younger days. His famous dimples were deeper than ever and he seemed so much more certain of himself since his brother had been lost on a scouting mission. He waved his hands to silence the Tribe.

That was no easy task. Everybody had crammed in together in a new Centre Square they had been made by knocking over the shanties of the Ship People. Children cried. Parents tried to shush them. Young hunters puffed up their chests, hoping to win the eyes of the remaining unmarried girls, or holding up fingers to show how many kills they would make.

"My people," Wallbreaker cried. "Many of you did not believe me when I said the Ancestors had spoken to me, and yet, here we are, in the new home that was promised to us. The Tribe lives and only one trial remains ... The final defeat of the Diggers."

"How do we know it will be final?"

Whistlenose jumped. The voice had been a woman's. Worse, it had been that of Ashsweeper, his own wife, right beside him. "The world we have crossed is full of nothing but Diggers," she said. "If we beat off one Tribe of them, what's to say there won't be an armful more?"

Luckily, Wallbreaker welcomed the question with a grin. "There are more Diggers than we can count, woman. But the Roof no longer supplies the enemy with new tribes to hunt when they've eaten the last of the old ones. They're starving out there. They're already planting each other in the ground, and far away, towards the centre of the streets they control, there is nothing for them to eat at all but rocks and trees. So, those distant from us, would starve to death before they could reach us, or be too weak to do us harm once they got here.

"If we can thwart their last attack—and it will be a big one, I don't deny it ... but if we can hold them off just a little bit longer, then I can promise you that nobody in this Tribe will ever have to volunteer after today. None of those children among us right now will be lost."

Whistlenose saw his wife was about to speak again, he grabbed her arm to shut her up, but Ashsweeper always had to have her say and he feared for her.

"But if there aren't going to be any new Tribes from the Roof for us either, what will *we* eat? What can we eat? *Rice?*"

They had heard of the new food—a sort of edible moss. A few had tried the crunchy grains, trying to choke them down with little success.

The Chief, rather than getting angry, nodded his head, acknowledging the wisdom of her questions. "Humans cannot live on rice. I know that. But Roof People can. They will have all the world to grow it in when the Diggers are gone. They will feed to their hearts content and live long lives without fear. And then, painlessly—I promise you!—painlessly, they will give their flesh to us, the true humans, and the ones who saved them from the agony of the fields."

There were oohs and aahs from the crowd as yet again, the Chief displayed his cleverness. Even Ashsweeper was nodding, but Whistlenose felt very uneasy all of a sudden. He couldn't put his finger on it. Yes, he loved the idea that neither his wife nor son should ever have to undergo the terror he had felt when he had been turned over to the Clawfolk. But horrible as it had been, his suffering had been no different to that of anybody else. In the end, even Chiefs gave up the flesh of their bodies so that all might make it Home. It was every bit as noble and brave as it was terrifying. This was different. Wrong even, although it was hard to say exactly how. He remembered Stopmouth looking down on a crowd of planted Ship People, saying, "And listen to their pain! That sounds human, doesn't it?"

None of these qualms prevented Whistlenose from obeying orders after the meeting when the Chief ordered a few hundred Roof People to be rounded up. He had ordered the capture of very specific people too. "I want the ones who can fight," he'd said. "This is very important. Once the Diggers are gone, it must be only our people who hold the spears." The power of the Talker was used to lure the weaponless victims into a place where they could be captured.

A day later, they had taken their prisoners and gone out onto the plain beyond the hills to a place where the sun spread its light for no more than a tenth every day. They tied the wrists and ankles of the Roof People together. They gagged them with choking black moss. Then, each hunter dug a knee-high pit for himself as quickly as possible. The holes were made in a broad crescent around the clumps of tear-streaked prisoners, to form the jaws of a huge beast.

"Good," Wallbreaker whispered. "Now, remove their gags ... "

Already shadows had been taking bites out of the sunlight, driving it back. Nothing could be seen beyond the circle of light, absolutely nothing. Some of the Ship People began to whimper then, to cry out for mercy. But the more sensible among them begged the others to shut up. It was too late for that. The Diggers would know. They would know that humans were here.

"Volunteers," Whistlenose whispered to himself, "think of them as volunteers." It wasn't the first time human hunting parties had used members of their own species to bait a trap. But never had they needed to be trussed up.

The only prisoners not struggling were Dharam and Yama. Like the hunters, they had been buried, but up to their chests, since half their bodies had been eaten away. Now, just before the last of the sun left them for good, Wallbreaker ordered these two men to be dug up. They came alive then, struggling and calling for their mothers, while the cries of the volunteers beyond them rose to a higher pitch of terror. Knives slit open the stomachs and lungs of the men to release the grubs that had made their homes there. Then, these were handed around to the hunters, small and warm and wriggling.

"Remember," shouted Wallbreaker. "Don't let them get into your throat! Hold the head against the inside of your cheek and let them fasten there. And don't worry! They eat slowly enough that they won't make it through in the course of a night. We'll be here far less time than that."

Whistlenose took the creature he'd been given into his hand, feeling it squirm there. He shuddered. Only two days before, under the Chief's orders, he had allowed a grub to feast on his cheek like this. The experience had lasted no more than a hundred heartbeats. Just enough time to sneak up on one of the enemy and kill it, while it made no effort to resist him. The Digger hadn't even seemed to see him! But as soon as the "mother" was dead, Whistlenose had bitten the vile grub in half.

Now, he had a new one, tiny, and hungry. The top of its body rose, as though questing. Then, it began sliding up his wrist. The thing was making for his nose or his ears. It was all he could do not to crush it in his fist and fling it away. To his left and his right, men were placing theirs carefully against the inside of their cheeks as Wallbreaker had taught them. They cursed and yelped as the creatures fastened there, but better that than swallowing the thing while it yet lived, or allowing it to crawl down your windpipe, which is what it really wanted to do.

Keeping his tongue towards the front of his mouth, Whistlenose shoved the creature in. For a heartbeat or two, there was no pain. This was followed by a small sting that made him wince a little.

Not so terrible, after all. Then, the flesh of his cheek grew warm the way he remembered. Tiny strands seemed to reach out from his face, passing through the back of his head, before racing along his spine. All at once, the strands flared into a burning, itching pain and he stifled a scream with only the greatest of effort.

"They'd better attack soon," said somebody beside him, the voice hoarse and unrecognisable. "Ancestors, but it hurts! I don't know how long I can stand it."

Whistlenose agreed. He held a single grub inside his mouth. Adult Diggers, on the other hand, had to suffer through dozens of their own young, crawling and gnawing at their mothers every moment of the day! And the only cure was to find another host to put them in. No wonder the creatures had consumed the whole world already!

But the Diggers were taking their time in coming today.

The hostages moaned. The hunters moaned too, uncaring after a while how unmanly they must have seemed, rocking with the pain, waiting, waiting for a chance to spit out the grubs. Soon, it was full dark and the only relief was the distant glow of fires from the ruined streets in the protection of the hills.

The Chief had been the first to experience this pain, the day he had jumped into a tunnel after Whistlenose to save his daughter. A grub had got into his mouth during the fighting and had been pinned against his cheek. Once it had attached itself, the Diggers had left him alone, even when he was killing them. But that situation had lasted no more than a few dozen heartbeats. Whistlenose's later experiment with the magic of the grubs had been briefer still. Nobody had expected the pain to intensify this much over a longer period. Even so, it was a brilliant plan and when the enemy finally came, they would be slaughtered in their thousands.

Now, Whistlenose tried every trick he knew to ease the growing agony. He daydreamed a future for his son; he planned hunts; he prayed and prayed to his grandfather, the great Slingcatcher who should have been a Chief. Nothing worked. Time passed, but he had no idea how long. He felt hot all over his body. Muscles loosened and his fingers twitched so that his spear fell to the ground.

No matter. He would look more convincing without it. If an attack came he could pick it up quick enough.

Soon, he forgot all about his grandfather. Instead, for the first time in hundreds of days, he thought about his mother. She had a triangular snout, he remembered, that dripped clear liquid. She dug with powerful claws, great tunnels where he could be warm and safe. She was coming! She was coming! So, he called for her and all around him, the other hunters were calling for their mothers too.

32.

FLIGHT

Wallbreaker waited until the others had taken grubs into their mouths. Then he waited some more. Darkness had almost fallen and he could still make out the shiny skin of the creature trapped in his hand. It would hurt, as it had before, that was certain. He wasn't ready for the pain yet and worse than that, he hated the thought of it consuming him with its tiny mouth. It was too close to the worst of his nightmares.

You're thinking too much.

Thinking was the gift the Ancestors had given him so that he might save the Tribe, but such a hard gift it was! Those terrible dreams of Armourback young had pursued him all the way across the world from the streets of ManWays.

I shouldn't put it in yet, anyway. Somebody would have to pay attention for the arrival of the Diggers and who better than the Chief? He would place the little creature against his cheek at the last minute, he decided. Yes. He would be the one to watch for danger.

As the light failed, he saw a few of the hostages struggling to free themselves, hissing urgently one to the other. "You untie me! Try and get your teeth down to the knot ... "

Wallbreaker felt sorry for them, as he always had for Volunteers. His father most of all, of course. He had looked so much like poor Stopmouth, but with a gift for joking and laughter that had left a terrible silence behind it when he had finally given his Flesh for the Tribe.

A man like that would never have to step forward now, not with so many useless mouths to feed. These Roof People were nothing, nothing compared to Father and he shouldn't waste pity on them ...

But they would feel the terror just as much in spite of that, wouldn't they? The pain of the grubs. The planting. The eating of their spirit and flesh and marrow that might last fifty days or more.

He felt sick at the thought of it and then reassured himself with the promise he had made to the bait when he had brought them here: "We won't let the Diggers have you. Or keep you, anyway. We aim to defeat them once and for all. Our hunters will be protected by grubs, so, once you have lured them out of their tunnels, we will slaughter them by the thousand!" And then, the bait would be slaughtered too: for they were the only hunters remaining to the Roof People. But at least it would be quick, and their flesh would be honoured and would feed the real humans for tens of days to come.

And Wallbreaker intended to thank each of them personally for their sacrifice.

However, as he imagined this triumph, he couldn't help wishing that Indrani were in there too amongst the rest of them. He still intended to keep his promise to let her live. Nor would he take her for a wife. But that didn't mean she would get away with what she had done to him. A Chief could not be seen to be weak. No. When all this was over, he would turn all his powers of imagination to finding some other way to make her pay. Oh yes. She would come crawling back to his bed before this ended!

It was too dark now to see the grub in his fist. The Volunteers moaned and his men too. All the better, he supposed. One of them even called out for his mother! Clever. The Ancestors would be pleased. Another man took up the call, and another. "Mmmmmoooother ... " Very convincing. Soon, they were all at it.

I should join them now. The pain won't last. But his hands were shaking. It was all he could do not to fling the grub away. He raised it towards his mouth.

"Mmmooother ... "

He paused. Something was terribly wrong. He didn't want to alert the Diggers that the Talker was out here—he had intended to save that for the ambush so the men could see the creatures they were killing. But he needed to know what was going on.

"A gentle glow," he ordered and the Talker obeyed. He stood up to his knees in a little hole, in the back rank of his hunters. Now he brought the globe forward towards the face of the man beside him, a wiry youth by the name of Drooplip.

Bulging eyes swivelled towards the Chief.

"Mmmooootherrr ... ."

"Oh, Ancestors ... "

Drooplip made a grab for him. It was clumsy enough that Wallbreaker should have had no trouble stepping back out of the way. But he had forgotten the hole he'd been standing in and he toppled over, the Talker spinning out of his hands.

As he fell, somebody else caught him in a clammy grip. He yanked himself free, then dived through a thicket of waving arms to pull up the Talker again, before crashing into the back of old Whistlenose.

"They're here!" shouted one of the hostages. "Oh, Gods! The Diggers! The Diggers are here!"

Wallbreaker could feel the truth of it himself in the trembling of the earth. They were coming. The Diggers! And all his hunters had trapped themselves because of him! Oh, Ancestors! What if he freed them? They had only one grub each in their mouths. But how many hunters could he get to before the Diggers arrived? And what was the point? The plan had failed. The Diggers would know now, they would know! But maybe ... a fighting chance ...

Another scream. The sounds of claws rushing towards him, directly towards *him*!

"Bright!" he shouted. "Brighter than the Roof!"

The sphere flared. Squinting, Wallbreaker could see the enemy driven back, grubs falling dead from their hides. But at

269

the very edge of the light, beyond his hunters and the Volunteers, great numbers of the enemy lay waiting for him. *Huge* numbers.

"I can burn you!" he shouted. "I can burn all of you!"

A single creature stepped forward. There was something different about it and it took Wallbreaker a moment or two to figure out what it was. Smaller, he decided, than the others. But that wasn't it. There was more. Its hide was smooth, completely unblemished.

No young, he realised. An *unmated* Digger, without grubs to worry about. Wallbreaker was done for. He was dead.

More claws rattled the stones behind him. And that was enough, more than enough. The next thing he knew, he was running for all he was worth, parting the horde of Diggers in front of him with the light of his Talker. But behind him, came the sounds of a smaller number of the creatures, those without any reason to fear him at all.

Rocks gave way beneath him. He skidded on patches of moss as shadows flickered and danced. He had no idea where he was going. He just had to get away from them, desperate for them to take the hostages, to take the hunters, anything and anyone so long as they just left him alone. But even as he ran, he realised his dilemma. The Talker. It was the last thing on this world the Diggers feared and they had to be certain of its destruction.

He felt the earth rumble, and he knew that it wasn't just a few younger, unmated creatures that pursued him now, but the entire swarm! They could return for the hostages any time, but he … he they meant to finish right away.

He wept and cursed and ran and tired. He had no sense of direction—he had lost sight of home in the glare he carried with him.

But slowly, ever so slowly, the light of the Talker began to dim.

33.

THE WOMEN

Flamehair cried when Stopmouth gave her the rice. Something was missing. So, one of the Religious women showed him how to mash the other stuff, called *vegetables*, until it looked for all the world like excrement. Then she made him feed it to his daughter, who gobbled it down like it was liver. And all might have been well, except that at the end, his girl said "mama?"

The word was identical to the one children of the Tribe used and he didn't know how to console her when no mama appeared.

Wallbreaker had ordered all of the Roof People to pack into the remains of HeadQuarters, and such were their numbers, that nobody had noticed when Stopmouth had been smuggled in amongst them. Lost in despair, he had barely noticed himself.

Now, he held his child tight to his chest, growling and weeping angrily at any who dared come too close. Eventually, he even drove off the gentle Religious woman.

"Ah, what's this now?" said Rockface. Sodasi hovered behind him, weaponless for once. Stopmouth didn't want to talk to them. He felt he was trying to vomit up his own heart and only the child in his arms, pleading for her mother, kept him present.

"You followed Indrani before," Rockface was saying. "Into your brother's house. All the way up to the Roof. But you can't follow her now, hey? Even you couldn't do that, boy. You mustn't do it."

Behind the big man, Sodasi was signing to one of the children.

They could have used real words, those two; they came from the same Religious community and spoke the same language. Sodasi's hands were almost as fluent as the child's, although sometimes she stopped him with a puzzled look on her face and he laughed at her. What a strange world it had become where the young taught the old and the old lived on and on!

"Listen," said Rockface. "We're going. Whether you come with us or not is up to you, hey? But you wouldn't want to miss it! A glorious charge!"

Stopmouth blinked with slow heavy eyes. What did Rockface mean by "glorious charge"? And what did it matter, anyway?

"Wallbreaker took some of our people, can you believe it? He took Religious to sacrifice to the Diggers when he could have had all the cowardly *Secular scum* he wanted!" Rockface spat the foreign words that he must have picked up from Sodasi. "He got Kubar too, hey? I'm fond of the old waster, though only the Ancestors know why. And that little friend of yours, what's her name? Taroona? Tar-something..."

"Tarini?" Stopmouth felt his arms tremble. Tarini was brave enough she might even have volunteered to be bait if she'd been asked, but he doubted Wallbreaker had asked anybody. He was Chief now and would suit himself. Stopmouth felt something stir within him. *Poor Tarini.*

"We're going to get them back," said Rockface.

Stopmouth found his voice. "What about the plan?"

"What plan? He's always making plans, your brother. Who cares about his plan? If he needs bait, I should be there, an old man. The sick should be there. The injured, hey? That's how it's done. But he can't seem to tell the difference. He's taken some of our best hunters, for the love of the Ancestors!"

It was true. The waste was breathtaking enough to push through Stopmouth's pain. Wallbreaker's contempt for even the best of the Roof people cast a dangerous light on the future.

Stopmouth raised his chin and forced his eyes to find those of the one friend who had stood by him from the very beginning.

"Rockface ... let me g-go with you. Find me that Religious woman who was looking after Flamehair. Let me come."

A massive palm slapped him hard enough across the back to jolt Flamehair and to set her wailing again. "Of course you're coming! It will be like the old days when we fought the Fliers, hey? I can't wait!"

But as the Religious woman returned to snatch Flamehair away from him, Rockface brought up what he called "a tiny problem." "We're blocked in here," he said.

"Blocked in? How?"

"The women of the Tribe—our old Tribe, that is ... well, you're not going to believe this, but they've been doing a bit of ... a bit of hunting during their journey. Mad, isn't it? The *women!*" Stopmouth, despite his loss, felt his mouth quirk up at these words.

"No, I'm serious! There are women outside with ... with *spears*, blocking us in. It's not a joke!" Lucky for Rockface, Sodasi, the best slinger in the Tribe, with a hundred days hunting behind her, didn't understand a word he was saying. Stopmouth just shook his head.

"Gather any hunters who are left and everybody who looks like they might be able to carry a weapon. There don't have to be enough of us to win a fight, just enough to look threatening."

"Welcome back," said Rockface nodding, and grimly, Stopmouth nodded back.

"I'm going outside," said Stopmouth.

On the way to the door, he spotted Ekta, the Warden. He doubted anybody could have made *her* do anything, and yet, here she sat, alone and useless. Instinct made him tap her on the shoulder. "Come with me, Warden," he said. She must have understood his gestures, for she shrugged and stood without bothering even to wipe the dust from her bottom.

The only remaining exit had indeed been blocked off by rubble and mossy rocks, so the two of them proceeded up to the roof to look down on a circle of armed women and children.

273

"You're supposed to be dead, Stopmouth!" one of them cried. "And yet, here you are, with a new wife already."

"Mossheart," he said, nodding. She was still very beautiful, he thought. She could never be as perfect as some of the Ship Women, but that didn't matter. She'd had such a hold over his younger self that when he spoke to her now, he felt he was in two places—two times—at once. "We n-need to leave," he said.

She smiled a hard smile. "I remember when you weren't able to look me in the face like that and talk at the same time. You're a man now, I see. A man who was supposed to have Volunteered. You couldn't keep your word? Well, never mind. You'll be staying where you are, Stopmouth. You can't force your way out when you have no fighters left, can you?"

She smiled again when she saw the shock register on his face. "He d-did this on purpose?" said Stopmouth. "Wallbreaker took our best fighters to use as volunteers on p-purpose?"

"Of course! He always could think circles around you. There can't be two Tribes any more than there can be two Chiefs."

Stopmouth felt dizzy. The implications for the future of his people were even worse than he had realised. Wallbreaker had no intentions of uniting the Tribes and using their skills. The old Tribe would dominate and what would it do then?

"Is that w-what you've become?" he asked. "V-volunteer the *young* and the *useful*?"

Some of the other women around Mossheart looked uncomfortable at the thought, but these people had already sacrificed the last of their traditions with the burning of the Tallies. Their own Ancestors wouldn't have recognised them now.

"Hey, Stopmouth," said another woman. This was Ashsweeper, Whistlenose's wife, and she held her spear easily. "What will you do if we let you out?" Mossheart glared at her, but Ashsweeper paid no heed.

"We will h-help," he said. "We'll provide them with some r-real volunteers and the rest of us will join in the fighting. There are more D-diggers than Wallbreaker thinks out there. We need him to succeed as much as you do."

"Oh, he will certainly succeed," said Mossheart. "But he can do without any of your help." And Ashsweeper was nodding her head in agreement.

"There's nobody left in there that can fight," said Ashsweeper. "Even Rockface is too old. He can't even stand straight."

Ekta shifted next to Stopmouth, bored and sad. He had to stop himself grinning. *Thank you Ancestors.* "You d-don't understand," he said now. "There are lots of people in here who can fight. They haven't done so before now because they don't want to hurt you. But if they don't get their friends back ... "

All the women below snorted in derision and made the grabbing "show us the flesh!" gesture they would have given to any idle, boasting man. He turned to Ekta. "I need your help," he whispered. He heaved a rock onto the parapet of the roof and the women below moved back out of range in case he planned to hit them with it.

"W-watch this!" he cried. He mimed for Ekta what he wanted her to do.

The Warden's arm became a blur, smashing down onto the rock and shattering it with a single blow. It happened suddenly enough that the women below yelped and stepped back even further, the pregnant ones holding their bellies.

"As I s-said. You have children w-with you. We d-don't want to hurt them if we don't have to. But we are leaving here to join the fighting when it starts. Do you intend to stand in our way?"

It took until nightfall to get everything organised. That meant they were probably too late: that the poor Volunteers had already been killed or captured or saved. Stopmouth's force would arri when the victory was already won.

Even so, he knew what he was doing still mattered. He to make his surviving friends appear dangerous enough could not be too easily dominated and destroyed by h

Language was a huge problem. The childre

always, half-bridging impossible gaps. Fulki led the way with that funny sneer of hers that the others seemed to fear. She ran off to try and recruit the Fourleggers, but returned empty-handed. The creatures would not be taking part. And that was probably for the best. Wallbreaker's hunters were nervous around them and might attack them.

When the people finally came outside under the stars, the women of the Tribe parted to let them go. All except Ashsweeper. "I'm coming with you," she said.

"You are?"

"And not just me. Some will stay behind with Mossheart to watch the children, but most of us are with you. I told my husband it was a waste to leave us out of this fight. We need to throw every spear at it. It's too important."

"Y-yes it is."

All around them, torches waved through the air and terrified people tried to stay quiet. They knew they were going into danger and Stopmouth had expected the Ship People amongst them to hold back the way they had when he had forced them to gather meat for the Fourleggers. But they did not. His rescue of their friends the day they had used the mirrors had won him their trust.

All the way to the edge of the ruined human streets, the women of the Old Tribe had built great bonfires of wood and bone that were tended by children too small to hunt. It was something they had learned during their migration, apparently, something that made the Diggers a little more reluctant to attack.

ᴬt the rocky area, just where the houses began to peter out, ˙ᶜʳᵉˢ remained to usher the reluctant humans into beyond, where the only illumination was

e, Wallbreaker's men had prepared a last 'eved would break the back of the enemy noring the talents and strengths of two ᵉe, he had chosen to bait his trap with to the New Tribe. Wasted. Horribly wasted and possibly dead or planted already far out in the darkness.

In spite of his anger, Stopmouth paused just before crossing the line of the last fires. There had been low levels of talk around him between those who shared languages. Prayers—even amongst the Seculars, along with the exchange of kisses and good-byes.

He signalled all of them to silence. The one thing he did not want to do was to ruin Wallbreaker's plan by running in at the wrong time. No, he would bring his people forward to a point where they could reach the fighting at a charge as soon as the cries and shouting began.

He took a last look around him. Rockface stood at his shoulder with Sodasi right behind. The children they had trained were there, hopping with excitement and signalling one to the other too fast to follow. Further back, Ekta, looking as serene as a Roof Goddess; a terrified, very tall old man clutching a sharpened stick; a young girl, totally unarmed; a bearded man, his mouth moving in silent prayer; and a thousand more stretching back through the streets.

He'd been a fool to ruin his night vision by looking behind him. Never mind. He took a deep breath and stepped into the darkness. Everybody followed—not in a column as he had expected and might have preferred. Instead they spread out until the whole crowd advanced like a palm sweeping bones from a plate.

Nobody had brought torches for fear of alerting the Diggers, so nothing could be seen. People to either side of him linked elbows and he imagined the same thing was happening right across the line.

It no longer moved in perfect silence. Untrained hunters cursed beneath their breaths or cried out when they stumbled. Behind them, the bonfires were still frustratingly close and Stopmouth felt sure the fighting would be over long before they could reach it. His friends might be dead already. He was worried in particular about poor Tarini, who had saved his life and his pride in the Roof.

He paused and unlinked from the arms holding him on either side. Something was very wrong: a certain unpleasant smell on the air. An invisible pressure at the front of his body, lighter than a flake of moss, but real enough. Everybody else must have felt it too for the whole line came to a halt and all those sounds of whispered curses over stubbed toes; all those muttered prayers; all the sliding of rocks and the scattering of pebbles, came to a stop.

"They're right in front of us," said Rockface, his voice calm, but sounding like a shout in the silence. "Look," he said. He must have brought an ember with him in a leather bag, for all too quickly he was able to light a torch, his face dancing in the flames. Nobody else spoke, not one of them. Stopmouth could feel them holding their breaths, just as he was. Rockface stepped forward out of the line, shrugging off Sodasi's hand that tried to hold him back.

Twenty paces he walked into the darkness, the light throwing up the crazy shadows of rocks and the torn shreds of moss or the stumps of trees the humans had cut for wood.

And then, the light found another place to rest. A row of glittering eyes, the snouts, the wiry pelts of Diggers, crawling with grubs that retreated from the torchlight.

Nobody of either species made a sound. It was much too shocking.

All of a sudden, one of the Diggers launched itself at Rockface, knocking the big man back and sending the torch spinning through the air. Panic broke out, everybody turned back, running for all they were worth towards the bonfires and the safety of the human streets.

Stopmouth found himself alone with Sodasi, standing over the fallen Rockface, expecting to be rushed.

Instead, the Digger that had attacked their friend hopped away from them, and the rest, the huge mass of them, began to move forward, at a pace no faster than a walk. The humans pulled their comrade to his feet and retrieved the torch. All three found themselves stumbling backwards before the advancing line of Diggers, while behind them, the Ship People ran for their lives.

"Why aren't the Diggers fighting?" asked Rockface. "Why aren't *we*? A man should charge!"

But he kept moving all the same.

Rockface, the Diggers, all of them, remained calm. It took Stopmouth a few moments to understand why. This is the end, he realised. The end of the struggle. A great moment, and both sides wanted to treat it with the reverence it deserved. The first people of this world, the humans, were about to leave it forever.

But Rockface had a different interpretation of what was going on. "They have killed Wallbreaker's lot. His foolishness has destroyed the Tribe and we are all that is left. These Diggers ... They're keeping their larder stocked, hey? After us, whatever will they eat? They want us around a bit longer now that they've picked the bones of the whole world clean."

The humans were pushed all the way back to the streets again and to the bonfires. The children who'd been tending them were herded away by the enemy so that the wood could be scattered and more places plunged into darkness.

"Are we going to take this?" asked Rockface. "You are the leader now, Stopmouth. You have to lead us in a last attack. Even the Ship People will fight, surely! I don't want to see any of my children planted."

Stopmouth agreed. "We'll fight, but not here. We'll do better from HeadQuarters with walls around us. We'll kill more of them that way."

"So what?" the bigger man muttered. He had fought Diggers from HeadQuarters before, Stopmouth remembered. Only the Talker had saved the last of the New Tribe then, but the Talker, like Wallbreaker's hunters, along with those of the Religious, was lost to humanity.

More Diggers must have been arriving by the many side-streets, for the main road was now packed with people. A thousand of them, maybe. Or fifteen-hundred. The long line stumbled backwards towards HeadQuarters.

Flamehair would be waiting back there for her father. Waiting

279

for the Diggers, too. Stopmouth would kill her first, not caring that her flesh would be wasted. He didn't want her to suffer such pain as the grubs would bring.

And still the enemy followed, gently pushing and pushing, breaking up the fires as they passed them, never more than ten paces away from their intended victims.

Oh, Ancestors. I'm sorry I have wasted our people like this.

The ground began to shake then and he thought the Diggers were burrowing beneath the streets as they had done in the past. Except... except that the confident enemy had stopped in their tracks. Were they uncertain? Was that possible? A cloud of dust was spreading through the air and Stopmouth looked up. He knew exactly where he was now. He recognised the big building he was standing beside and suddenly, a great urgency gripped him.

"Back!" he screamed. "Everybody, get back! Back!" And the crowd, sensing the desperation of his words, obeyed. They were close to panic anyway, expecting pointy snouts to burst up between their feet at any moment. But that wasn't it at all. No, the ground held firm. Instead, the wall of one of the few remaining buildings in the area—the giant warehouse that had been given over to the Fourleggers—shattered, collapsing onto the street, burying dozens of Diggers, but not the humans who had just passed it by.

A hundred Fourleggers, maybe two hundred, of all ages, shot out of the building beyond, their claws bared, flinging burning bundles of moss and twigs into the confused ranks of Diggers. They crashed into the startled enemy, burning and stabbing. Diggers lost their throats in gouts of blood, but worse by far were the bodies of grubs, popping open at the slightest touch of a flame—and the flame was everywhere.

Fourleggers killed Diggers by the dozen, and the fallen, with few grubs to keep them alive, stayed down. Stopmouth saw enemies scrambling backwards, clawing at each other, panicking, desperate to get out of the packed, burning road.

Stopmouth wouldn't give them the chance.

"Charge!" he cried and sprang forward, Rockface at his side. He felt the wind of one of Sodasi's uncannily accurate slingstones as it flew past his ear. He heard chilling human screams—of rage. The women were here, the women of his old Tribe, mourning their men with blood and spears and rocks and flaming torches.

Stopmouth stabbed one enemy after another. Sometimes their grubs kept them alive long enough to start crawling away, but these were quickly finished off by Ship People who brought concrete down on their skulls. Rockface was laughing and the children, oh Ancestors, the children he had trained, were the fingers of a single hand, swarming one victim after another, licking blood from their weapons, signalling to each other, as the Diggers fled before them.

Many of the Ship People fought too. Clumsily, with tears on their faces and in constant terror. Ekta led them and she dashed creatures against walls and snapped their backs across her knees, while shouting orders at people who might or might not have understood what she meant.

And yet, while dozens of Diggers fell, the enemy resolve began to stiffen, to push back. People screamed and fell, hamstrung rather than killed so that they might still be planted later on. They lay there in terror beside fallen Fourleggers as clawed feet used them for a road and pushed the humans and their remaining allies back again, crowding them all together. Ashsweeper fell into the press, her spear, ripped away from her by a dying enemy. Three Diggers worked together to keep Stopmouth back from her, trying to trap his spear in their bodies.

He saw her face, though, on the ground, frightened, but brave enough to cry, "They've bitten through my leg. Kill Nighttracker! Kill my son!"

Poor Fulki went down too, snatched away from the other children with a screech. Rockface burrowed down after her and came back alone, his spear red with her blood, his face streaked with tears.

The Diggers disengaged again, but only a little.

It had taken them a few hundred heartbeats to reassert their mastery, to resume their gentle herding of their future food-supply back towards HeadQuarters. The remains of the U stood no more than a few hundred paces behind them, but the people who had been hiding in it came pouring out of it now.

Stopmouth found Mossheart at his side, her daughter in her arms. She had brought the Religious woman with her, the one who had been looking after Flamehair.

"The Diggers are inside those buildings," Mossheart told him. "They burst up from the floor. We have nowhere left to go."

Stopmouth hung his head.

"It's not you who failed, Stopmouth," she told him. She spoke calmly and seemed almost relieved. "The Tribe failed when we let my husband lead us away from what the Ancestors had taught us. And so, we are no longer worthy of them. He was planning to eat the Roof People, you know? Not just the weak. They would have grown food for themselves only to become food for us. We were going to plant them, as if *we* were the Diggers."

"No ... " he said, but he knew she was telling the truth. "No ... "

"If you kill my daughter," Mossheart said, "I will do the same for yours. Although ... they are both my husband's children, aren't they? Aren't they? I worked it out. There wasn't time for her to be yours ... "

"Flamehair is *my* d-daughter," he said.

She sighed. "Oh, what does it matter now? We are dead. We were dead all along and never knew it. Even back then, when you were a broken-tongued boy and your brother was so beautiful. Now," she said. "Are you strong enough to kill the children? Or do you prefer that the Diggers will have them?"

34.
GRUBS AND V⊕LUNTEERS

Something, or somebody, banged into Whistlenose's back. He cried out for his mother, but then, he was lost, all alone in the streets beyond ManWays where no child should be. He coughed, his body racked with agony, doubling over on itself. A great light ripped away the darkness, searing his eyes under closed lids.

He cried out again, surprising himself, for his voice was that of a man, rather than a child. He rolled, hacking up phlegm on the earth, barely aware as the light seemed to move away and hundreds of clawed feet gave chase.

Darkness returned and the voices of people weeping nearby. It took him a full hundred heartbeats to remember where he was, and a hundred more to figure out what had happened. The grub had taken him over completely until somebody or something had hit him hard enough in the back to knock it free of his mouth.

Of the Diggers, there was no sign, but the Roof People were still there, whimpering in the dark a few dozen paces away. All he could see now was the light of what had to be the Talker disappearing off into the distance.

"The ambush has failed then," he said. The best he could hope for was to get as many of the hunters out of here as possible before the Diggers caught up with whoever was leading them away.

He groped forward in the dark until arms grabbed him, wrapping him tight in an embrace, while a voice moaned and called for its mother. Whistlenose had been expecting this and he managed to keep his arms free and above his head.

"What woman would admit to birthing you, Clickstone?" He shoved fingers into the man's mouth and pulled the grub free. He bit through it as Clickstone gasped and fell away. "That's one," he said. He had freed a half-dozen others before Clickstone had recovered enough wits to help, and the numbers of hunters rose quickly until all two hundred or so were either groaning on the ground or groping around for their fallen weapons. Now and again somebody would try to light a torch only to be scolded by their comrades. Nobody wanted to alert the Diggers to the escape.

"I'm going to free the bait now," Whistlenose said. "Can somebody find a knife for me? And be careful not to stab me when you're handing it over."

"No fear of that! I can hear the sound of your nose from here!"

"No you can't! I don't do that any— Oh, never mind. Just get me a knife."

"Whistlenose?" He felt a hand touch him on the shoulder. He recognised the worn out voice.

"Laughlong?"

"Are you sure you want to free the bait? They might keep the Diggers off our backs when we're making our escape. Volunteers, you know?"

Whistlenose did know, and took a few heartbeats to think it over. "I don't think it matters," he said at last. "The Diggers aren't stupid. They were happy chasing after the Talker knowing we couldn't move and that they could come back for us any time it suited them. It's the people who can walk they'll want to catch, so, the more of us there are heading back, the better." What he didn't say was that the Chief's brother had convinced him that these people were human too, and worthy of respect. "Come on," he told Laughlong. "Help me free them."

They made shushing noises so the Volunteers would stay quiet, and everybody obeyed. They stank of urine and terror, but at least one voice in there was collected enough to whisper commands of its own, and in a surprisingly quick time, they had all formed a chain of hands in the darkness.

"Now," he said. "We just need to figure out which way we came from ... "

But the gravelly-voiced man amongst the bait seemed completely sure of himself in that regard too. So, the hunters, who had little experience in this place, found themselves trailing after their supposed prisoners.

It was slow going and Whistlenose had no idea how much time was passing. His eyes began to play tricks on him in the darkness. People cursed and fell and the sounds of breathing seemed loud enough to bring the Roof down on their heads. If only the sun would return! This would all be so easy. They'd see its light from ten thousand paces away.

People gasped up ahead and voices babbled in Roof language. Whistlenose pushed forward and for the first time since Wallbreaker had run off with the Talker, he could see something. Fires! The shadowy outlines of houses! And an oily mass of Diggers, pouring in between those buildings. This was the horde their trap had been set up to destroy, but instead, it was going to wipe out their families!

Whistlenose started running. He had no need to say anything—the rest of the hunters were with him too. The Volunteers joined in, weaponless though they were, and before Whistlenose's astonished gaze, many of them began clumping together into the same little groups that had come to save the Tribe when it lay trapped against the river.

He felt a terrible shame then and understood why the Ancestors had allowed the ambush to fail. But he pushed such thoughts away. Ashsweeper was in there somewhere and Nighttracker too, the son he was never supposed to have had.

The back ranks of the enemy turned to face the charge, but the humans barely slowed. Men fought as though insane, desperate to reach their families, while the Diggers still seemed to think they could take prisoners for their fields. Spears jammed in corpses and men used knives and teeth instead. A few of them risked putting grubs from dead Diggers in their mouths again and these were able to kill without being attacked in return, taking dozens and dozens of enemies each before the pain began to lead them astray.

The Volunteers proved no less effective. They knew the buildings here better than anybody. They climbed walls to rain rocks down on Diggers or led them into traps, careless of their own lives and brave as any hunters Whistlenose had ever seen.

The little, malnourished one, a pet of Stopmouth's called Tarini, had a magical ability to pass through knots of combatants without being touched to pull injured people free of trouble.

Whistlenose killed and killed. His terror of the Diggers and their grubs had gone entirely away. He didn't care if they caught him now; he'd been planted, he'd felt what it was like and not even that pain could compare to the deaths of his precious wife; his innocent son. Wounds had no effect on him, his spear cut the air so fast it hummed and every hunter around him fought the same way. Every volunteer too. The Ancestors possessed them all and filled them with a cold and bitter fury.

And then, he faced a new creature altogether. A human being, dripping with gore from tooth and fingernail and the shattered grip of a spear. They almost fought, each holding himself back with the greatest of effort. It couldn't be over. It couldn't be. But already a touch of sunlight reddened the sky enough to drive off the stars and Whistlenose realised he'd been fighting an entire night already.

In all directions, lay a layer of enemy corpses two or three thick, while a small number of survivors fled in all directions. A few men had been overcome again by the grubs in their mouths and these raved for their mothers. This was the only sound.

The filthy creature spoke. "You will n-not eat them, Whistlenose, you hear me? I w-won't l-let him t-touch a h-hair on their heads."

Whistlenose was confused. The Diggers had been killed in great numbers. Did Stopmouth—for that is who the creature was—intend to waste so much flesh? But the young hunter had used the word "him." "I won't let *him* touch a hair on their heads."

"Wallbreaker's gone, Stopmouth. He…he led the Diggers away from us with the light of the Talker. He gave us a chance to escape so that we could come to you here."

A sigh and Stopmouth, an exhausted Stopmouth, fell to his knees amongst the enemy corpses. "He Volunteered? W-wallbreaker *V-volunteered*?" His tone was both incredulous and hopeful at once.

Whistlenose found himself on the ground too, all of a sudden. He was bleeding everywhere. His very bones ached, especially his knee. It had given way to dump him on the ground. But he didn't care about that.

"I want my wife," he said to Stopmouth. "I want my son."

35.
MANY WORLDS IN ONE

As always, these days, a pall of smoke hung over the streets. Digger meat cooked and popped on a hundred fires of dried bones and moss kindling. But nobody tended to them today or hauled rubble, or worked in the fields.

Hands clapped. Drums pounded and throats pealed with the first easy laughter in what seemed like ten thousand days. Ship People shared food with Religious who made clumsy hand signals to men and women of the old Tribe. Fourleggers sniffed curiously at everything, and Ashsweeper, leaning on the shaft of a spear, hobbled after that mad little boy of hers.

Alone, out of everybody, Mossheart seemed unhappy. "Look at that old fool, Rockface!"

Mossheart had taken to spending time with Stopmouth. "Oh, I won't marry you," she had told him, as if he had been thinking to replace Indrani before her soup had even cooled! "But, I miss that brother of yours. I don't care that he was a coward or that he tried to bring in other wives to set above me. He was a man who dreamt of more than the next slice of meat from the spit. And you can do that too."

Mossheart's daughter had taken to playing gently with Flamehair and was a comfort to her while her father was off dealing with Digger attacks. New generations of the enemy were maturing all the time, away out there in the dark. But they arrived in scattered, disoriented groups, many of them with no grubs of their own so that they died easily. With no new flesh coming from the Roof, the rest of the enemy would soon starve.

Stopmouth closed his eyes, listening to the strange songs of the Roof People and feeling the heat on his face from the fire. But Mossheart wouldn't let him rest. "Oh won't you look at him!" she said. "That old man should be soup long ago."

She was still talking about Rockface. The hunter had just landed from a leap over the fire. His face was flushed with pleasure and only the slightest hint of pain. But he waved towards his bride, beckoning her forward. "Jump!" he cried, repeating the word with his hands as all the children did.

"It's a waste of food feeding him," Mossheart continued. "The Tribe needs the strongest to survive."

"It's n-not about the strongest any more. It's the best we need to survive now. And Rockface is the best."

"Stupid Roof talk. That Indrani poisoned you."

Sodasi leapt without hesitation, crashing into Rockface as everybody cheered. But then, worried hunters were stepping in to help the couple back to their feet. "It's all right!" Rockface cried. "It's just my back! It does that sometimes, hey?"

Flamehair squirmed in Stopmouth's lap. "You want some rice, baba?" he asked her.

"Rice!" Mossheart spat.

"She'll have to g-get used to it. There won't be any m-more Diggers to eat when she's older."

"Pah! There's no strength in it. She'll never get a name like that."

"She already has a name."

"A proper name. Her *own* name. Not something you just stole from your poor mother."

The time had come for Sodasi's last dance among her unmarried friends. Far too many people were joining in to suit tradition, even men. Tarini was there, making friends with Vishwakarma and a few others. But Rockface knew the proper way to do things and he came over to lie beside them in a cloud of his own sweat.

"Oh, I know I should Volunteer," he said to Mossheart's disapproving look. "But she wants me, my poor girl, and I won't refuse her anything, hey?"

"You won't last her the time it takes to make a child!" said Mossheart.

"I don't know." He grinned at his dancing bride and she waved back from the far side of the fire. "We have to talk with our hands, so I don't always get what she means. But she says I'm only forty—whatever that is! Forty what? Days? I ask her. But she says no, that's not it. She says I'll be around a long time. Long enough. We'll see. Things are different now. I know it's not right." He grinned. "But I don't care, hey? I mean, look at her!" He shouted, "I don't care!" And all the dancers cried gibberish of their own in time to the drums and Flamehair laughed.

"I love you," Stopmouth told his child. "R-rockface? Show F-flamehair how to s-say 'I love you' with the signs."

"I'll show her. I'll show both of you, hey? And you'll never have to worry about that tongue of yours again."

Stopmouth had stopped worrying about that long ago, but he grabbed Rockface with his free hand and pulled him into a fierce hug. He wished more than anything Indrani could be here now. At the end of the world with him. At the beginning of everything.

EPIL⊕GUE.
F⊕UR M⊕THERS

There were four of them left. Their children burrowed tunnels through their flesh and they felt the pain of it as a glorious web of fire. Their poor, unmated sisters would never know this joy; would never share the pain of the universe: the cries of stars longing for the love of their creator; the screaming, eternal dying of the comets. Only their children allowed them to be part of all that. Only their grubs.

But agony should not be hoarded selfishly. It must be shared.

And so they ran. Deeper and deeper into the darkness. Nowhere could they find new hosts for the grubs. Everywhere they went were fields planted with their own sisters until even these petered out into desert. By the time their energy had left them, they saw a place where light shone by day. A glare that caused their grubs to shrink deep inside their mothers' bodies. Perhaps some hosts might live there? But no, they had not the strength left to do the right thing; to subdue even one lucky creature.

They found a single planted human there, high on the side of a hill so that he faced down to where the light shone and from where the smell of smoke and wasted, cooked flesh must have tickled his nose. A metal ball lay at his hip, and a broken spear.

They lapped gratefully at the nutritious drool from his mouth.

"Mother ... " he moaned. He suffered an agony greater than any member of his species had ever known. They felt particularly tender towards him in that moment and they chose this spot to plant each other so that they might be near him and share in his pain as they all sank into the soil together.

Each of their deaths would mean the birth of a single child. There would be no more Diggers after that, and this too, was beautiful.

ACKNΘWLEDGEMENTS

I won't write anything fancy here, but I want to say that everybody who helped out on the first two books, *The Inferior* and *The Deserter*, gets my love and thanks all over again. This includes family and friends, work colleagues and neighbours. It includes commenters and tricksters from the Brotherhood Without Banners. It includes an elite band of booksellers from Dublin to St. Andrews, to Liverpool and Lansing. It includes everybody at Conville & Walsh, at Random House Children's Books and at that mighty forge of the imagination known as David Fickling Books in Oxford.

Who else? Who else? Gabrielle Harbowy swooped mercilessly on typos. Fiona Jayde provided a great and bony cover ...

But most of all—because this is a book that should not exist—I want to thank all of those people in every part of the world, who stormed their piggy-banks to buy the first two volumes, and who pestered me for years afterwards with questions such as, "What part of the word trilogy *don't* you understand?"

It's all done now. Let's go back to sleep.

Also by Peadar Ó Guilín

The Inferior (The Bone World Trilogy, Book 1)
The Deserter (The Bone World Trilogy, Book 2)

Forever in the Memory of God and Other Stories (ebook)

Coming Soon:
Eat the Drink

Please check www.frozenstories.com for the latest releases

Made in the USA
Lexington, KY
28 November 2015